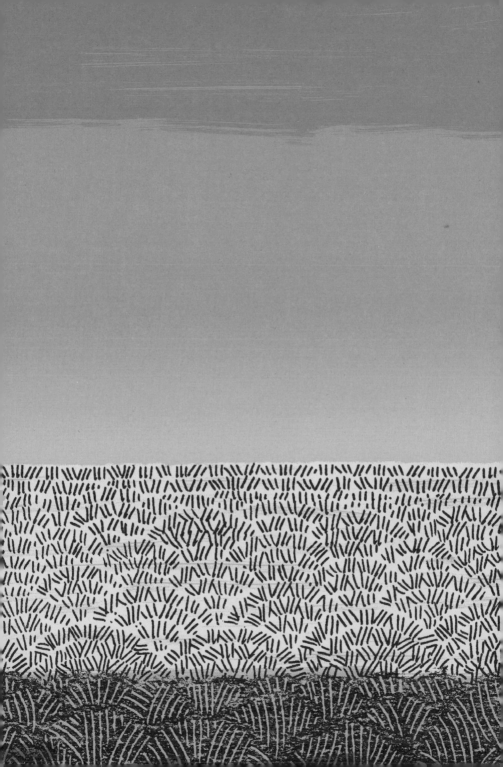

Also by Andi Watson

Glister
Princess Decomposia and Count Spatula

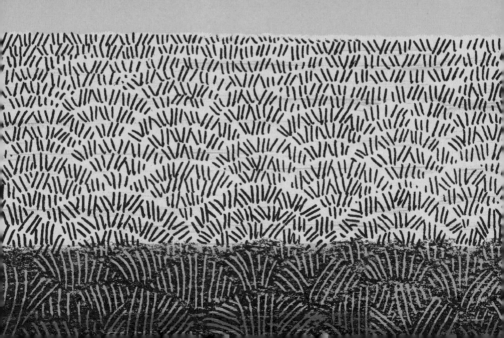

KERRY and the Knight of the Forest

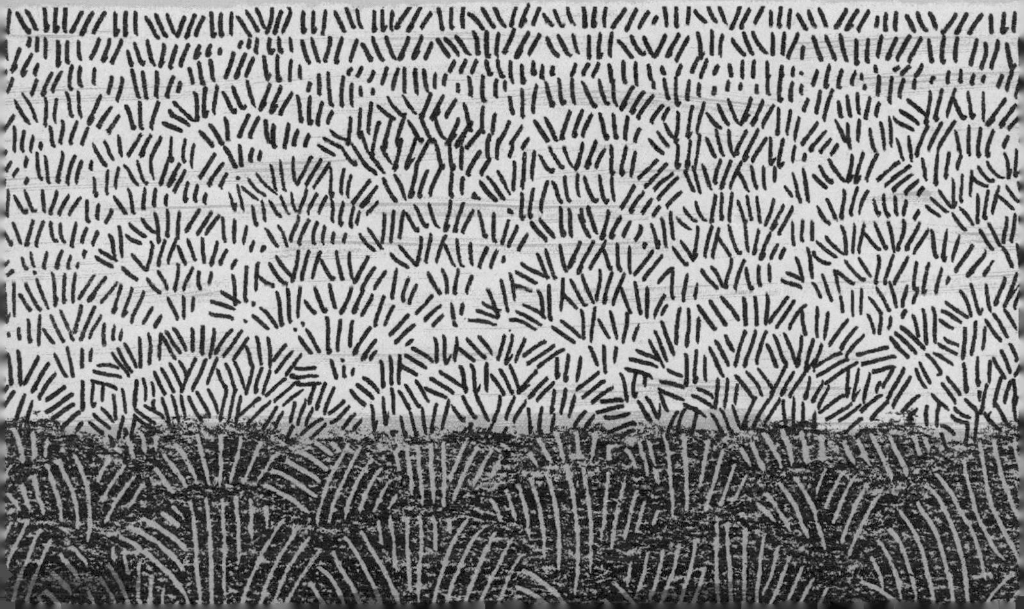

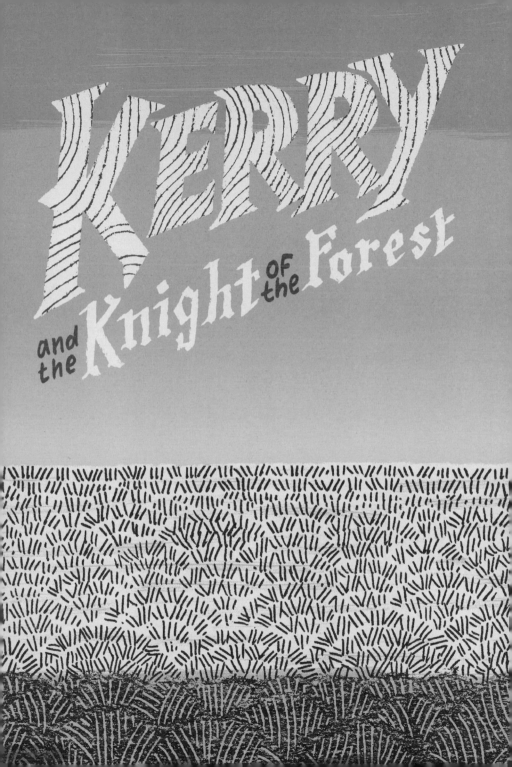

Cover art, text, and interior illustrations copyright © 2020 by Andi Watson

All rights reserved. Published in the United States by RH Graphic, an imprint of Random House Children's Books, a division of Penguin Random House LLC, New York.

RH Graphic with the book design is a trademark of Penguin Random House LLC.

Visit us on the Web! RHKidsGraphic.com • @RHKidsGraphic

Educators and librarians, for a variety of teaching tools, visit us at RHTeachersLibrarians.com

Library of Congress Cataloging-in-Publication Data
Names: Watson, Andi, author.
Title: Kerry and the knight of the forest / Andi Watson.
Description: First edition. | New York : RH Graphic, [2020] | Audience: Ages 8–12 | Audience: Grades 4–6 | Summary: "Kerry gets lost on his way home and has to navigate through a fantastical forest to find his way out, only most of the creatures in the forest are not there to help him"—Provided by publisher.
Identifiers: LCCN 2019025827 | ISBN 978-1-9848-9330-7 (library binding) | ISBN 978-0-593-12523-6 (hardcover) | ISBN 978-1-9848-9329-1 (paperback) | ISBN 978-1-9848-9331-4 (ebook)
Subjects: LCSH: Graphic novels. | CYAC: Graphic novels. | Lost children—Fiction. | Forests and forestry—Fiction. | Fantasy.
Classification: LCC PZ7.7.W375 Ke 2020 | DDC 741.5/973—dc23

Designed by Patrick Crotty

MANUFACTURED IN CHINA
10 9 8 7 6 5 4 3 2 1
First Edition

A comic on every bookshelf.

To my Family

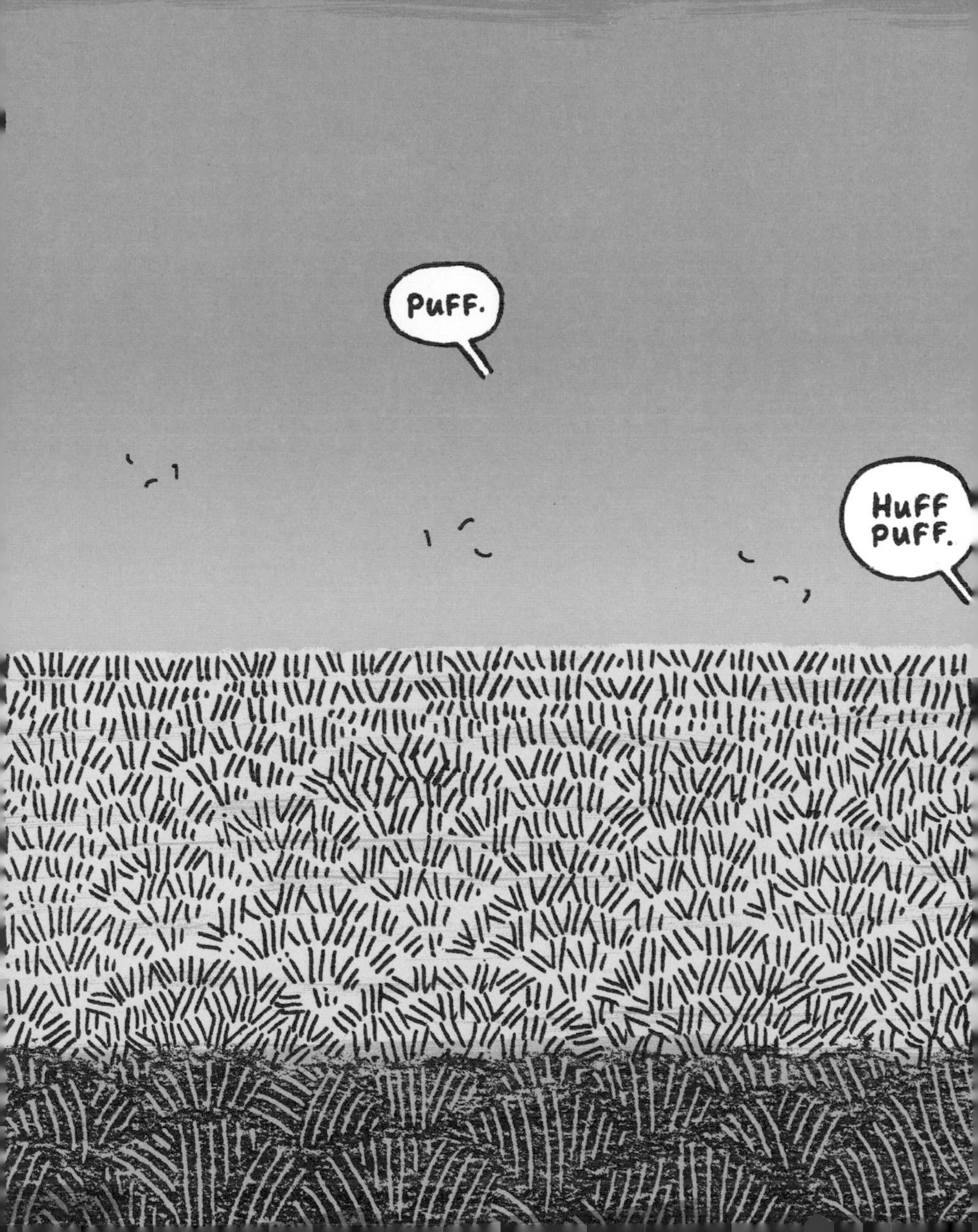
PUFF.
HUFF PUFF.

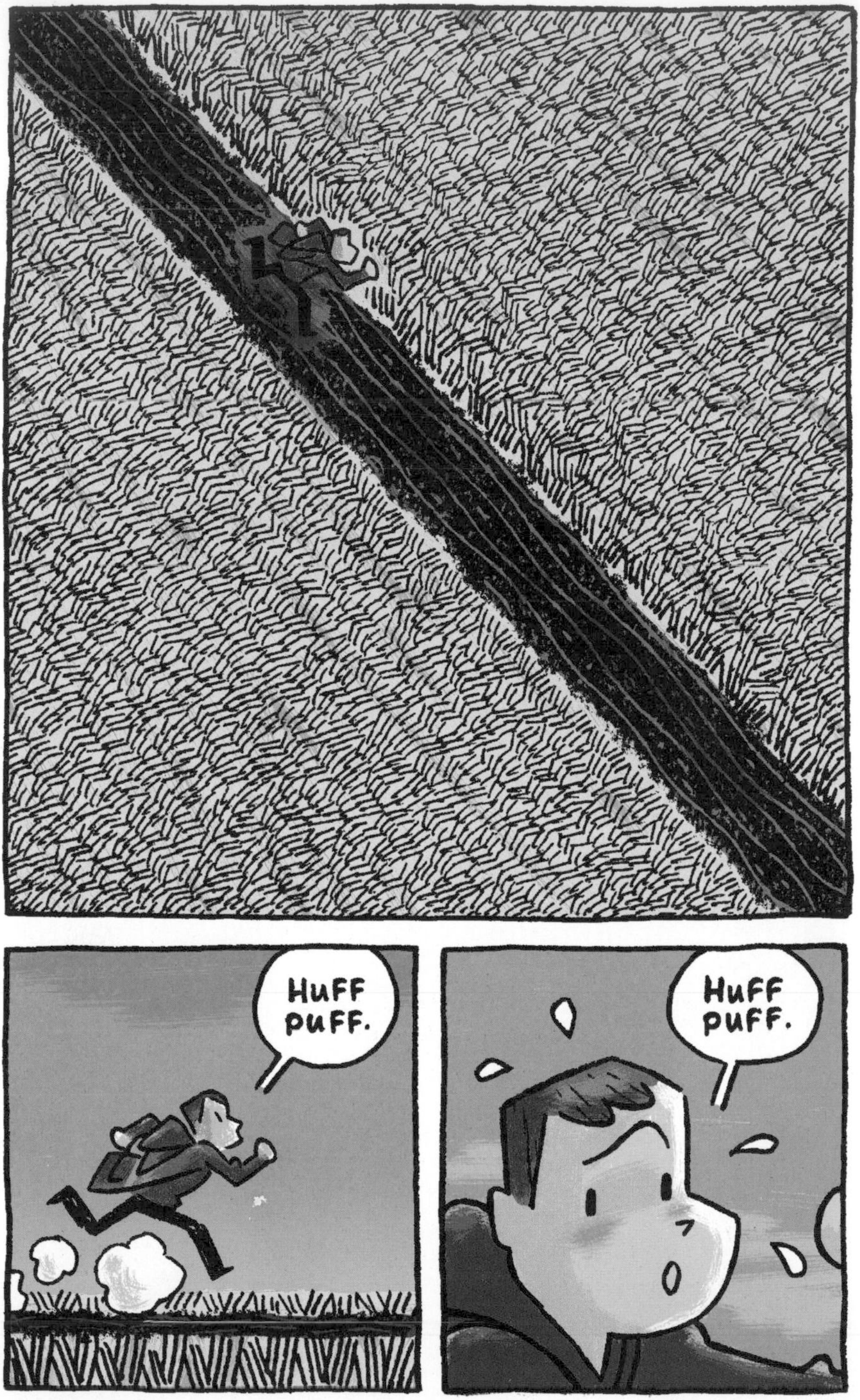
HuFF puFF.
HuFF puFF.

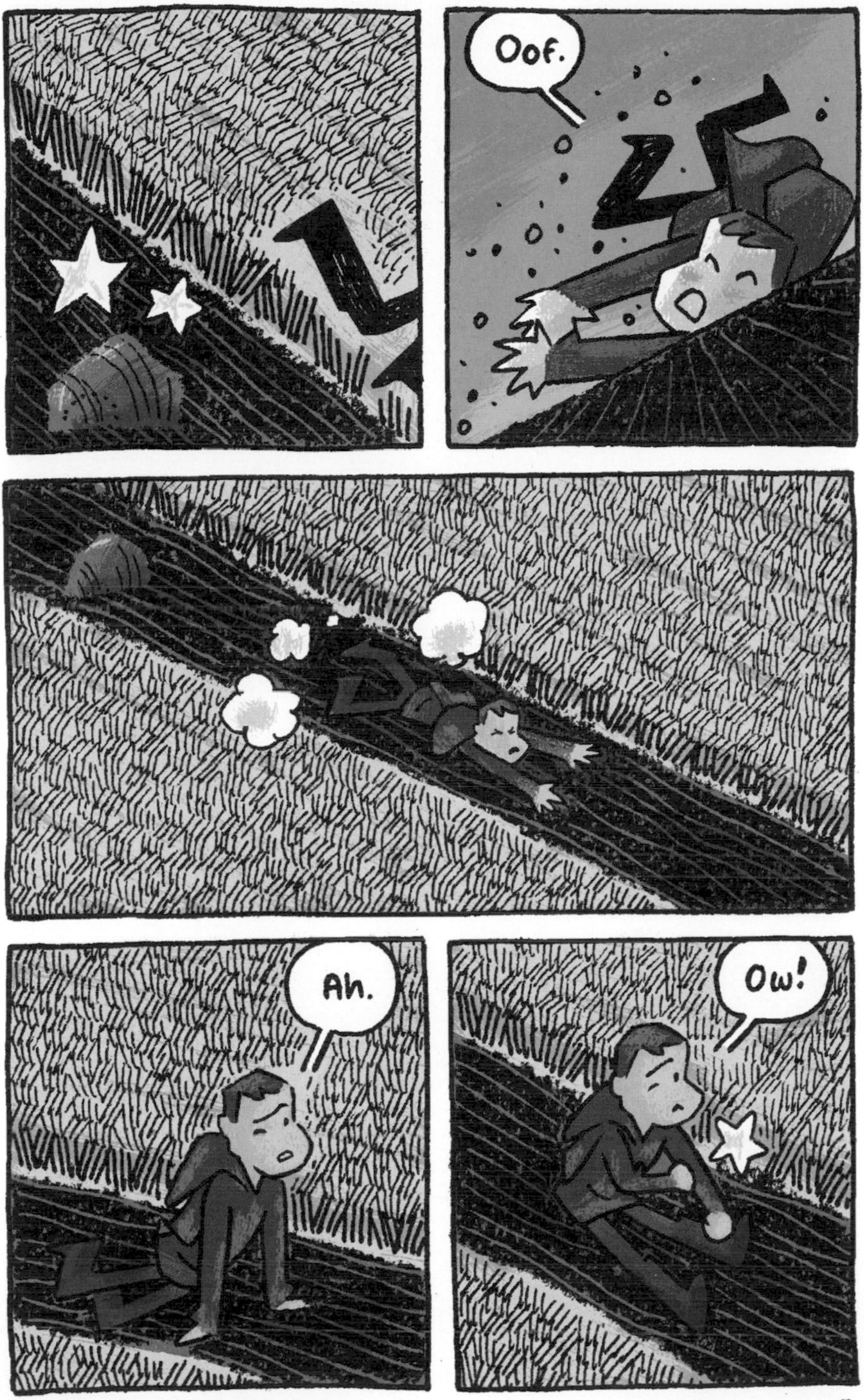
Oof.
Ah.
Ow!

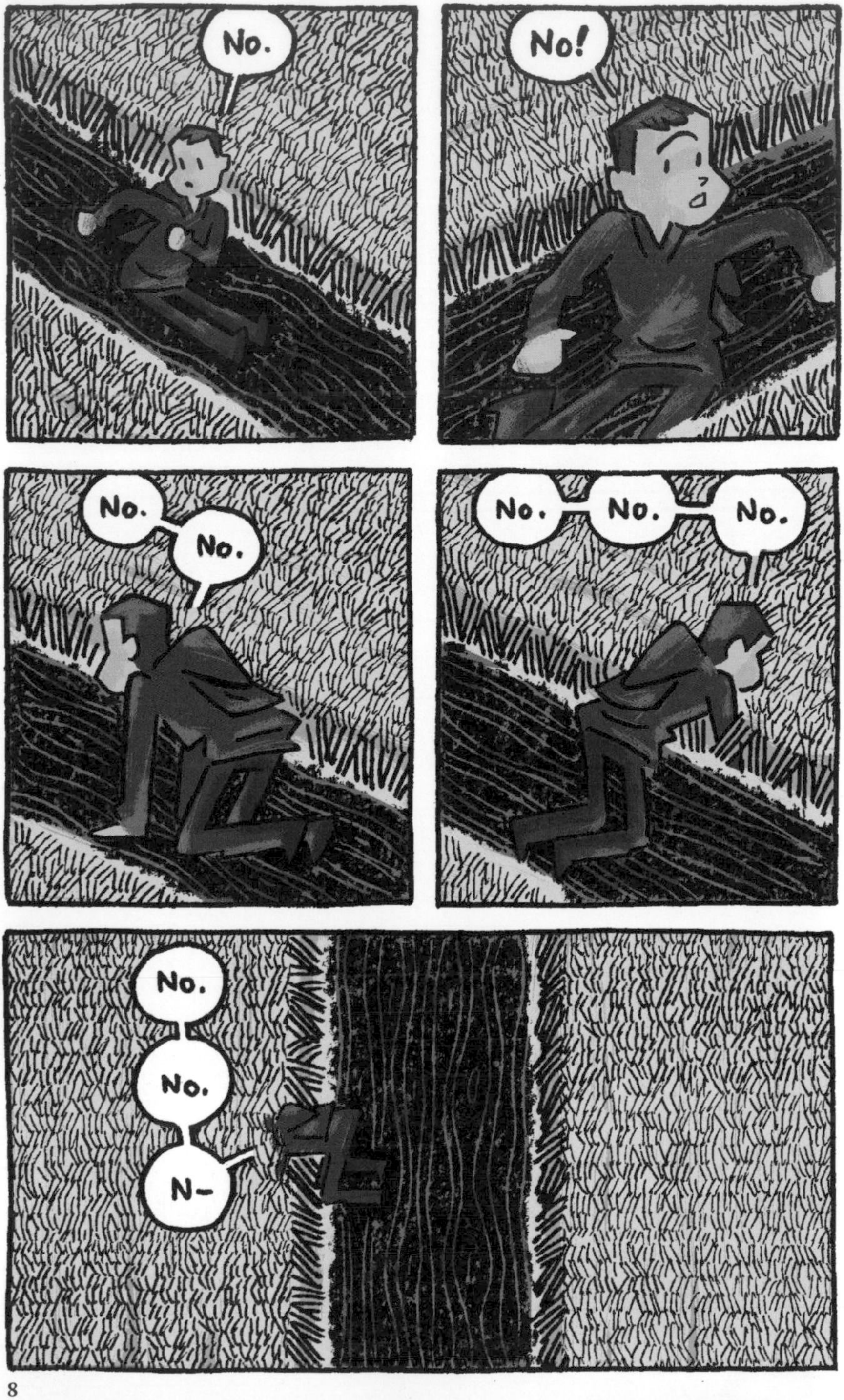
No.
No!
No.
No.
No.
No.
No.
No.
No.
N-

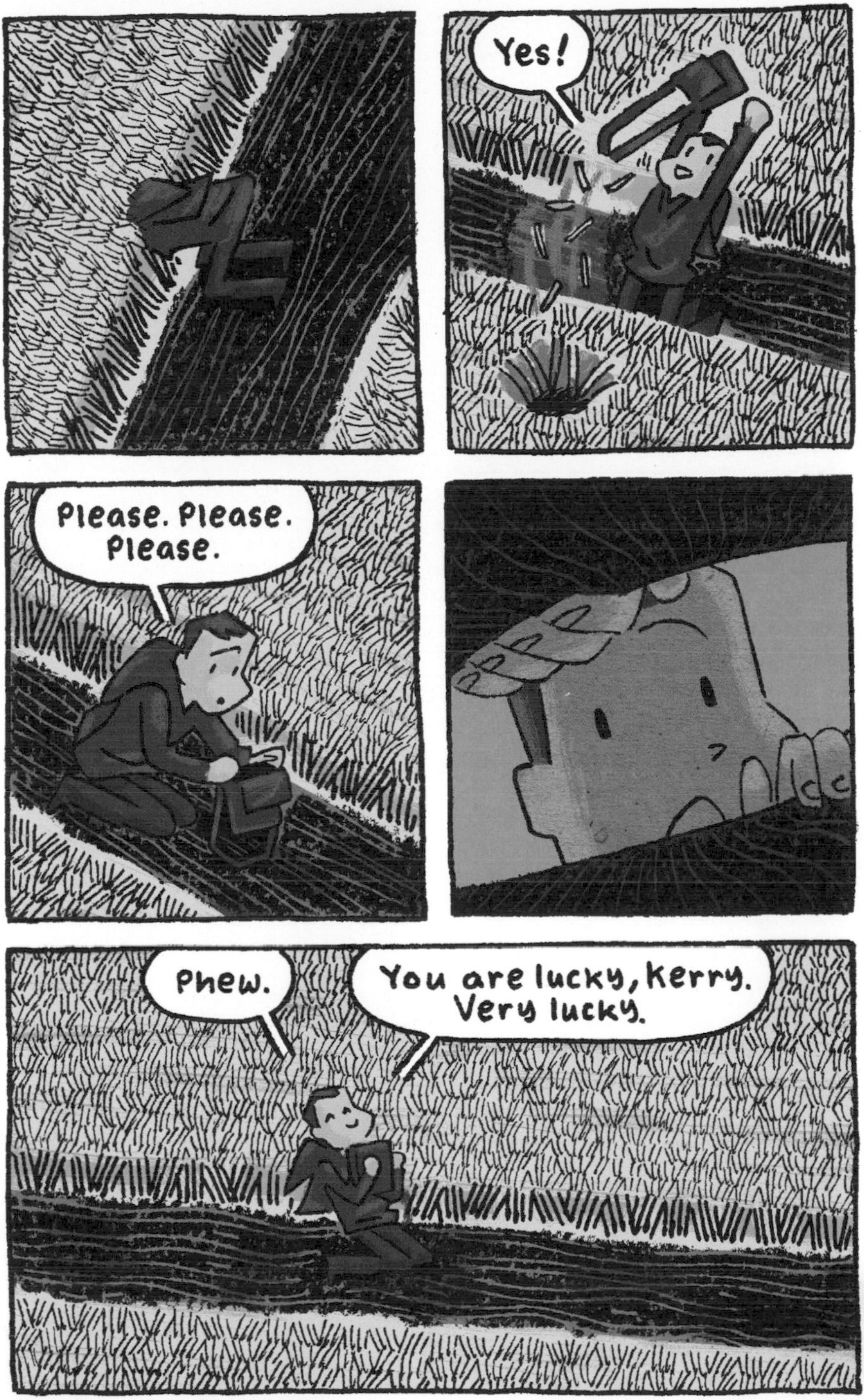
Yes!
Please. Please. Please.
Phew.
You are lucky, Kerry. Very lucky.

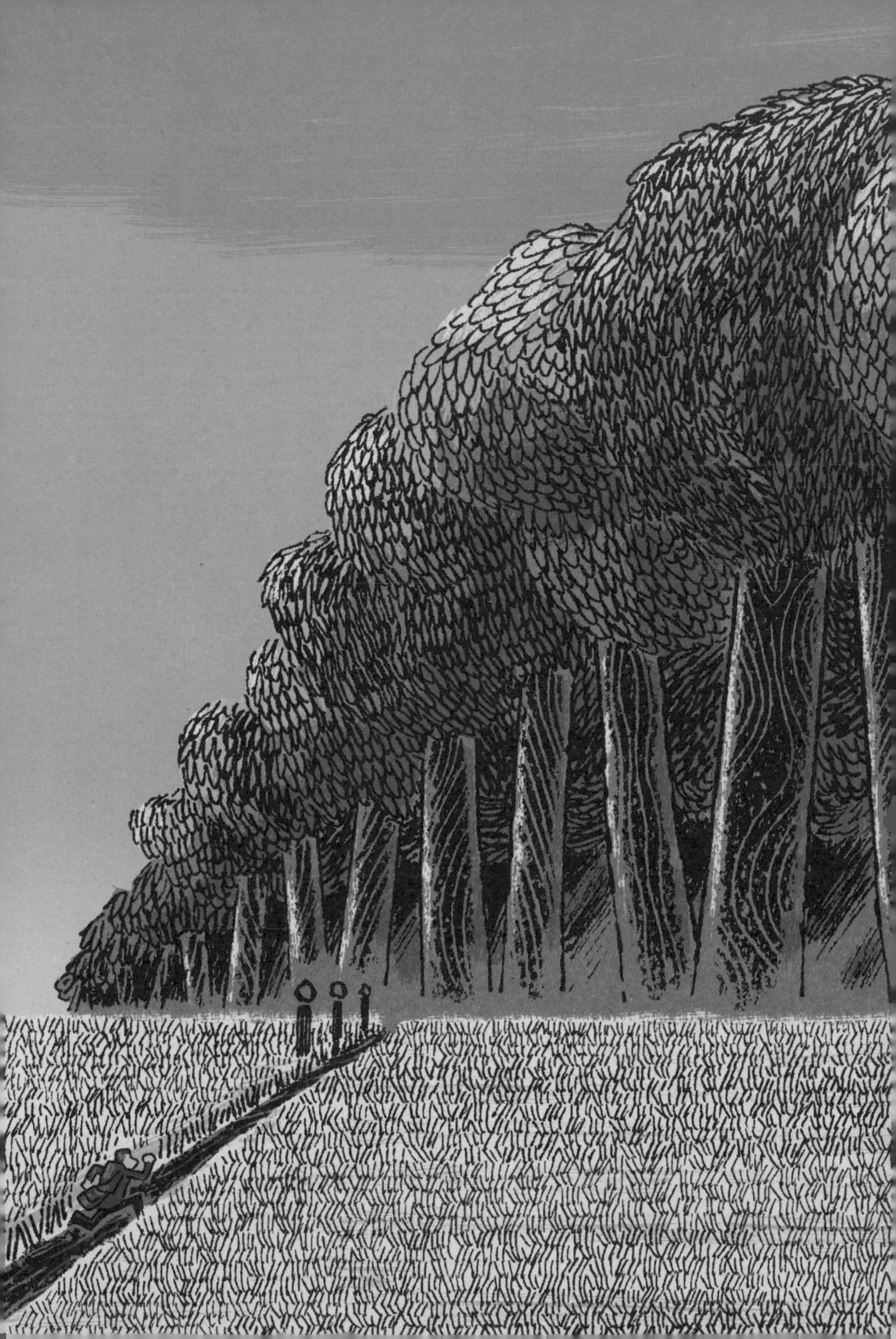

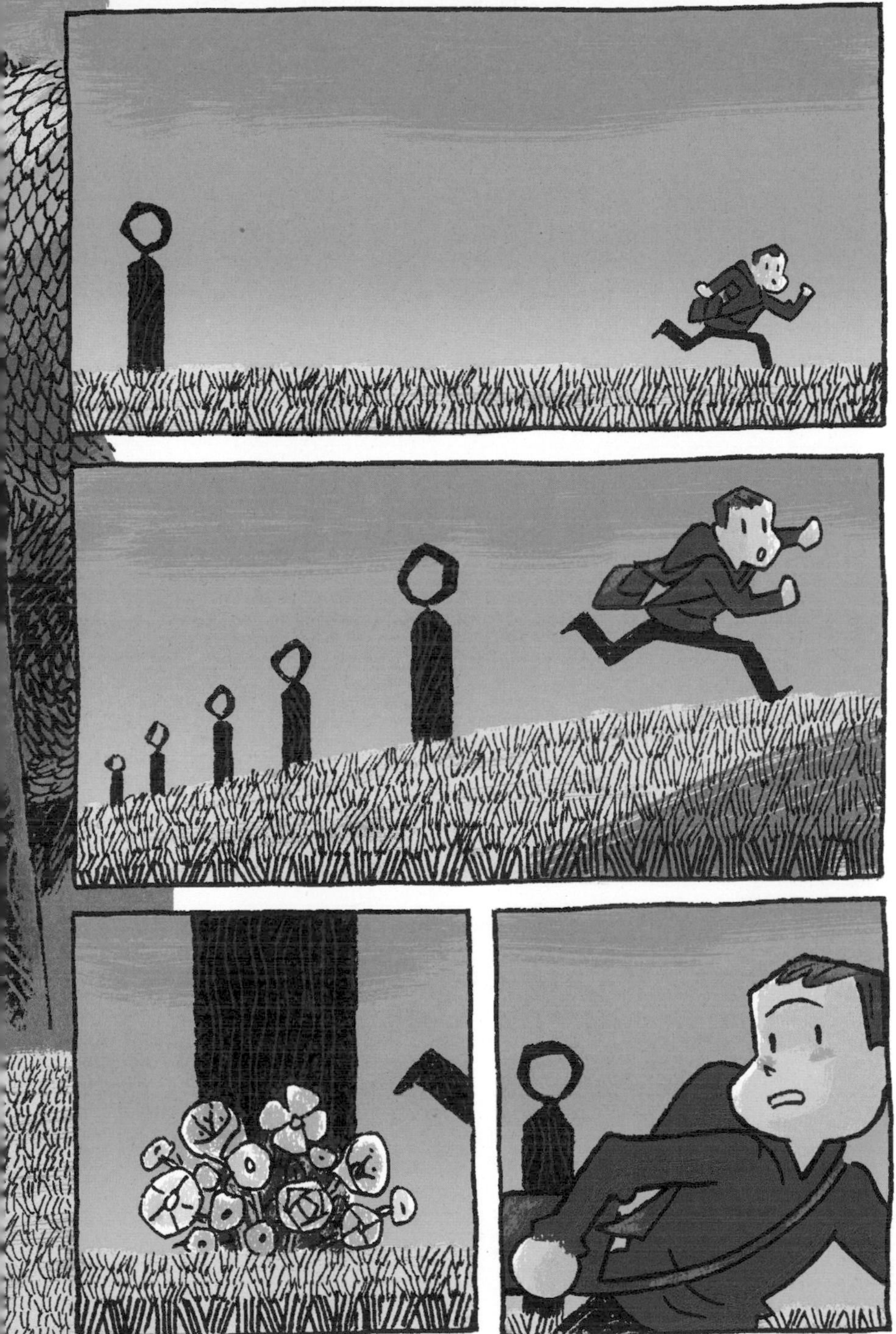

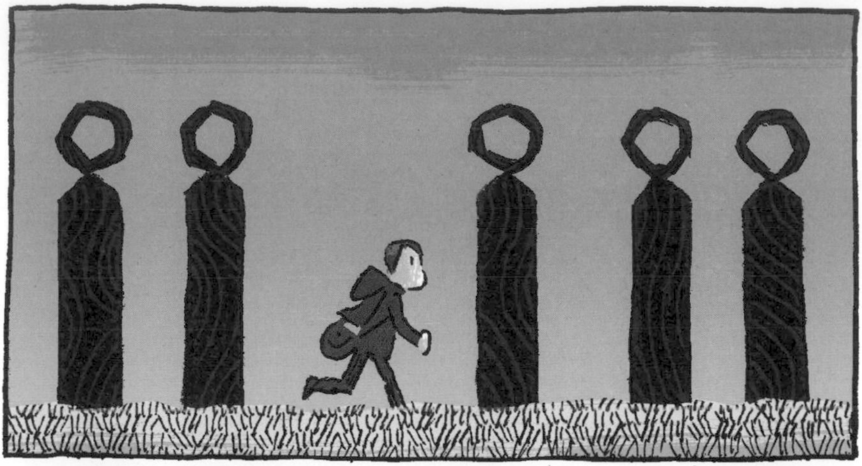

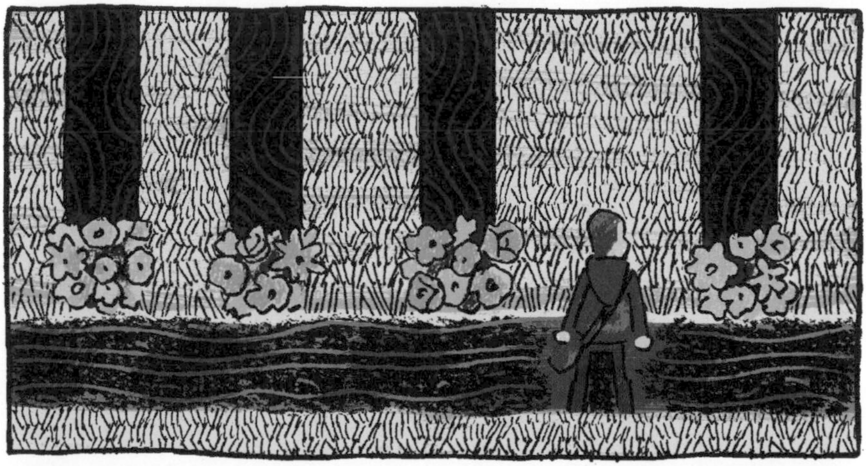

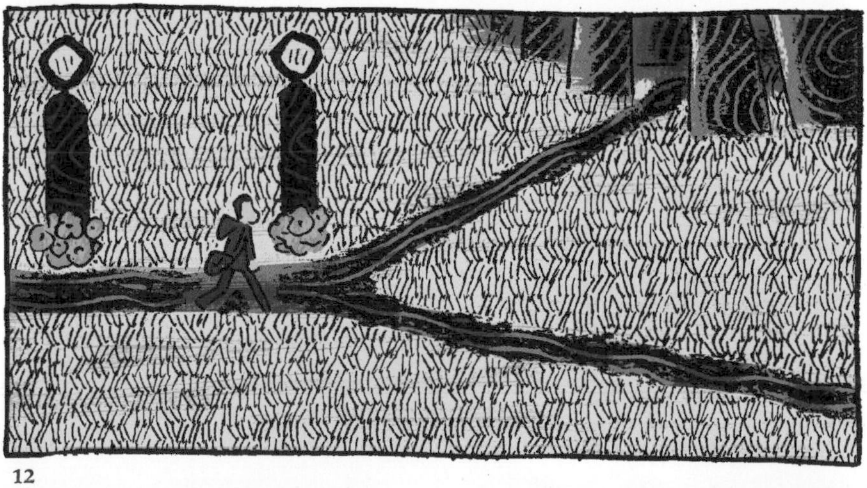

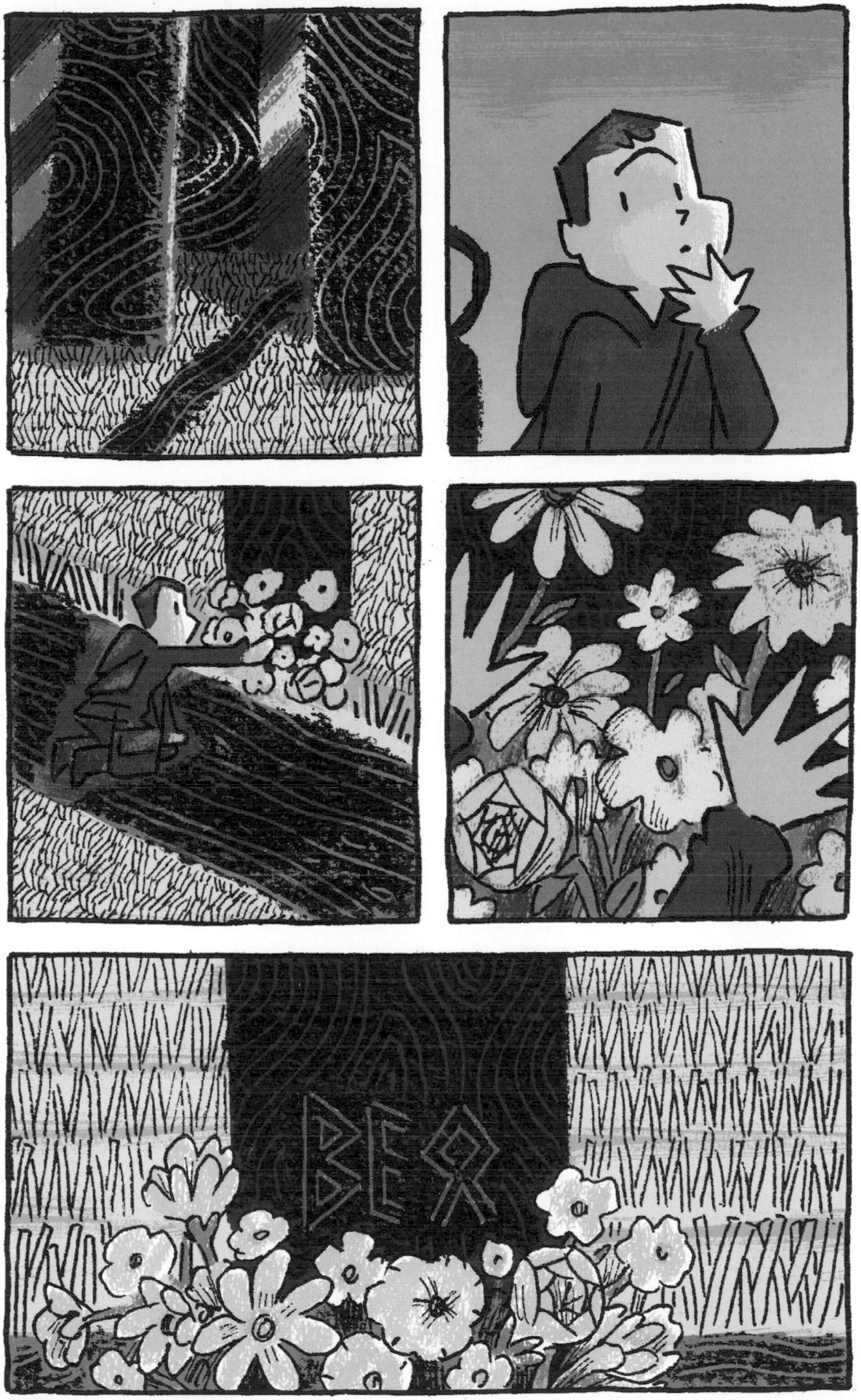

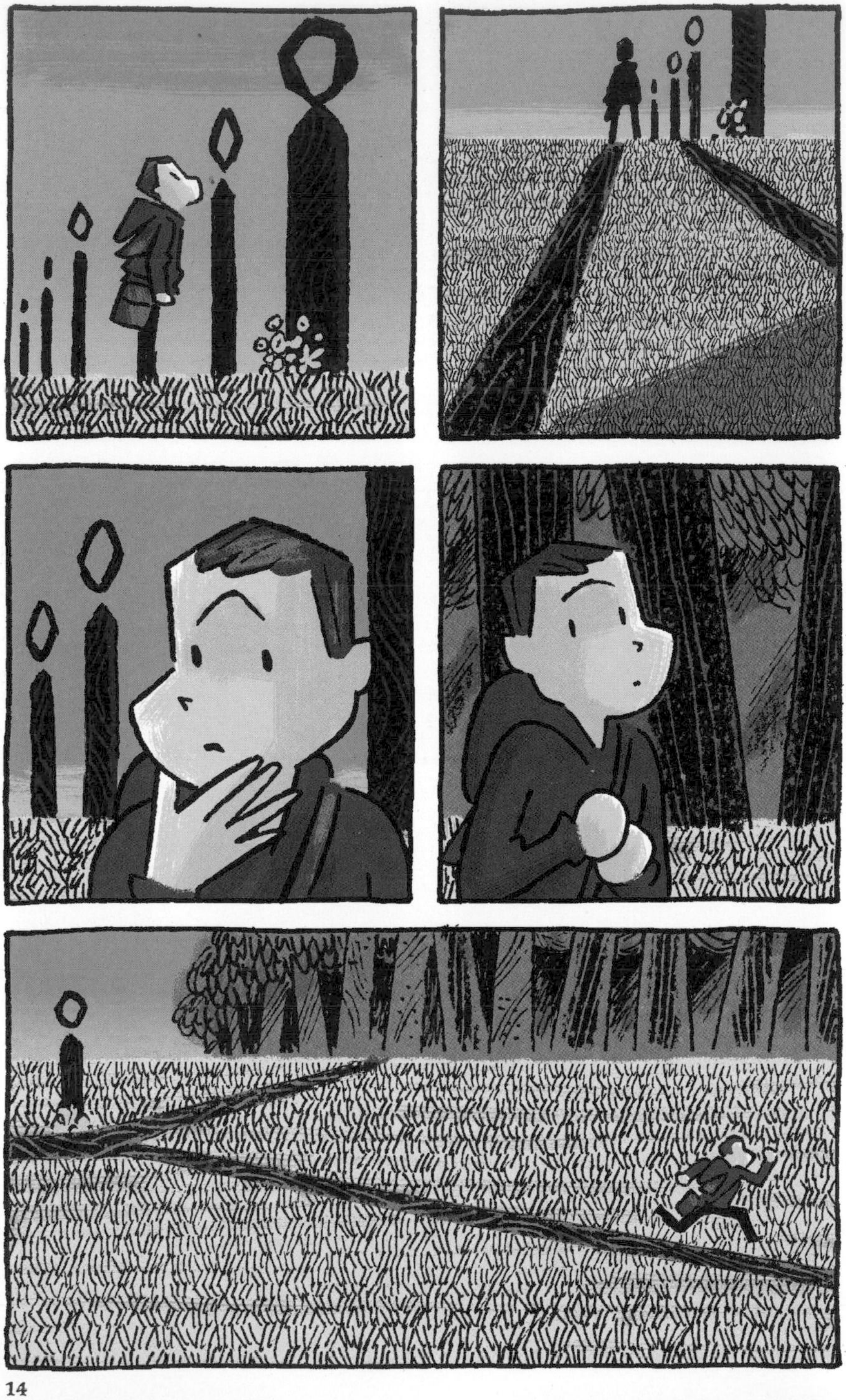

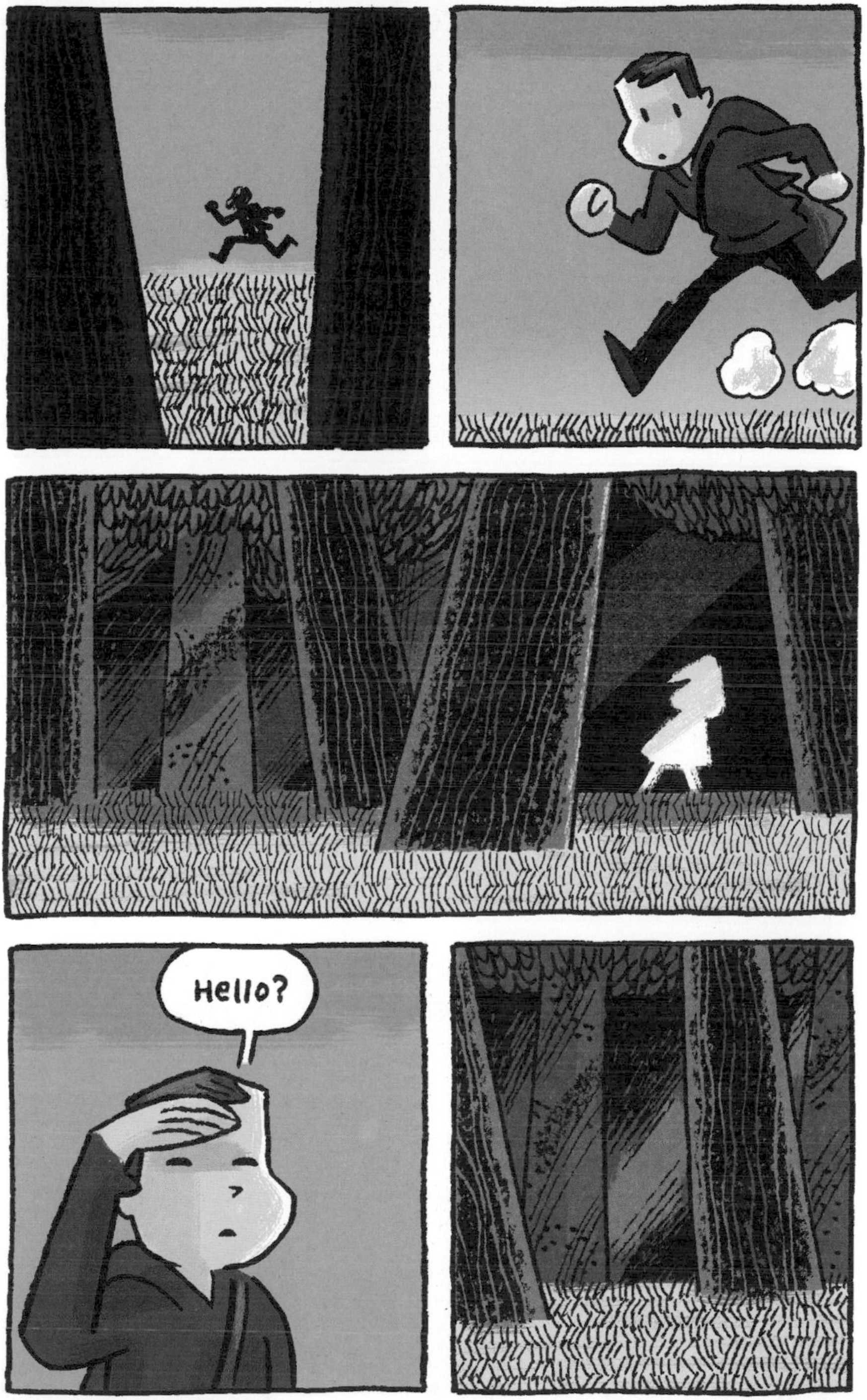
Hello?

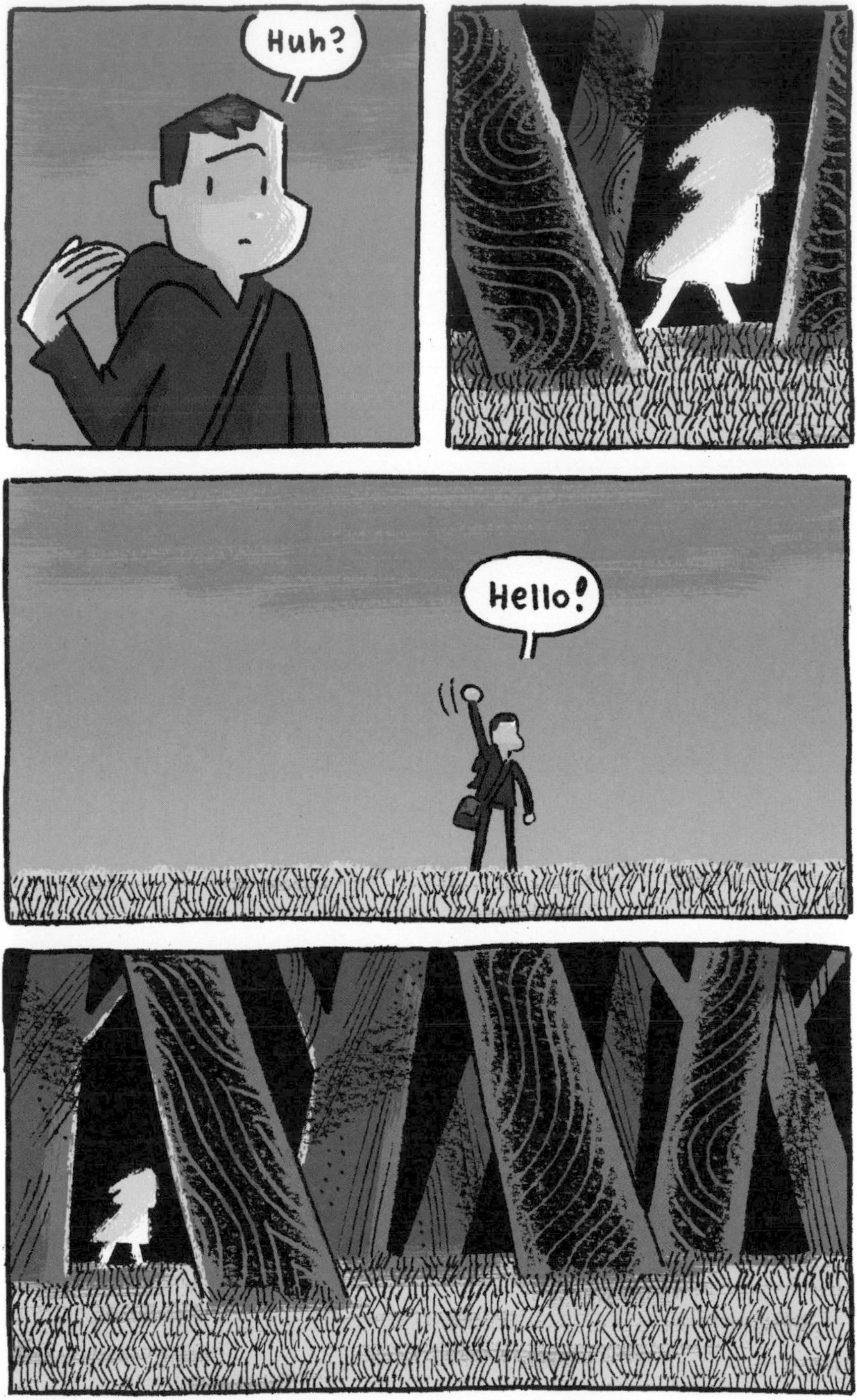
Huh?
Hello!

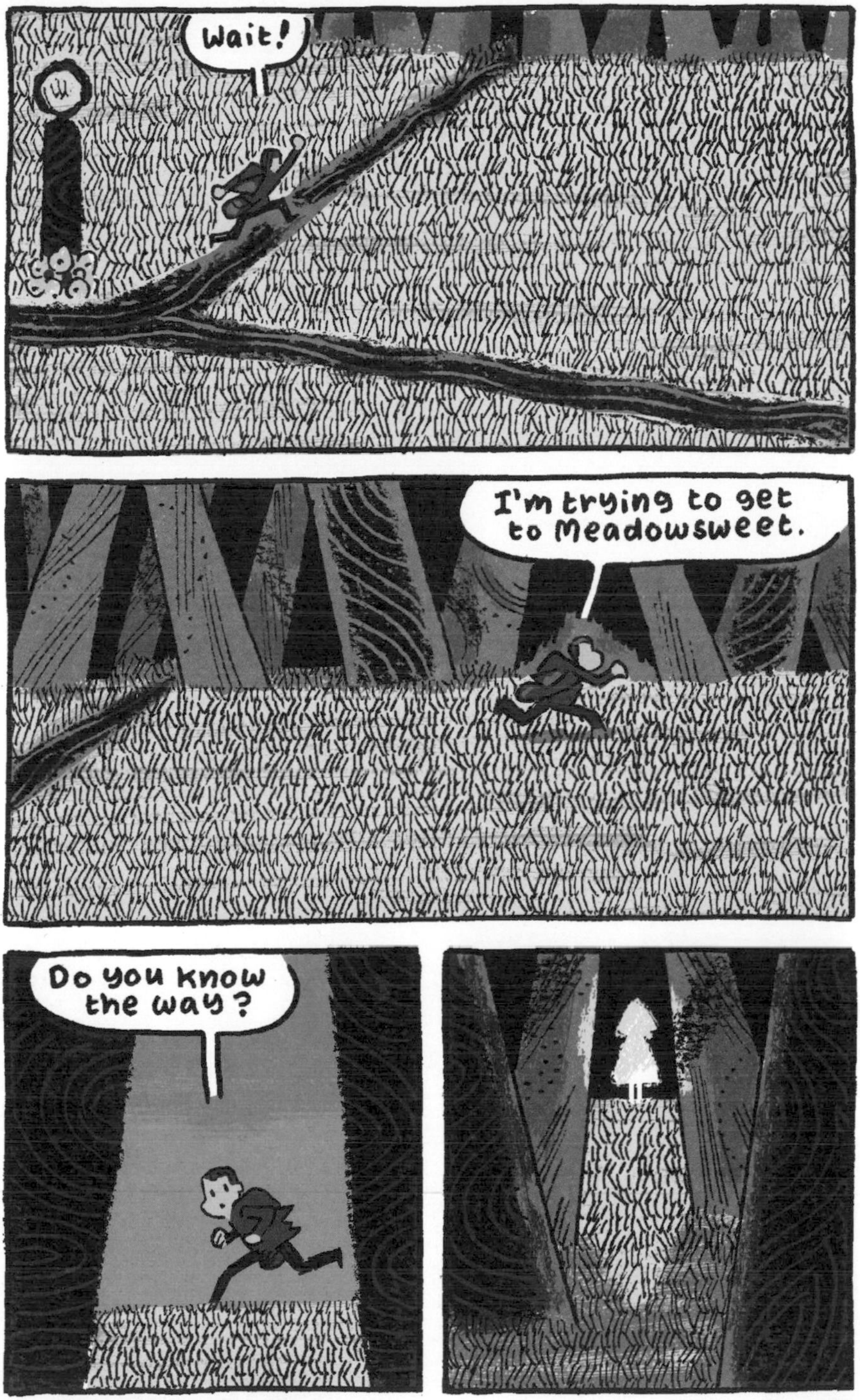
Wait!
I'm trying to get to Meadowsweet.
Do you know the way?

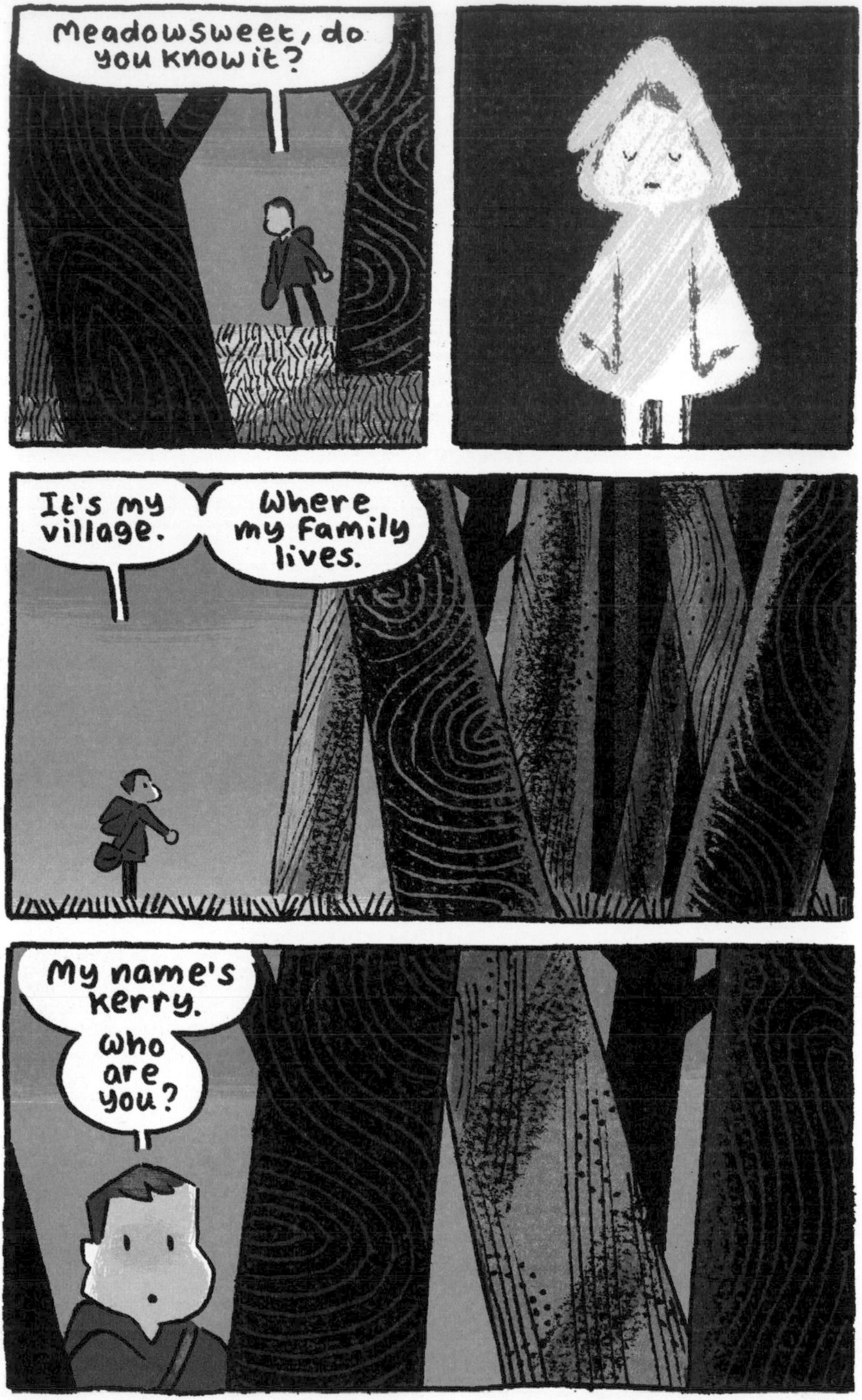
Meadowsweet, do you know it?
It's my village.
Where my family lives.
My name's Kerry.
Who are you?

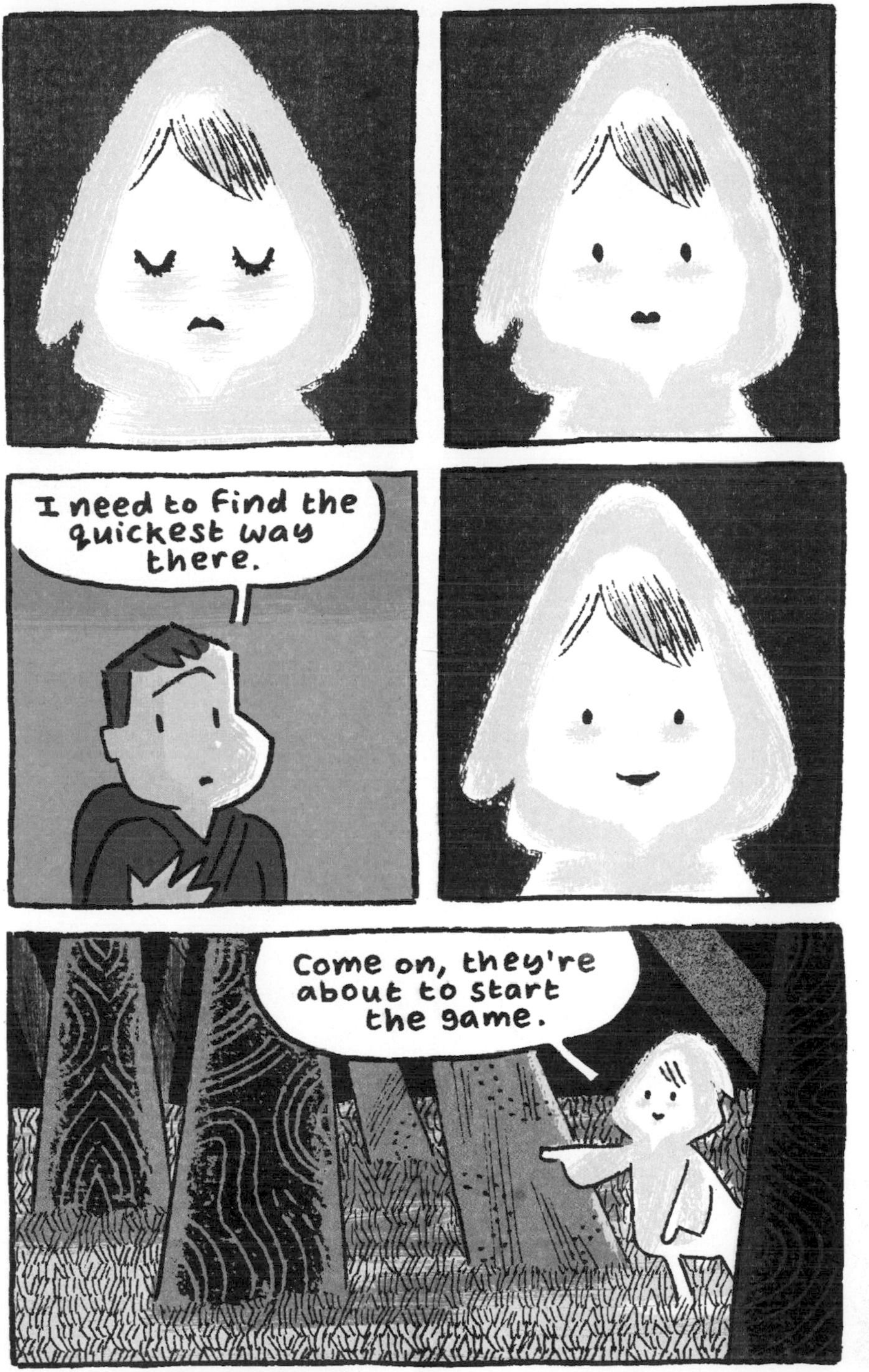
I need to find the quickest way there.
Come on, they're about to start the game.

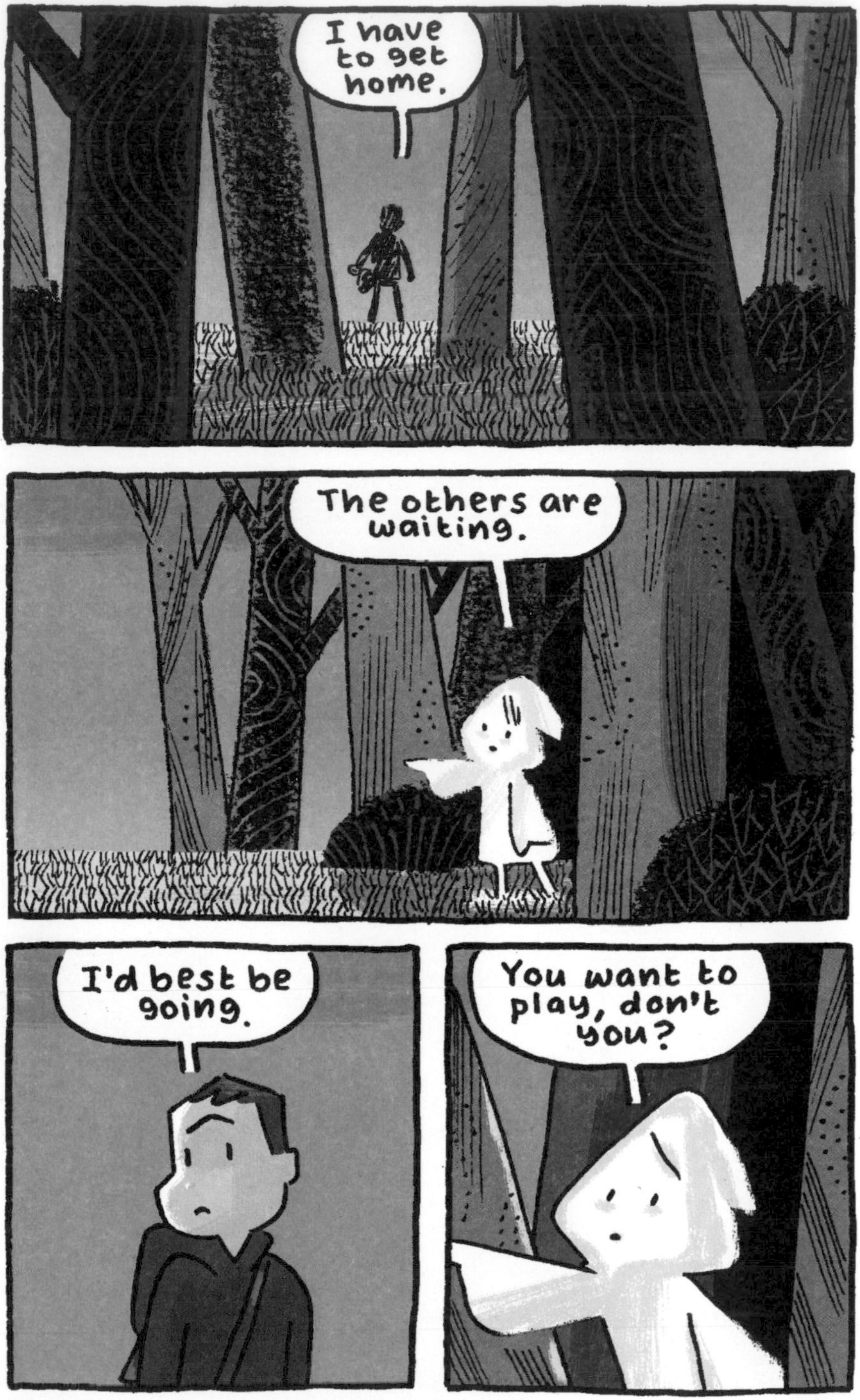
I have to get home.
The others are waiting.
I'd best be going.
You want to play, don't you?

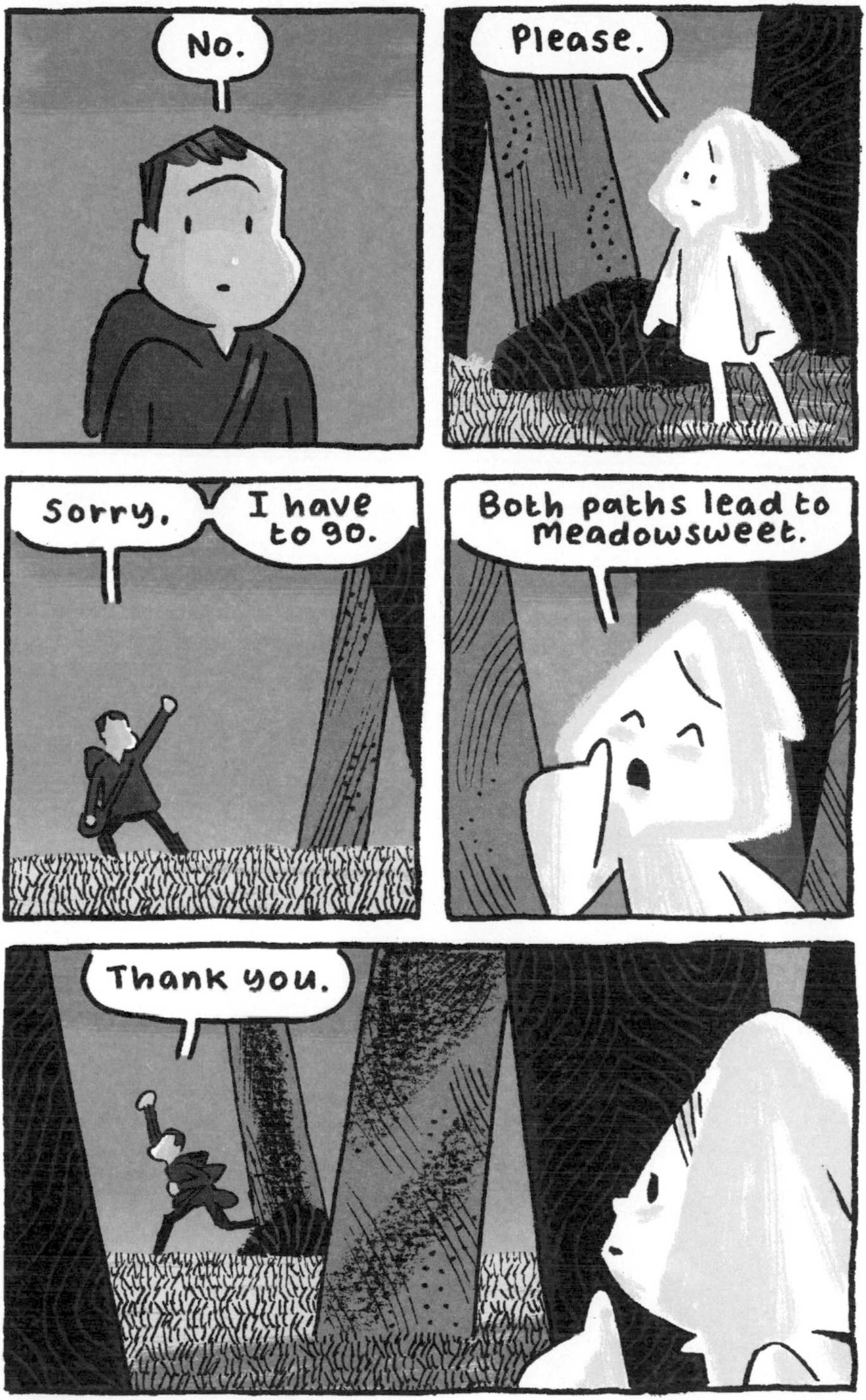
No.
Please.
Sorry.
I have to go.
Both paths lead to Meadowsweet.
Thank you.

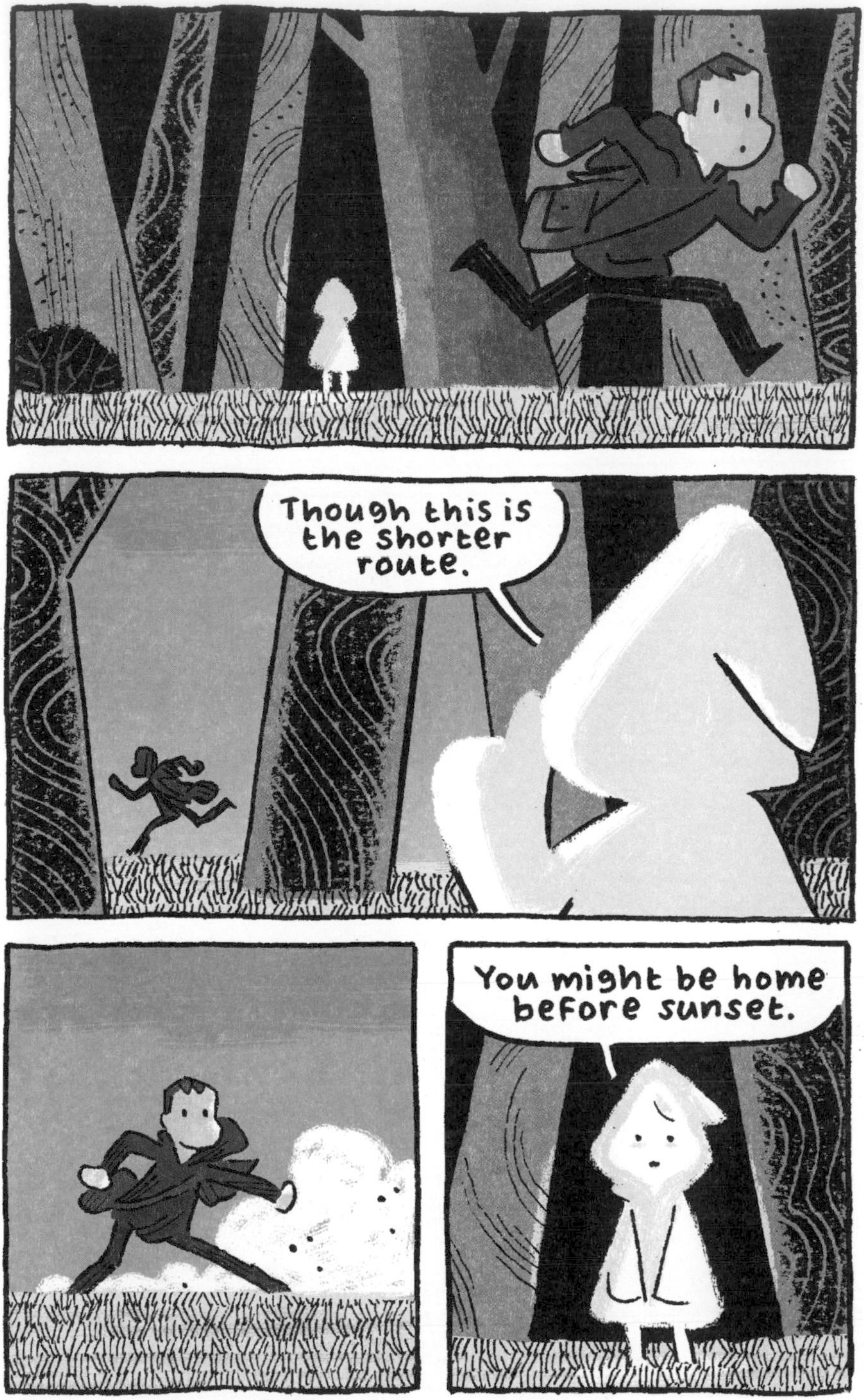
Though this is the shorter route.
You might be home before sunset.

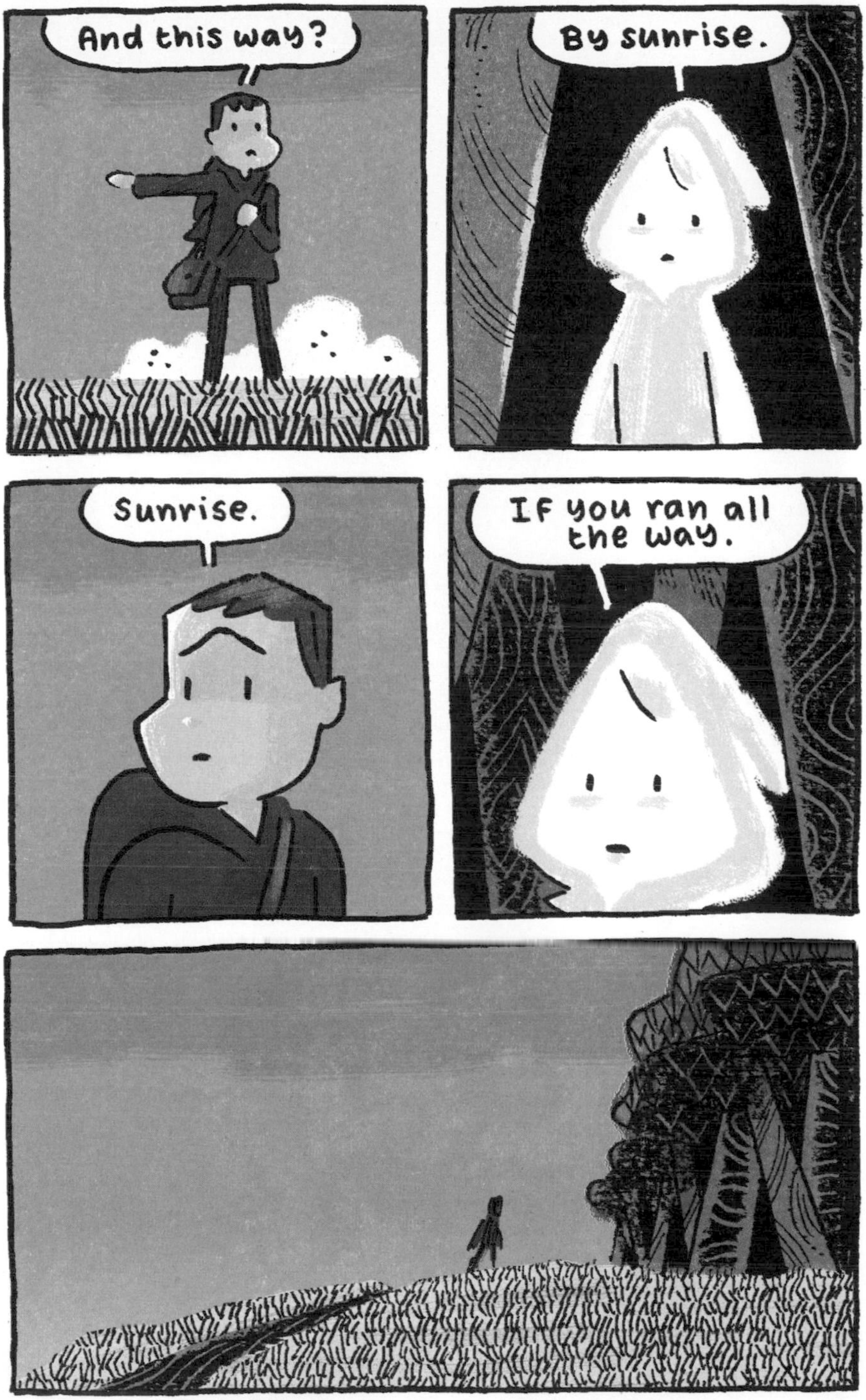
And this way?
By sunrise.
Sunrise.
If you ran all the way.

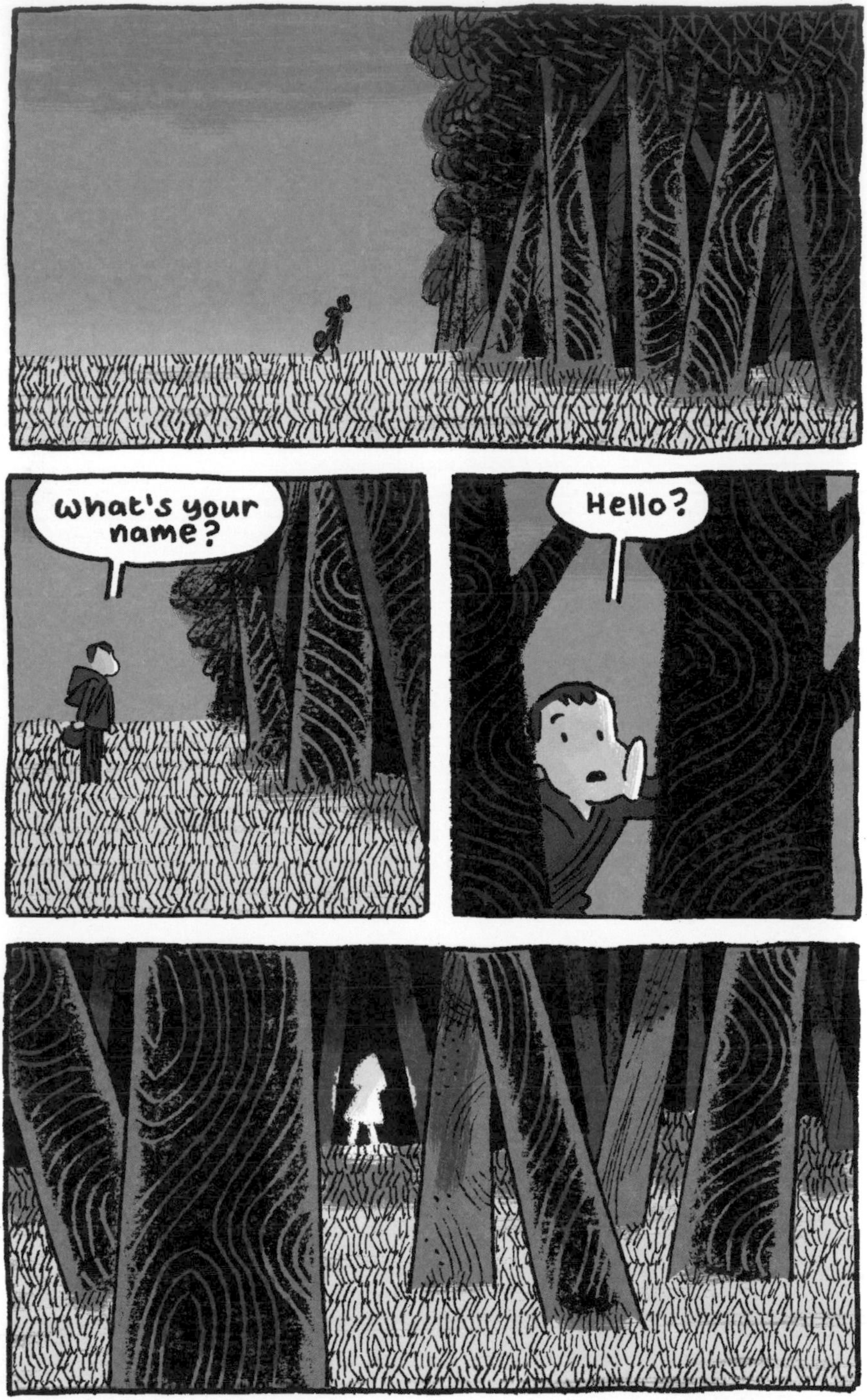
What's your name?
Hello?

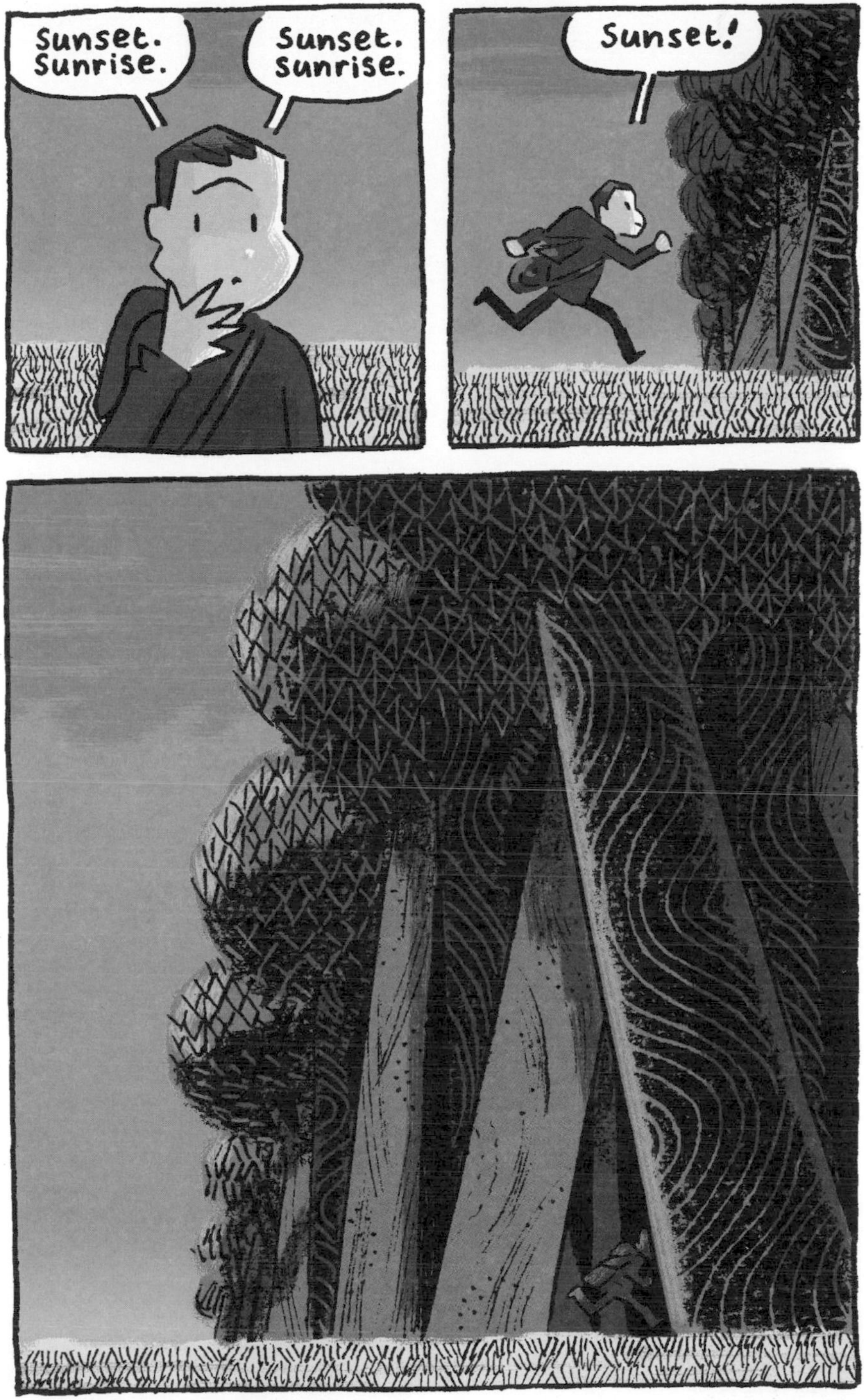
Sunset.
Sunrise.
Sunset.
sunrise.
Sunset!

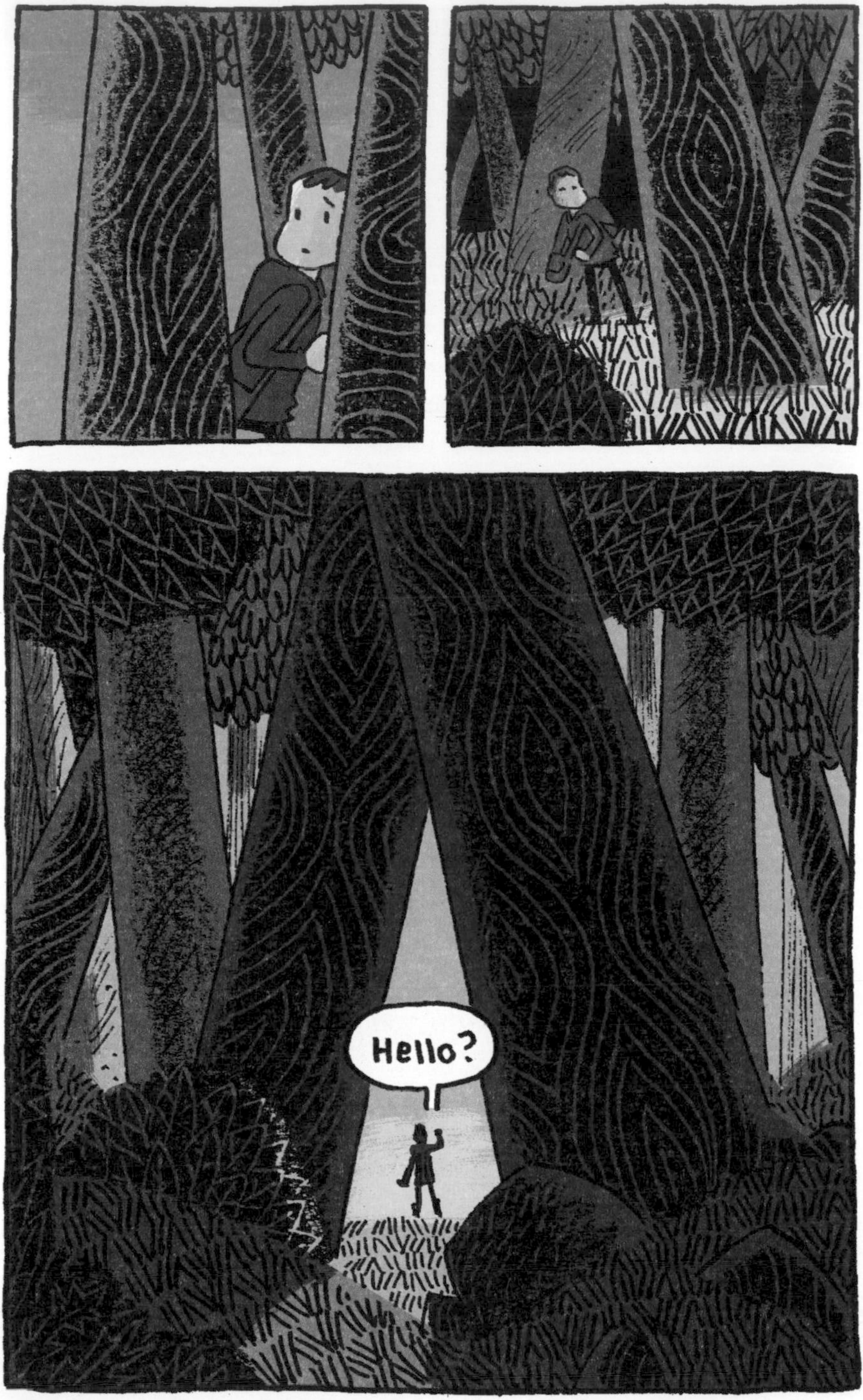
Hello?

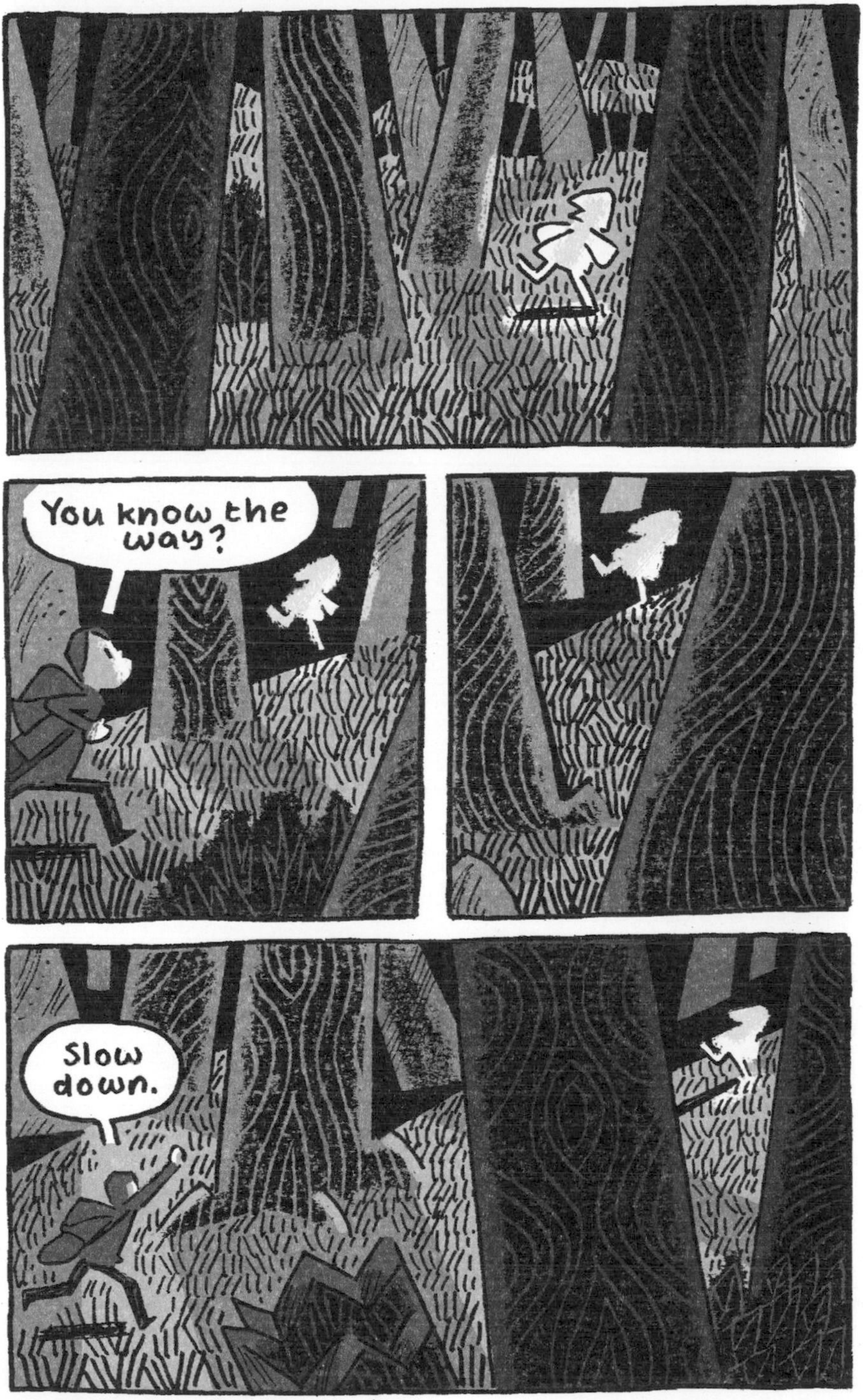
You know the way?
Slow down.

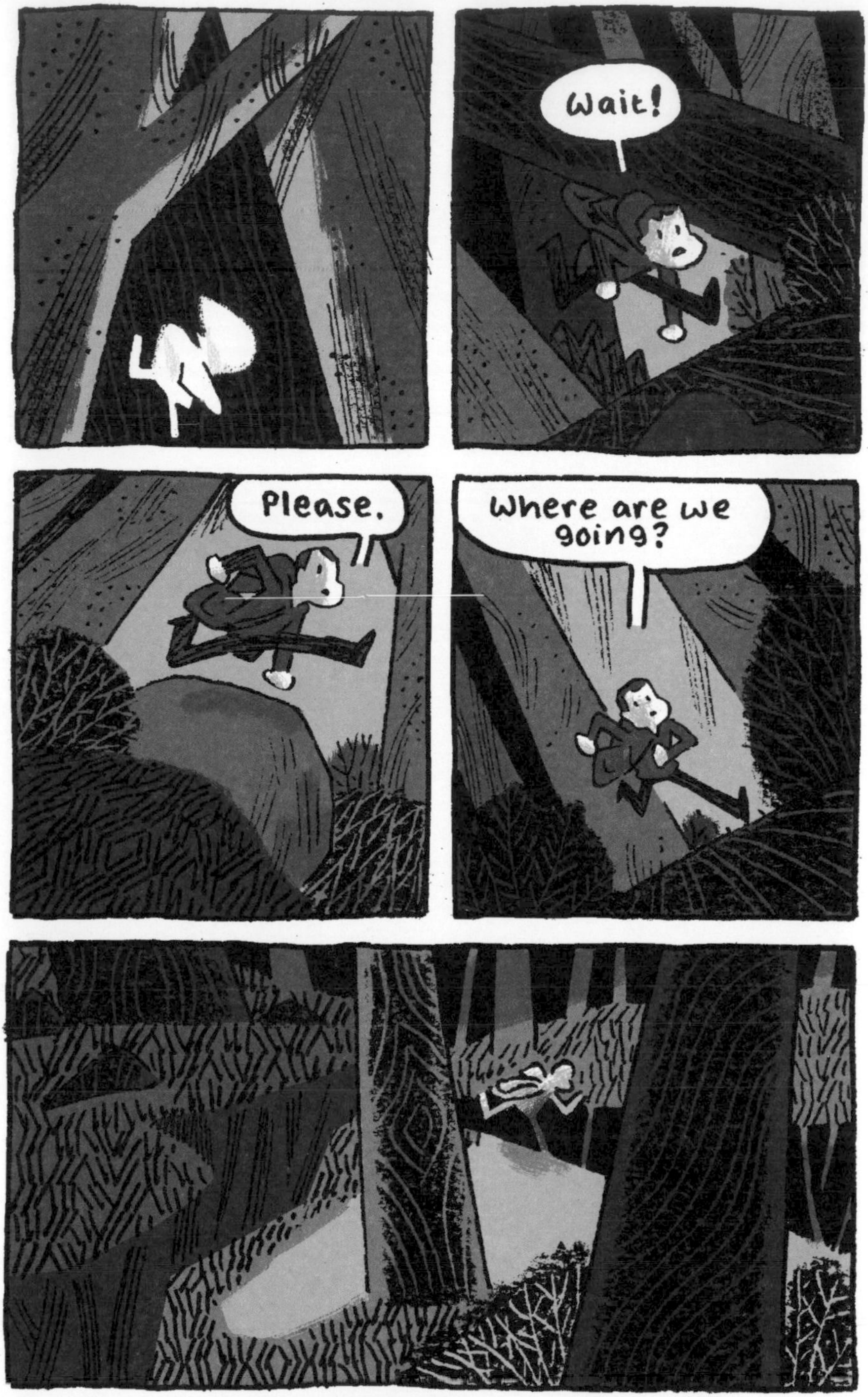
Wait!
Please.
Where are we going?

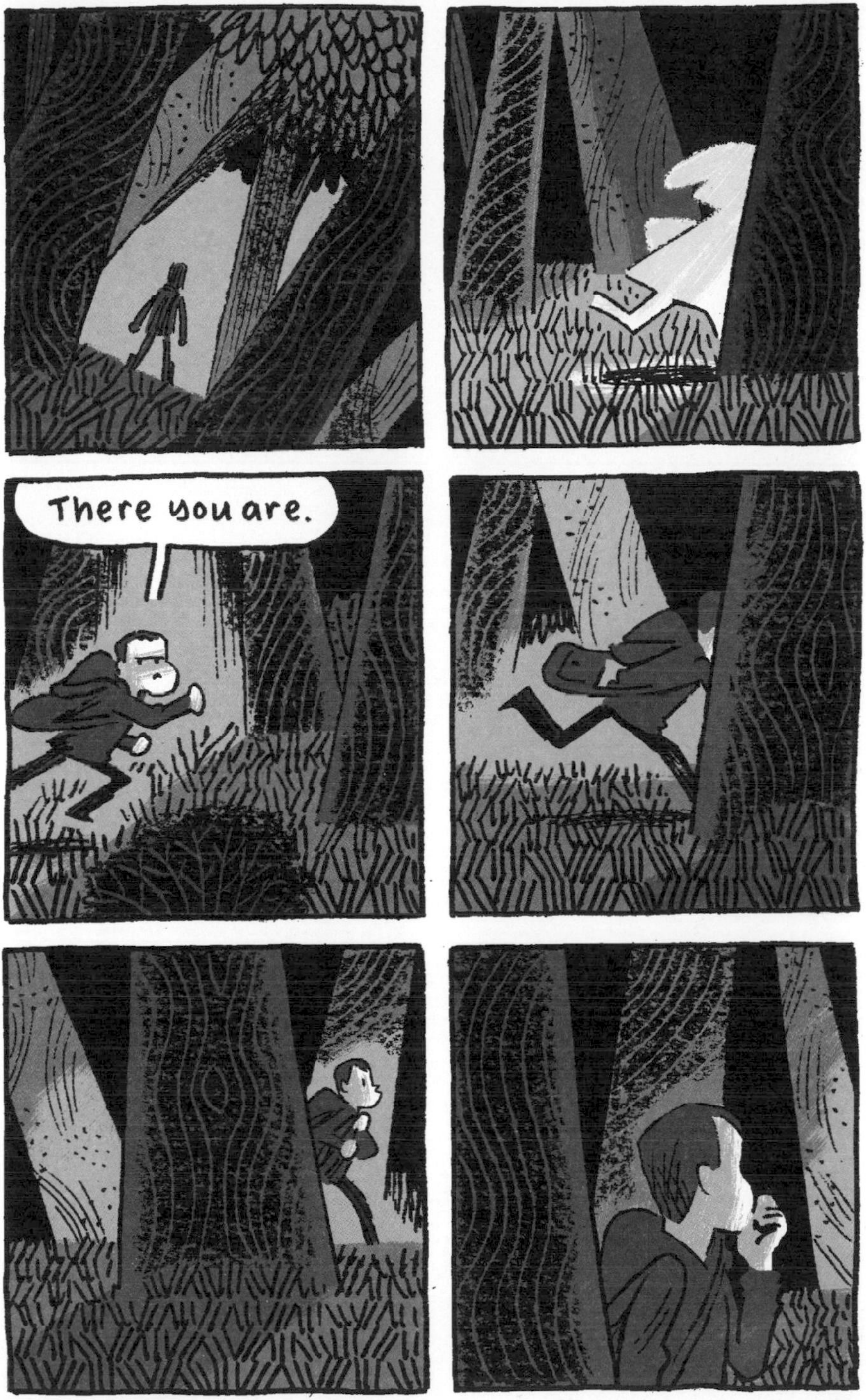
There you are.

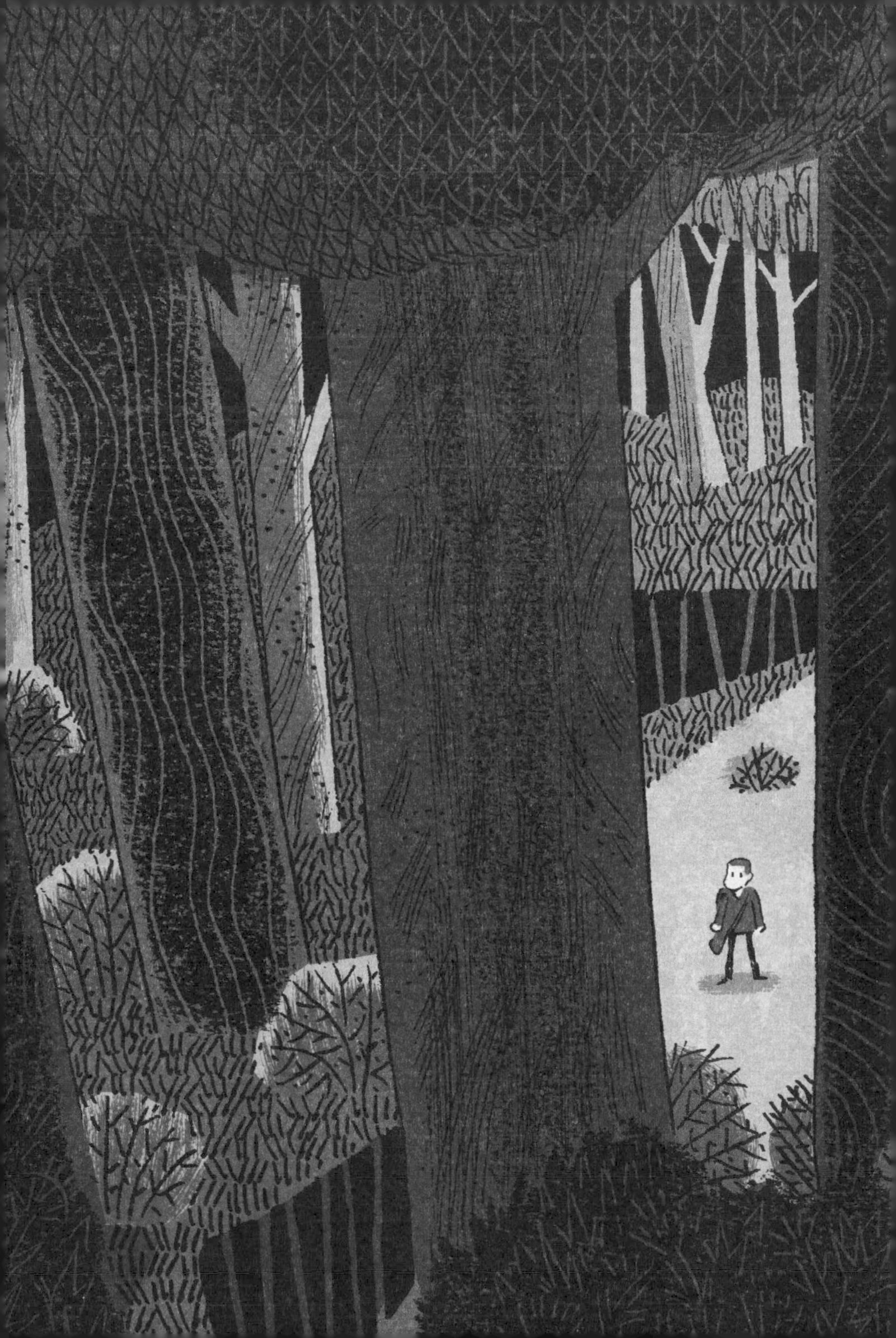

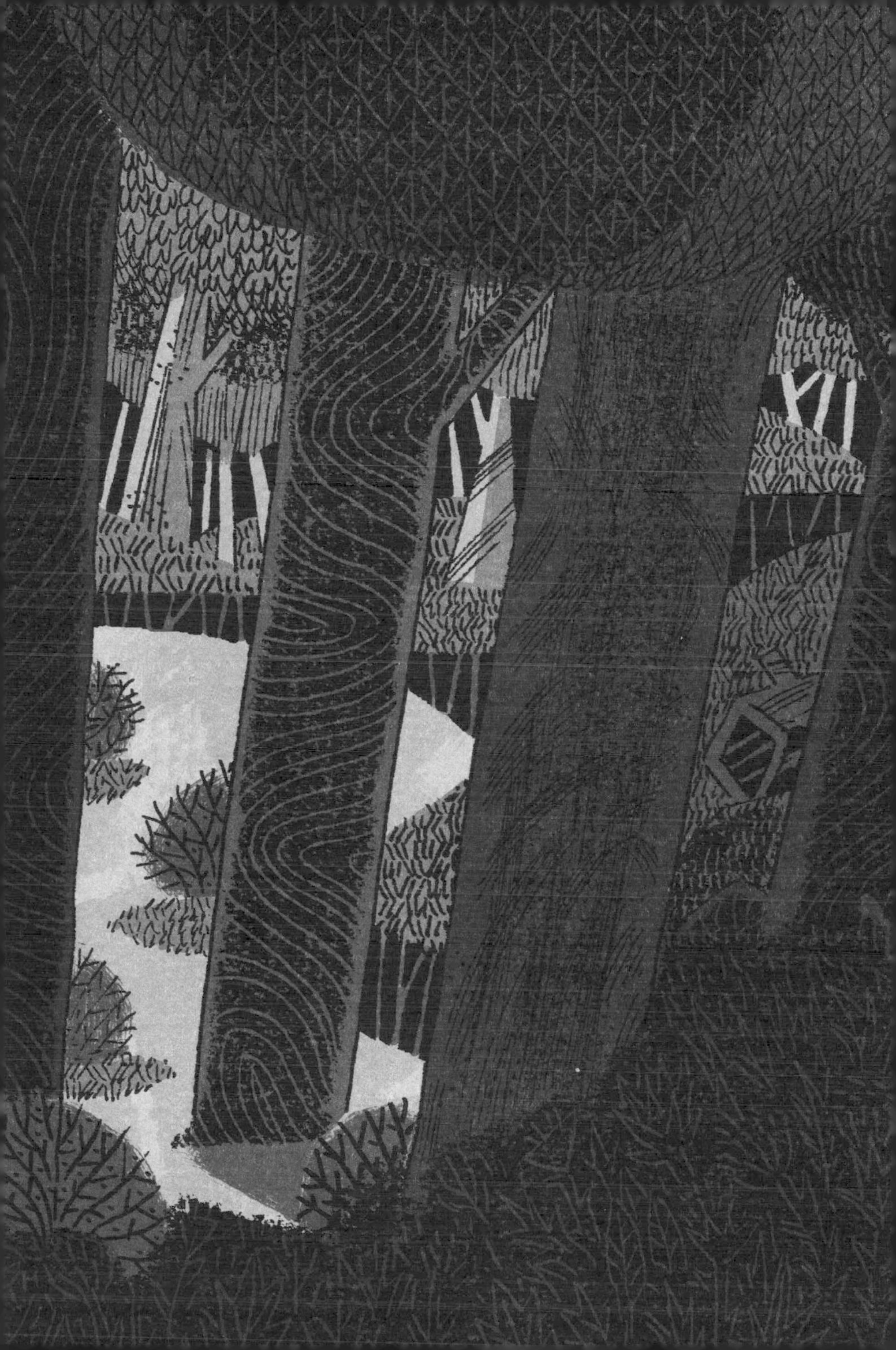

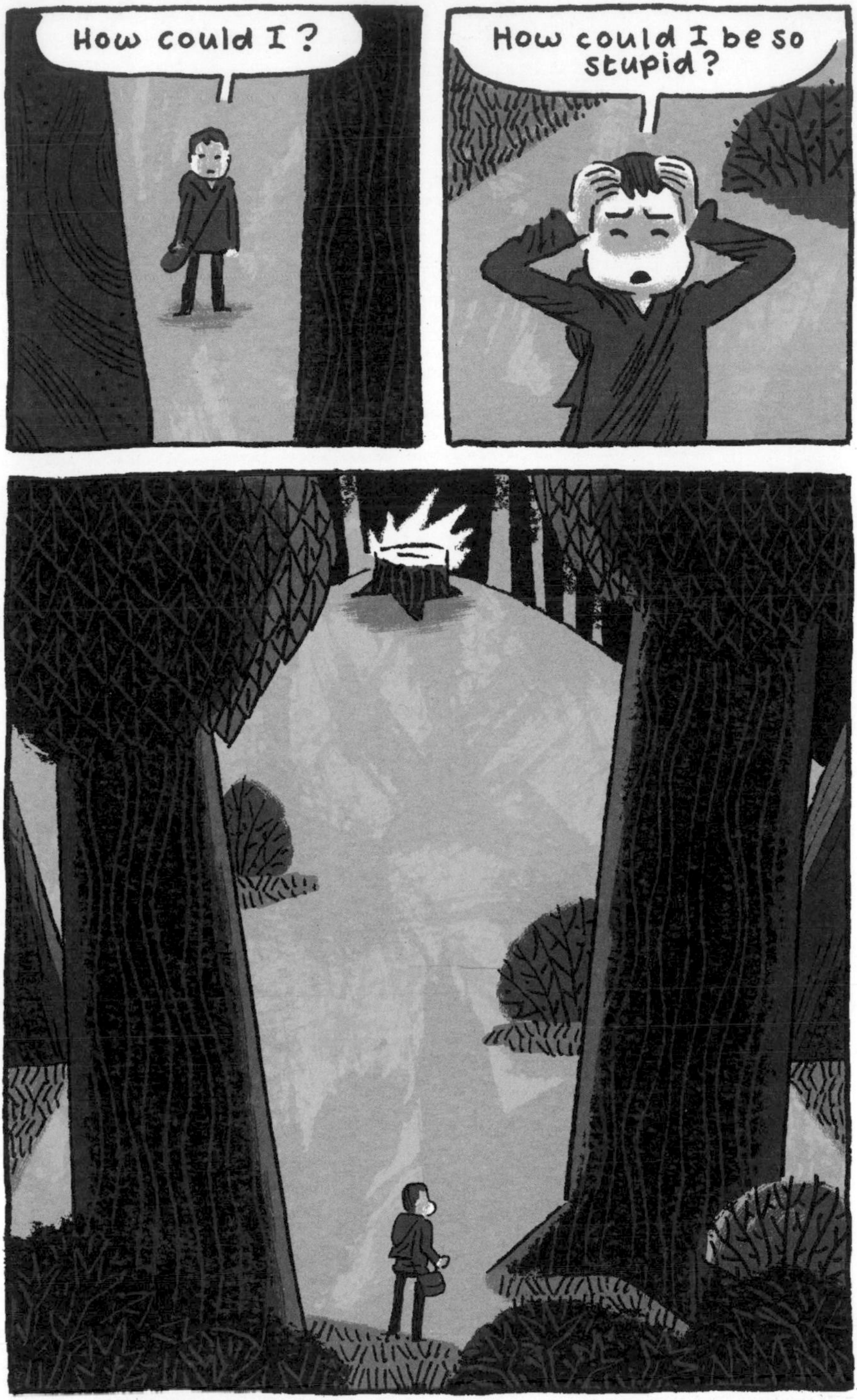
How could I?
How could I be so stupid?

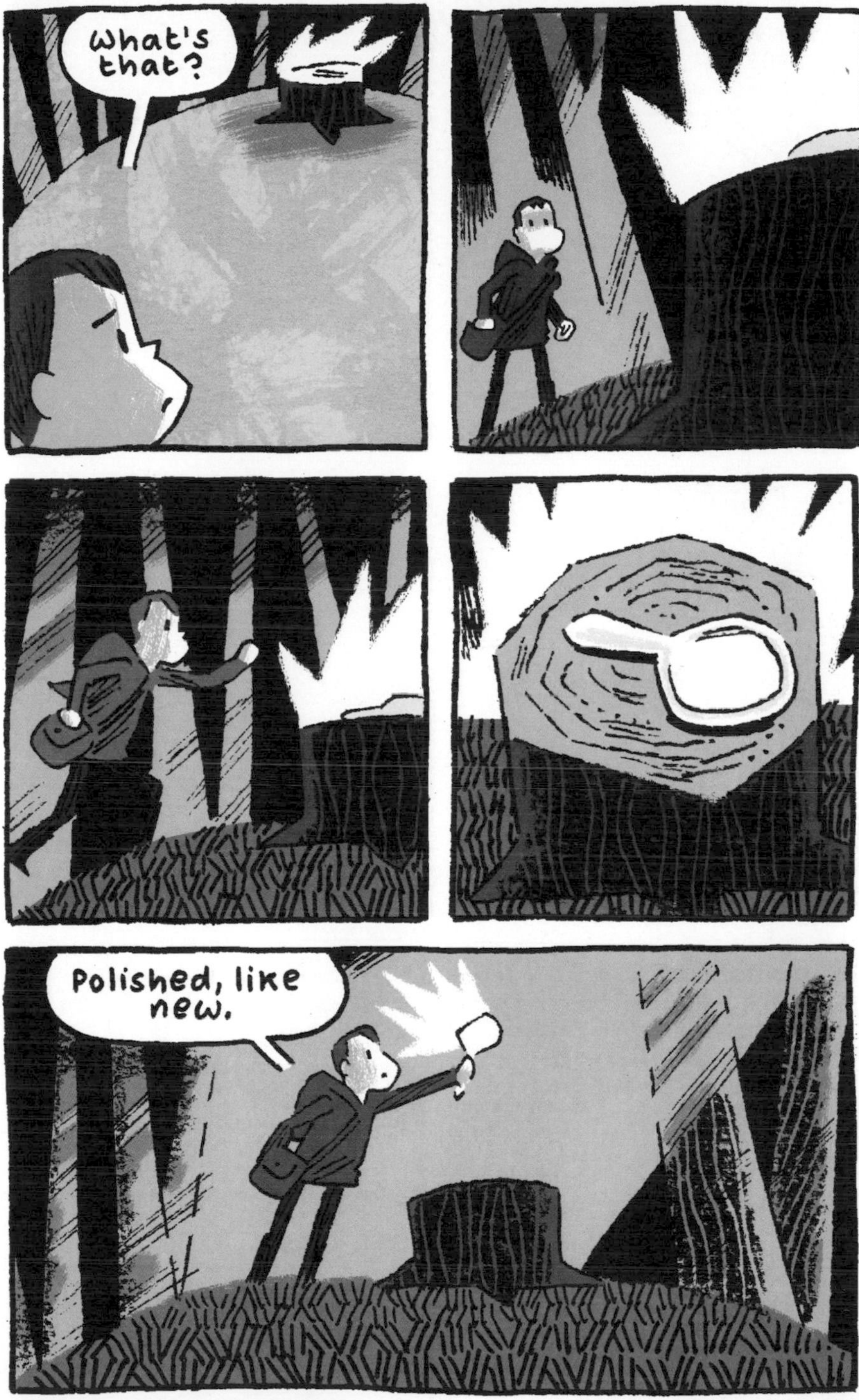
What's that?
Polished, like new.

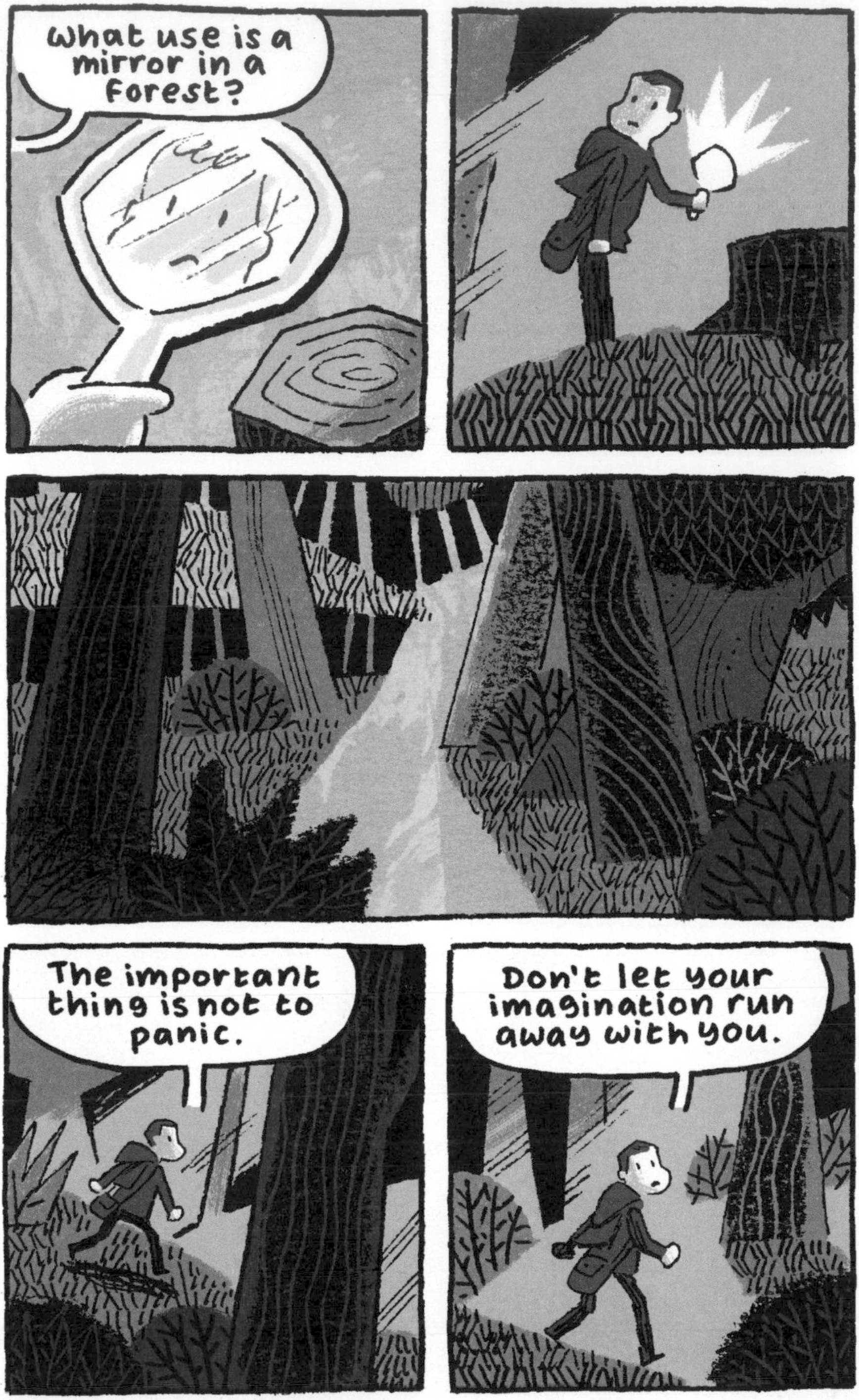
What use is a mirror in a forest?
The important thing is not to panic.
Don't let your imagination run away with you.

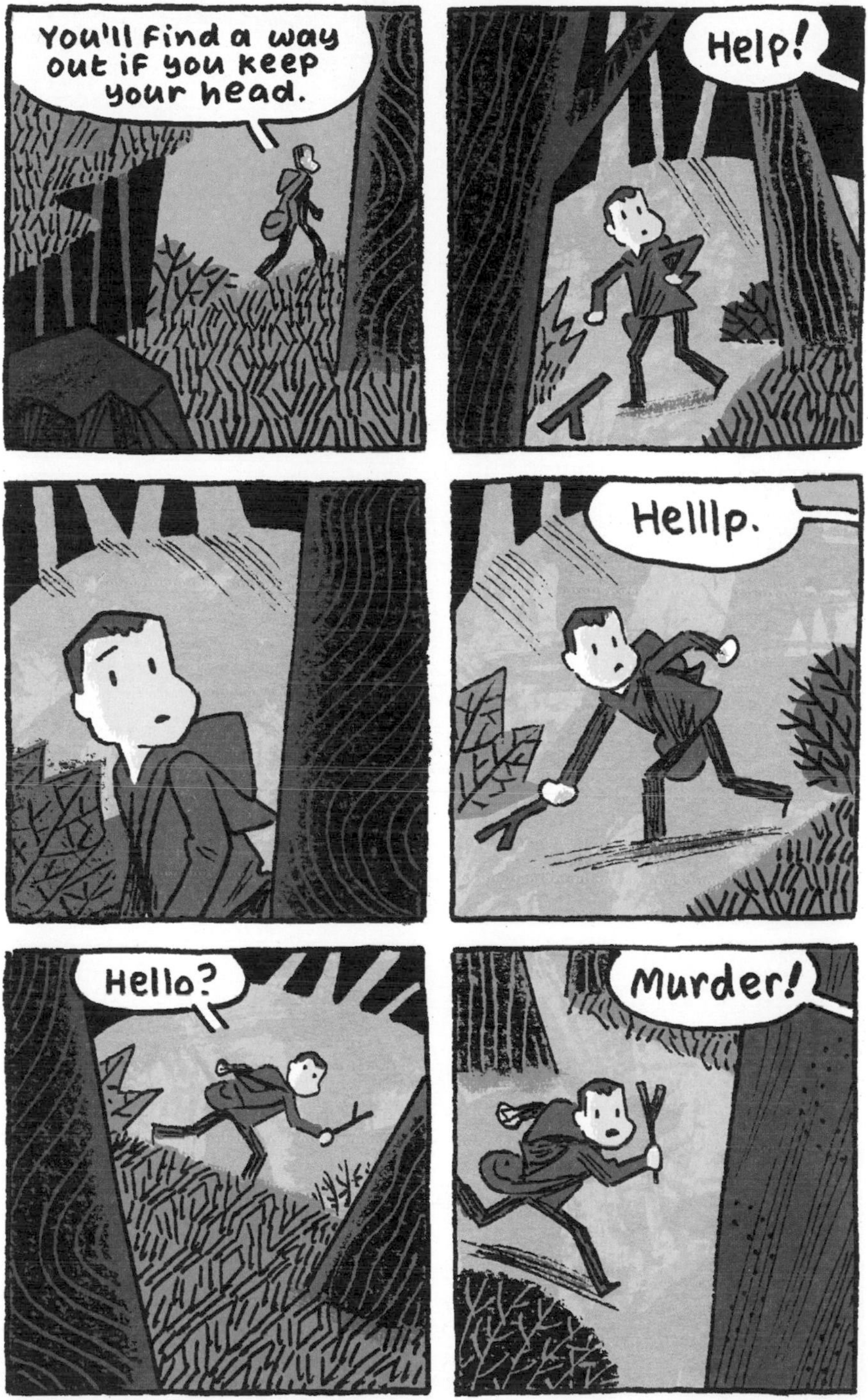
You'll find a way out if you keep your head.
Help!
Helllp.
Hello?
Murder!

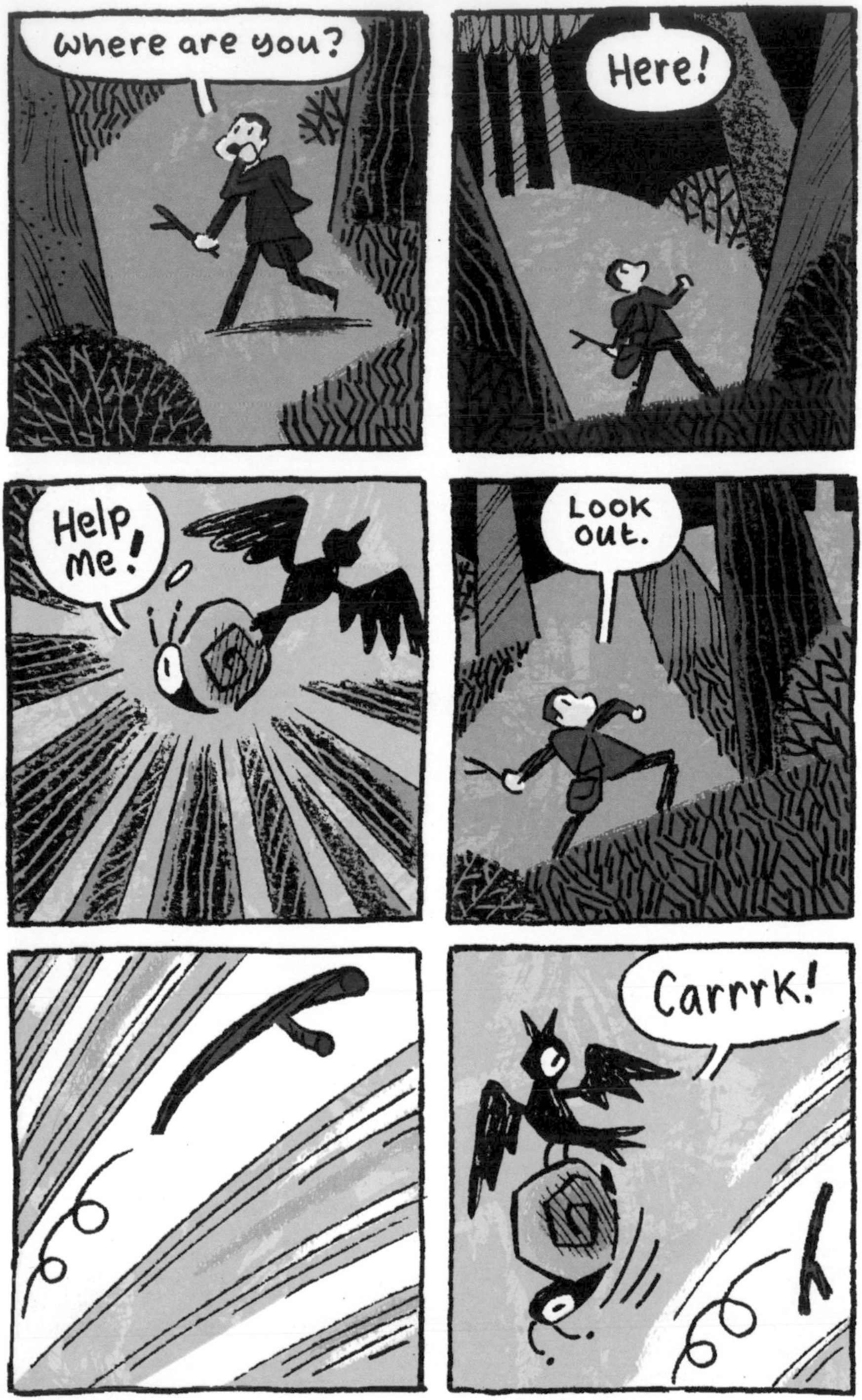
Where are you?
Here!
Help me!
Look out.
Carrrk!

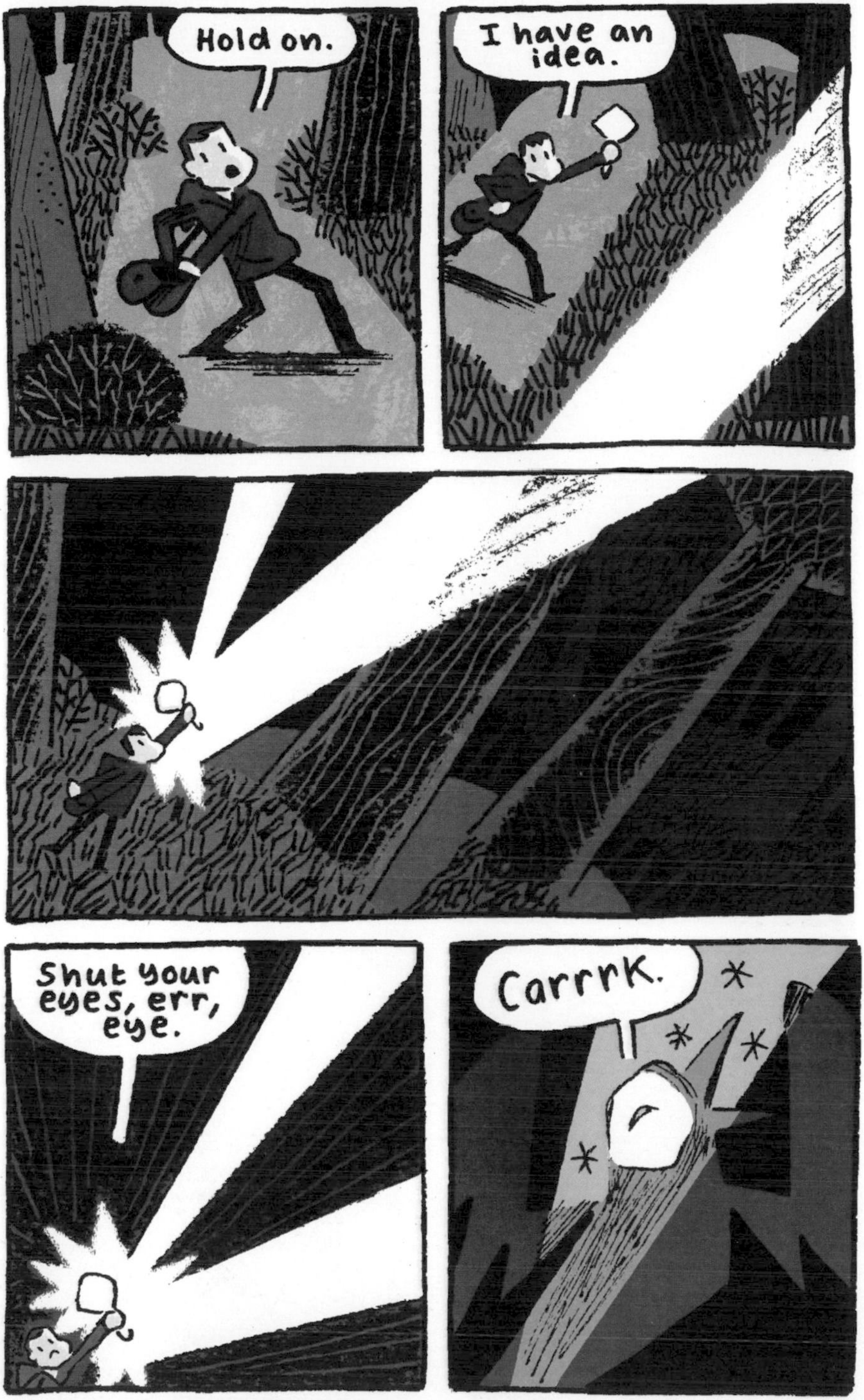
Hold on.
I have an idea.
Shut your eyes, err, eye.
Carrrk.

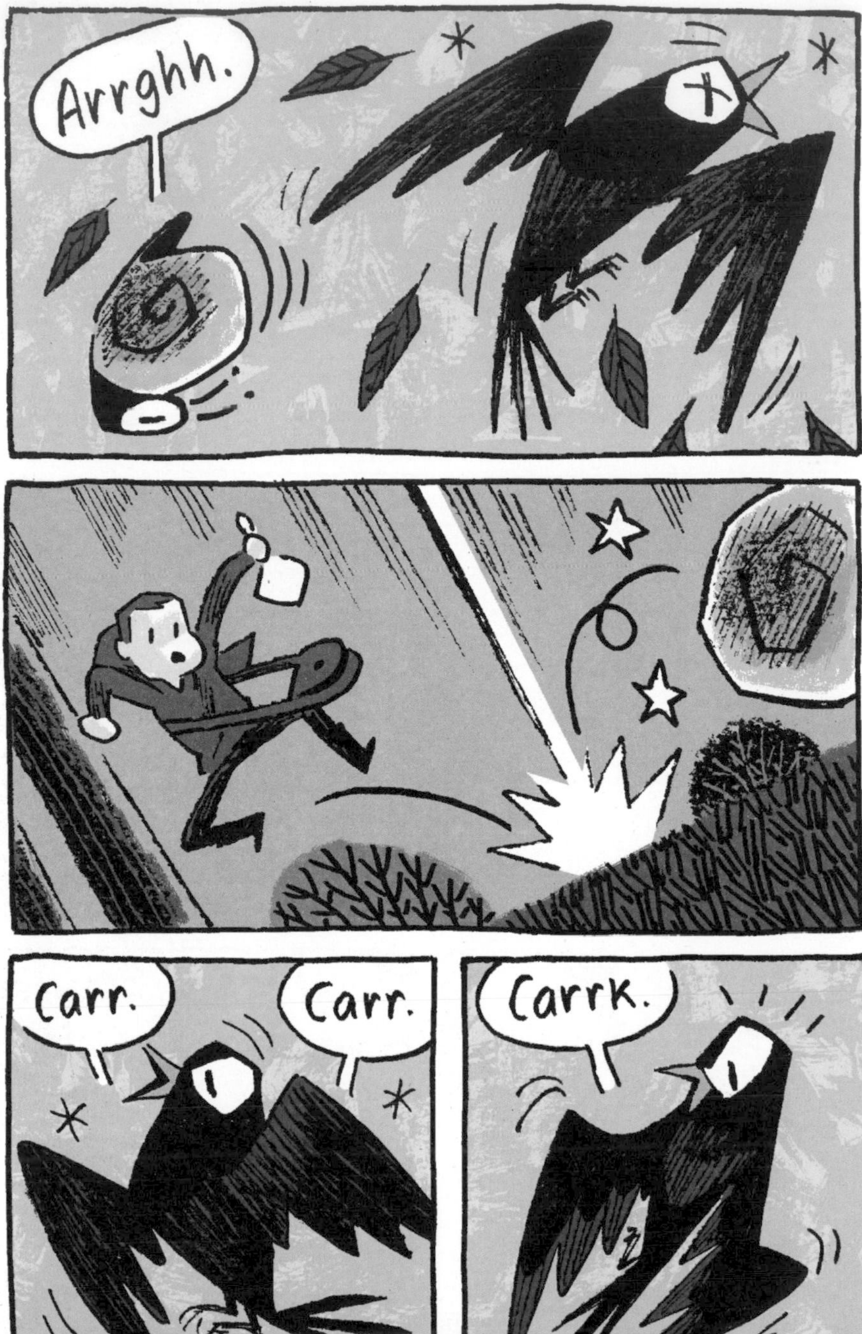
Arrghh.
Carr.
Carr.
Carrk.

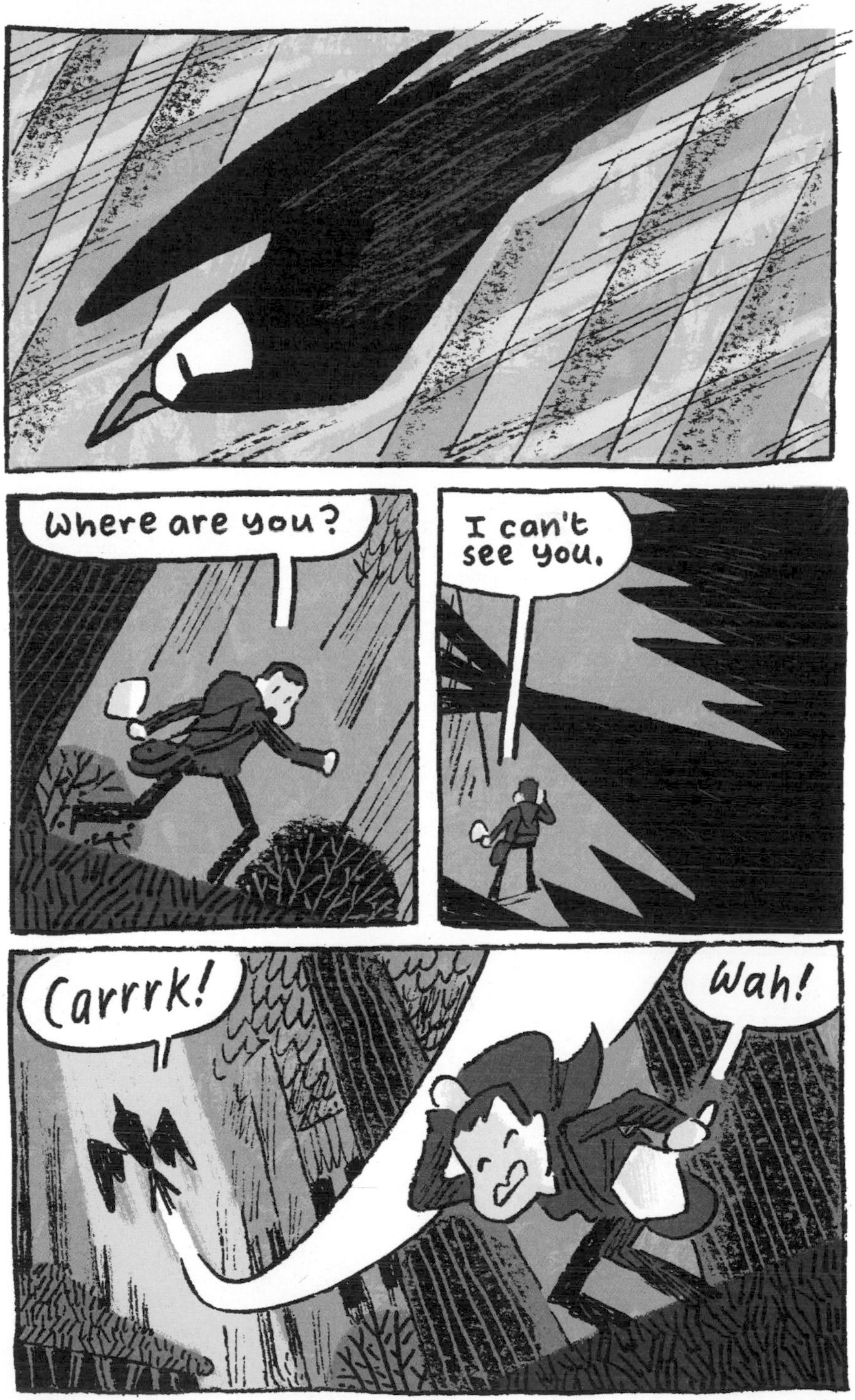
Where are you?
I can't see you.
Carrrk!
Wah!

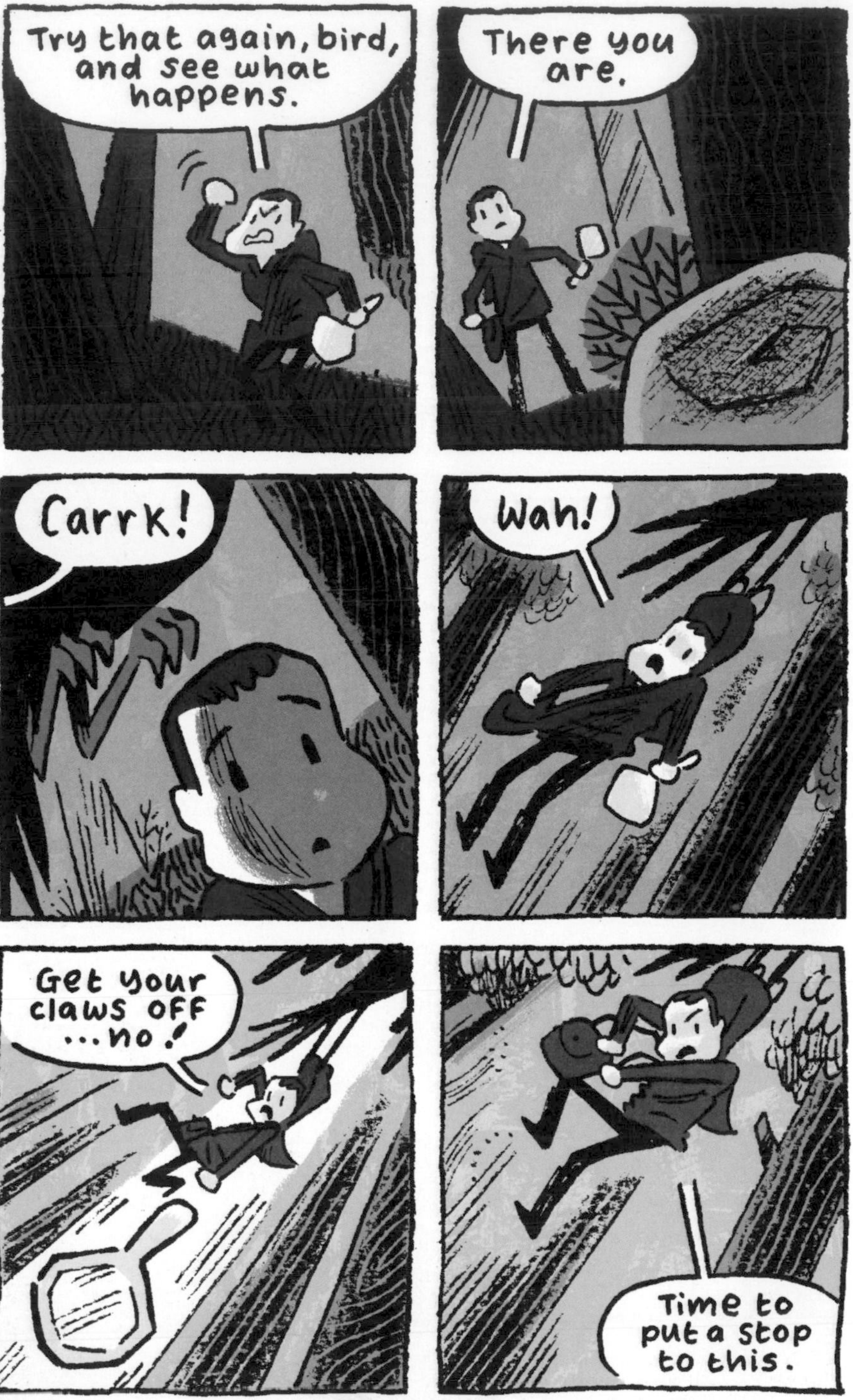
Try that again, bird, and see what happens.
There you are.
Carrk!
Wah!
Get your claws off ...no!
Time to put a stop to this.

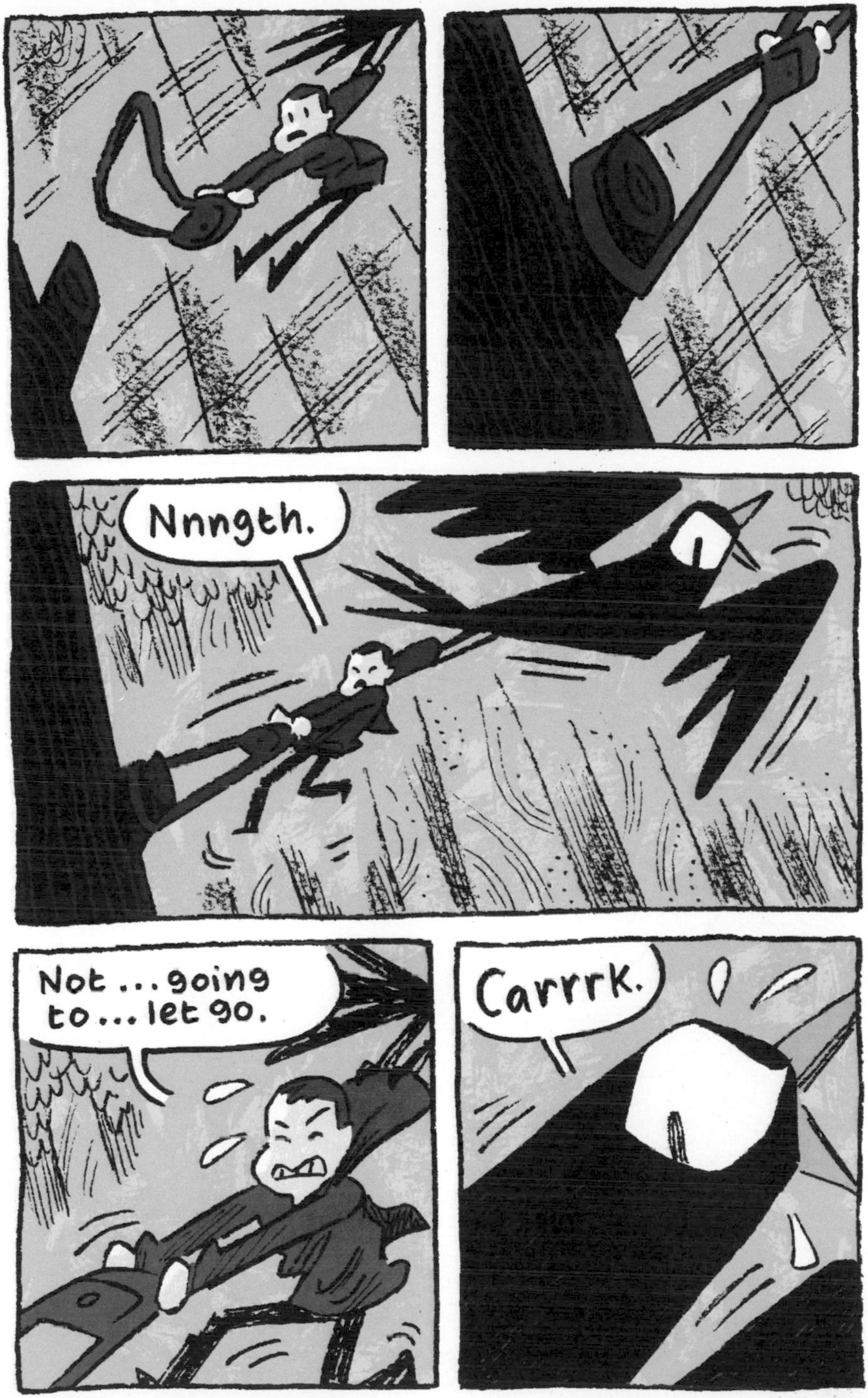
Nnngth.
Not ... going to ... let go.
Carrrk.

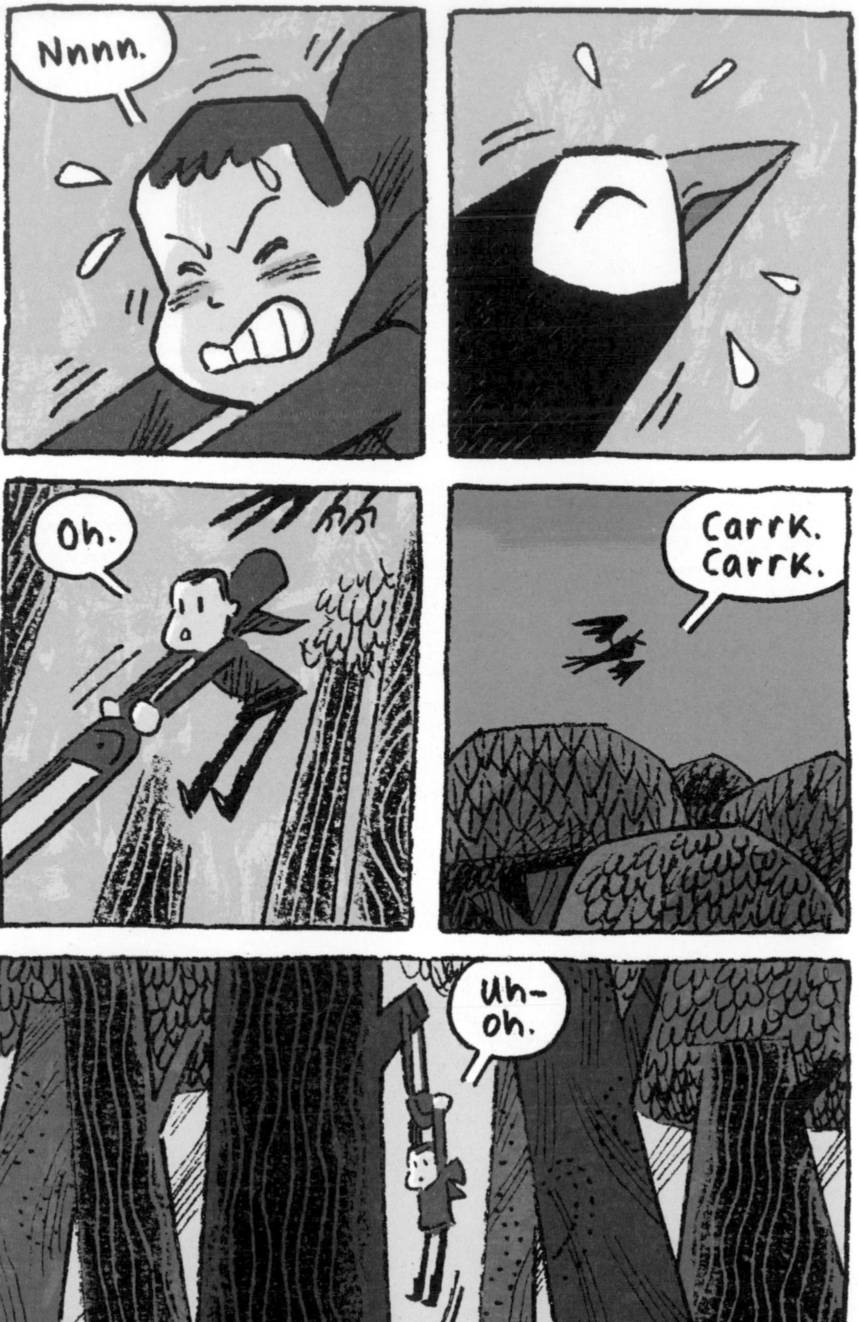
Nnnn.
Oh.
Carrk. Carrk.
Uh-oh.

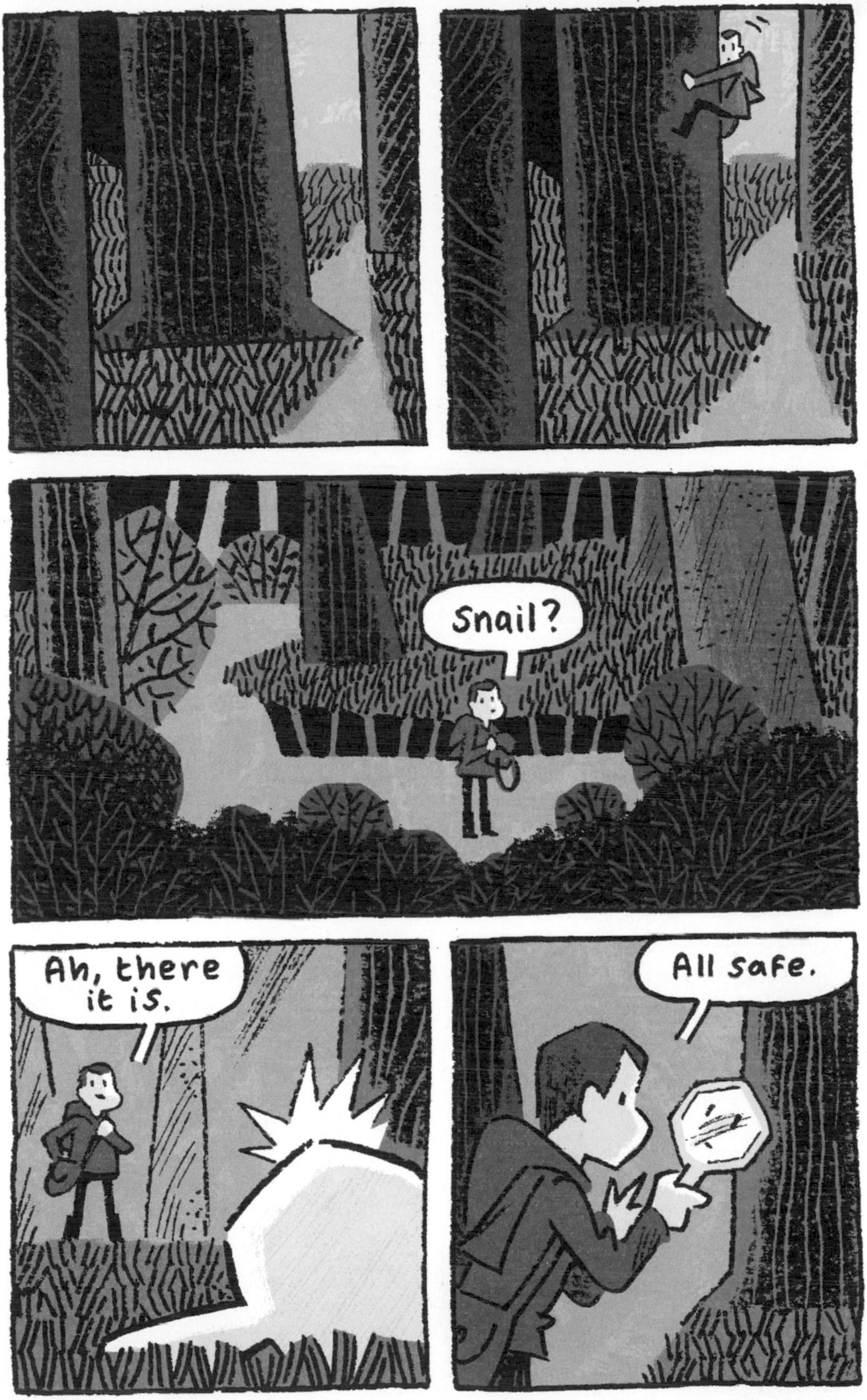
Snail?
Ah, there it is.
All safe.

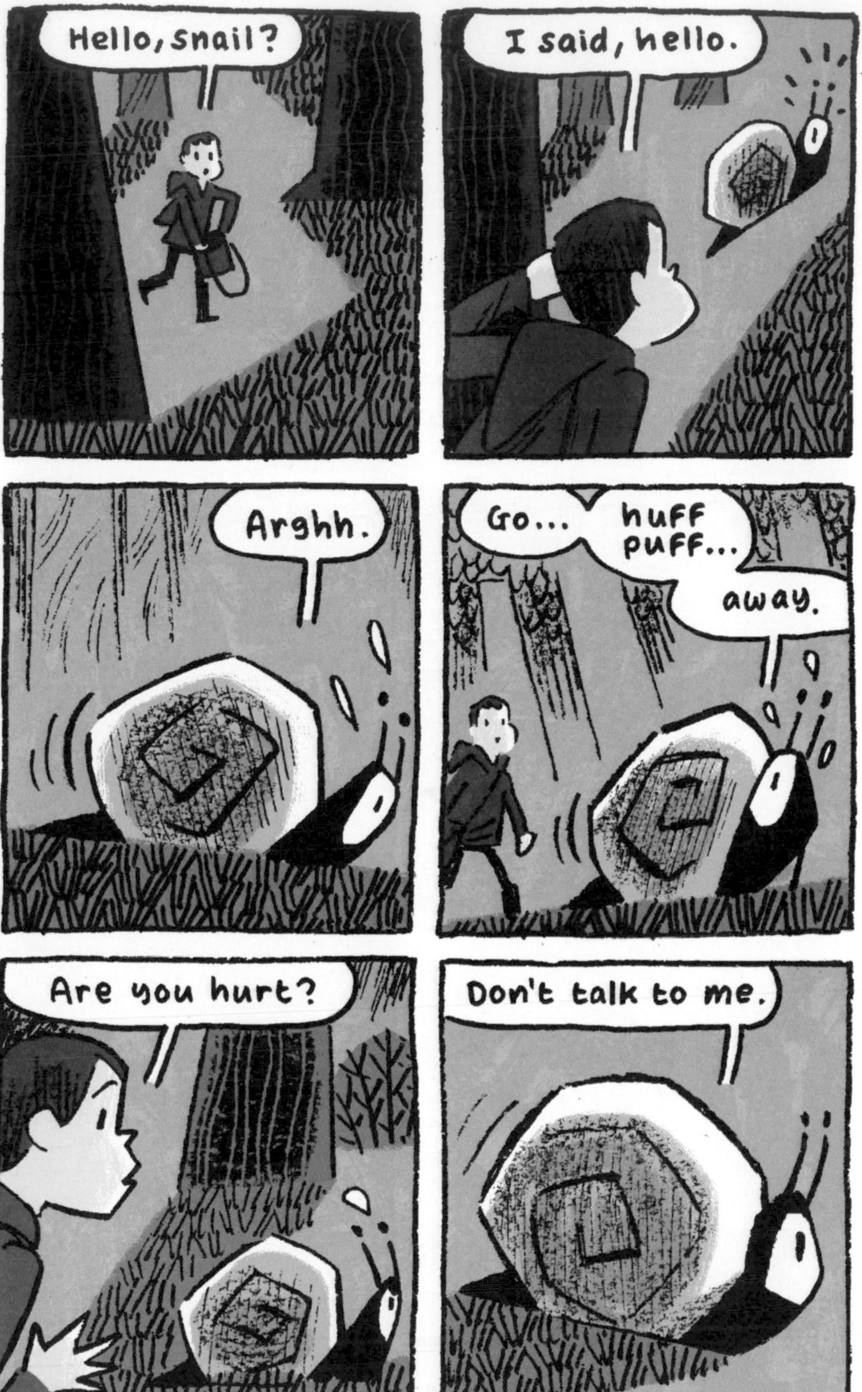
Hello, snail?
I said, hello.
Arghh.
Go...
huff puff...
away.
Are you hurt?
Don't talk to me.

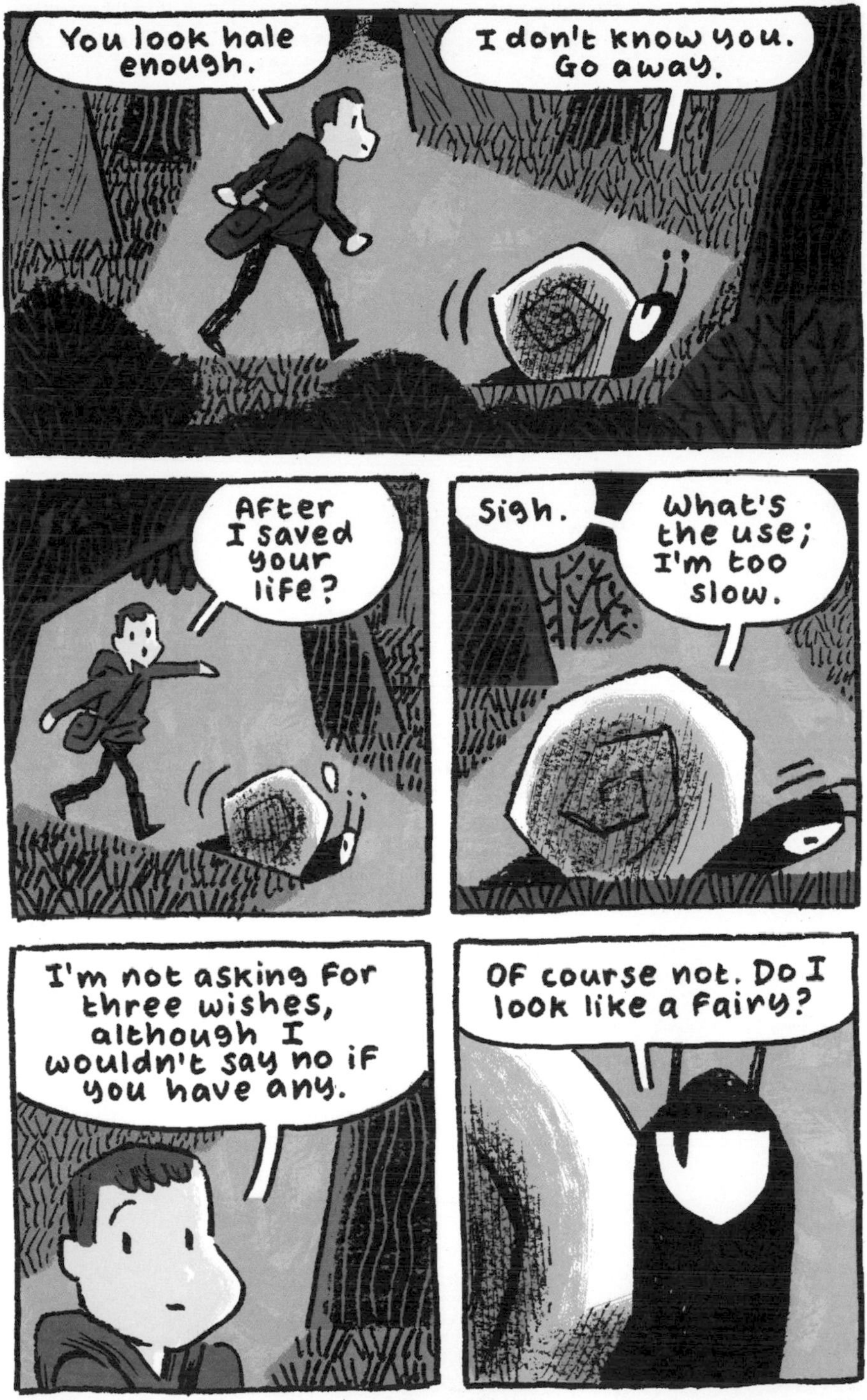
You look hale enough.
I don't know you. Go away.
After I saved your life?
Sigh.
What's the use; I'm too slow.
I'm not asking for three wishes, although I wouldn't say no if you have any.
Of course not. Do I look like a fairy?

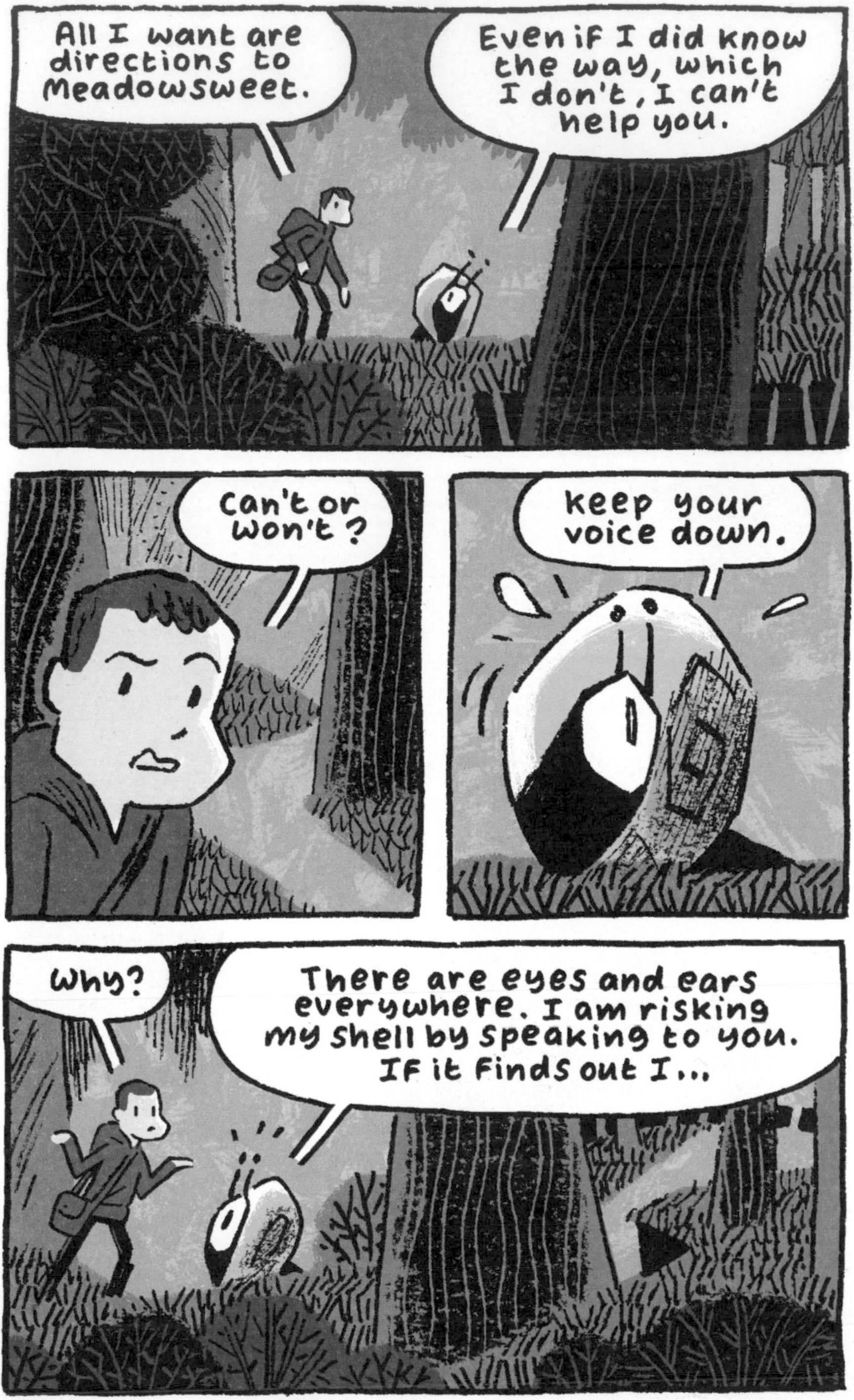
All I want are directions to Meadowsweet.
Even if I did know the way, which I don't, I can't help you.
Can't or won't?
Keep your voice down.
Why?
There are eyes and ears everywhere. I am risking my shell by speaking to you. If it finds out I...

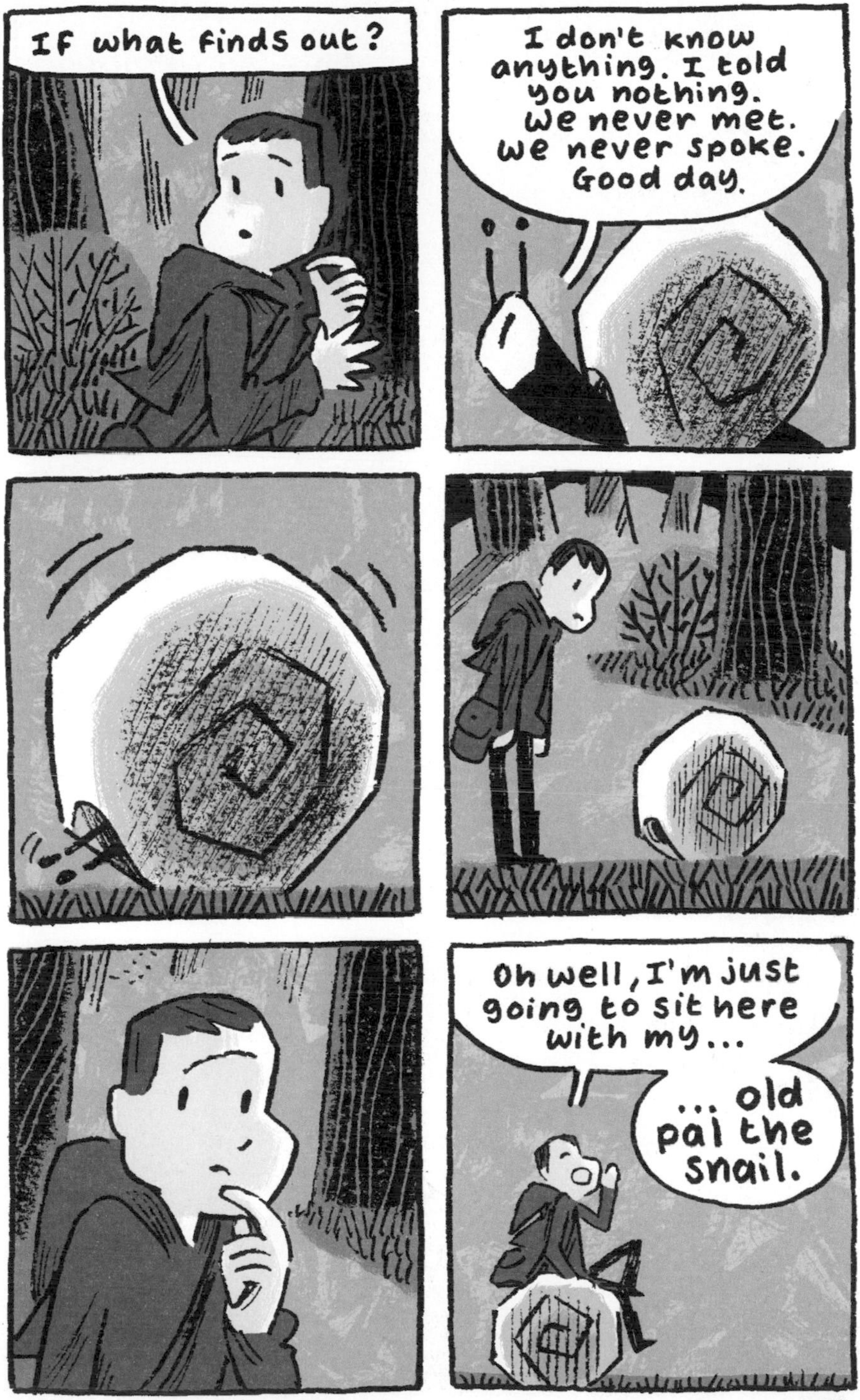
If what finds out?
I don't know anything. I told you nothing. We never met. We never spoke. Good day.
Oh well, I'm just going to sit here with my...
... old pal the snail.

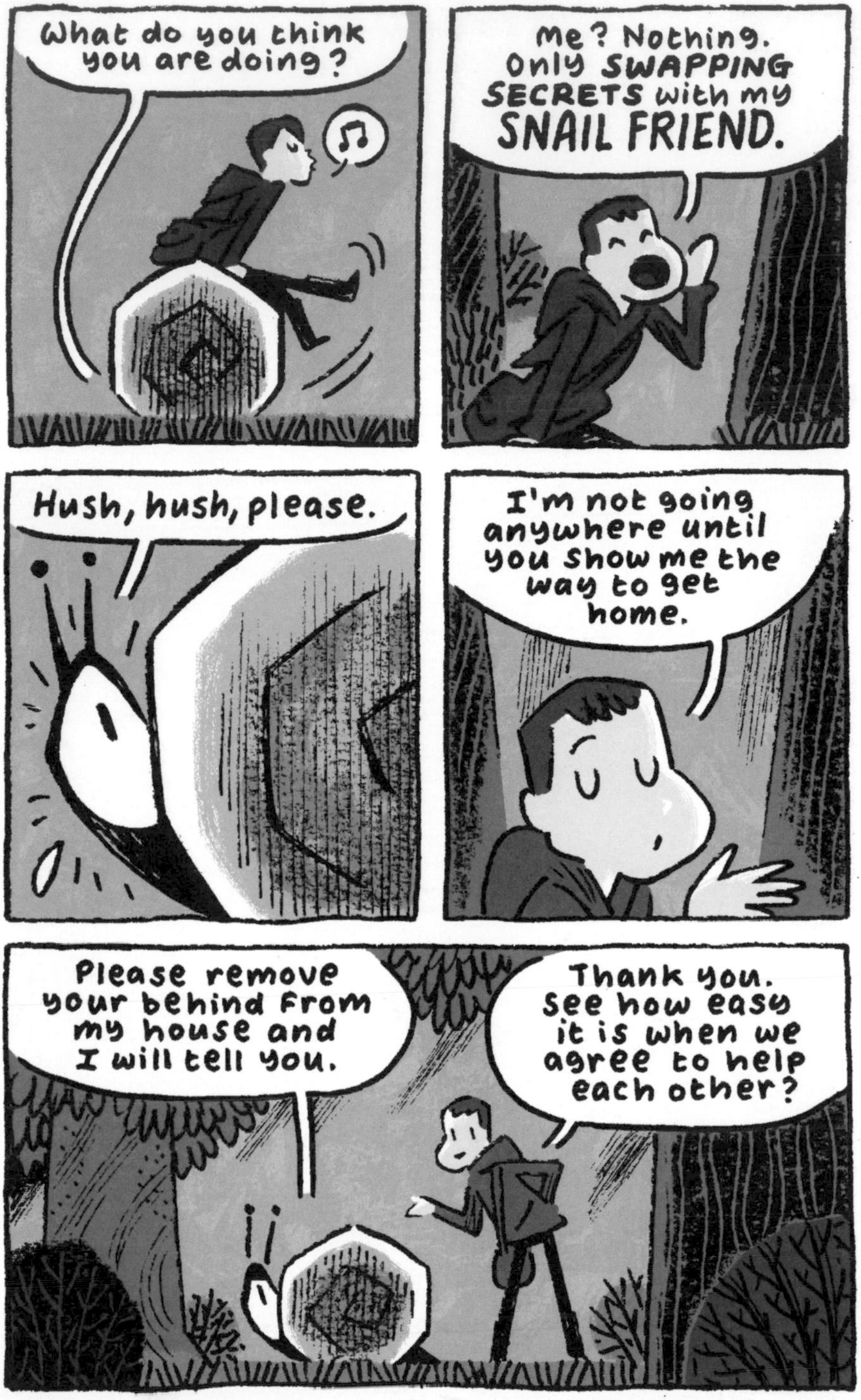
What do you think you are doing?
Me? Nothing. Only SWAPPING SECRETS with my SNAIL FRIEND.
Hush, hush, please.
I'm not going anywhere until you show me the way to get home.
Please remove your behind from my house and I will tell you.
Thank you. See how easy it is when we agree to help each other?

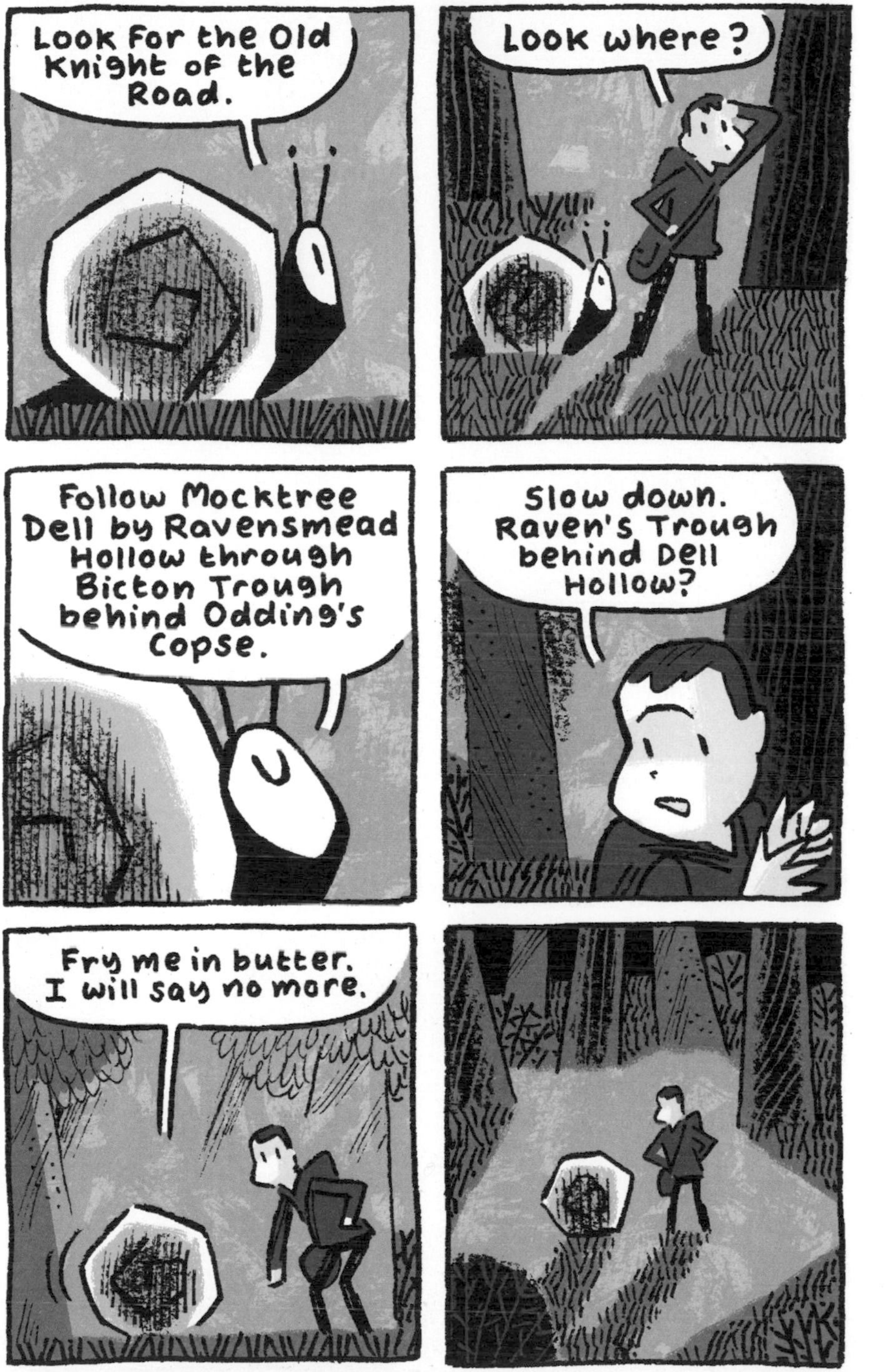
Look for the Old Knight of the Road.
Look where?
Follow Mocktree Dell by Ravensmead Hollow through Bicton Trough behind Odding's Copse.
Slow down. Raven's Trough behind Dell Hollow?
Fry me in butter. I will say no more.

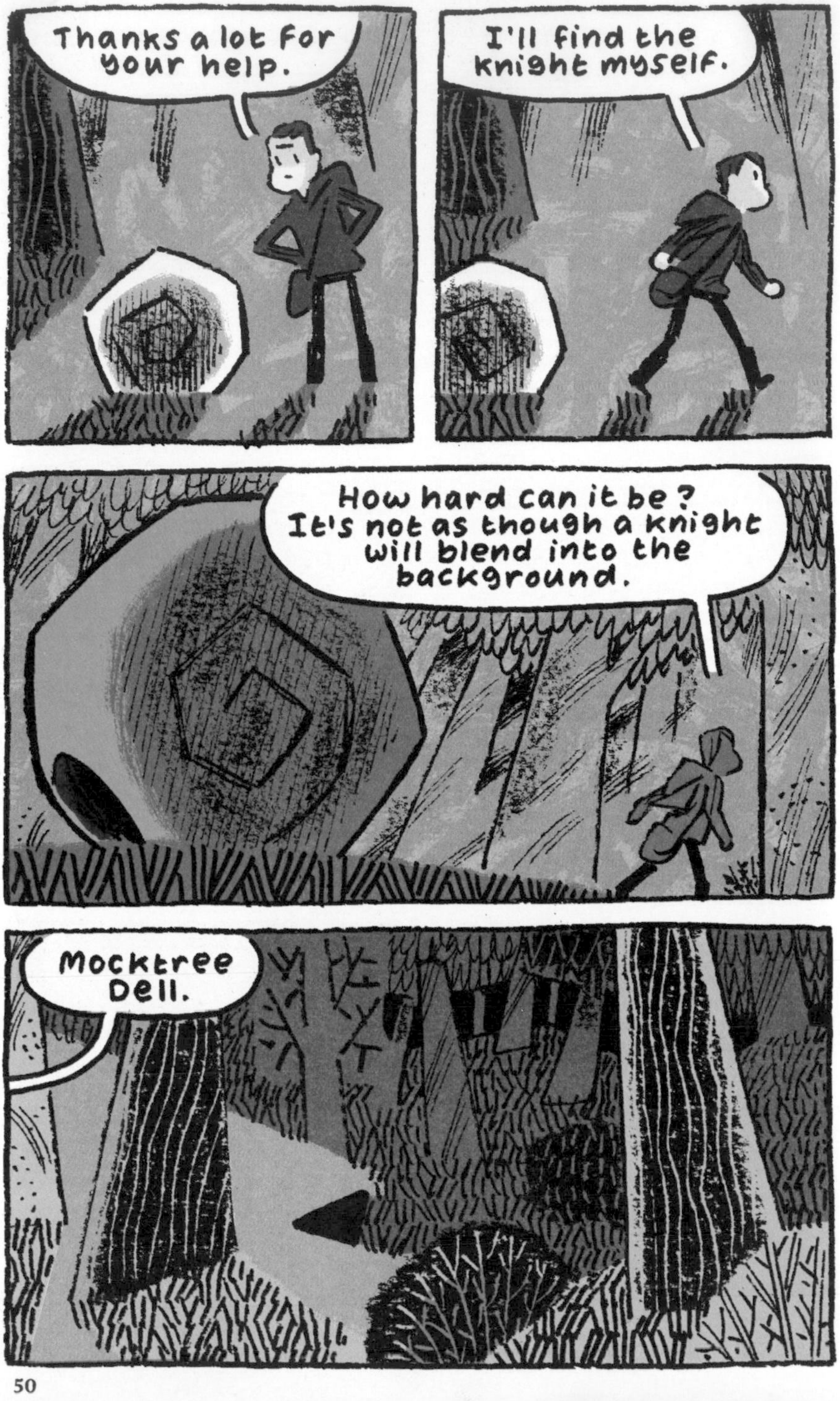
Thanks a lot for your help.
I'll find the knight myself.
How hard can it be? It's not as though a knight will blend into the background.
Mocktree Dell.

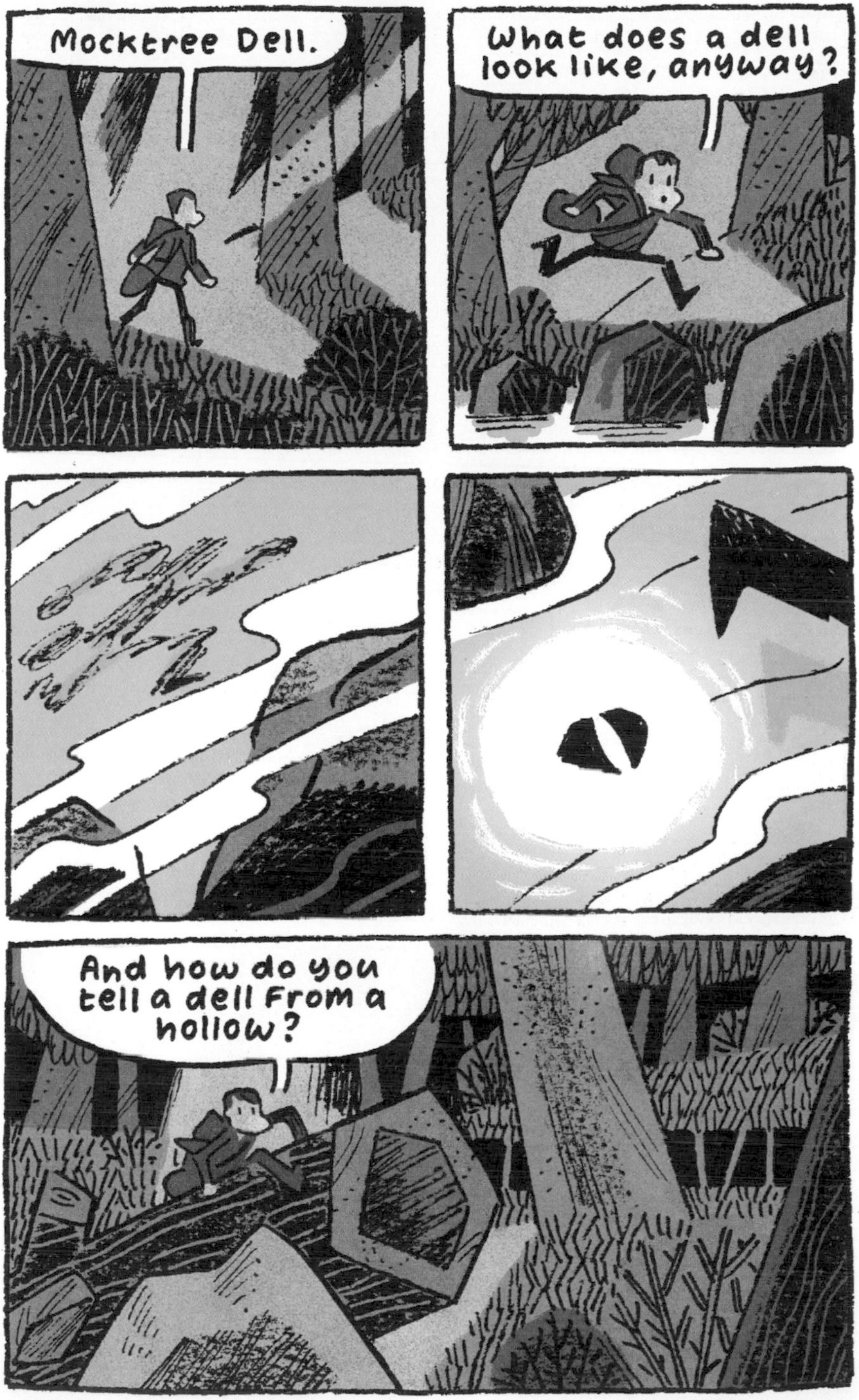
Mocktree Dell.
What does a dell look like, anyway?
And how do you tell a dell from a hollow?

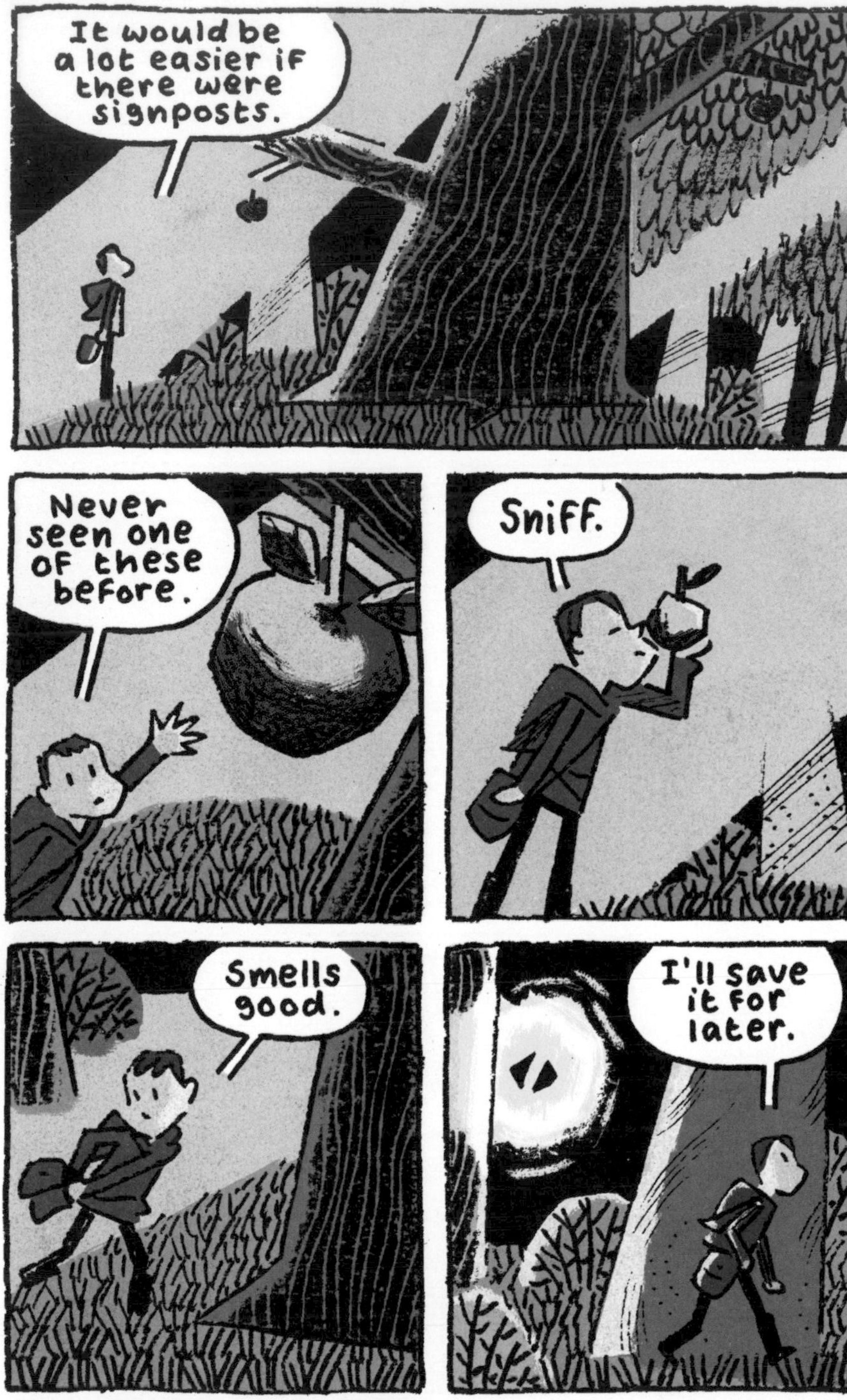
It would be a lot easier if there were signposts.
Never seen one of these before.
Sniff.
Smells good.
I'll save it for later.

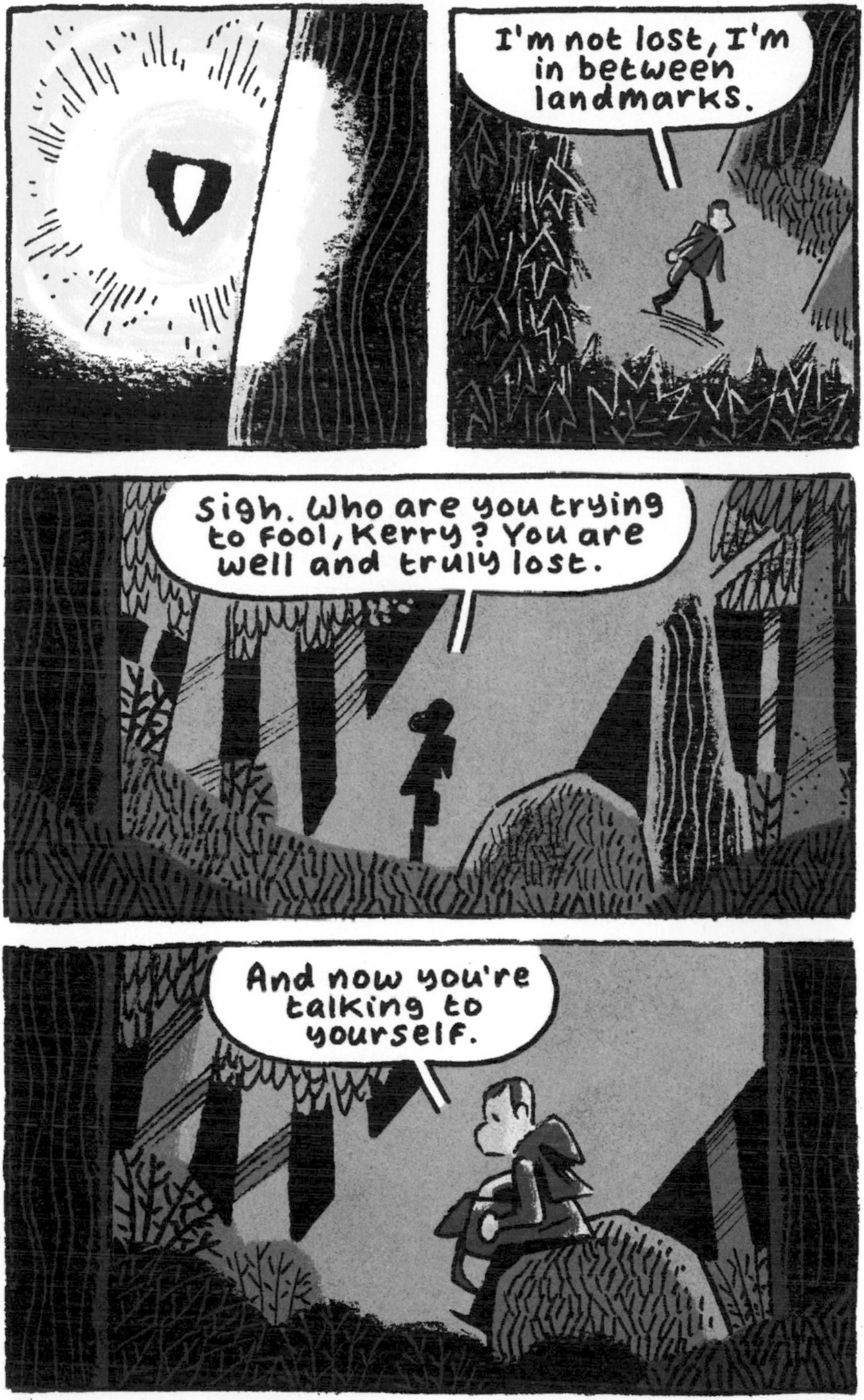
I'm not lost, I'm in between landmarks.
Sigh. Who are you trying to fool, Kerry? You are well and truly lost.
And now you're talking to yourself.

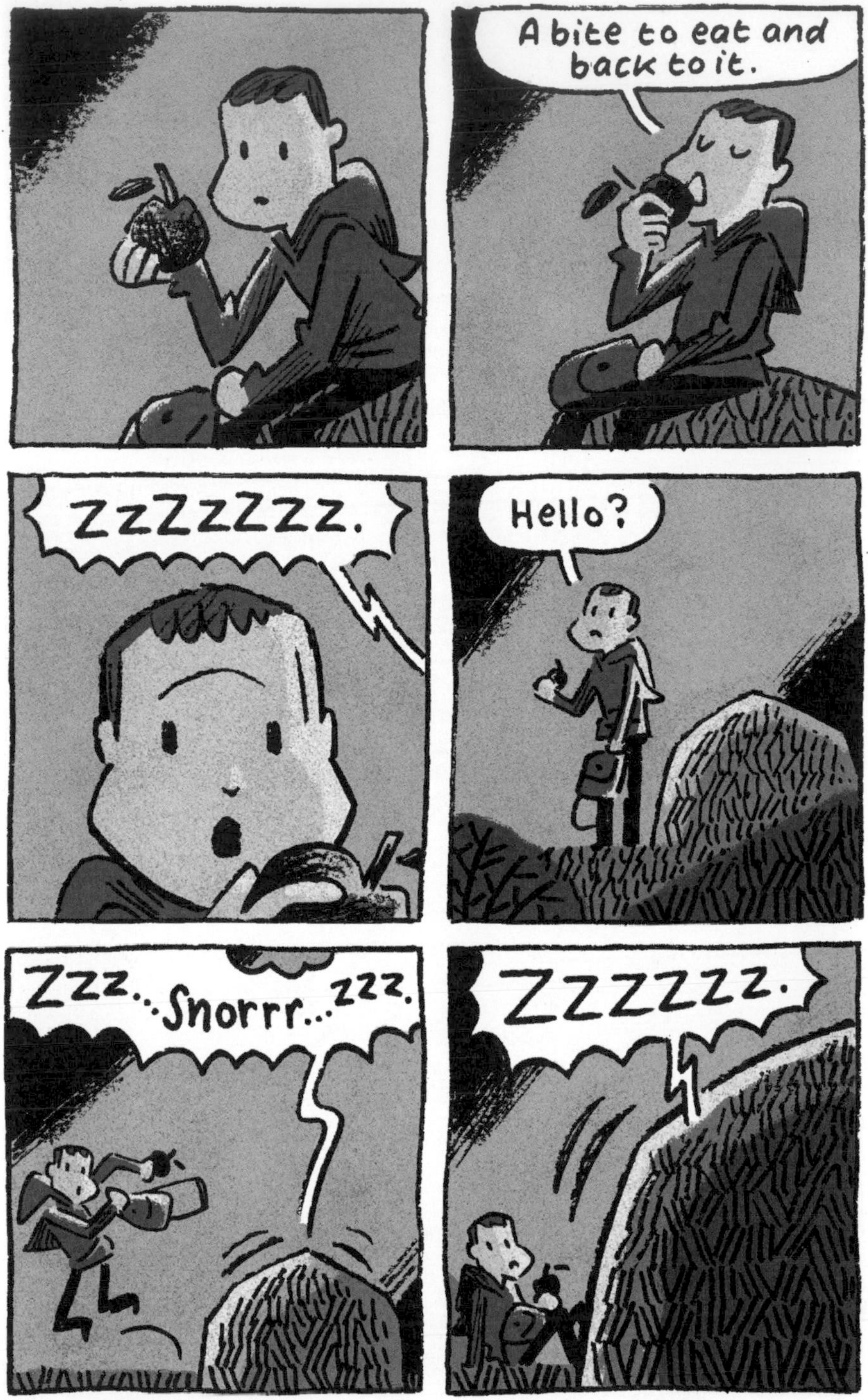
A bite to eat and back to it.
ZzZzZZz.
Hello?
Zzz... Snorrr... zzz.
ZZZZZZ.

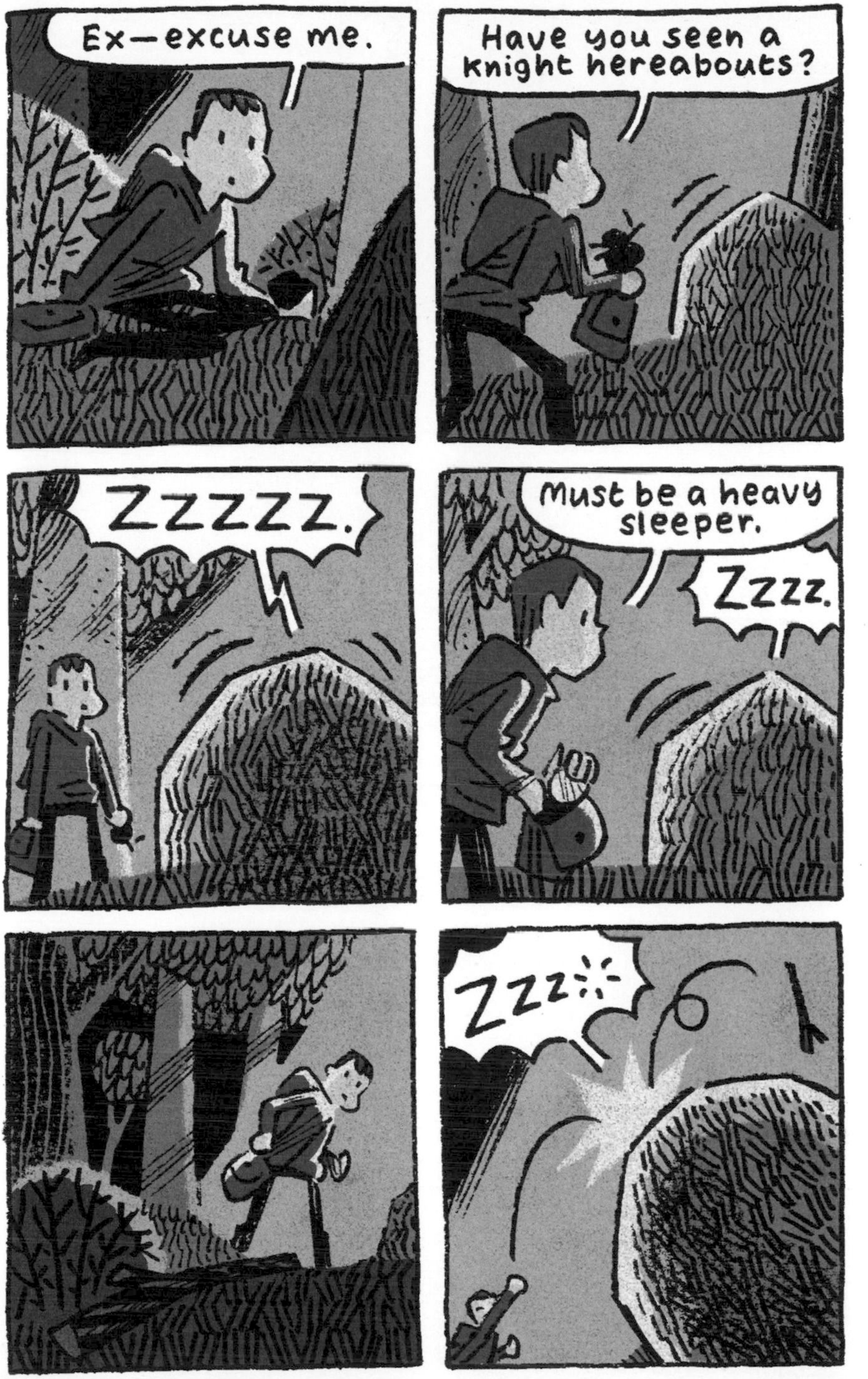
Ex—excuse me.
Have you seen a knight hereabouts?
Zzzzz.
Must be a heavy sleeper.
Zzzz.
Zzz

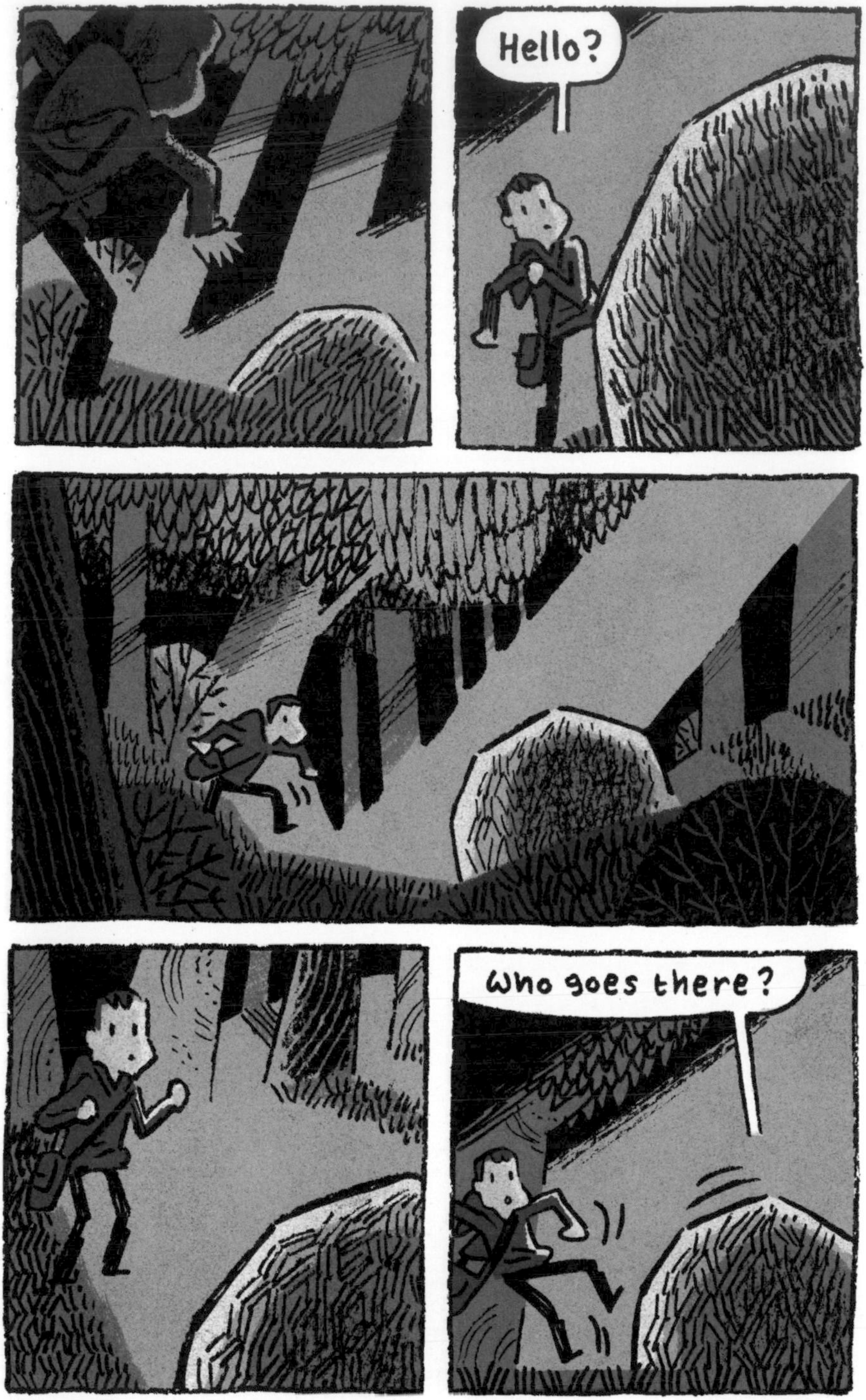
Hello?
Who goes there?

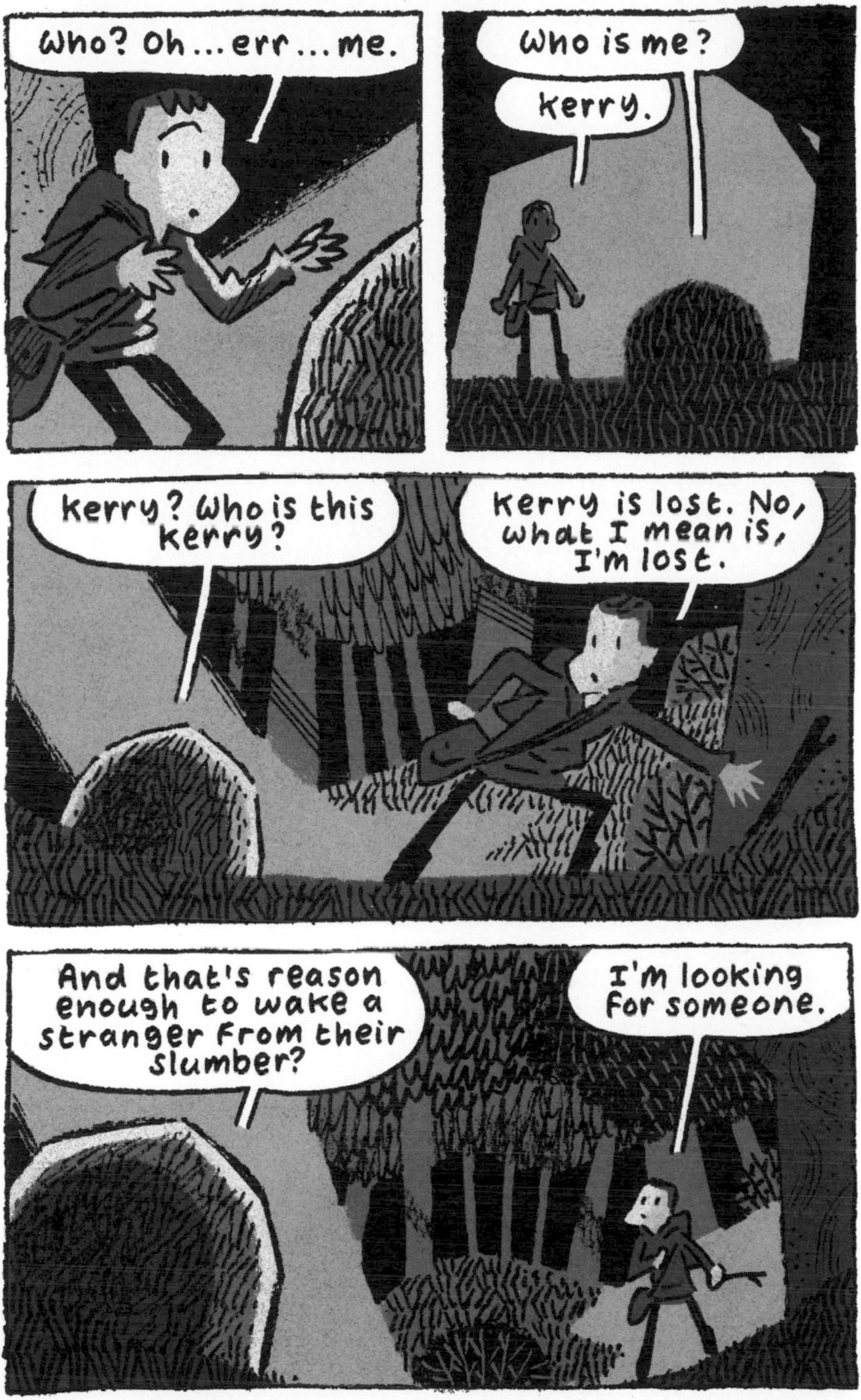
Who? Oh... err... me.
Who is me?
Kerry.
Kerry? Who is this Kerry?
Kerry is lost. No, what I mean is, I'm lost.
And that's reason enough to wake a stranger from their slumber?
I'm looking for someone.

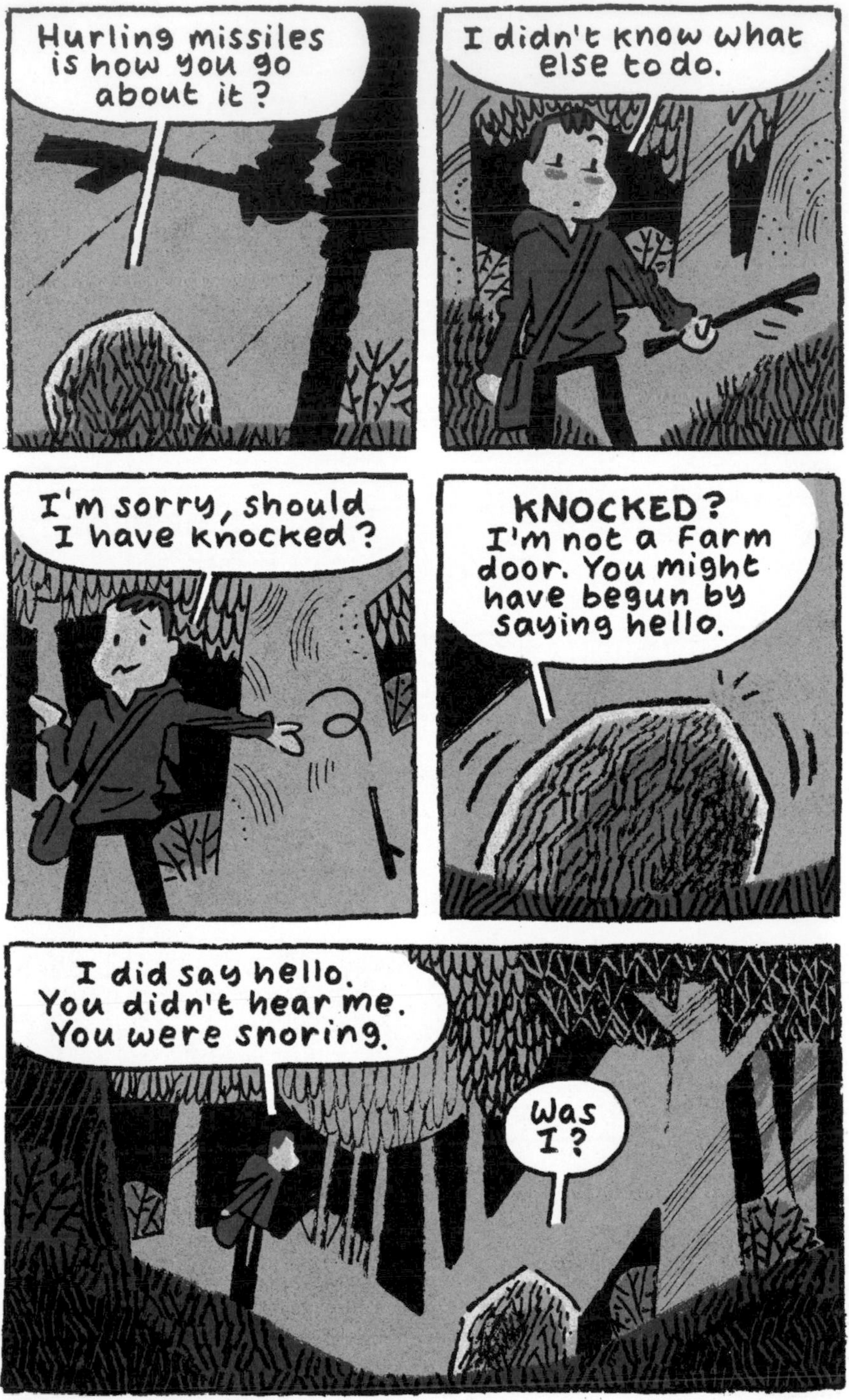
Hurling missiles is how you go about it?
I didn't know what else to do.
I'm sorry, should I have knocked?
KNOCKED? I'm not a farm door. You might have begun by saying hello.
I did say hello. You didn't hear me. You were snoring.
Was I?

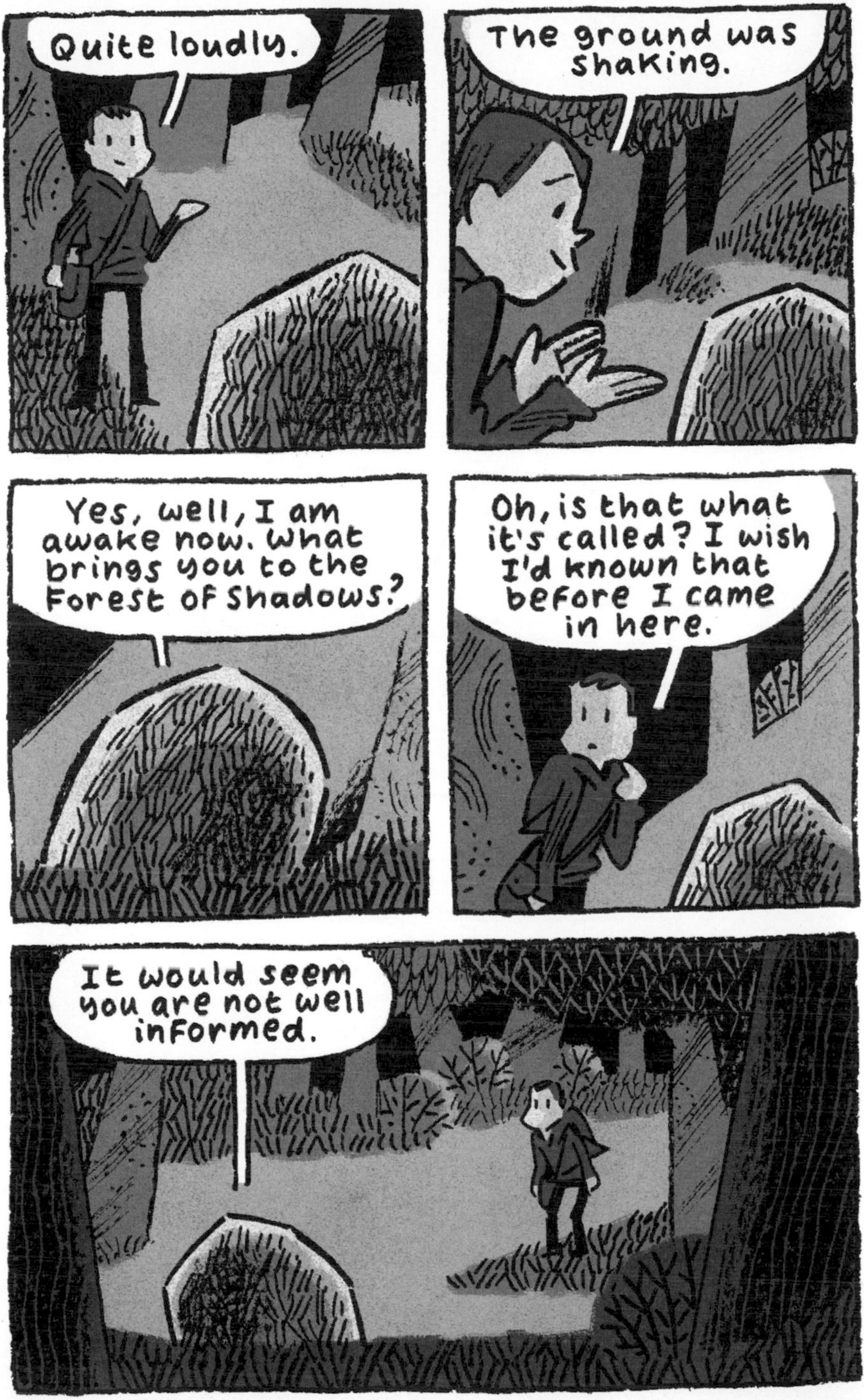
Quite loudly.
The ground was shaking.
Yes, well, I am awake now. What brings you to the Forest of Shadows?
Oh, is that what it's called? I wish I'd known that before I came in here.
It would seem you are not well informed.

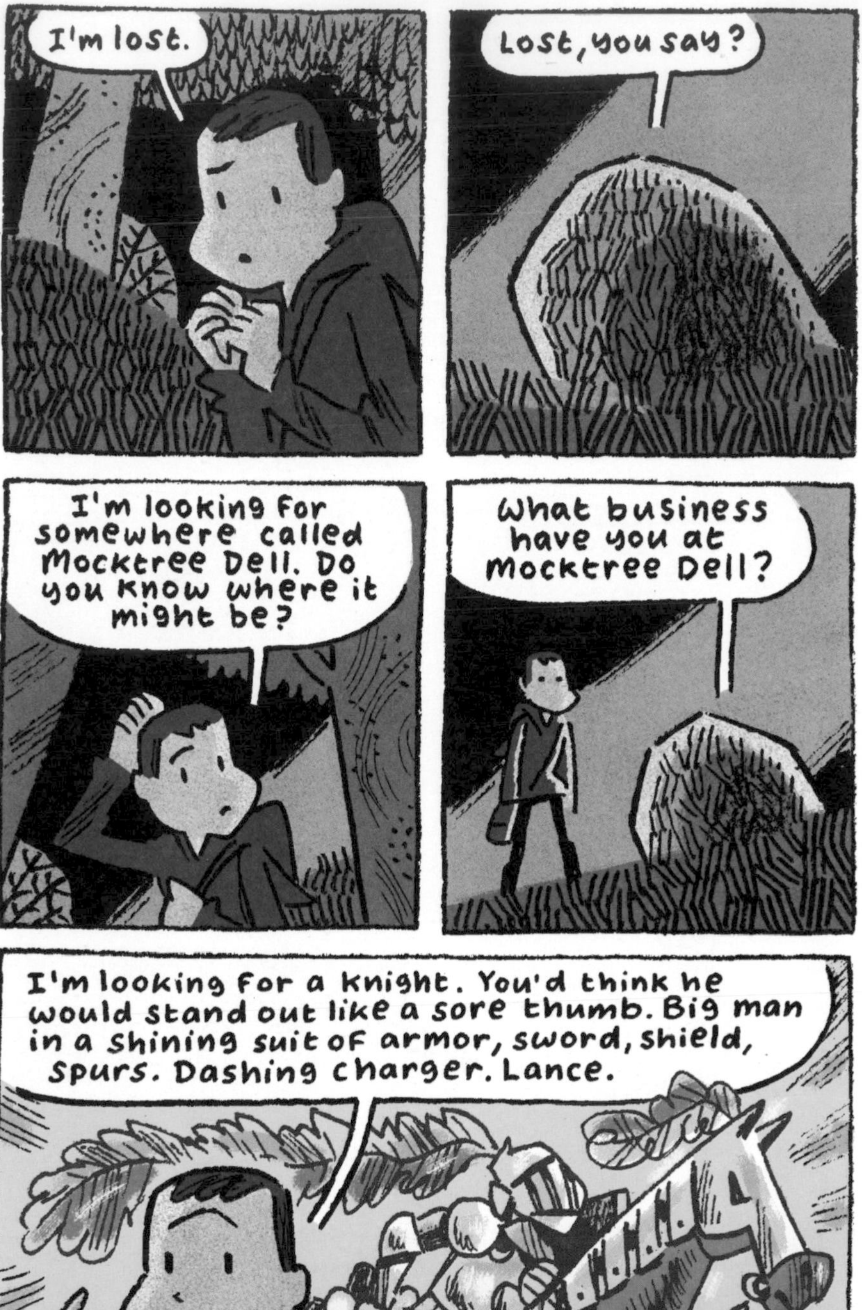
I'm lost.
Lost, you say?
I'm looking for somewhere called Mocktree Dell. Do you know where it might be?
What business have you at Mocktree Dell?
I'm looking for a knight. You'd think he would stand out like a sore thumb. Big man in a shining suit of armor, sword, shield, spurs. Dashing charger. Lance.

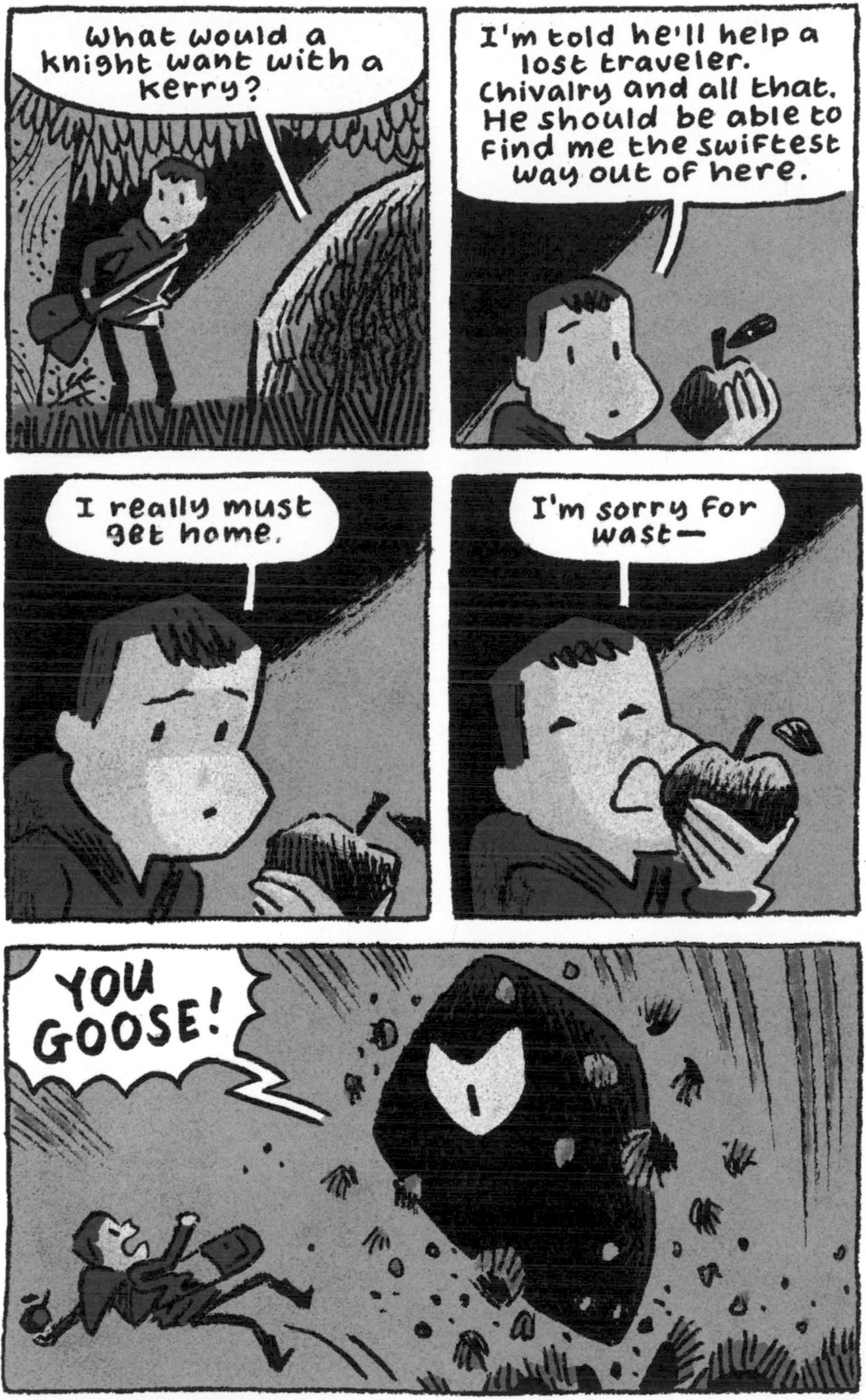
What would a knight want with a kerry?
I'm told he'll help a lost traveler. Chivalry and all that. He should be able to find me the swiftest way out of here.
I really must get home.
I'm sorry for wast—
YOU GOOSE!

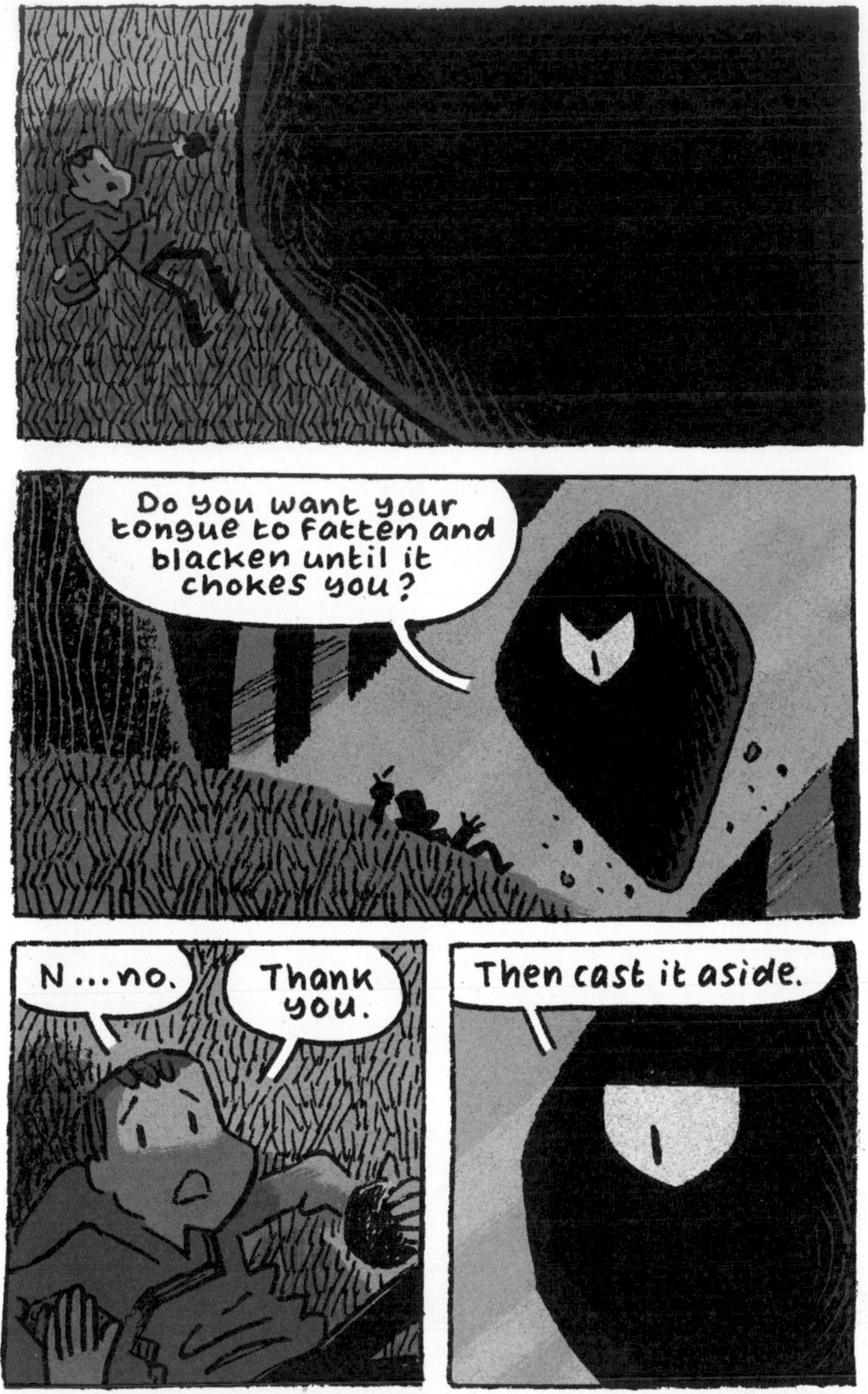
Do you want your tongue to fatten and blacken until it chokes you?
N...no.
Thank you.
Then cast it aside.

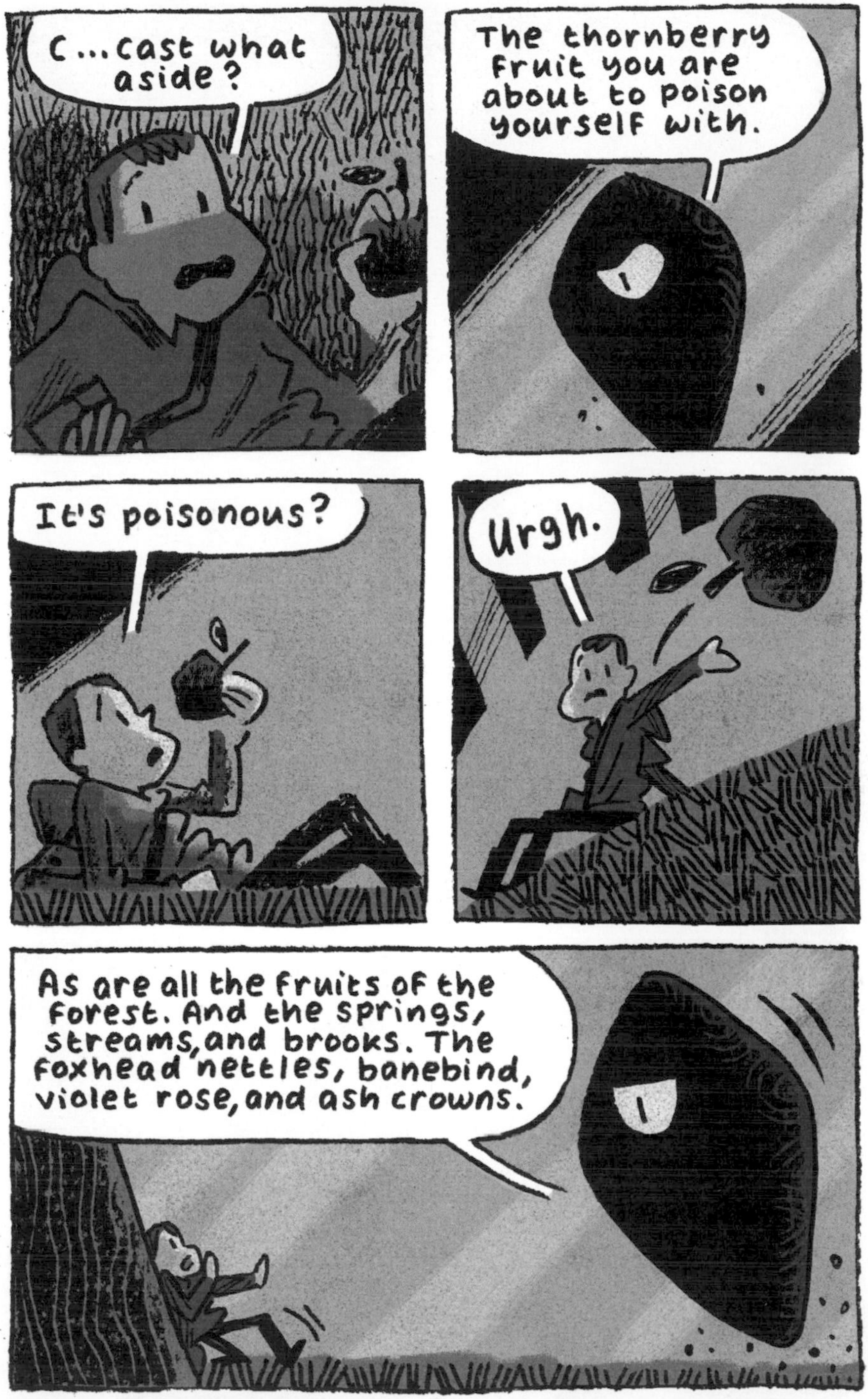
C...cast what aside?
The thornberry fruit you are about to poison yourself with.
It's poisonous?
Urgh.
As are all the fruits of the forest. And the springs, streams, and brooks. The foxhead nettles, banebind, violet rose, and ash crowns.

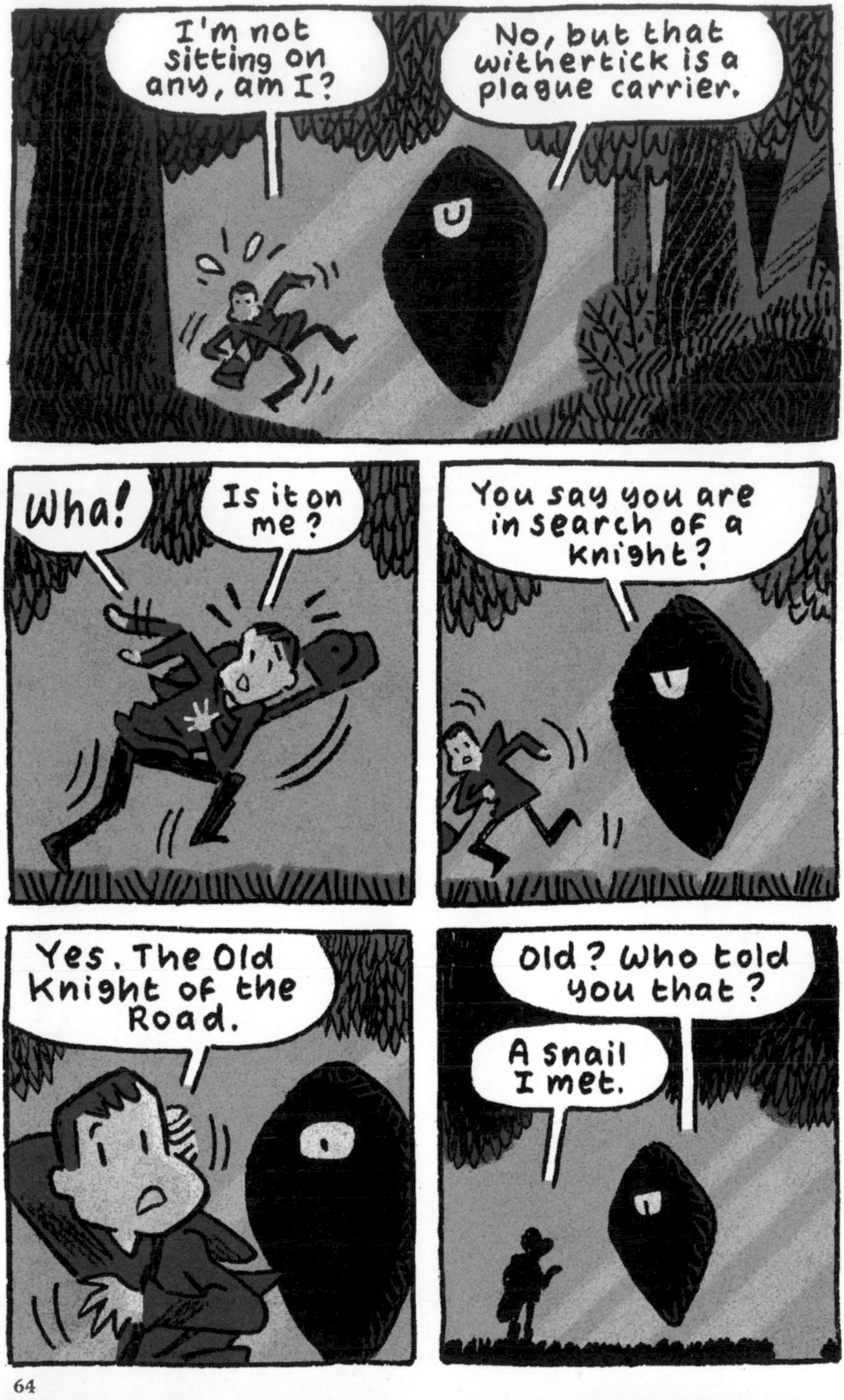
I'm not sitting on any, am I?
No, but that withertick is a plague carrier.
Wha!
Is it on me?
You say you are in search of a knight?
Yes. The Old Knight of the Road.
Old? Who told you that?
A snail I met.

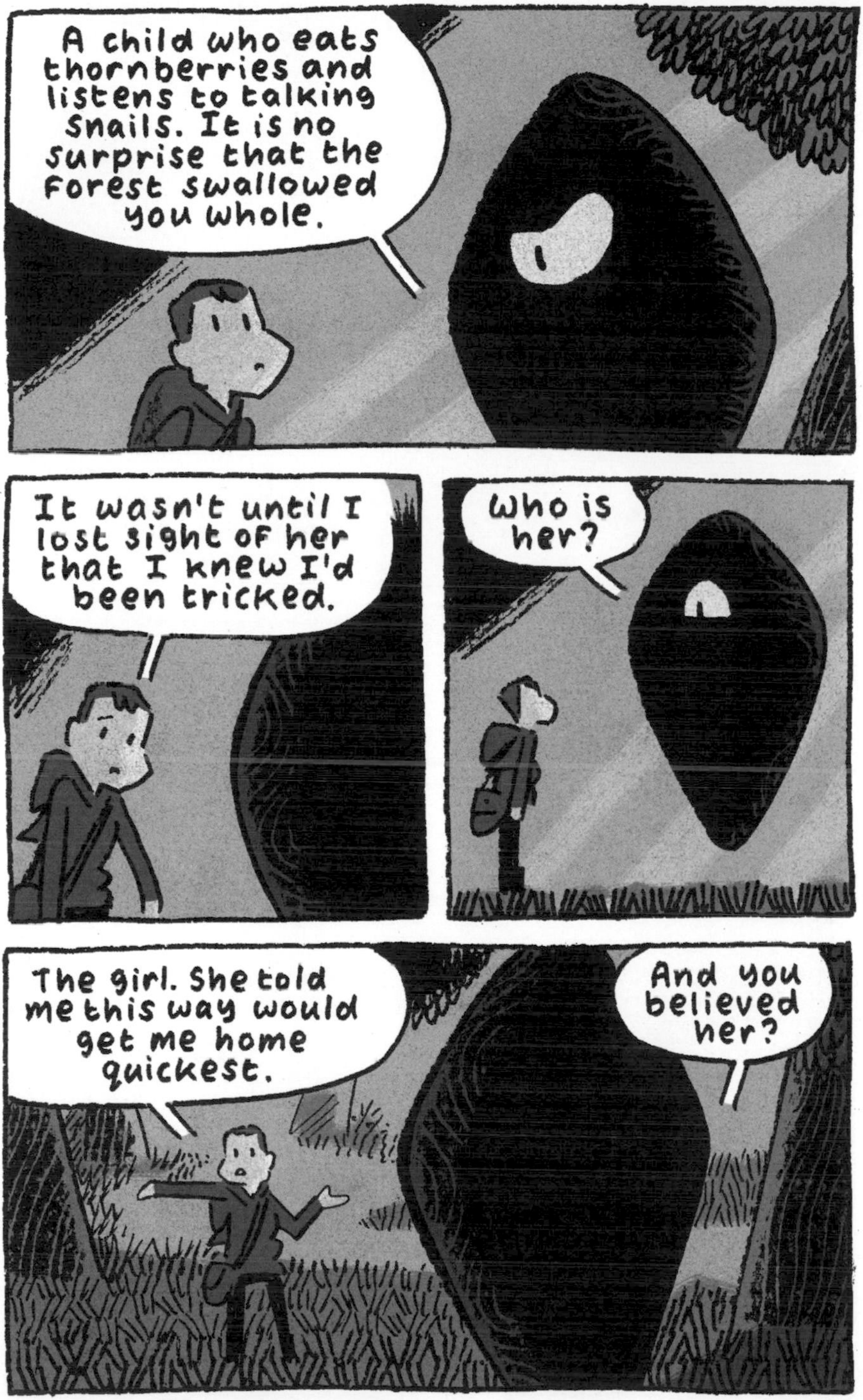
A child who eats thornberries and listens to talking snails. It is no surprise that the forest swallowed you whole.
It wasn't until I lost sight of her that I knew I'd been tricked.
Who is her?
The girl. She told me this way would get me home quickest.
And you believed her?

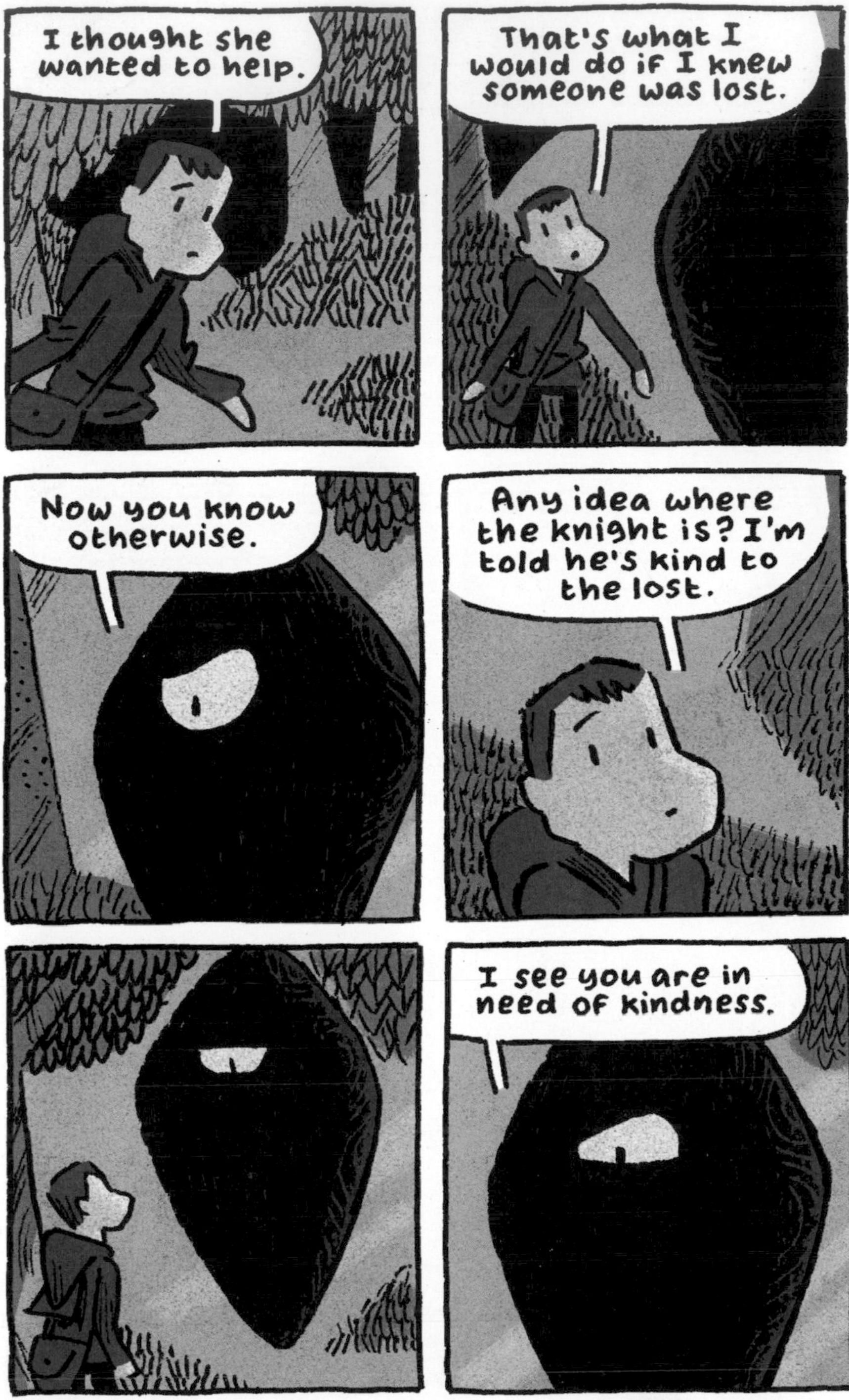
I thought she wanted to help.
That's what I would do if I knew someone was lost.
Now you know otherwise.
Any idea where the knight is? I'm told he's kind to the lost.
I see you are in need of kindness.

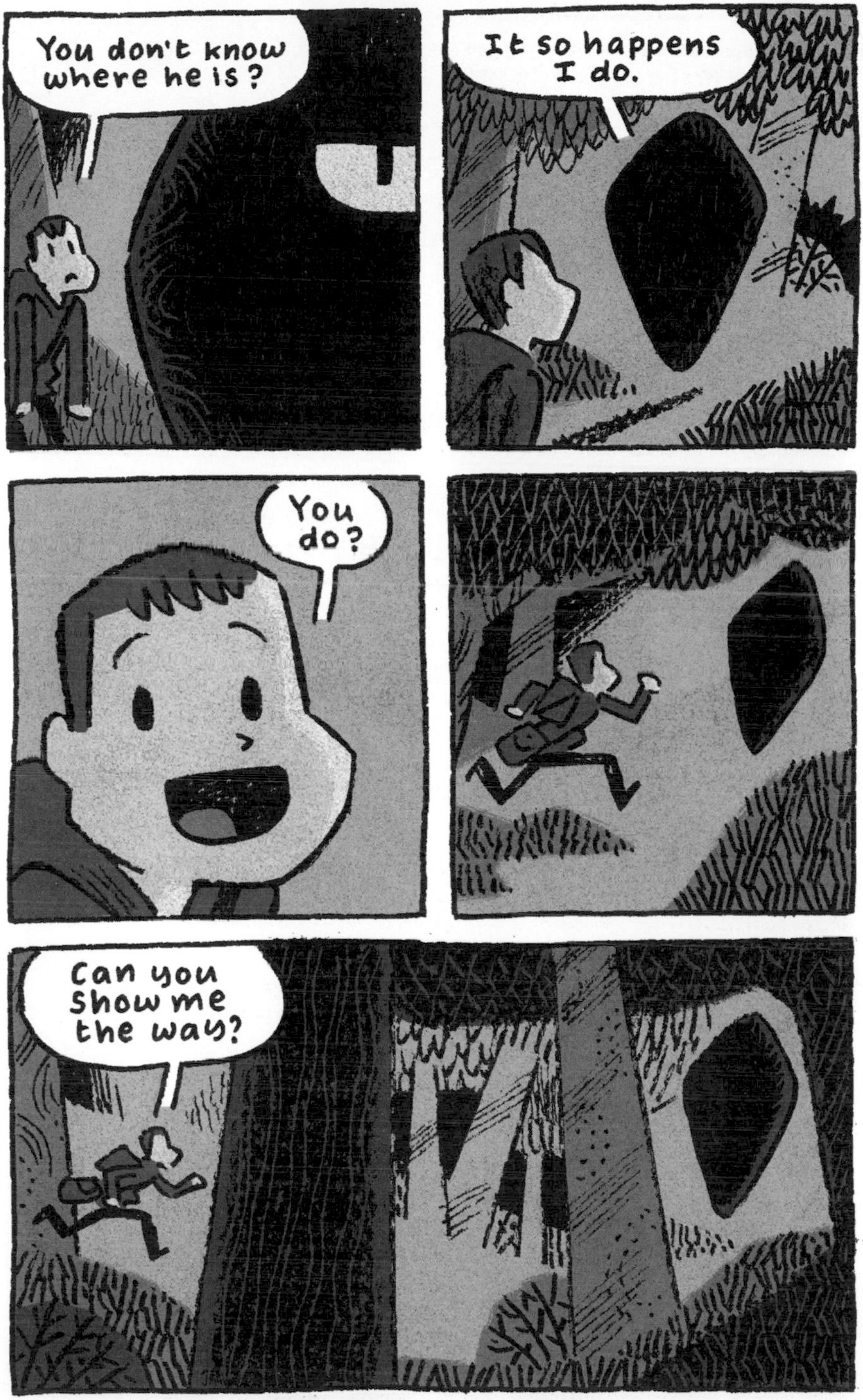
You don't know where he is?
It so happens I do.
You do?
Can you show me the way?

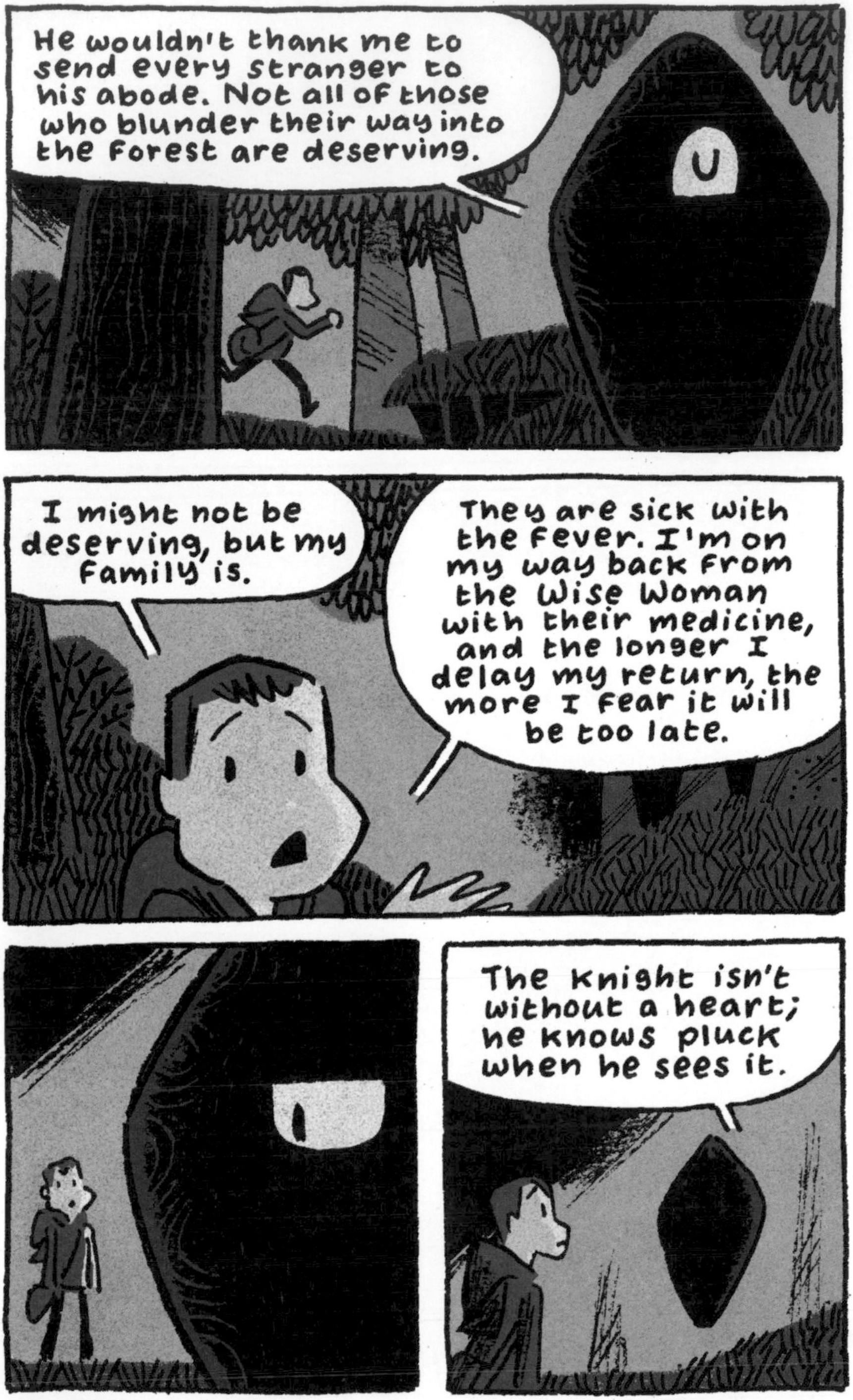
He wouldn't thank me to send every stranger to his abode. Not all of those who blunder their way into the forest are deserving.
I might not be deserving, but my family is.
They are sick with the fever. I'm on my way back from the Wise Woman with their medicine, and the longer I delay my return, the more I fear it will be too late.
The Knight isn't without a heart; he knows pluck when he sees it.

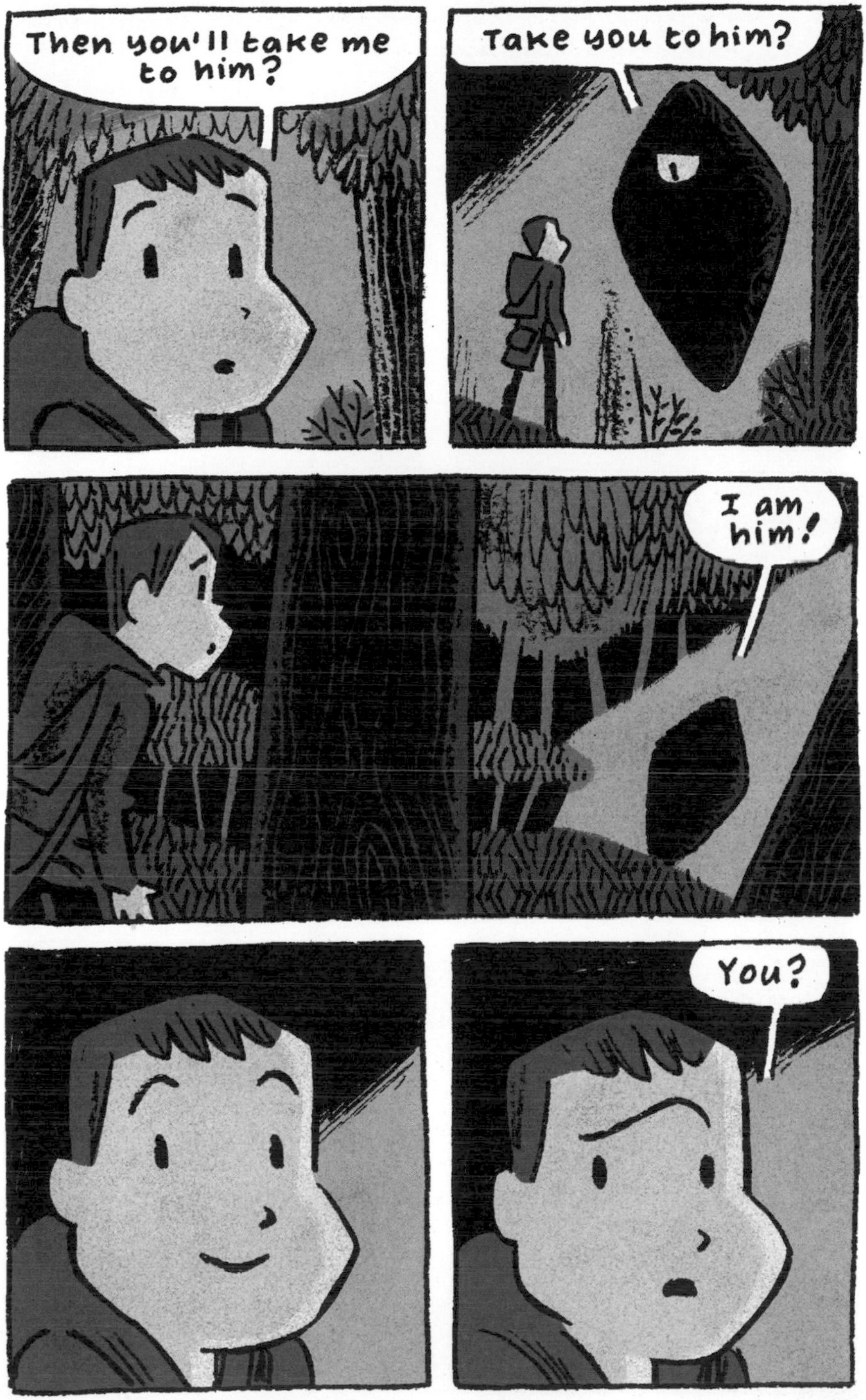
Then you'll take me to him?
Take you to him?
I am him!
You?

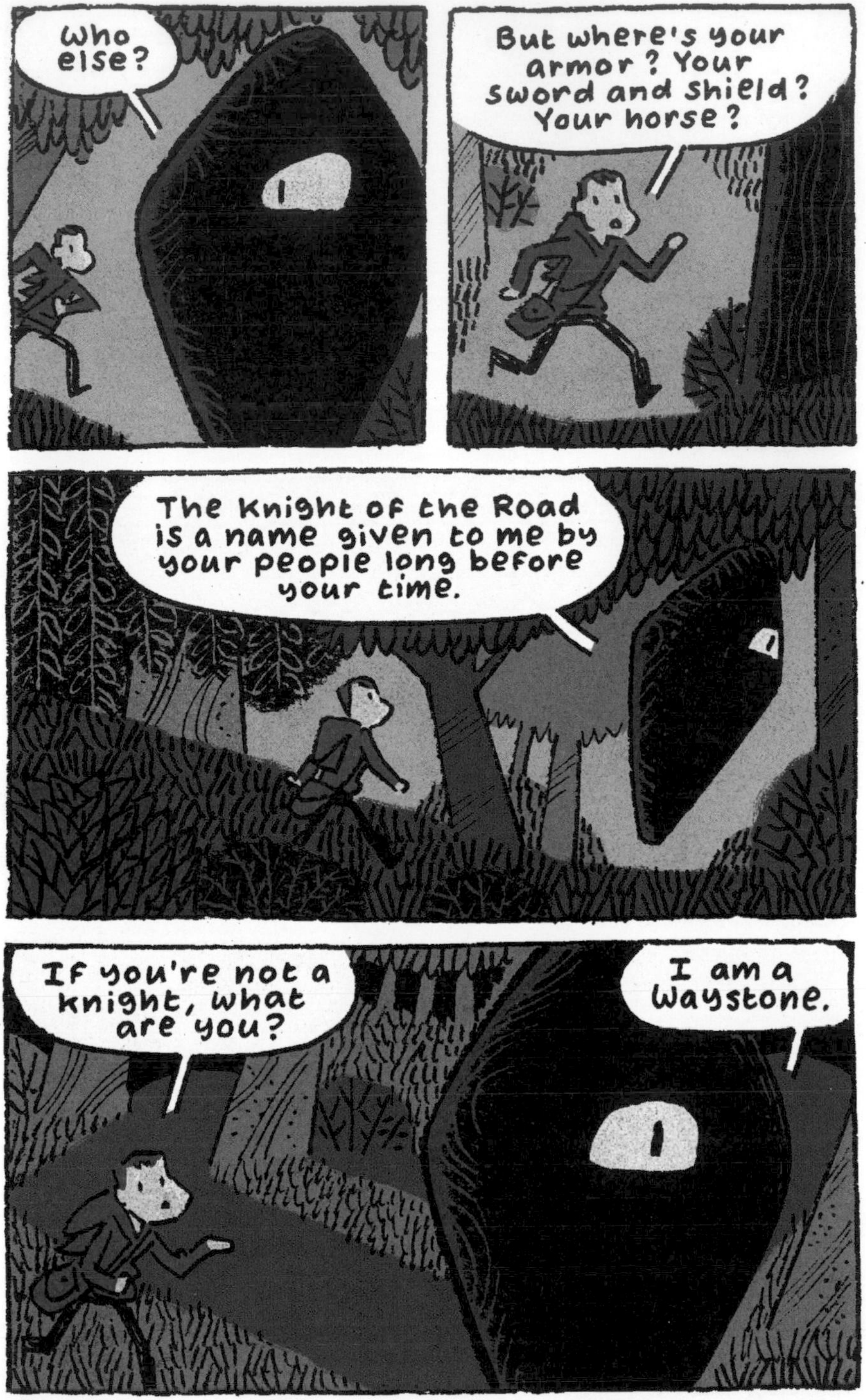

Who else?
But where's your armor? Your sword and shield? Your horse?
The Knight of the Road is a name given to me by your people long before your time.
If you're not a knight, what are you?
I am a Waystone.

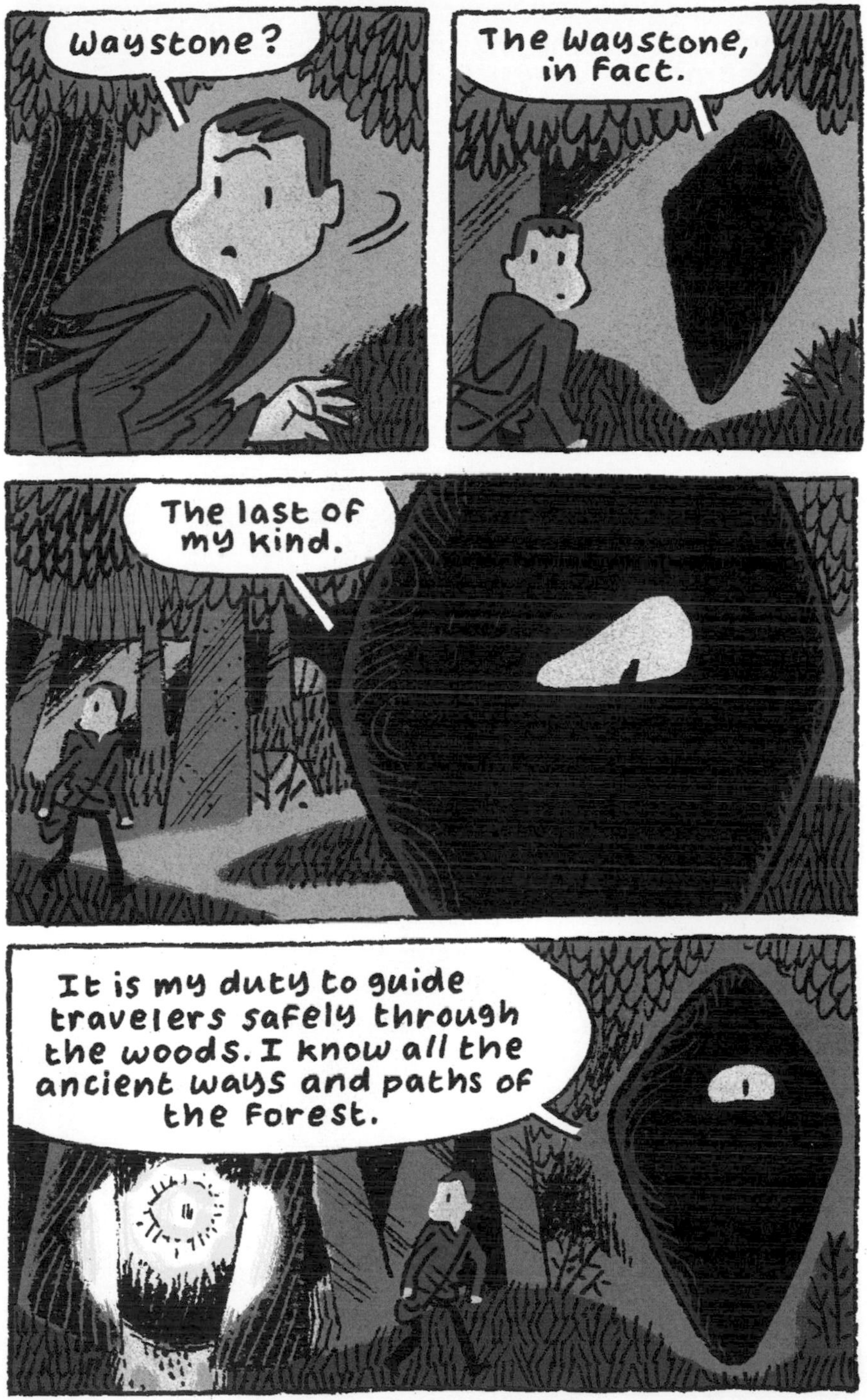
Waystone?
The Waystone, in fact.
The last of my kind.
It is my duty to guide travelers safely through the woods. I know all the ancient ways and paths of the forest.

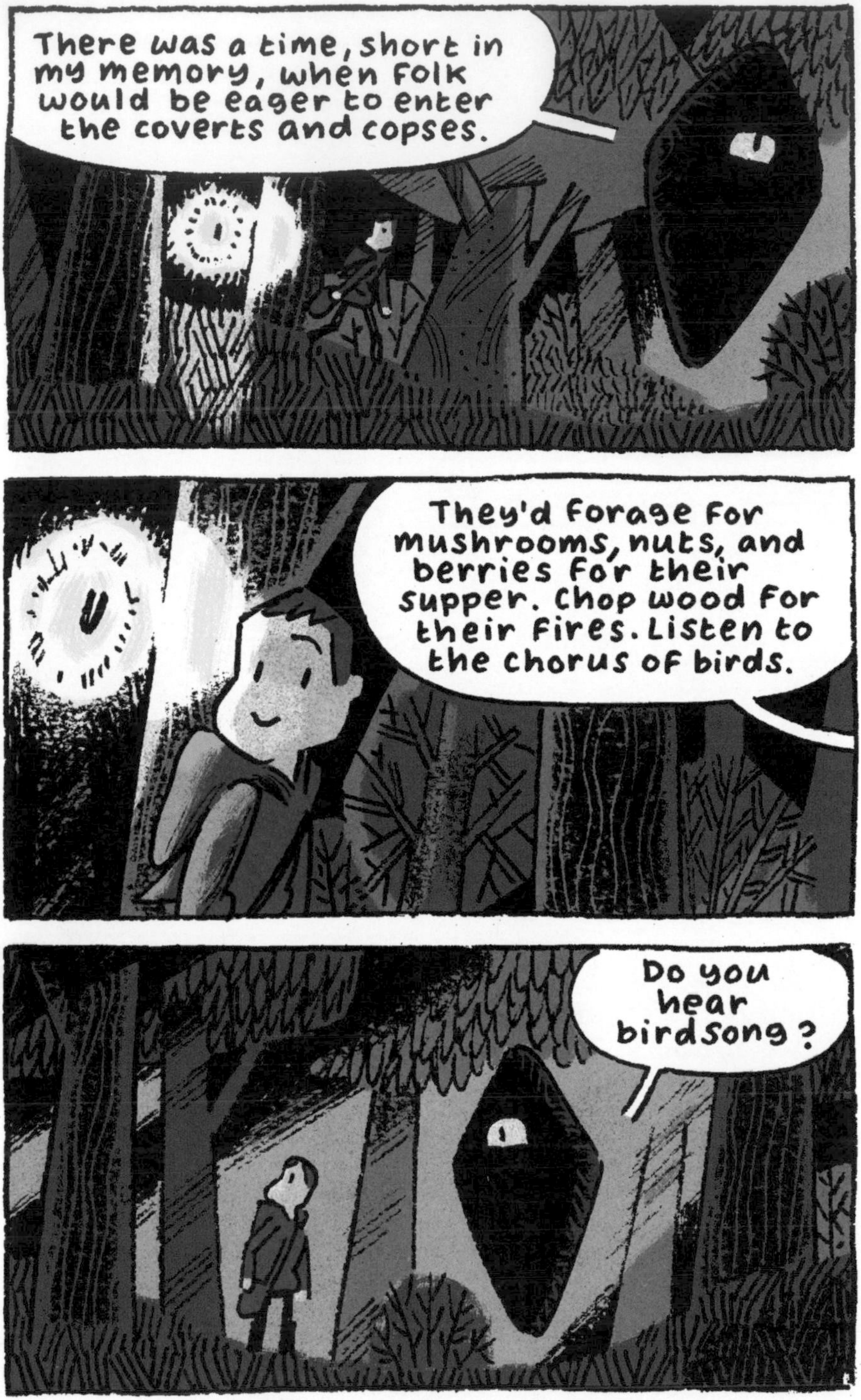
There was a time, short in my memory, when folk would be eager to enter the coverts and copses.
They'd forage for mushrooms, nuts, and berries for their supper. Chop wood for their fires. Listen to the chorus of birds.
Do you hear birdsong?

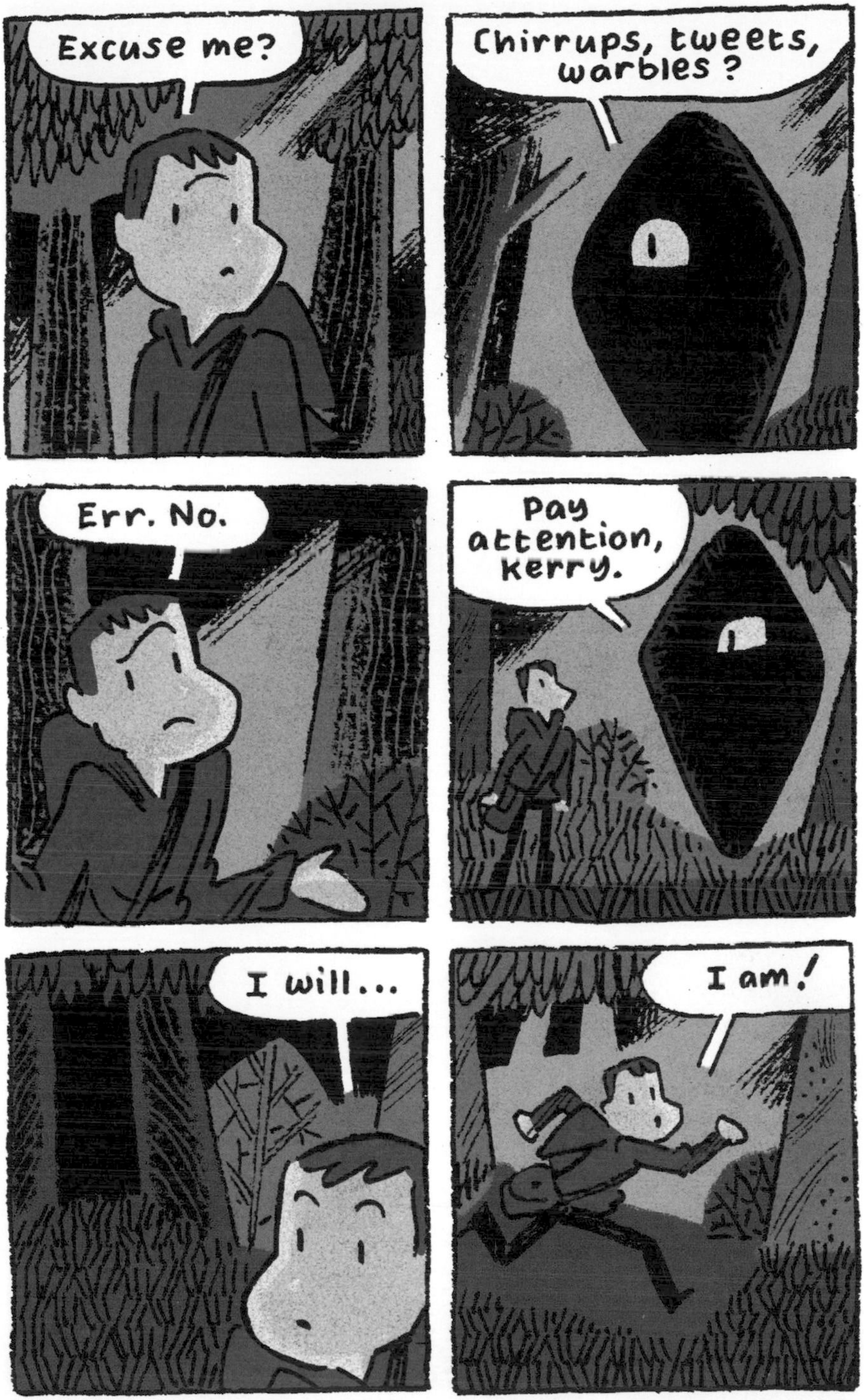
Excuse me?
Chirrups, tweets, warbles?
Err. No.
Pay attention, kerry.
I will...
I am!

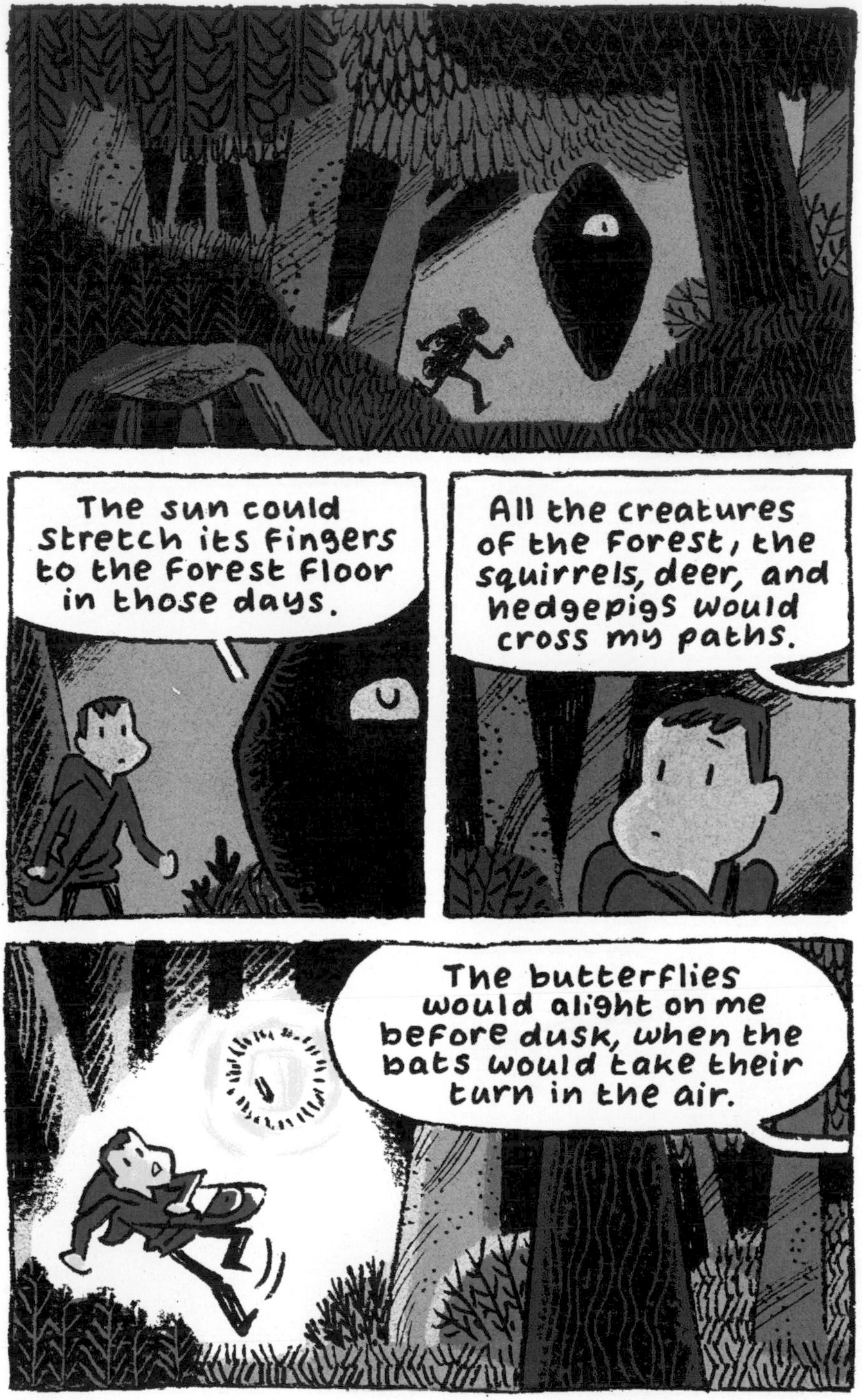

The sun could stretch its fingers to the forest floor in those days.
All the creatures of the forest, the squirrels, deer, and hedgepigs would cross my paths.
The butterflies would alight on me before dusk, when the bats would take their turn in the air.

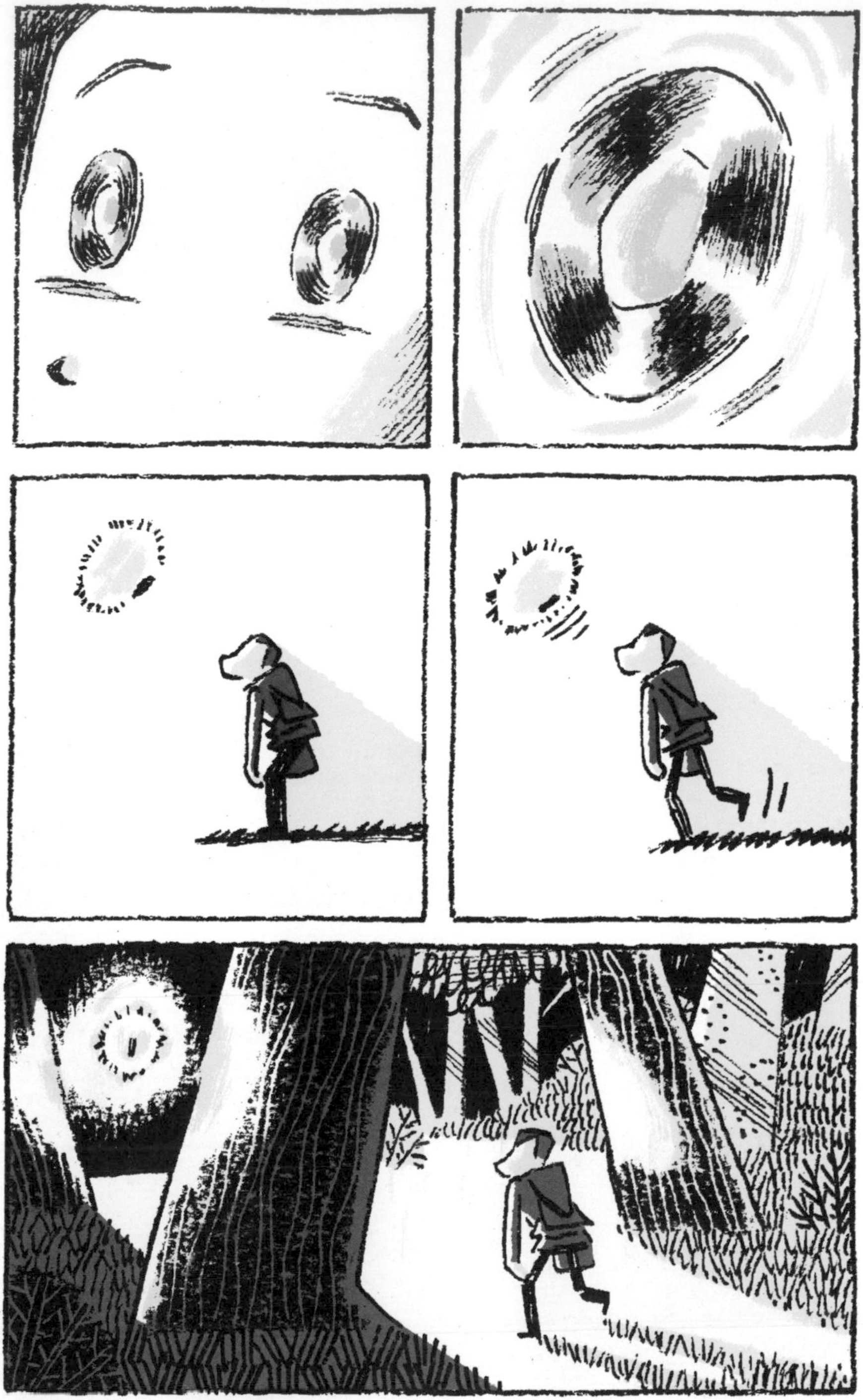

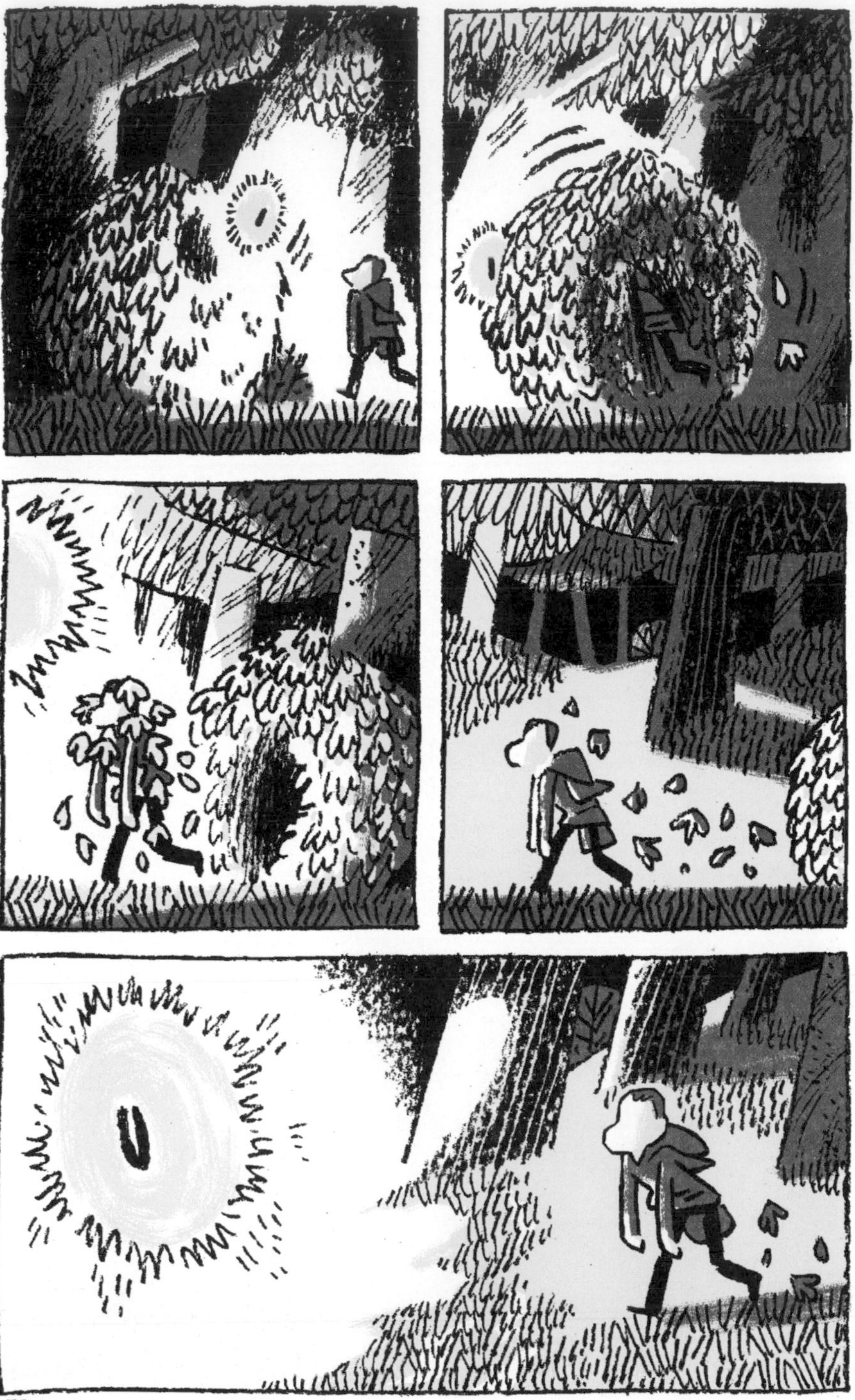

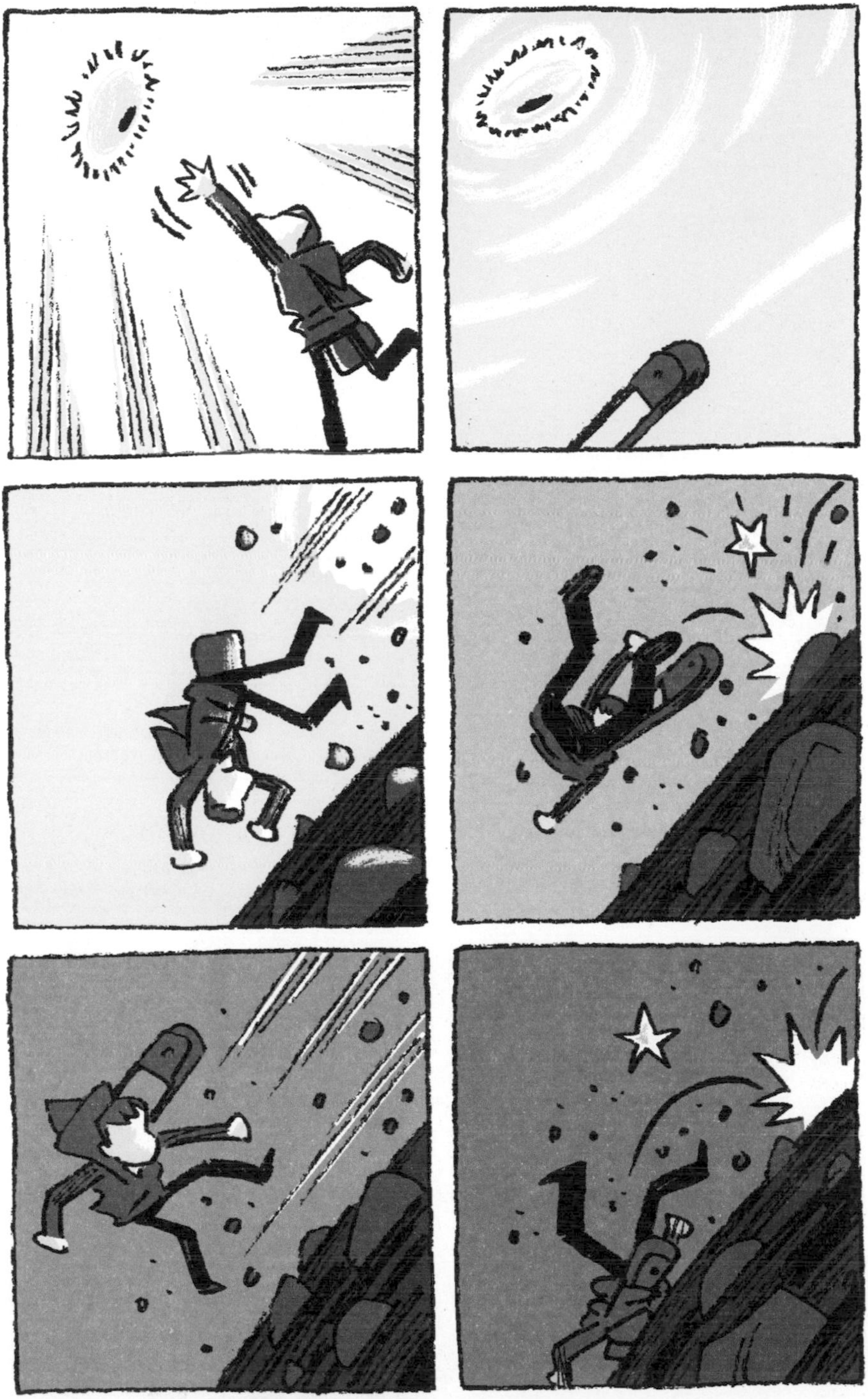

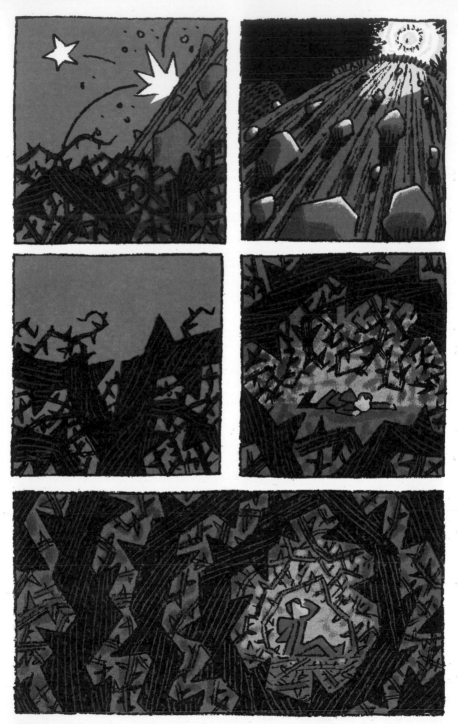

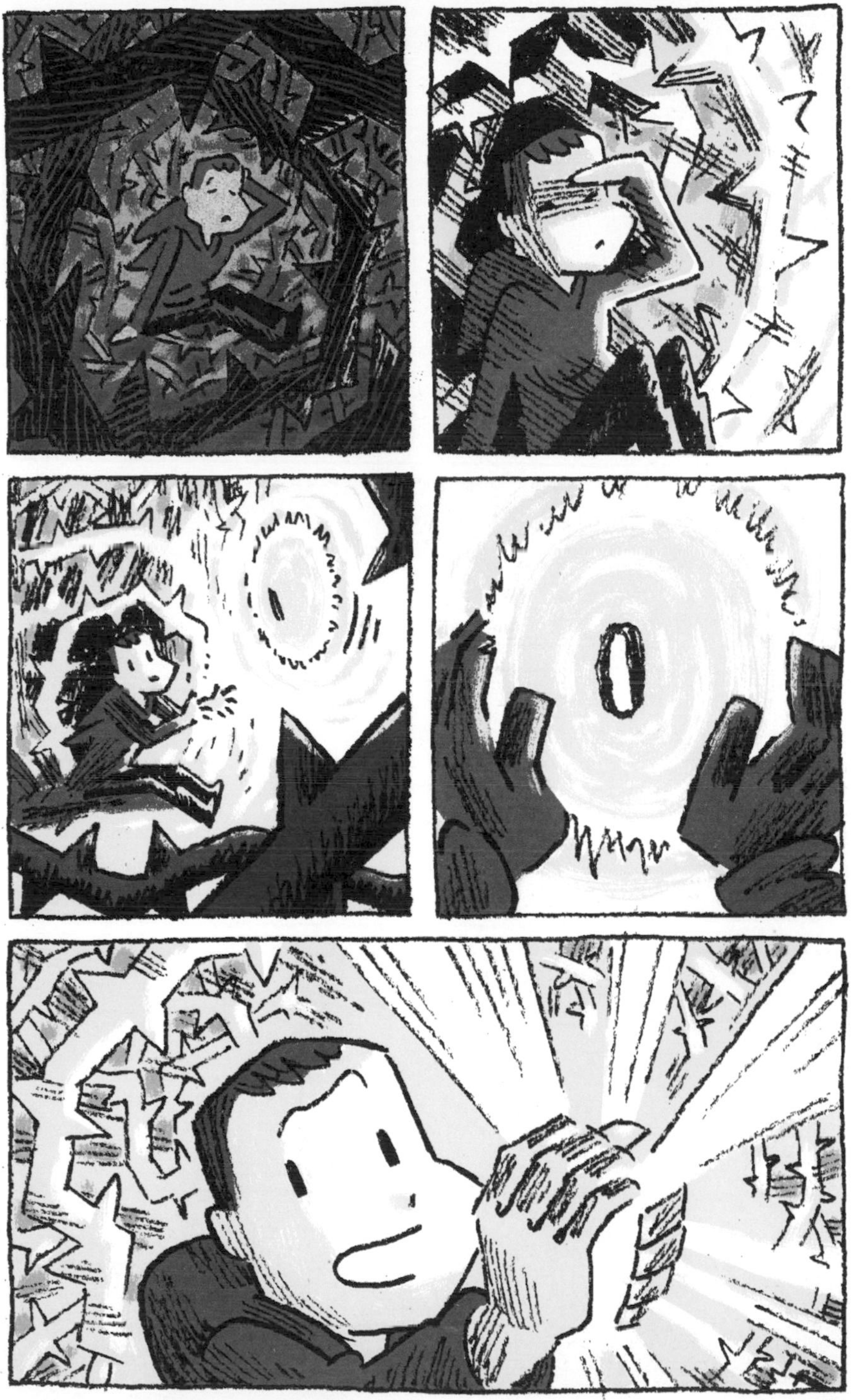

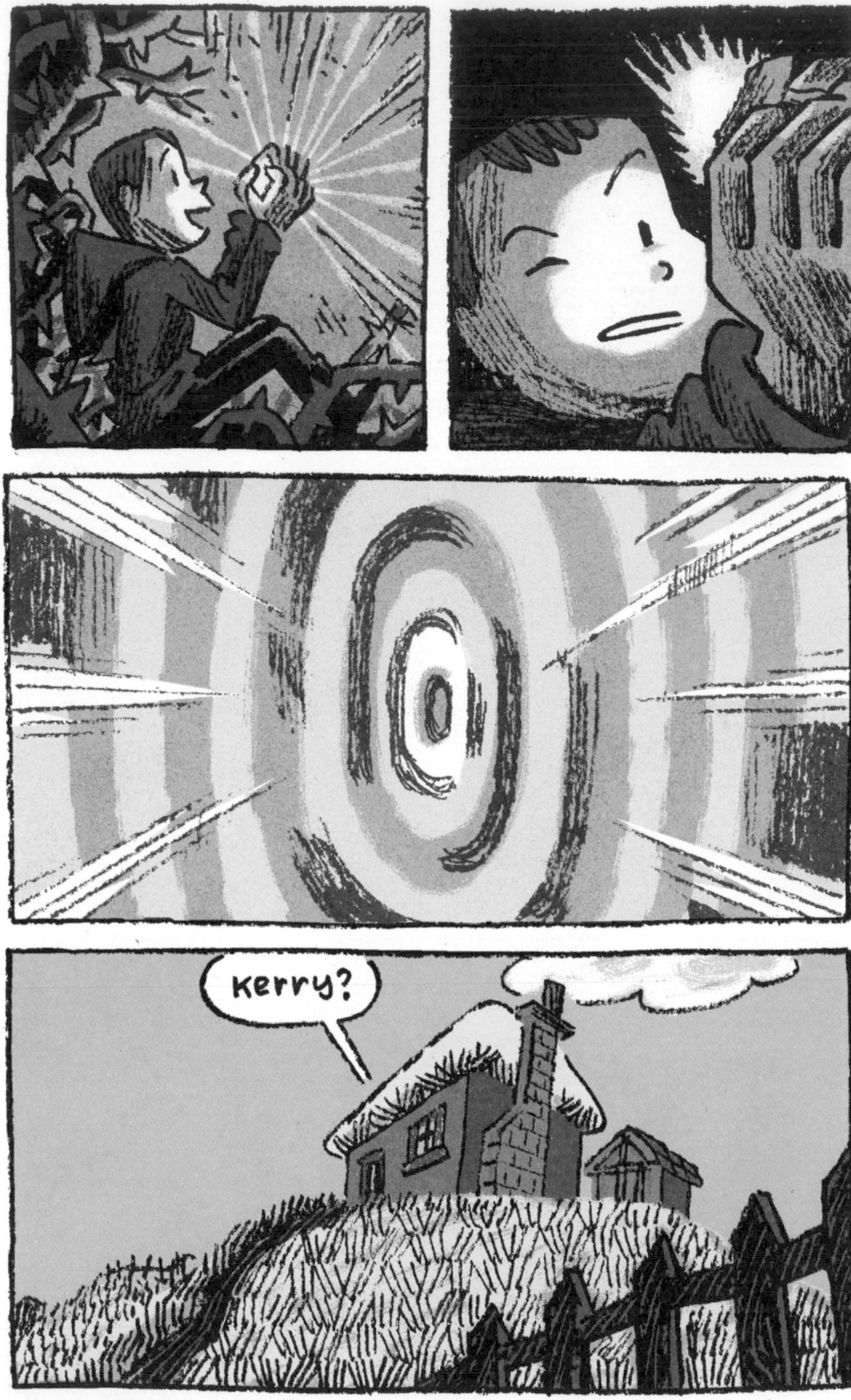
Kerry?

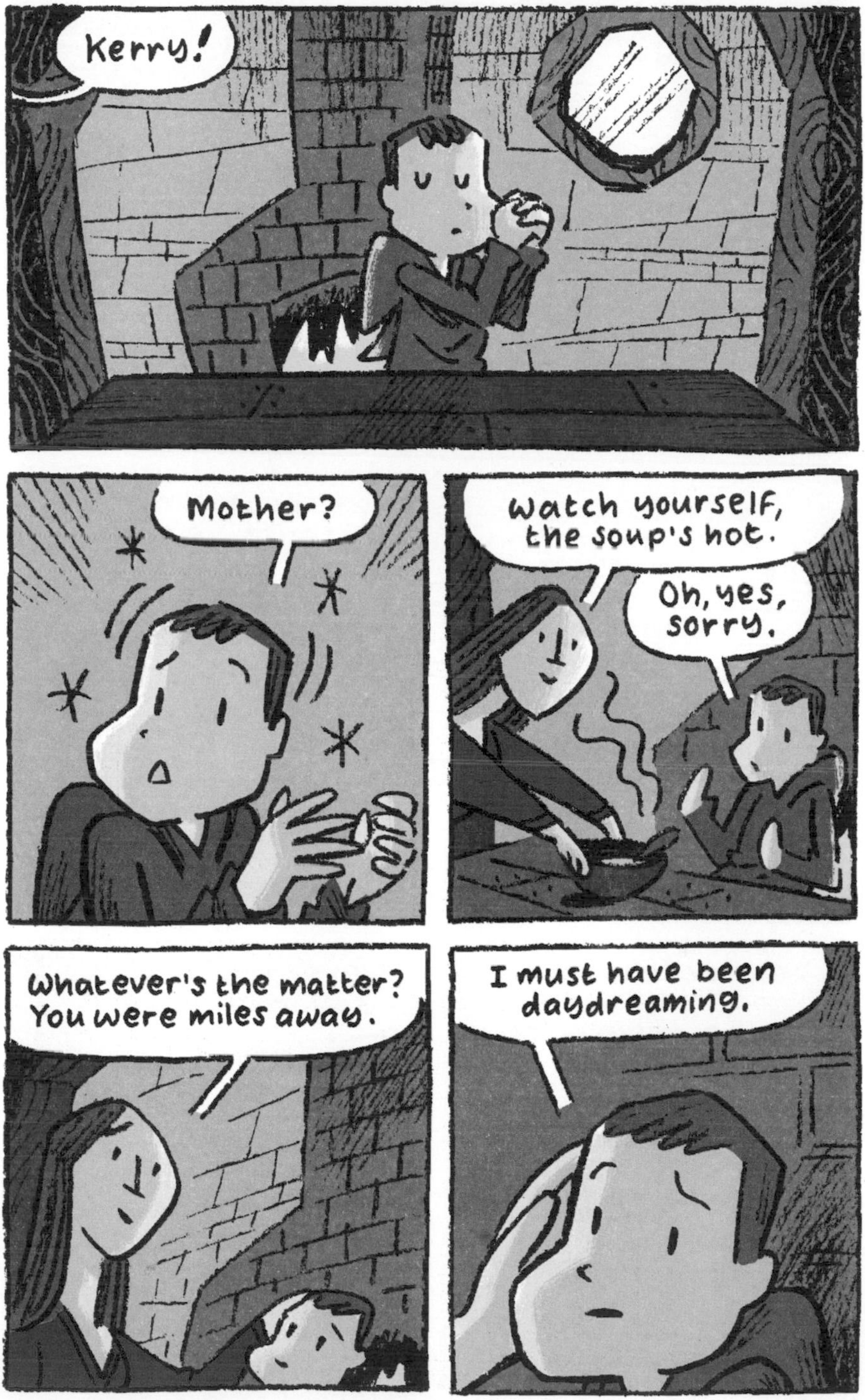
Kerry!
Mother?
Watch yourself, the soup's hot.
Oh, yes, sorry.
Whatever's the matter? You were miles away.
I must have been daydreaming.

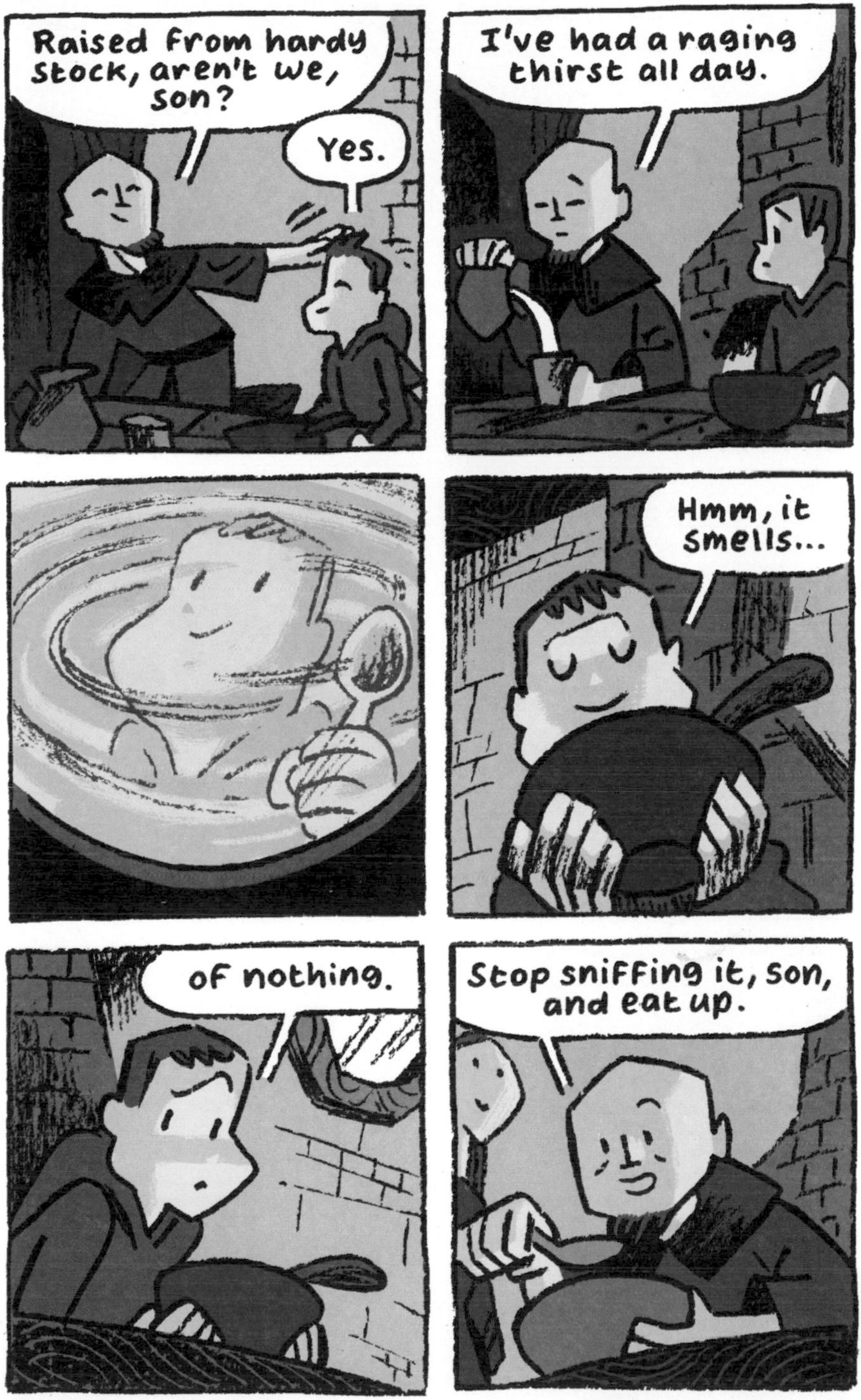
Raised from hardy stock, aren't we, son?
Yes.
I've had a raging thirst all day.
Hmm, it smells...
of nothing.
Stop sniffing it, son, and eat up.

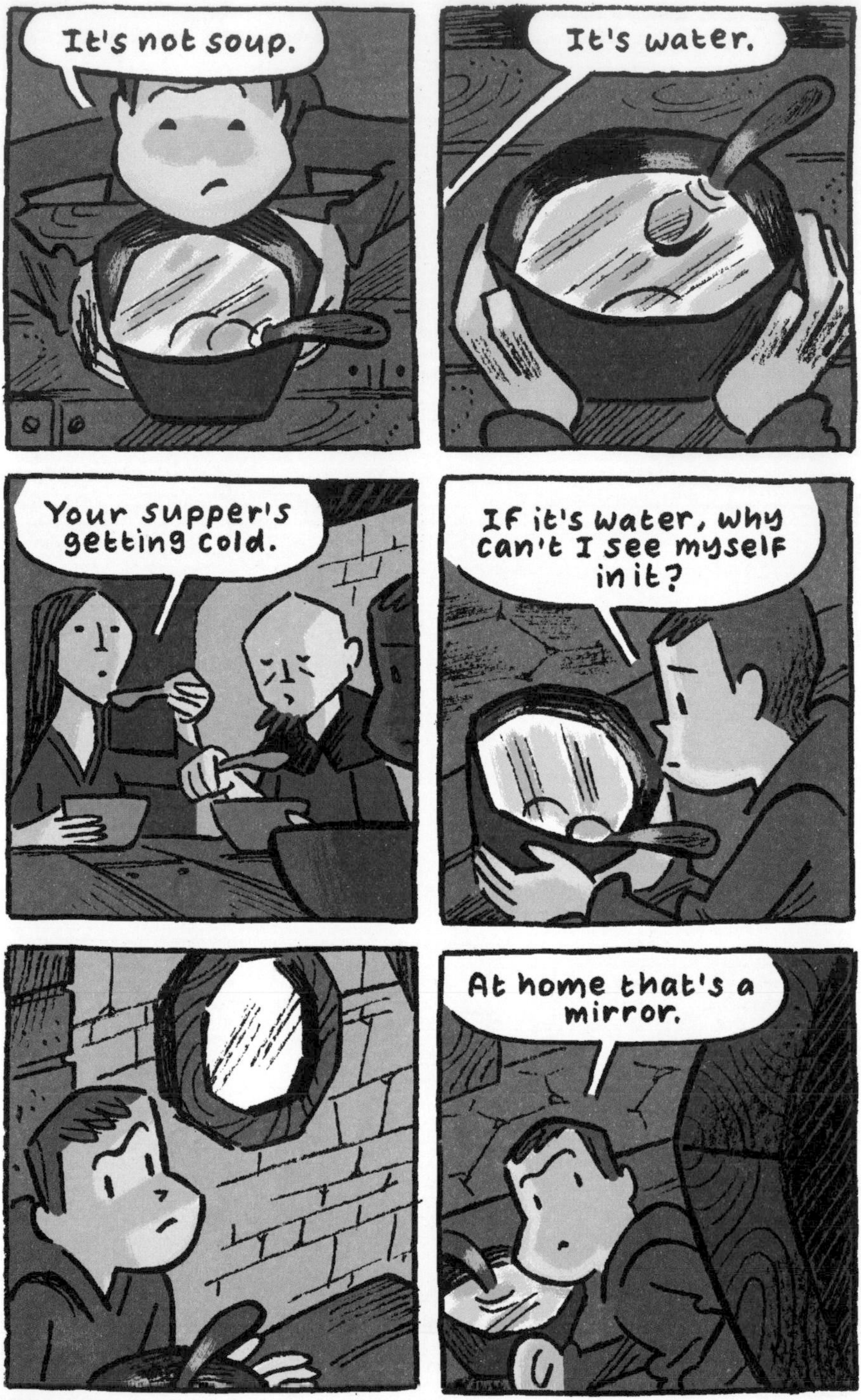
It's not soup.
It's water.
Your supper's getting cold.
If it's water, why can't I see myself in it?
At home that's a mirror.

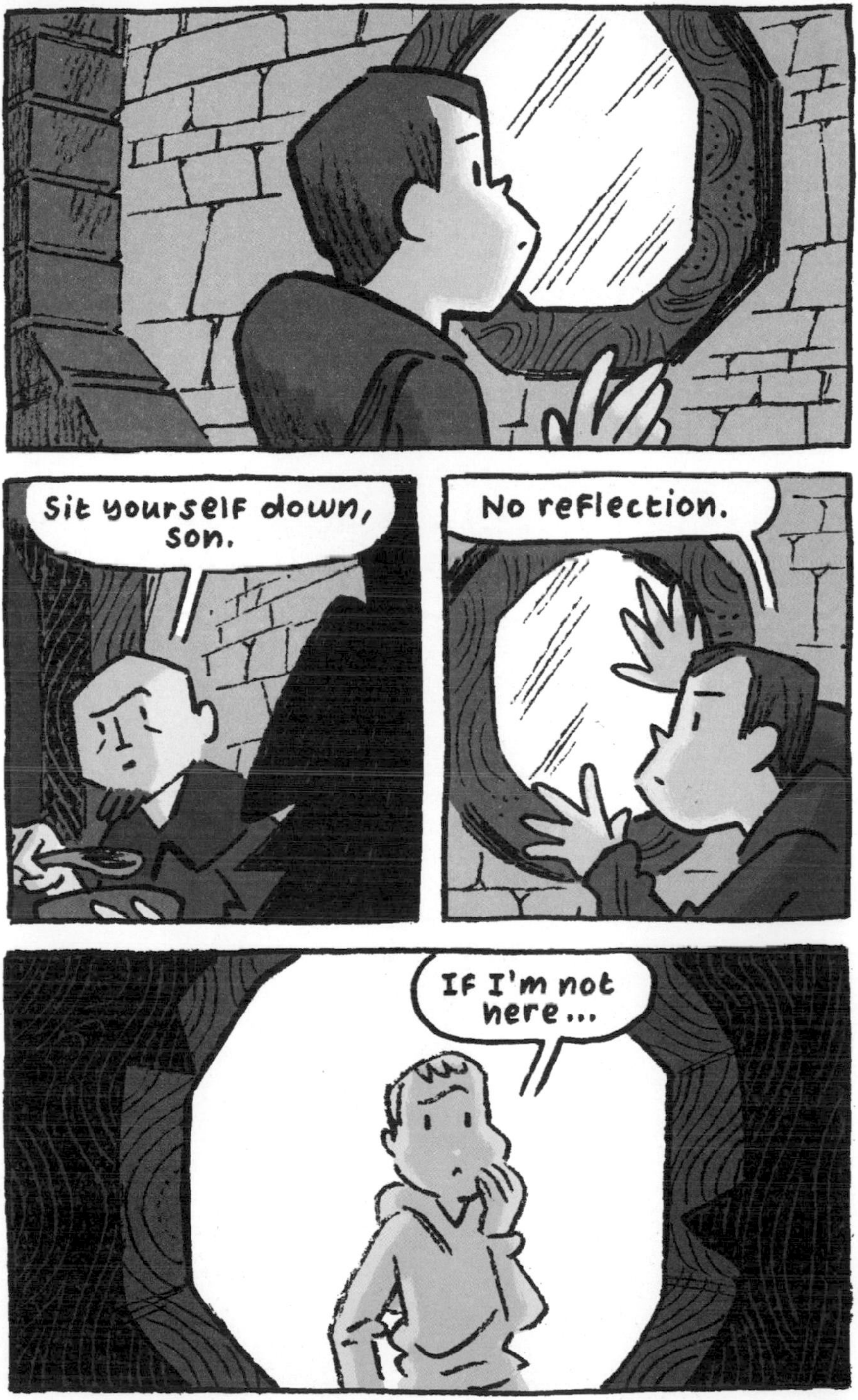

Sit yourself down, son.
No reflection.
If I'm not here...

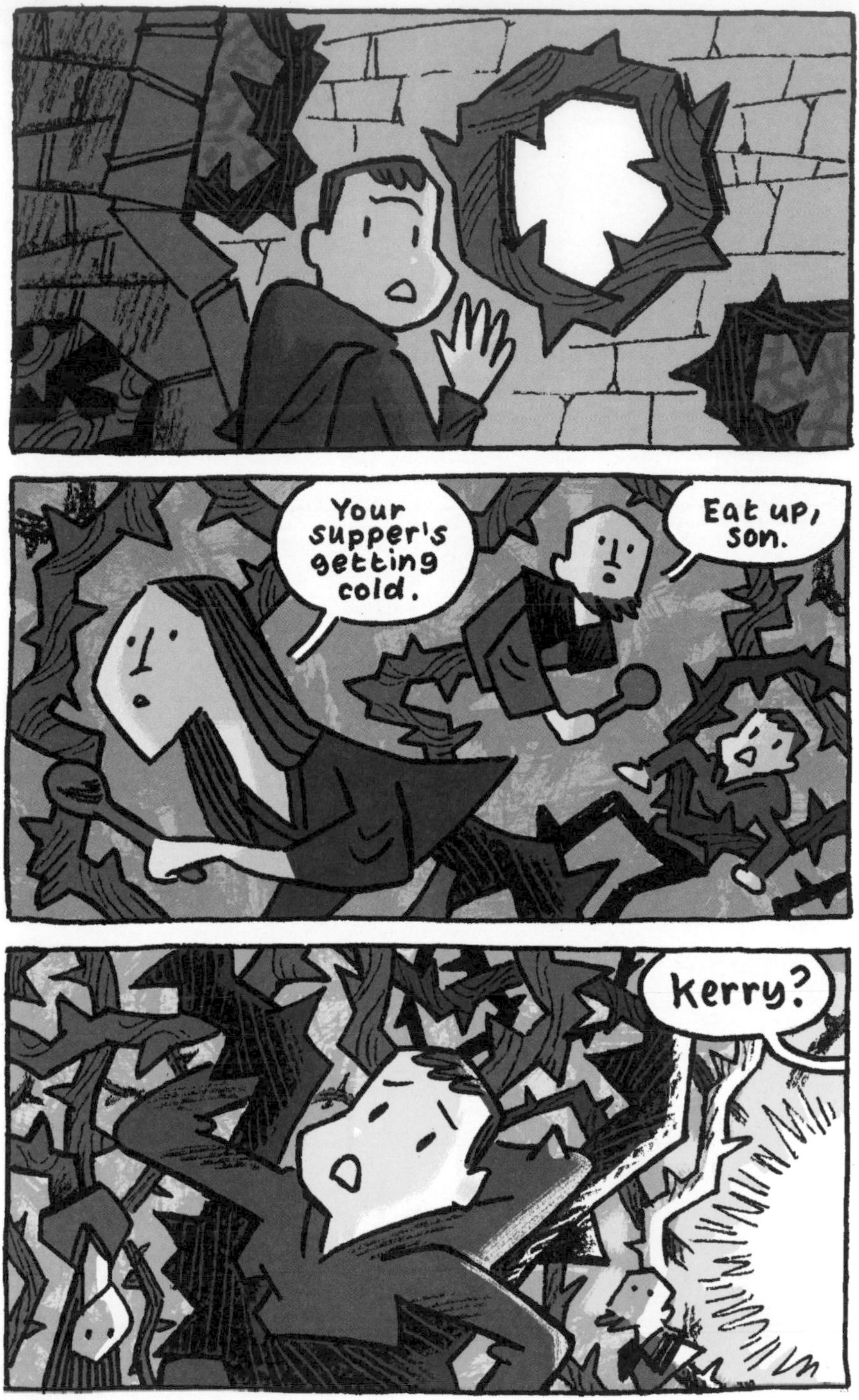
Your supper's getting cold.
Eat up, son.
Kerry?

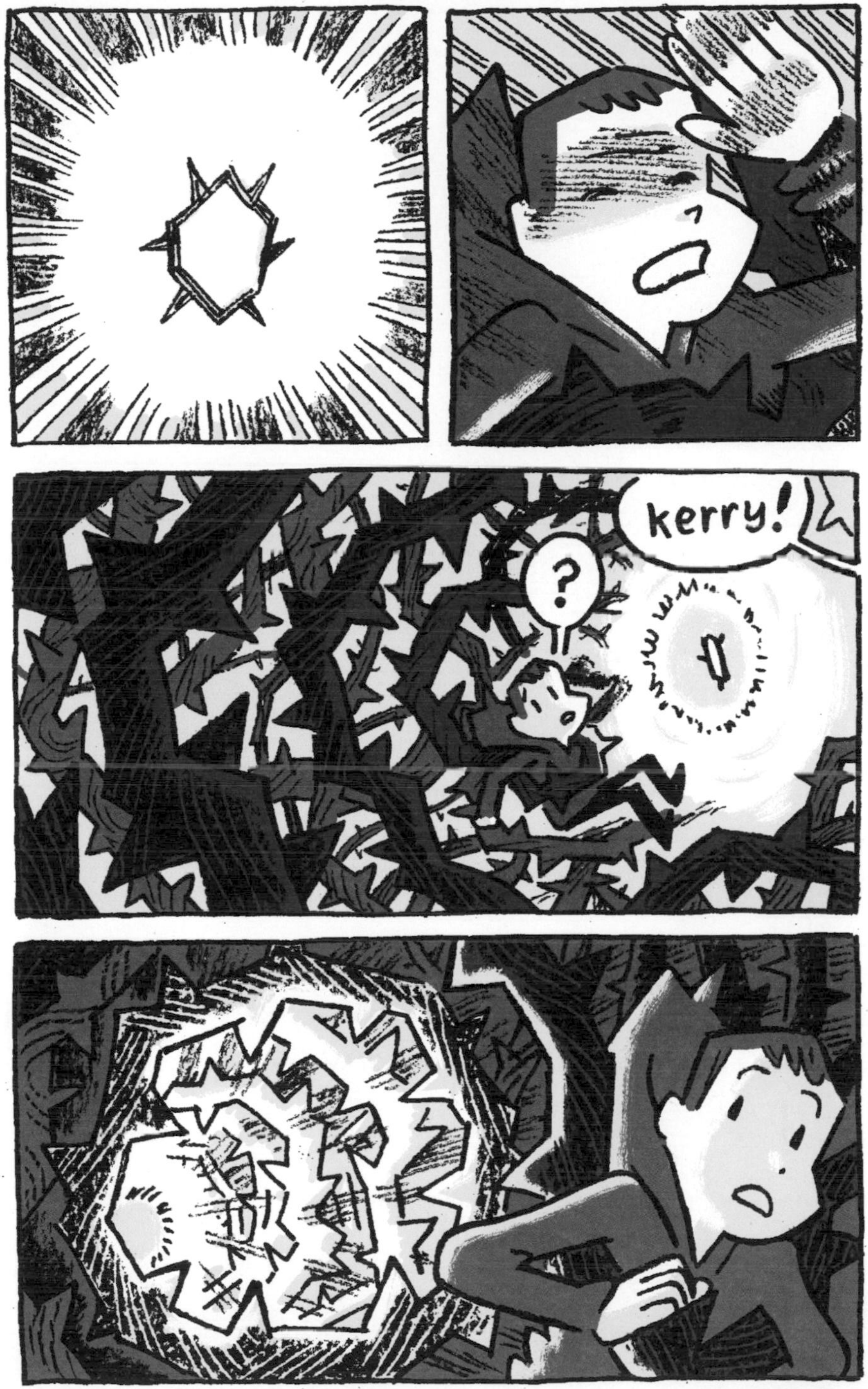
kerry!
?

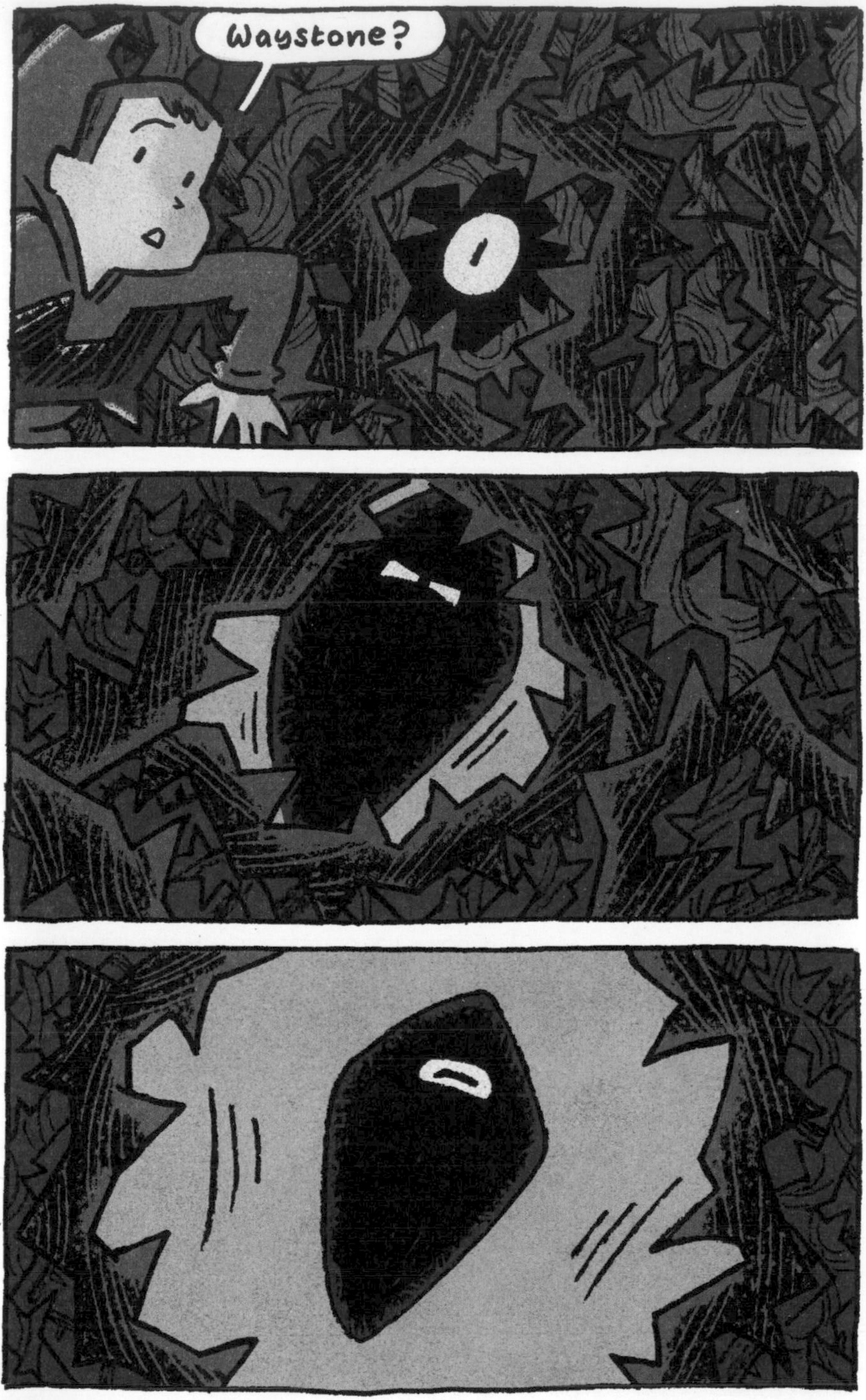
Waystone?

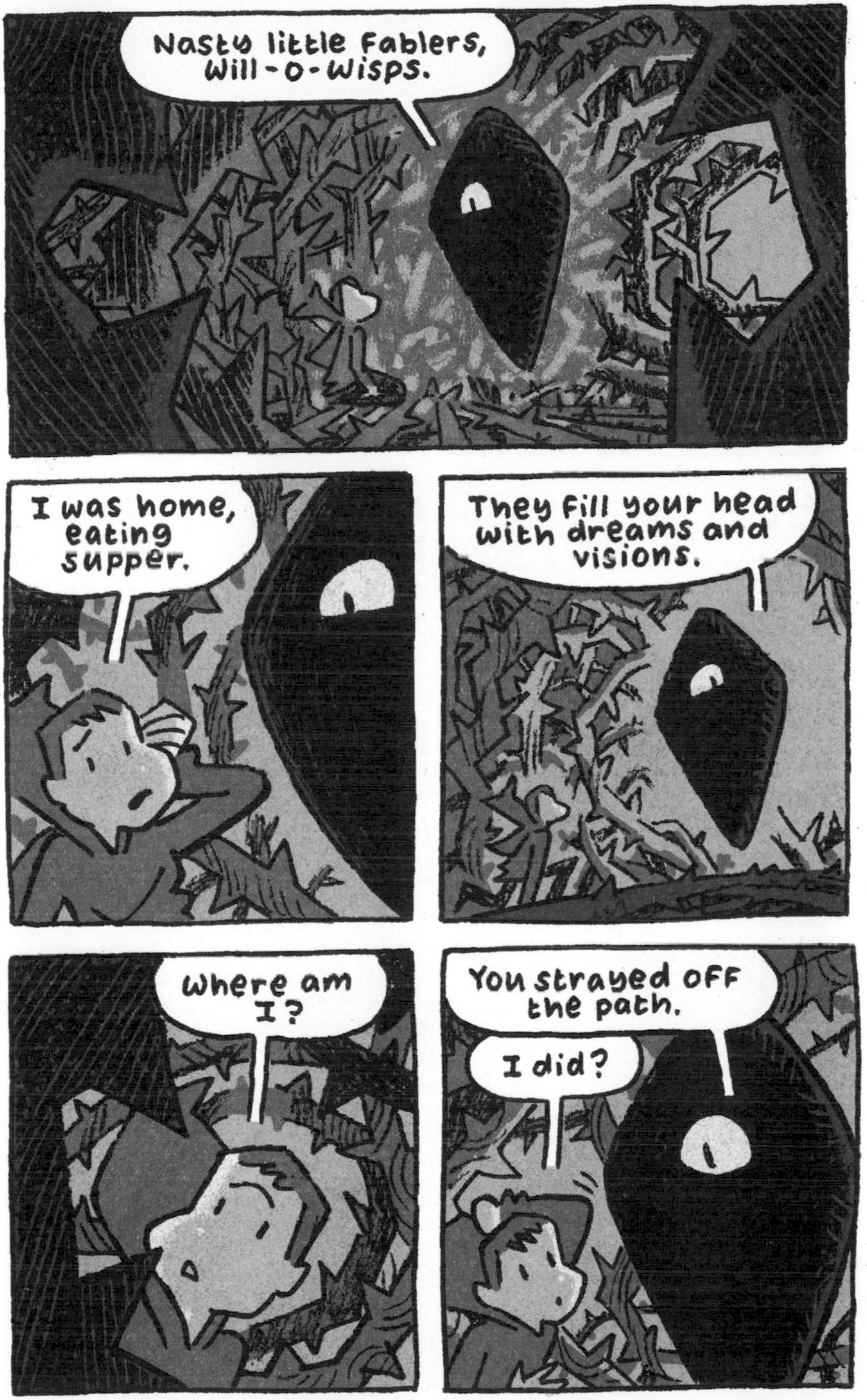
Nasty little Fablers, Will-O-Wisps.
I was home, eating supper.
They fill your head with dreams and visions.
Where am I?
You strayed off the path.
I did?

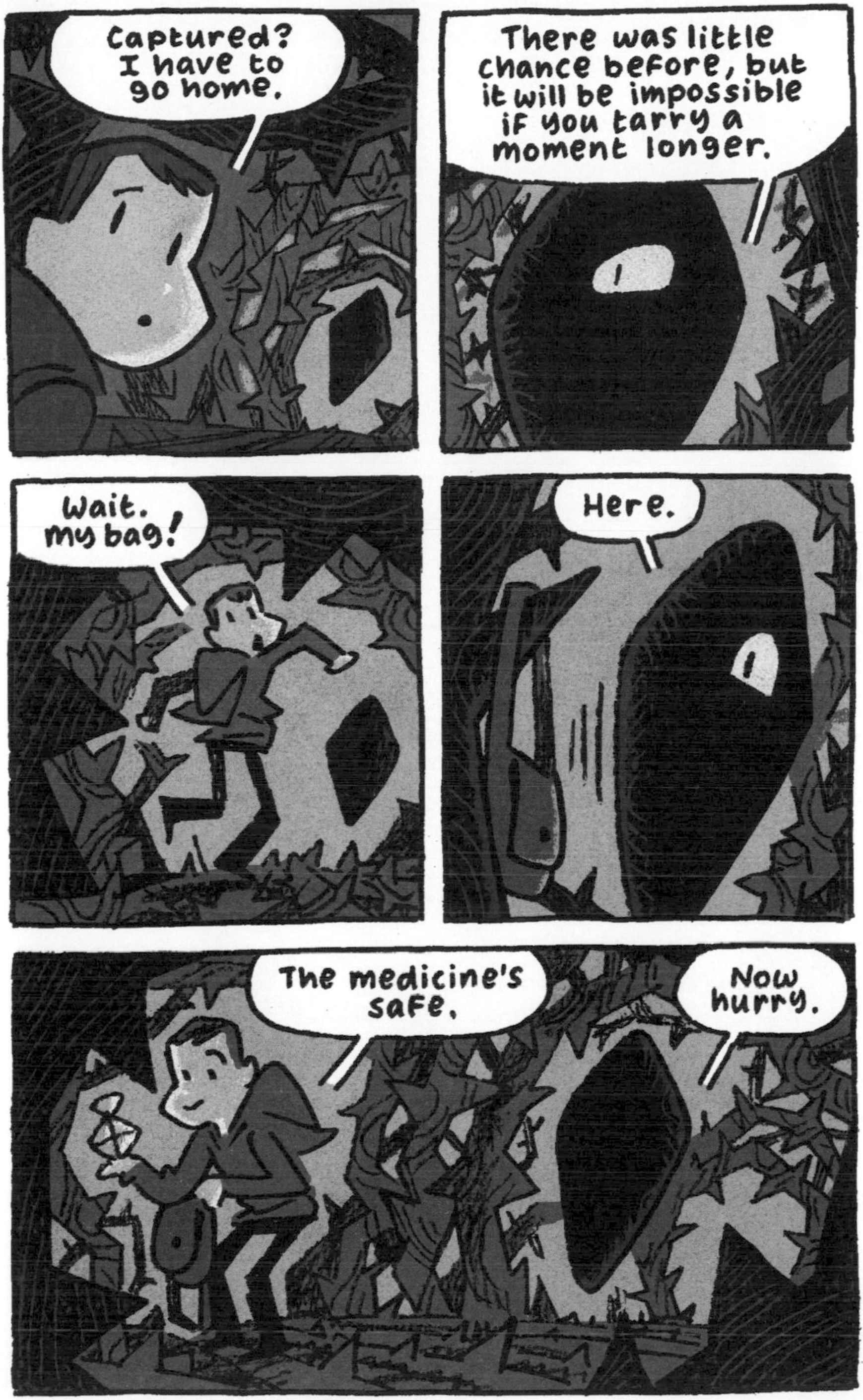
Captured? I have to go home.
There was little chance before, but it will be impossible if you tarry a moment longer.
Wait. my bag!
Here.
The medicine's safe.
Now hurry.

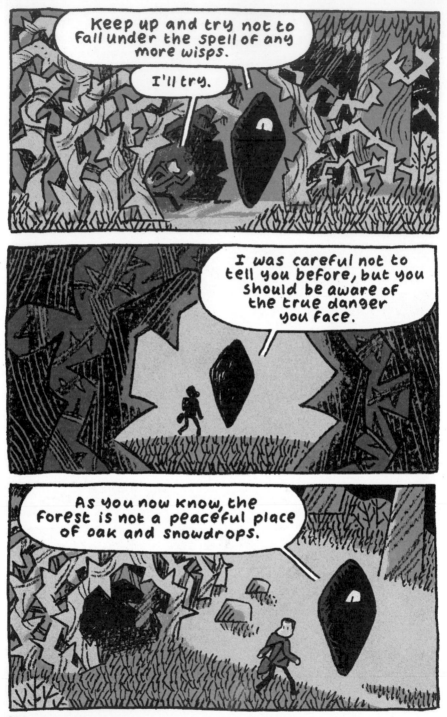

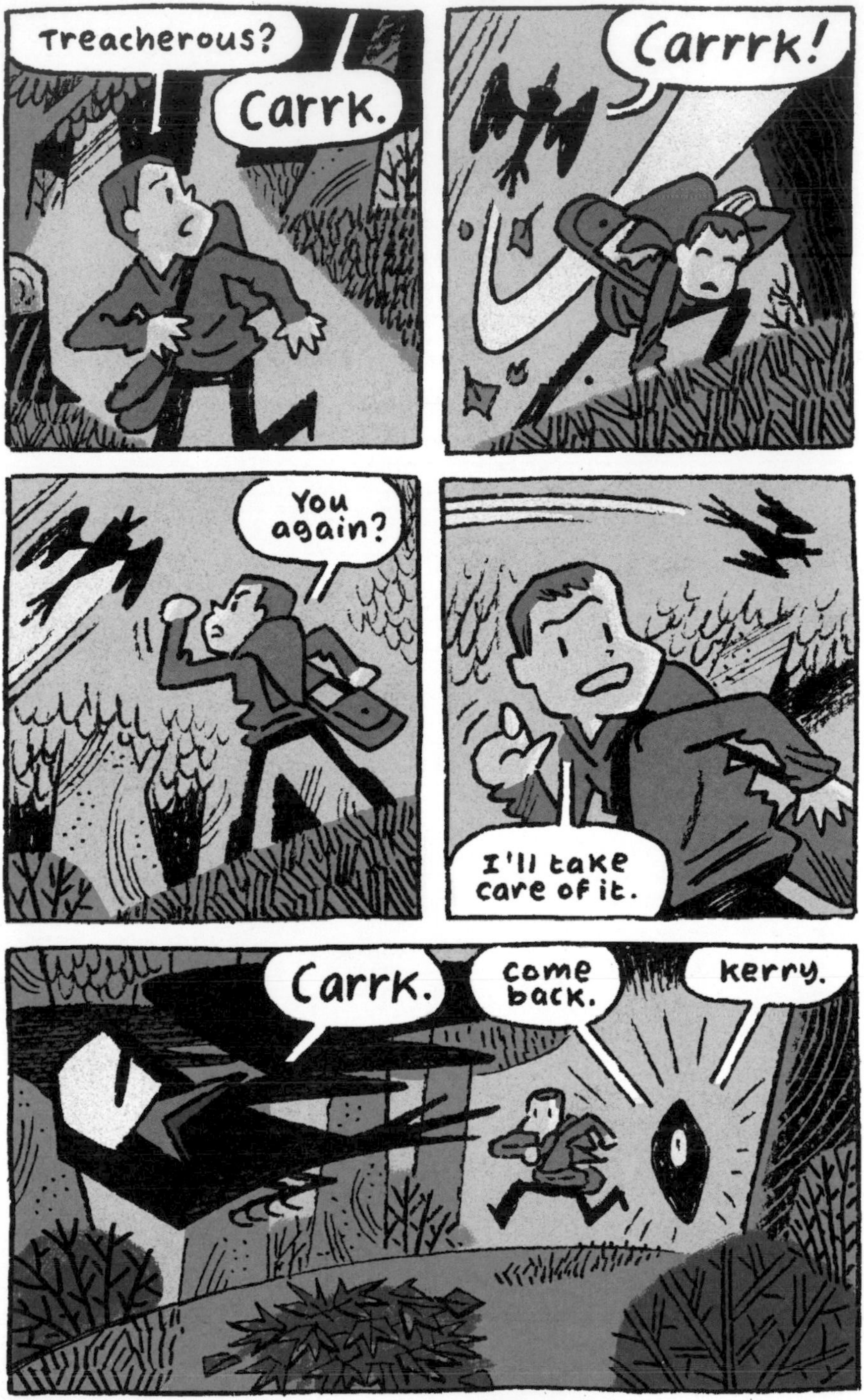
Treacherous?
Carrk.
Carrrk!
You again?
I'll take care of it.
Carrk.
come back.
kerry.

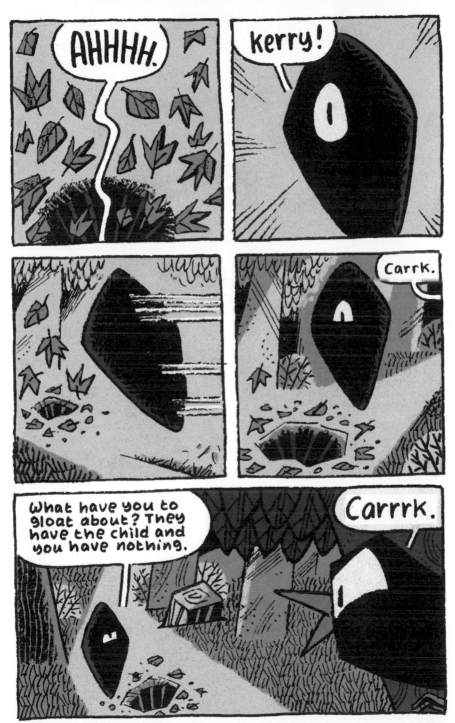

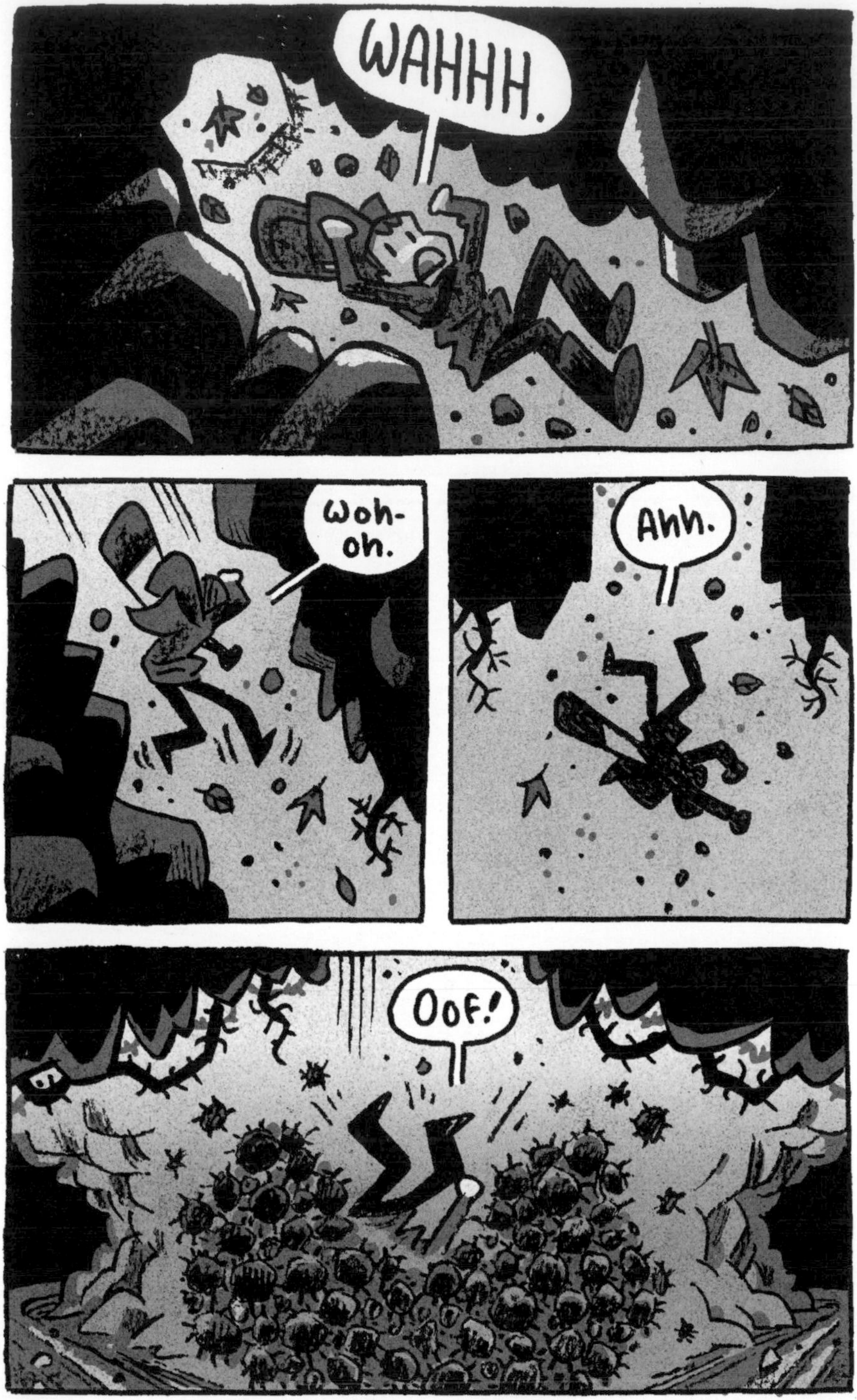
WAHHH.
Woh-oh.
Ahh.
Oof!

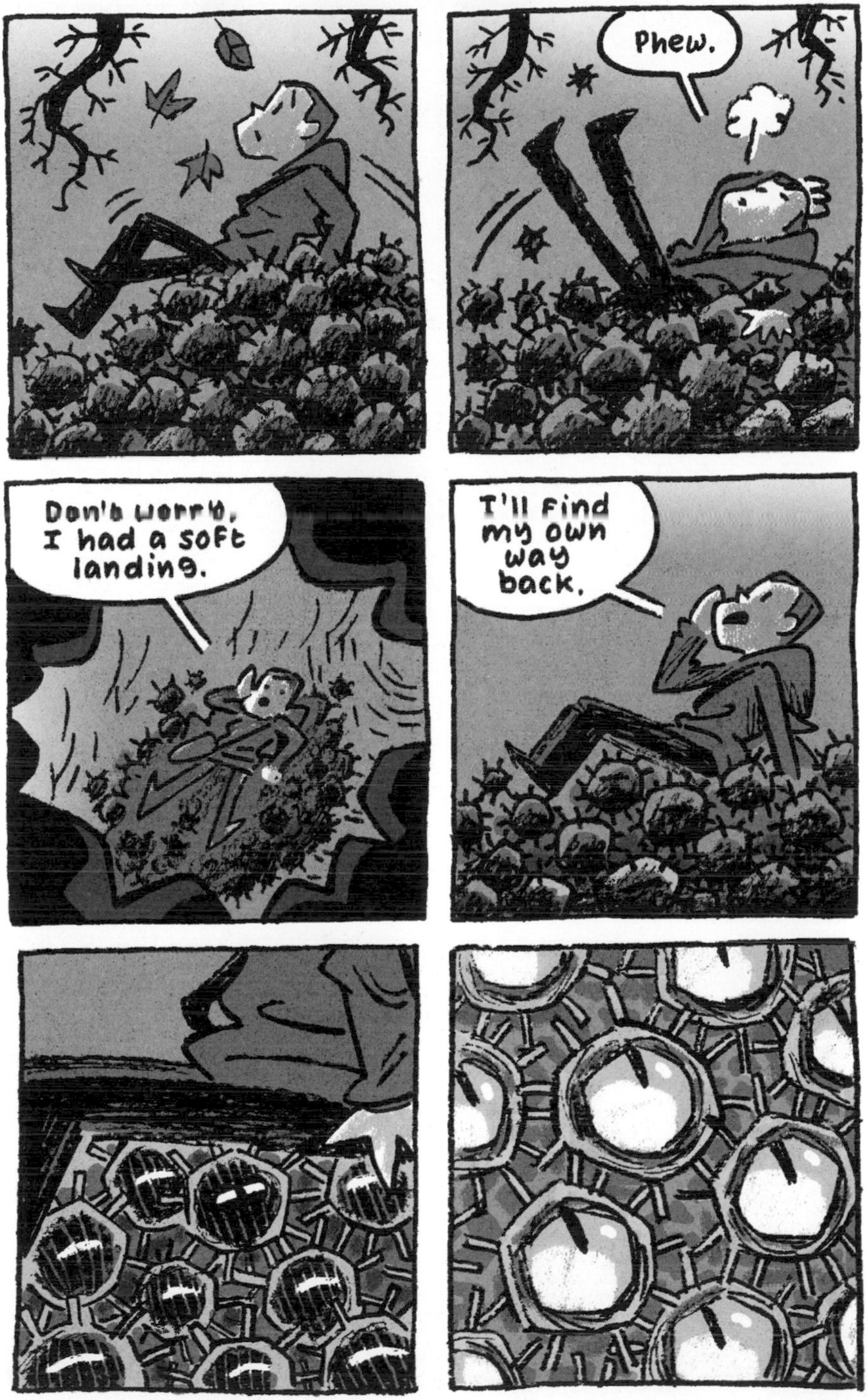
Phew.
Don't worry, I had a soft landing.
I'll find my own way back.

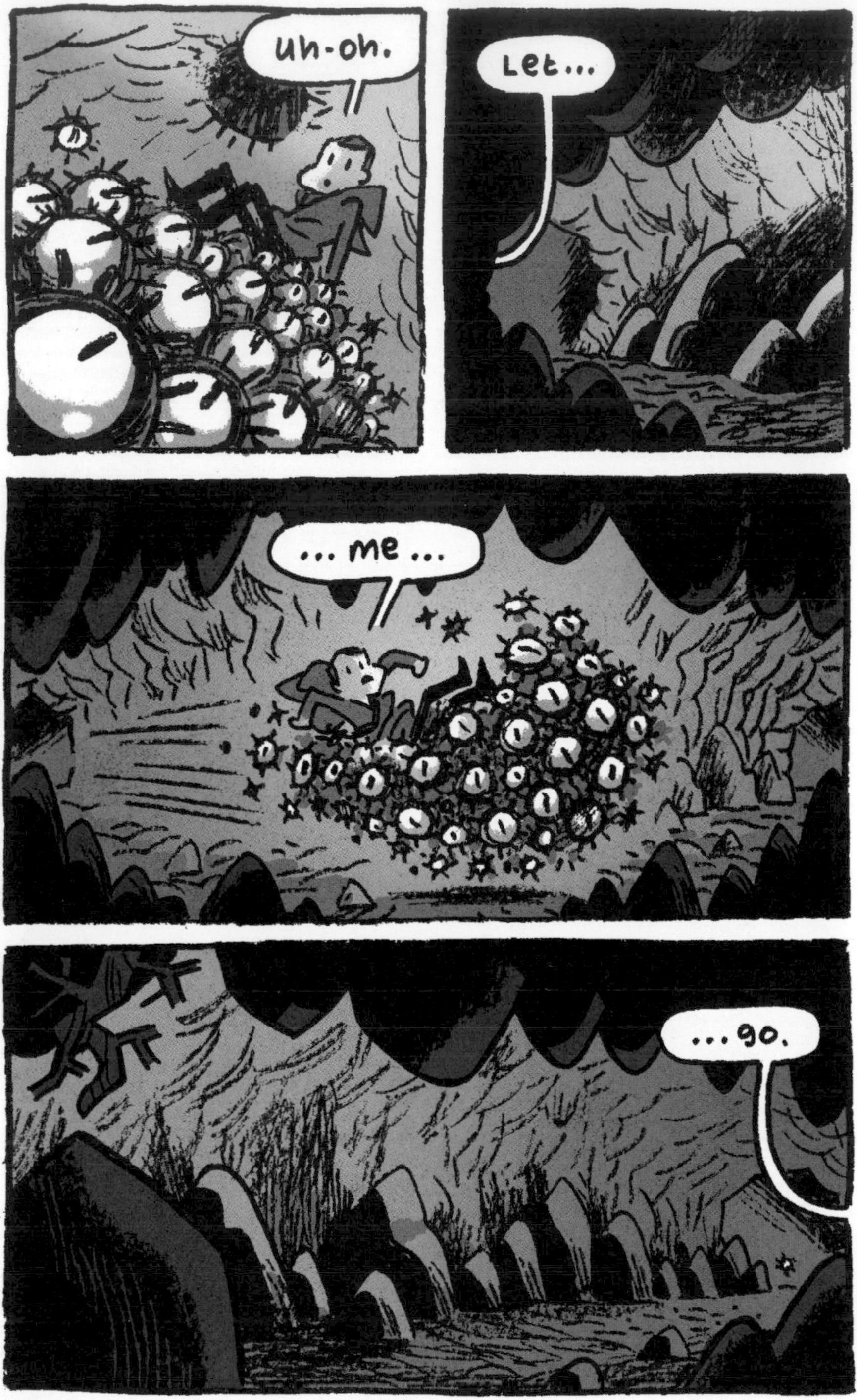
uh-oh.
Let...
... me ...
...go.

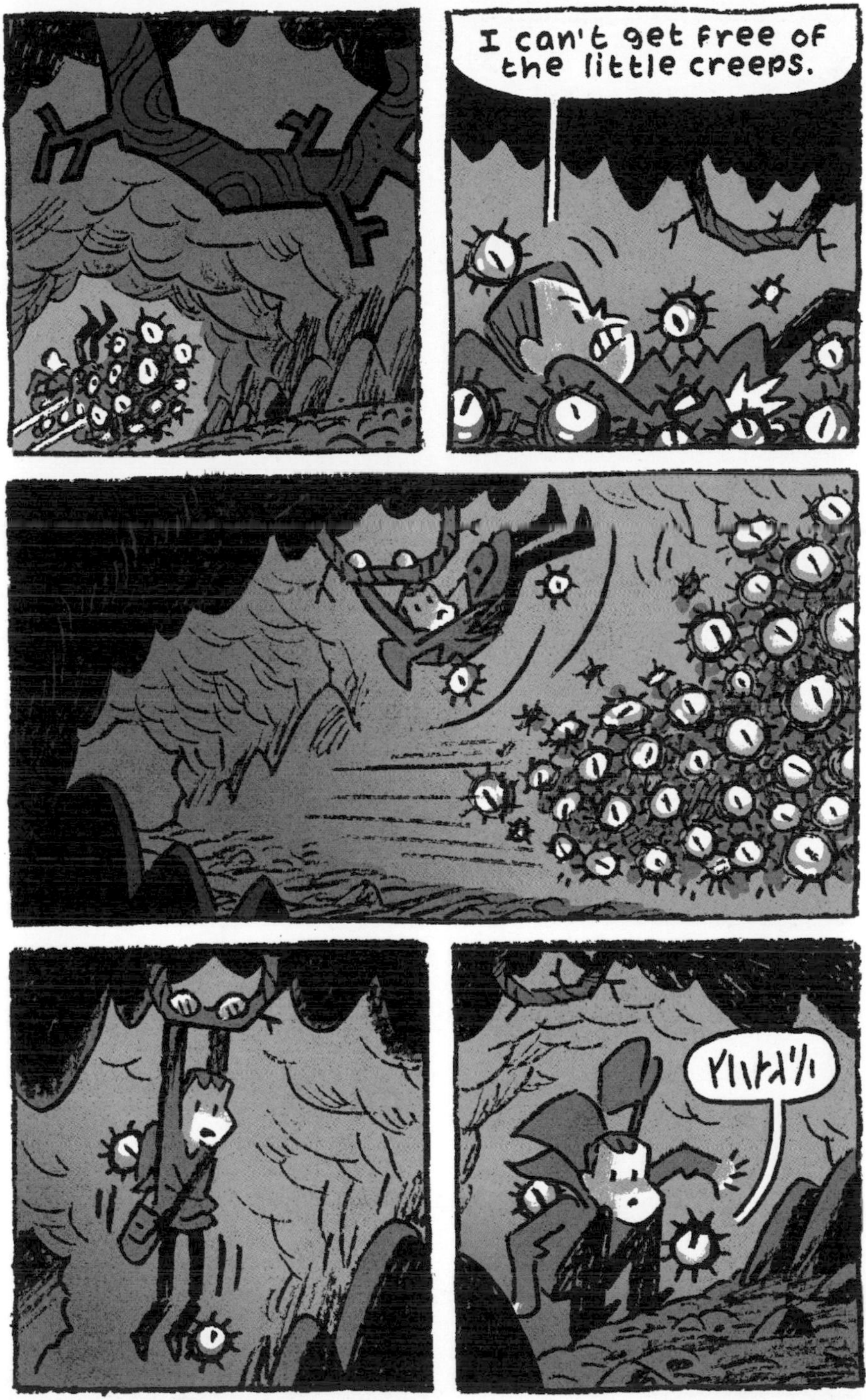
I can't get free of the little creeps.

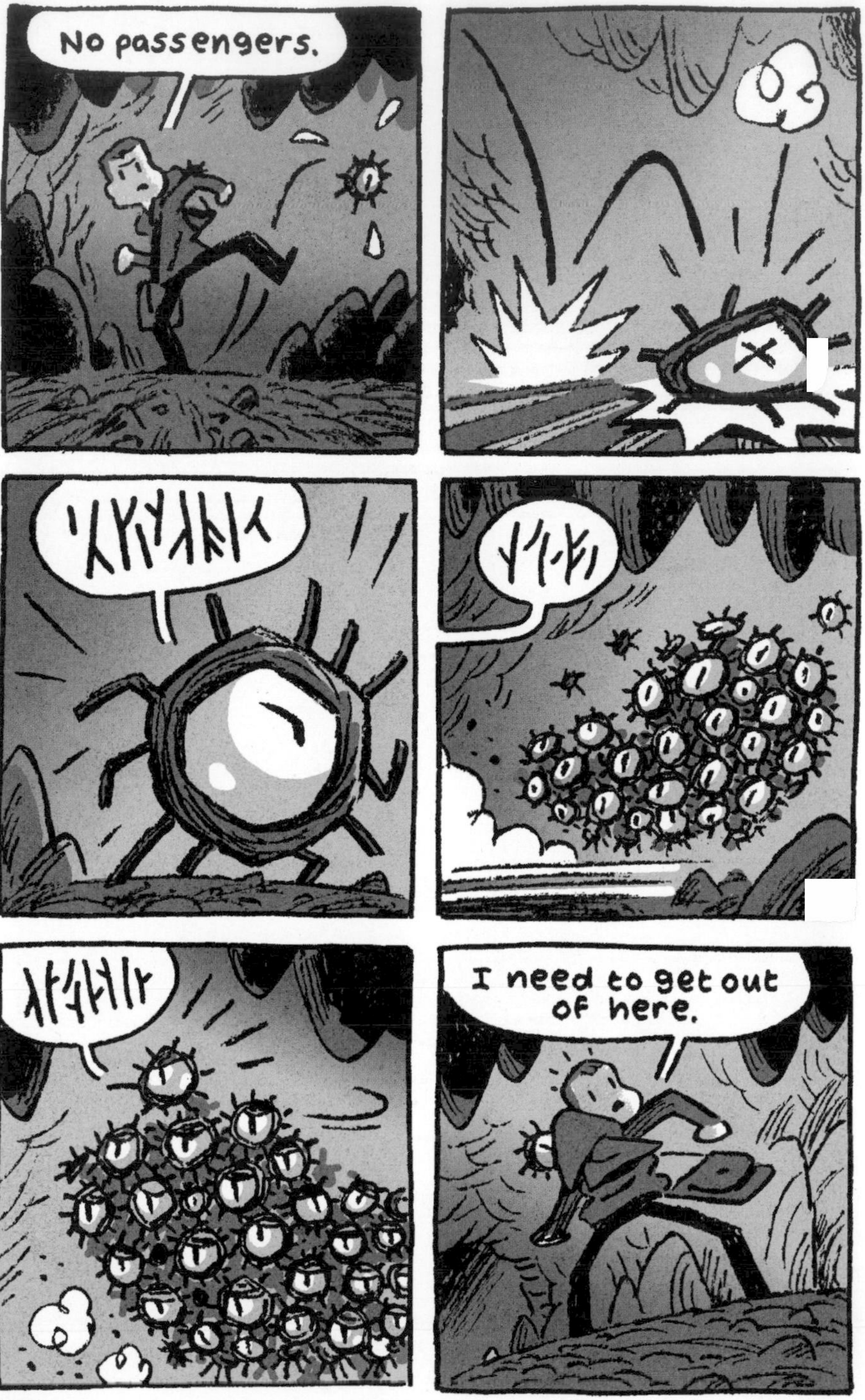
No passengers.
I need to get out of here.

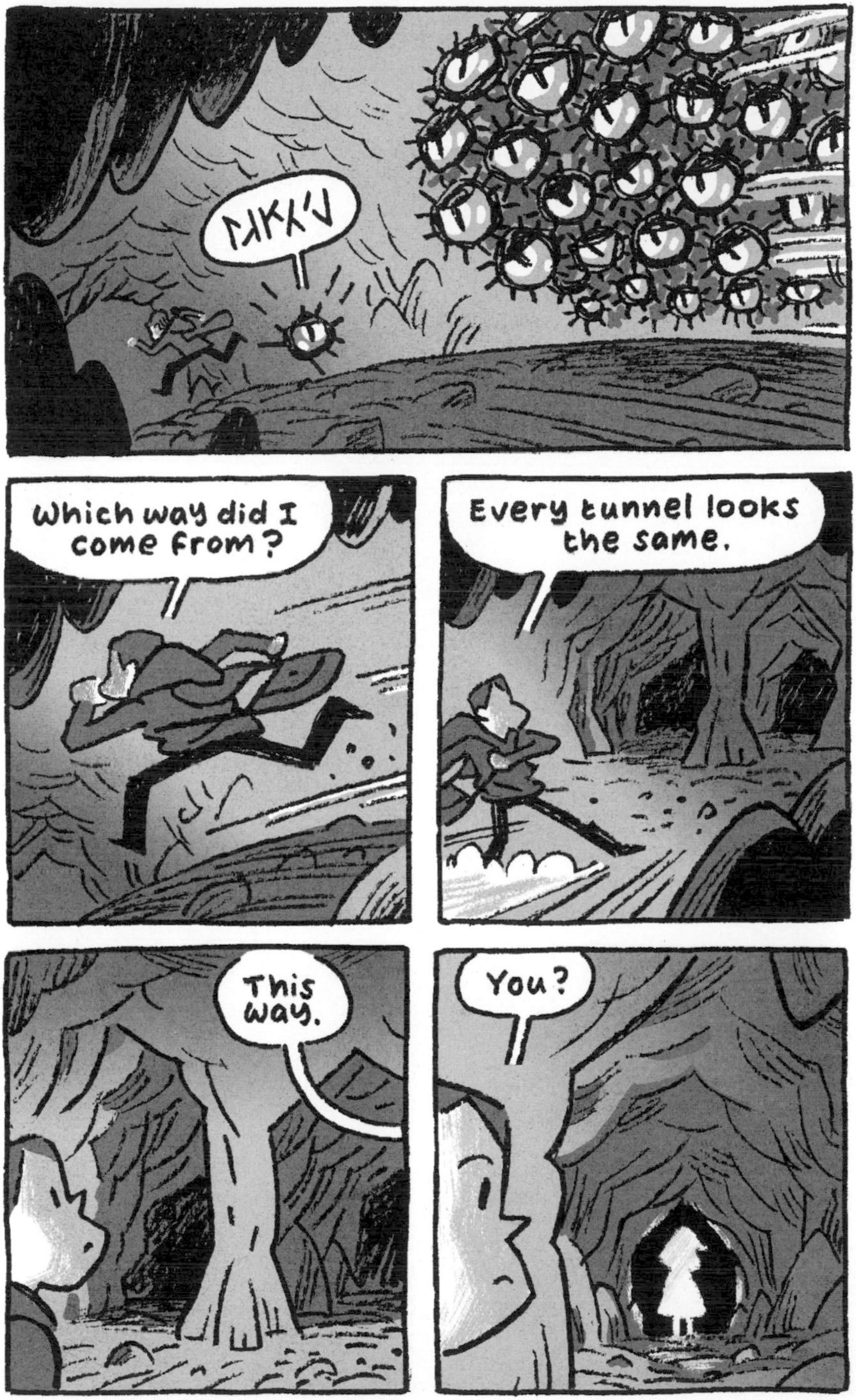
Which way did I come from?
Every tunnel looks the same.
This way.
You?

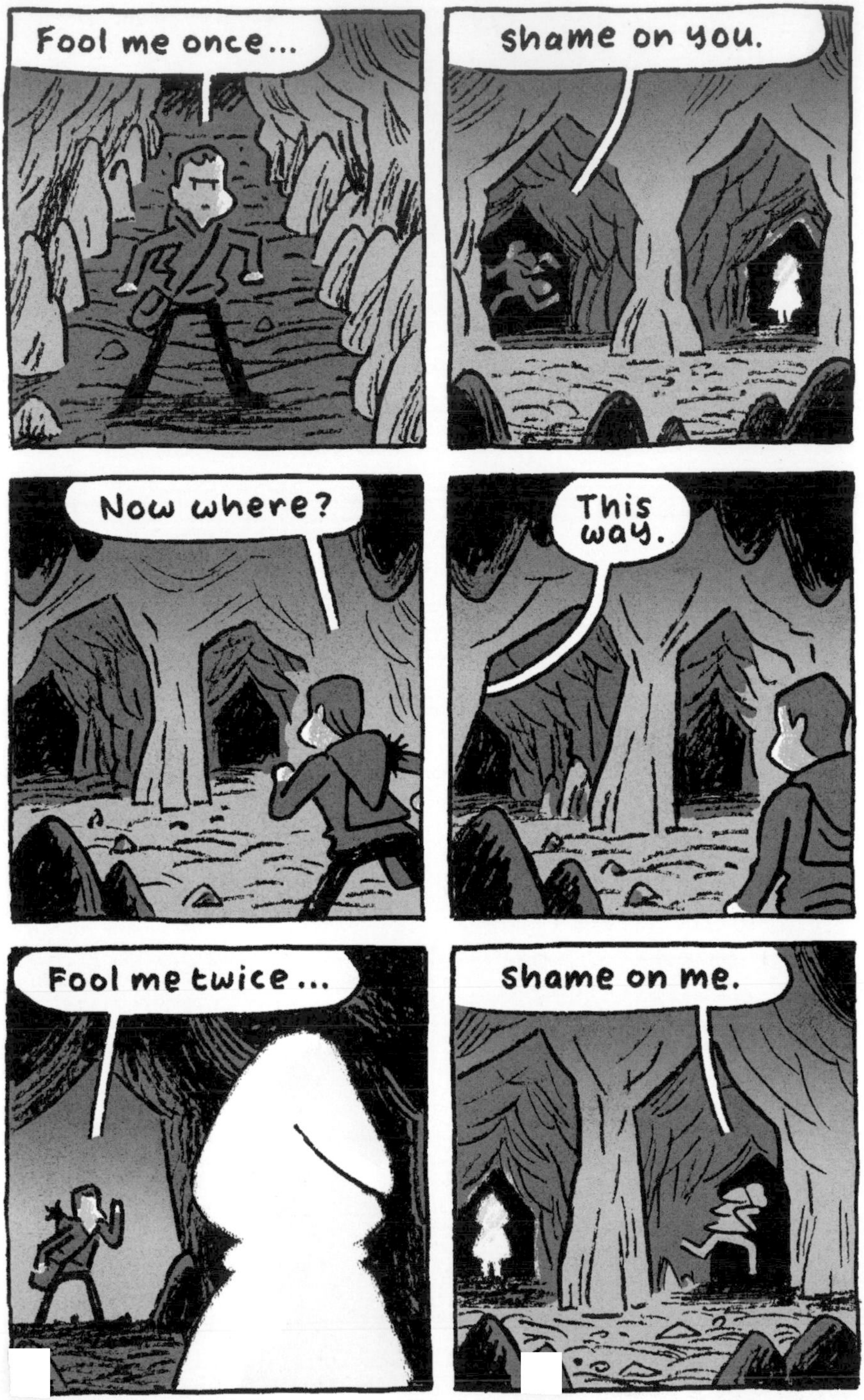
Fool me once...
shame on you.
Now where?
This way.
Fool me twice...
Shame on me.

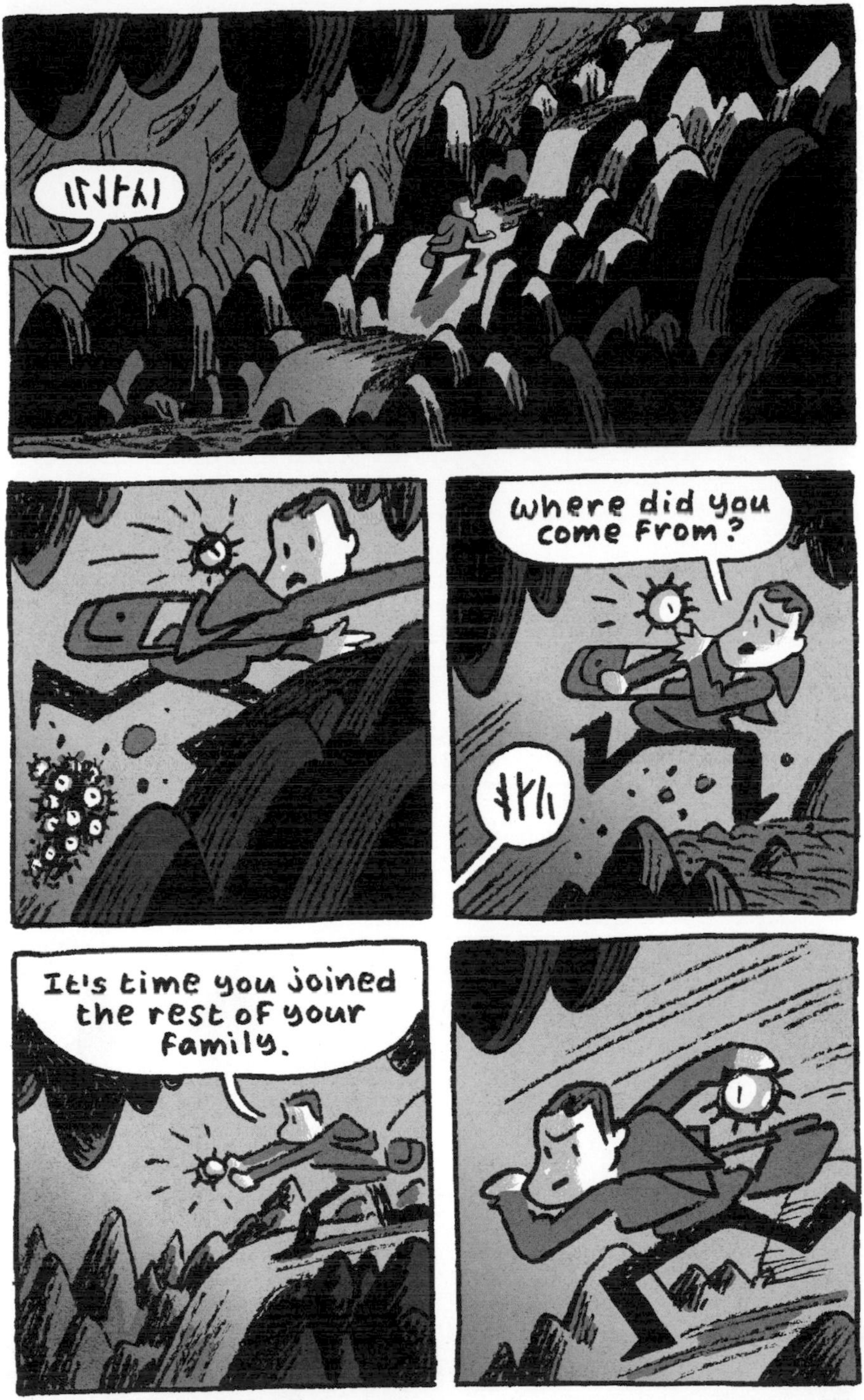

Where did you come from?
It's time you joined the rest of your family.

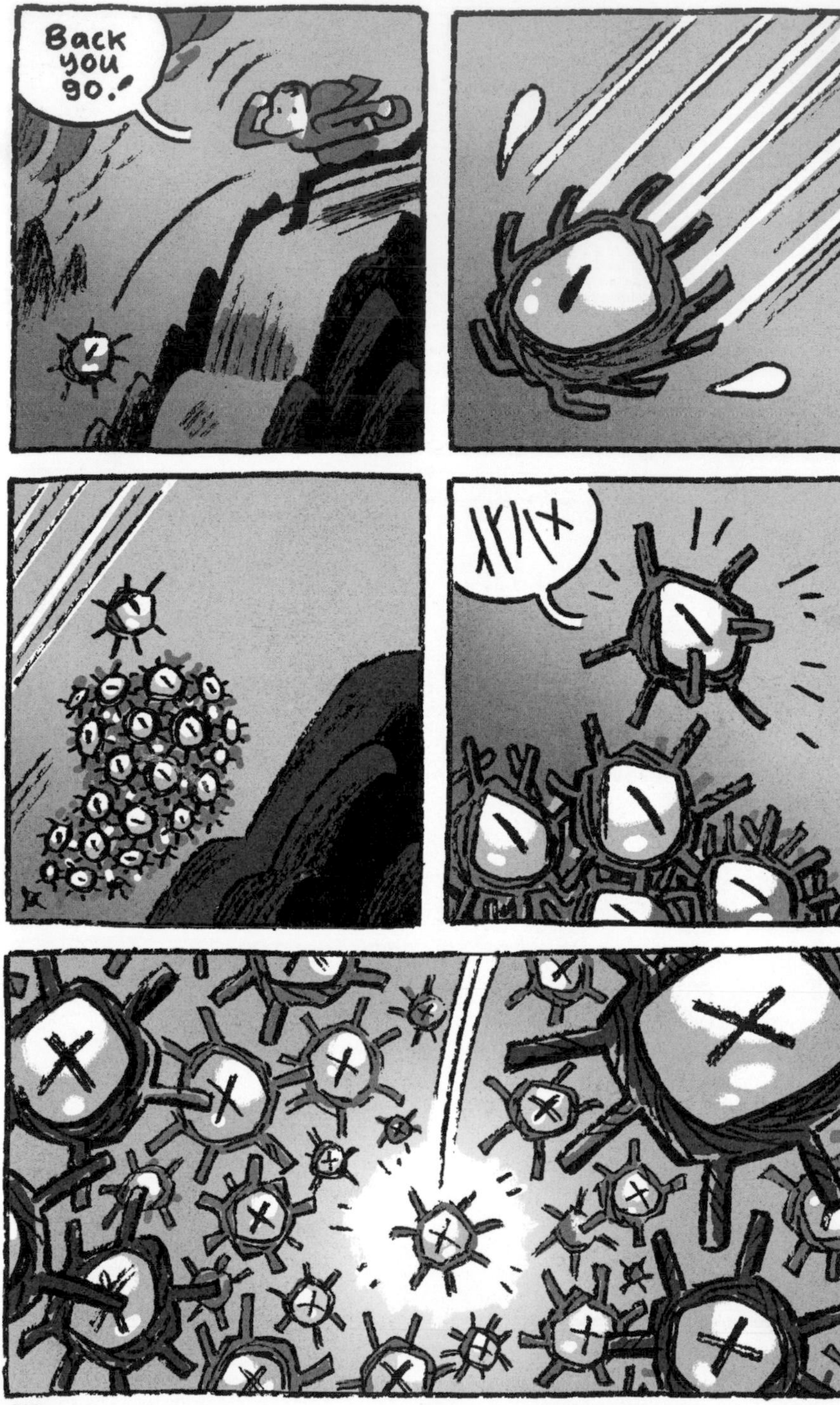
Back you go.

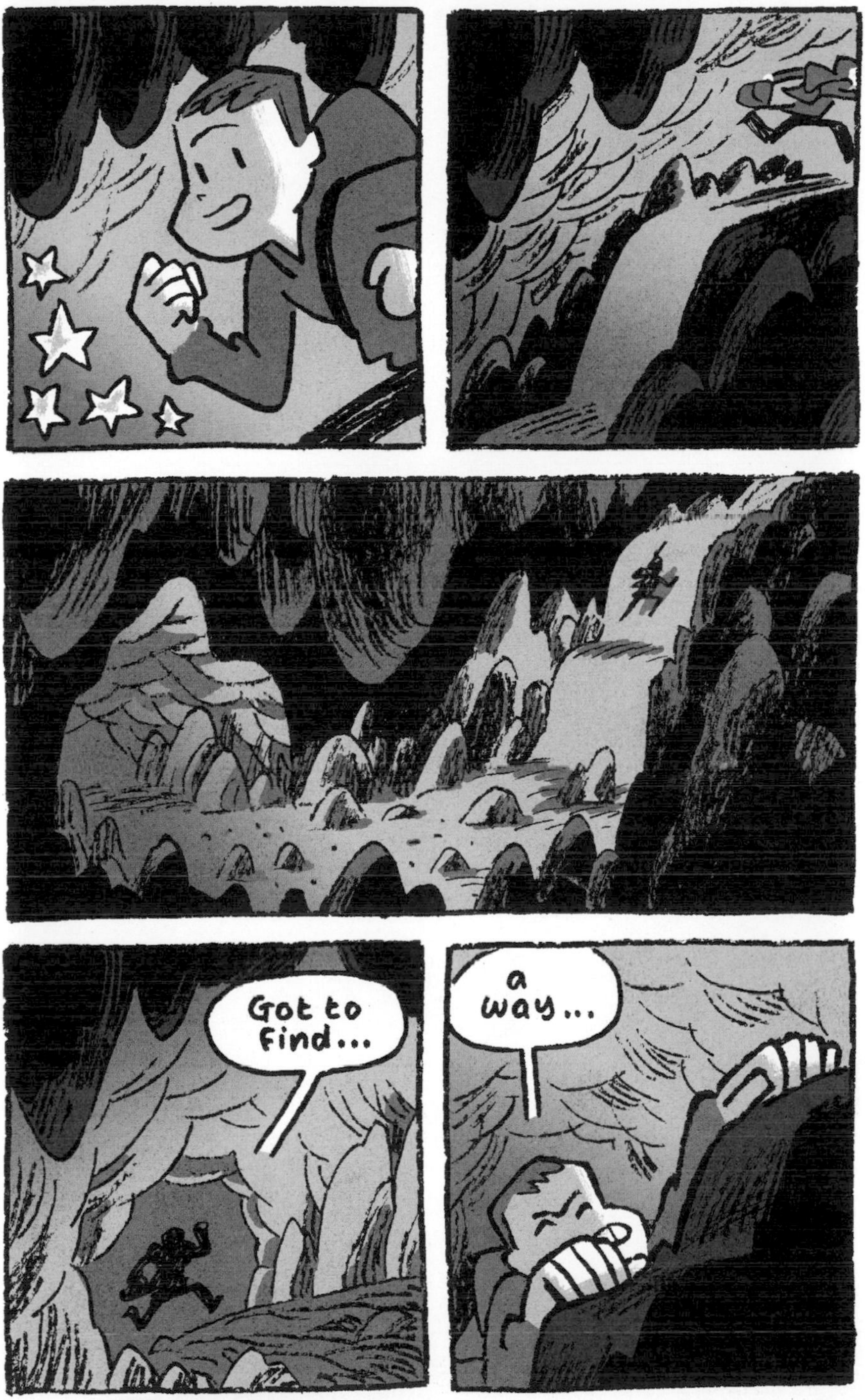
Got to find...
a way...

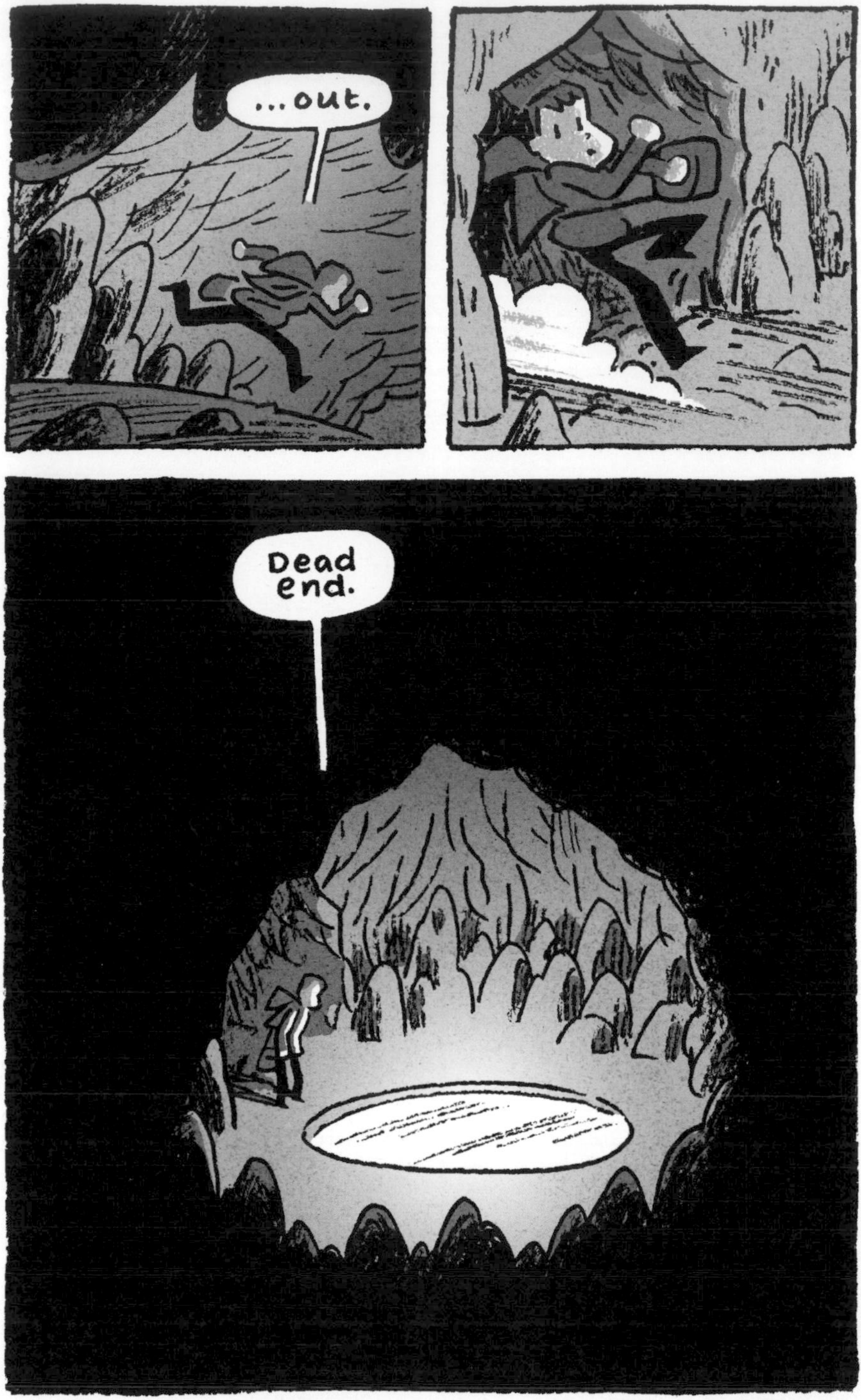
...out.
Dead end.

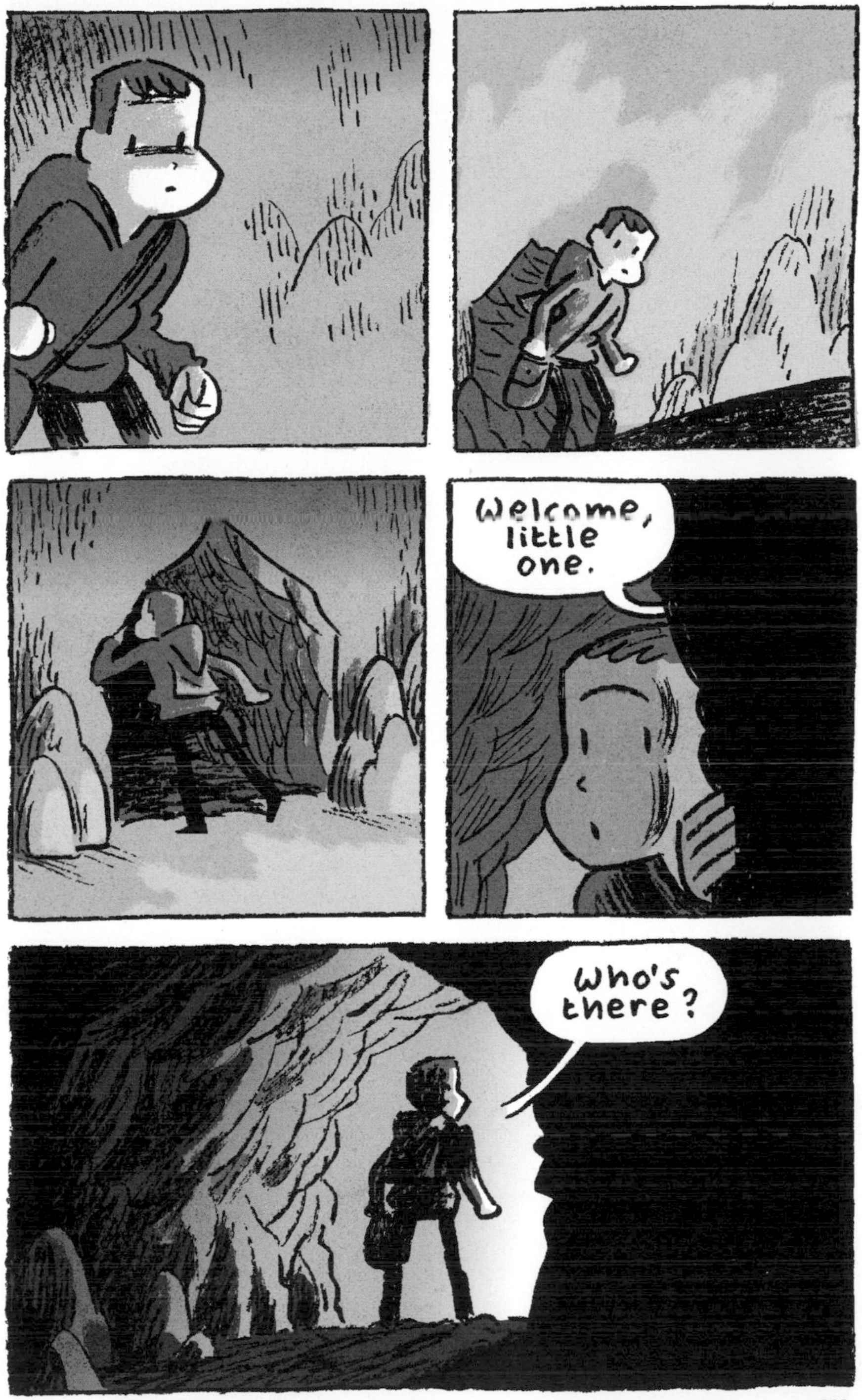
Welcome, little one.
Who's there?

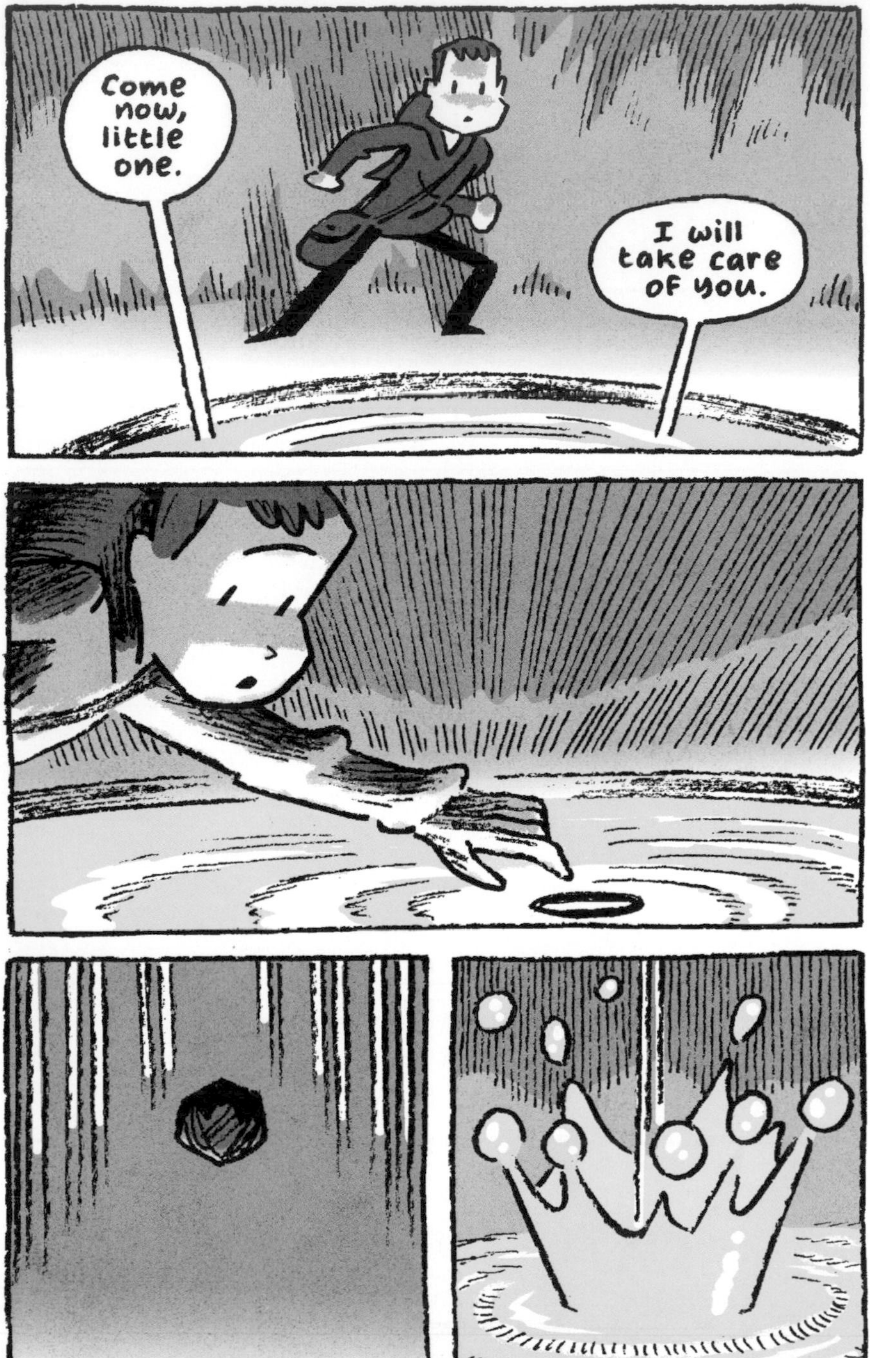
Come now, little one.
I will take care of you.

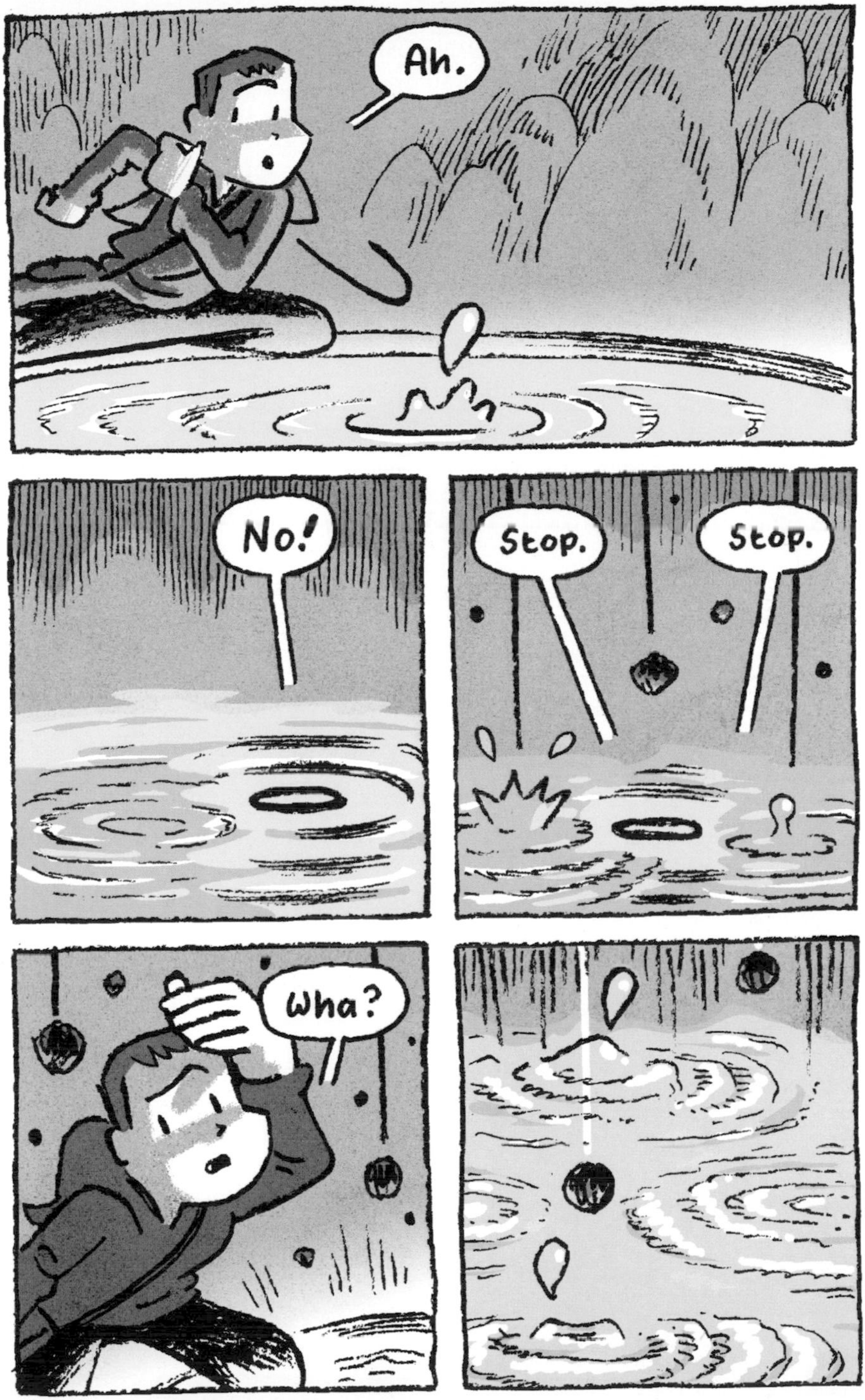
Ah.
No!
Stop.
Stop.
Wha?

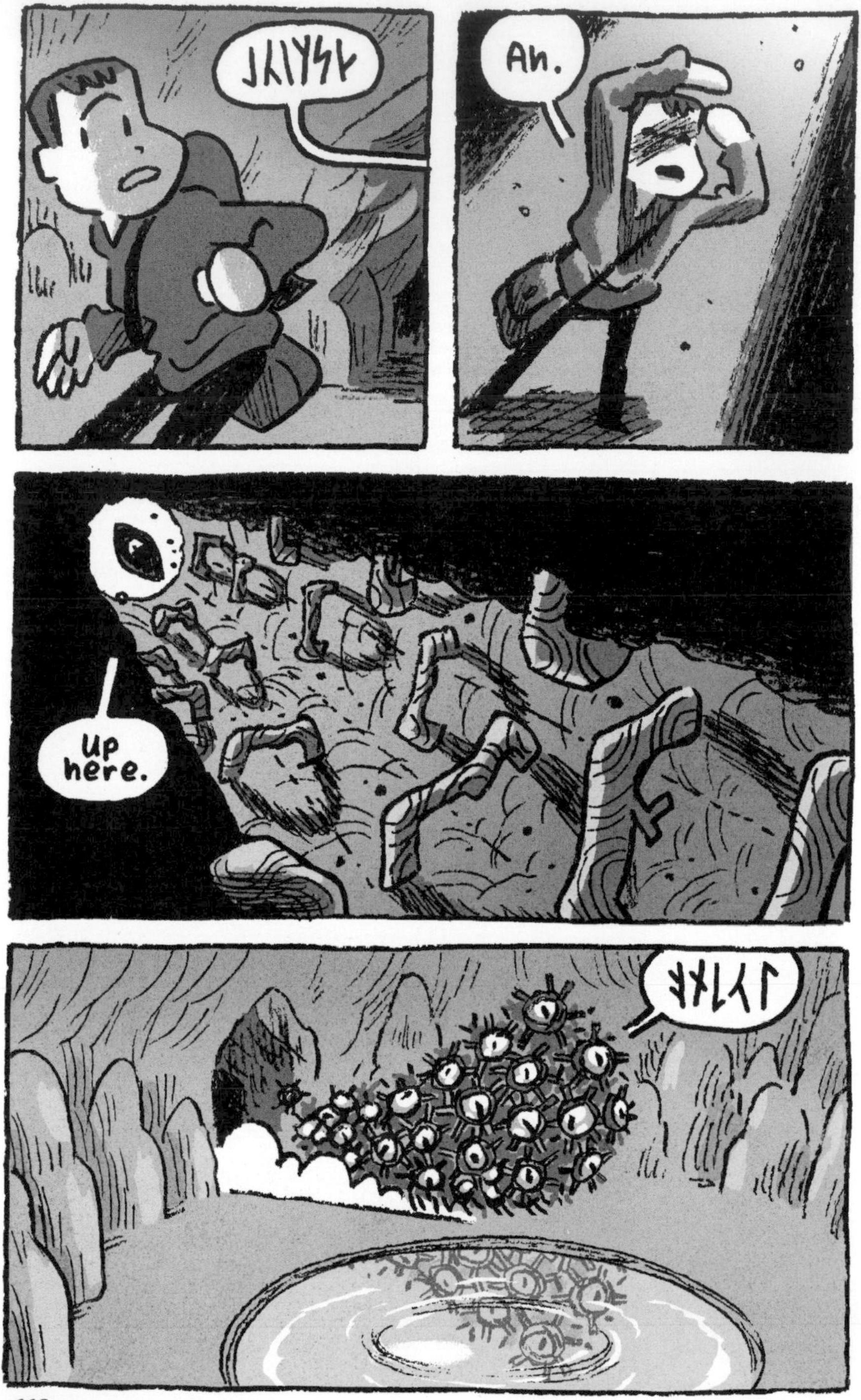
Ah.
Up here.

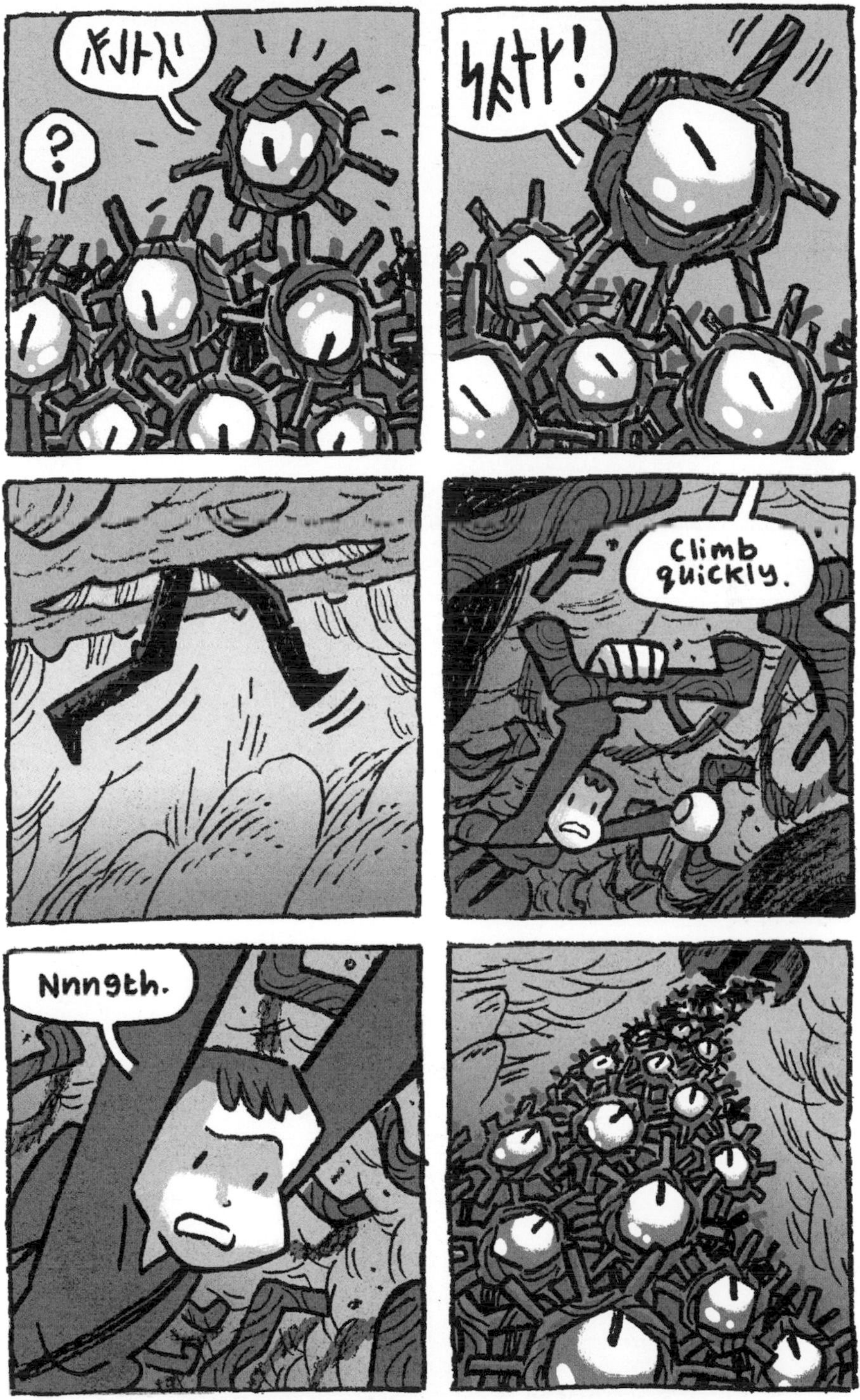
?
Climb quickly.
Nnngth.

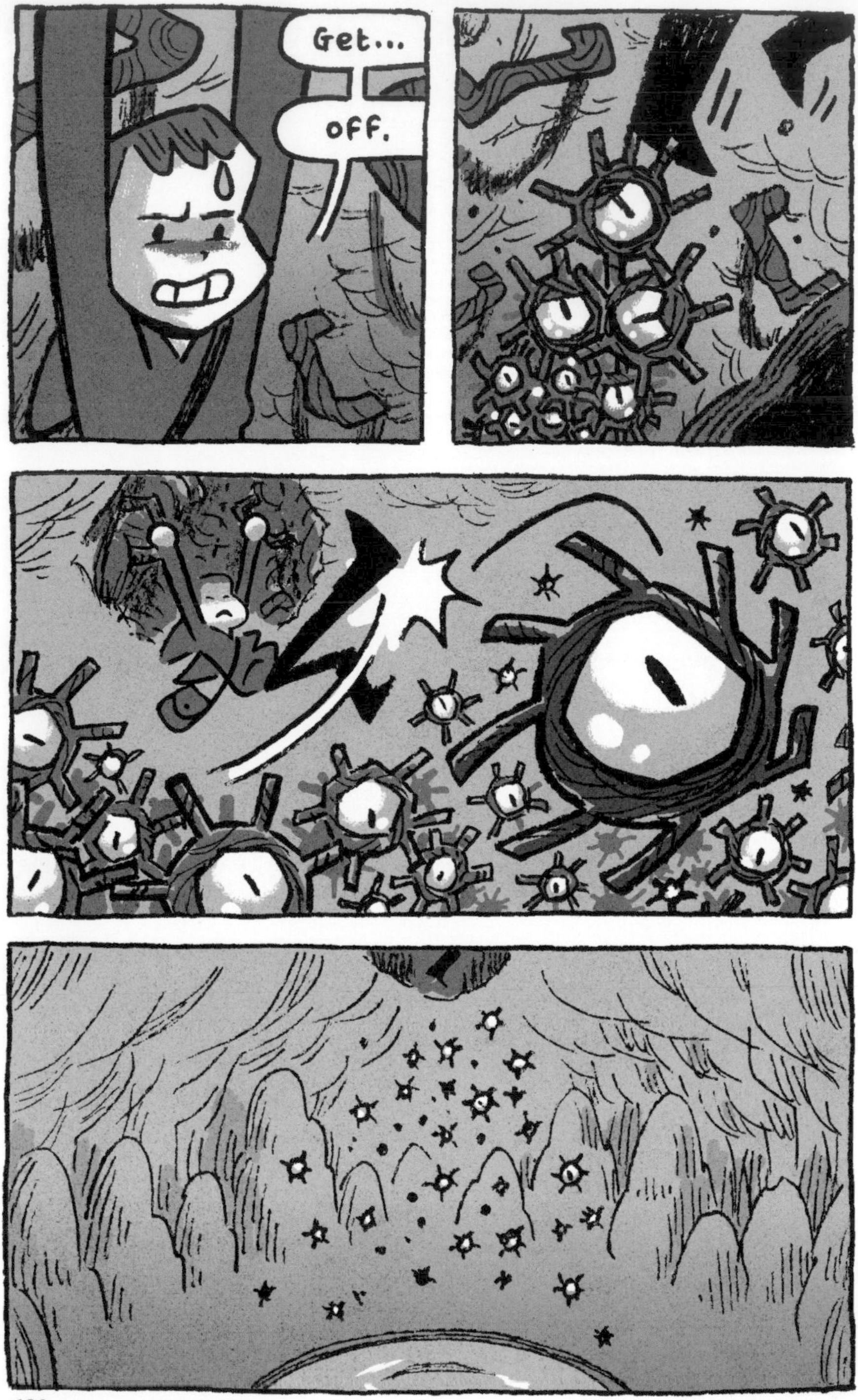
Get...
off.

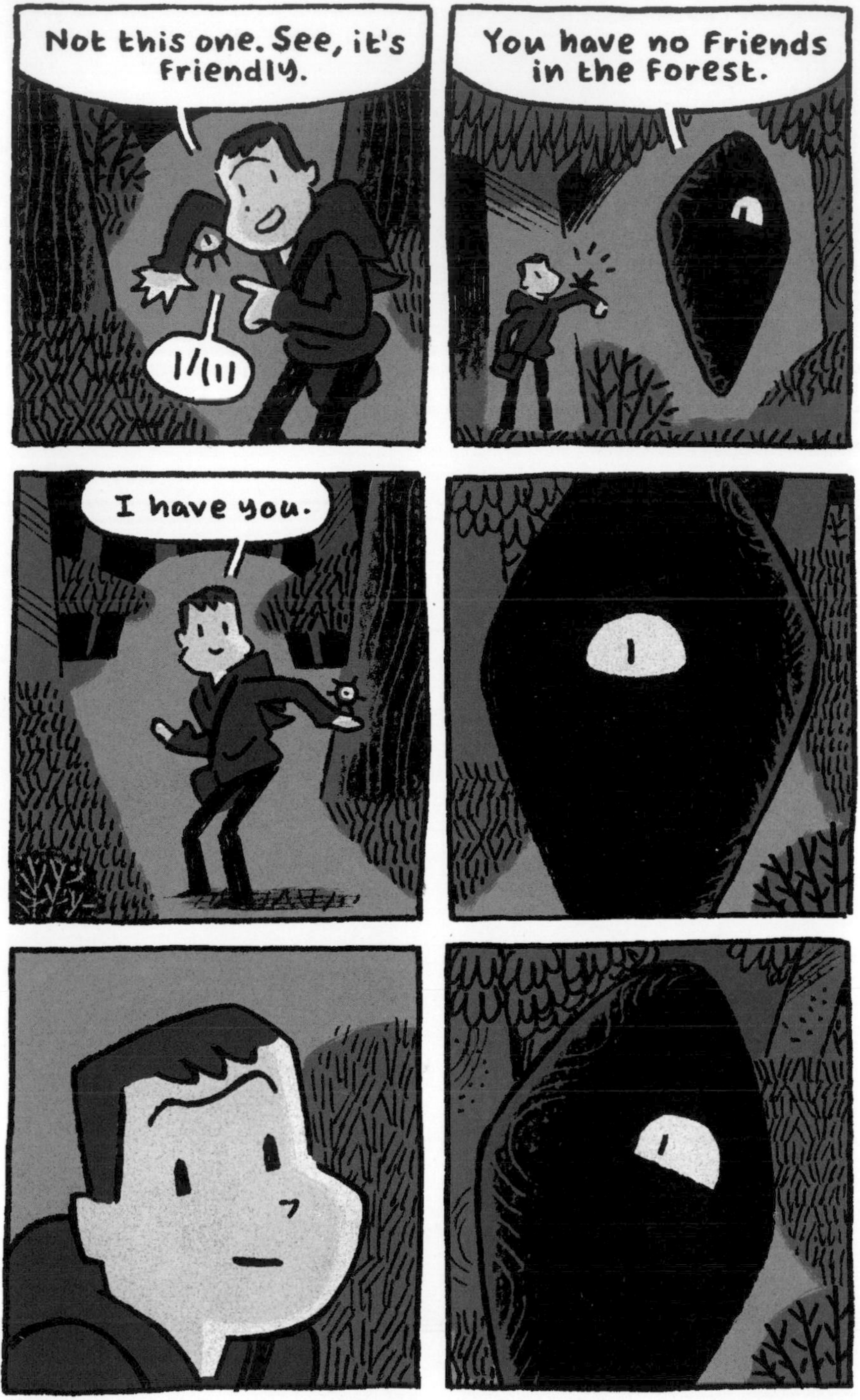
Not this one. See, it's friendly.
You have no friends in the forest.
I have you.

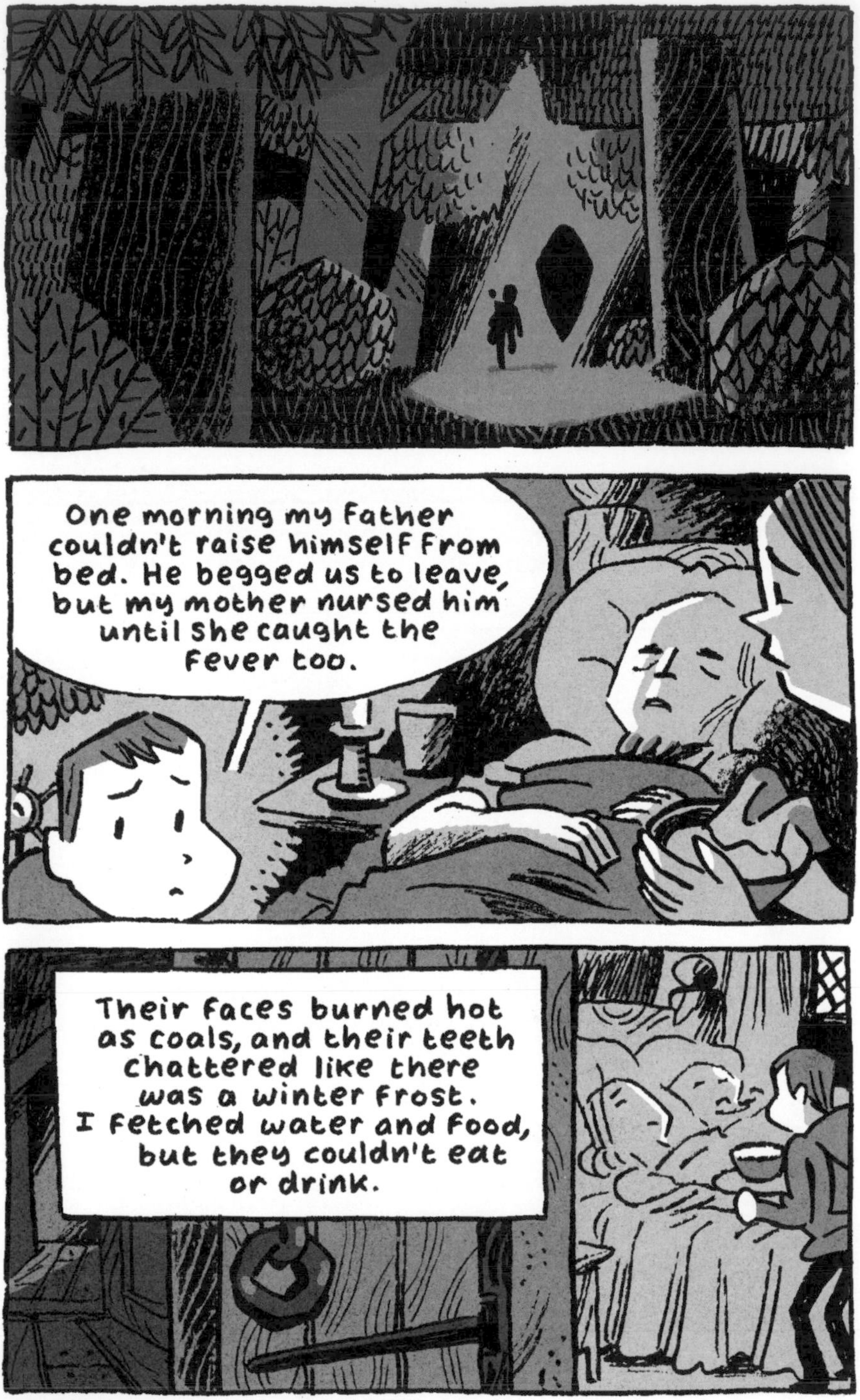
One morning my father couldn't raise himself from bed. He begged us to leave, but my mother nursed him until she caught the fever too.
Their faces burned hot as coals, and their teeth chattered like there was a winter frost. I fetched water and food, but they couldn't eat or drink.

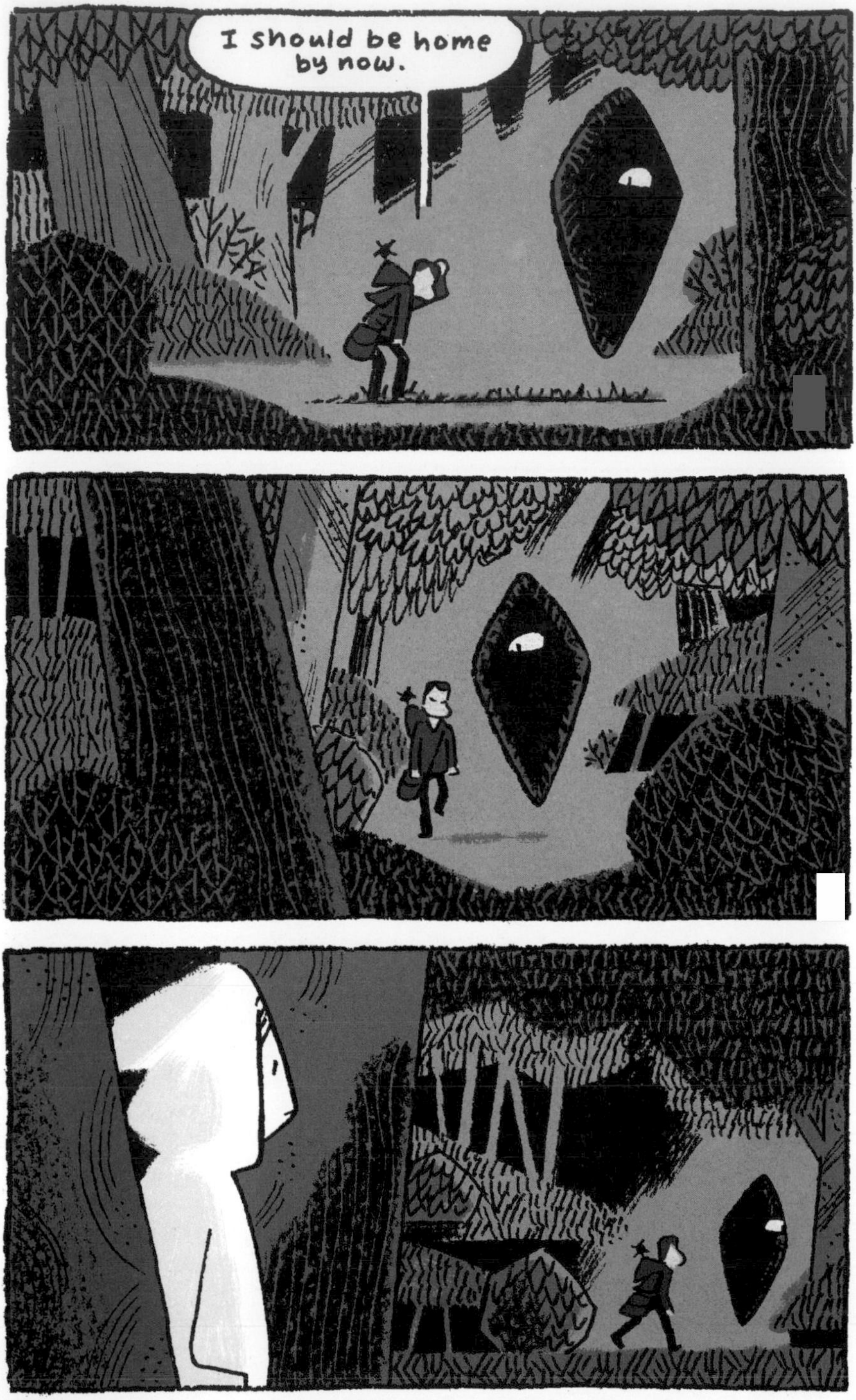
I should be home by now.

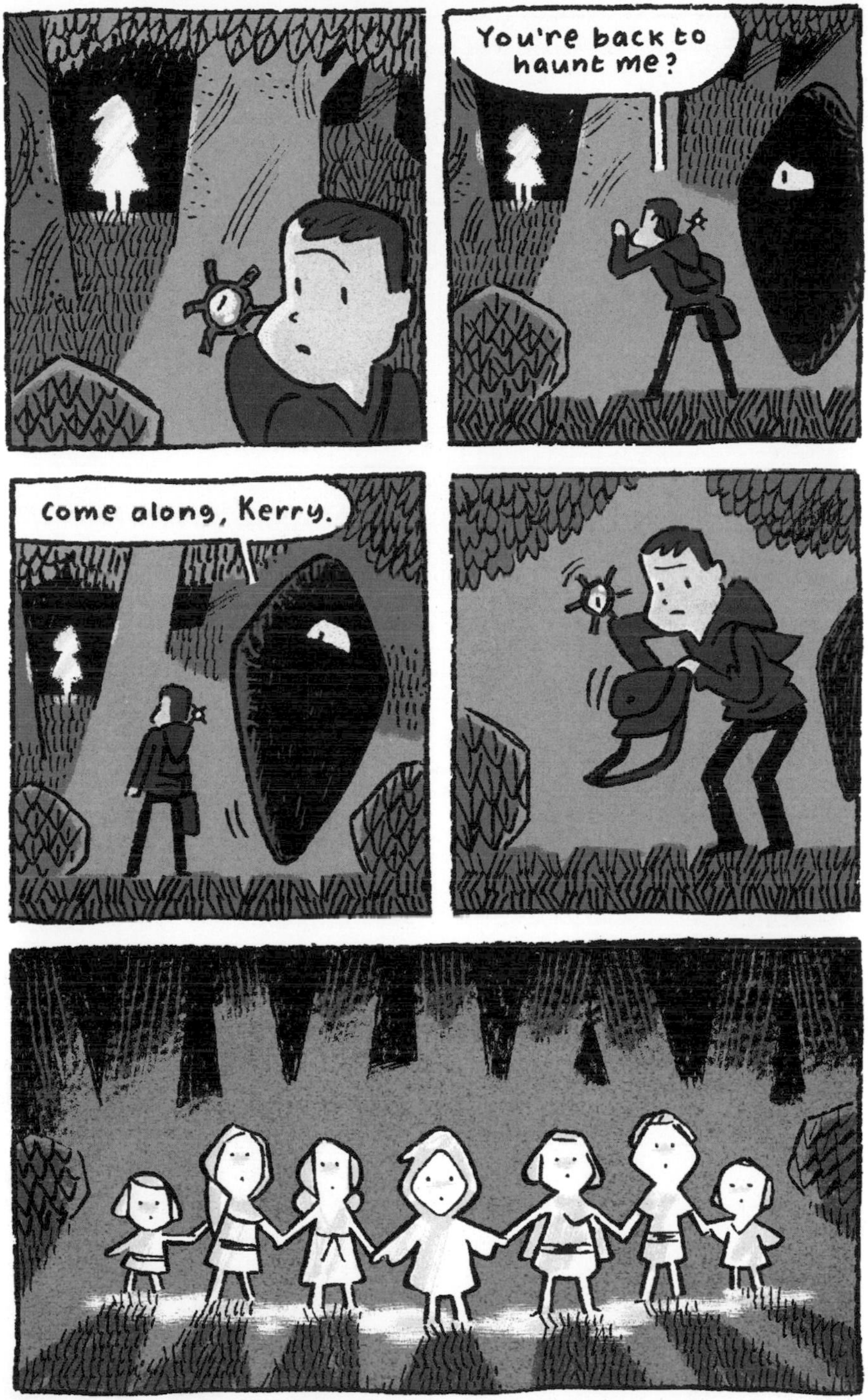
You're back to haunt me?
Come along, Kerry.

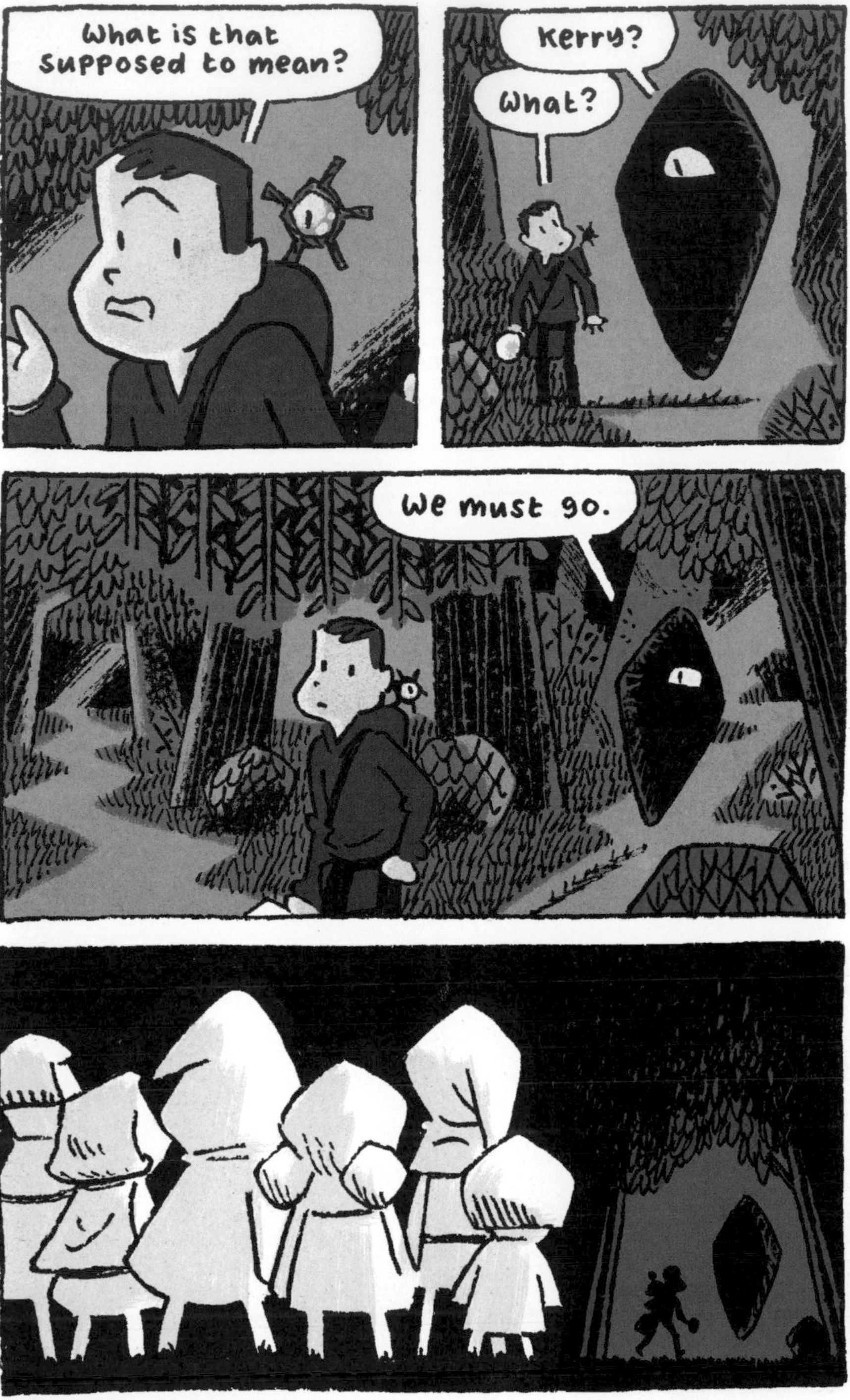
What is that supposed to mean?
Kerry?
What?
We must go.

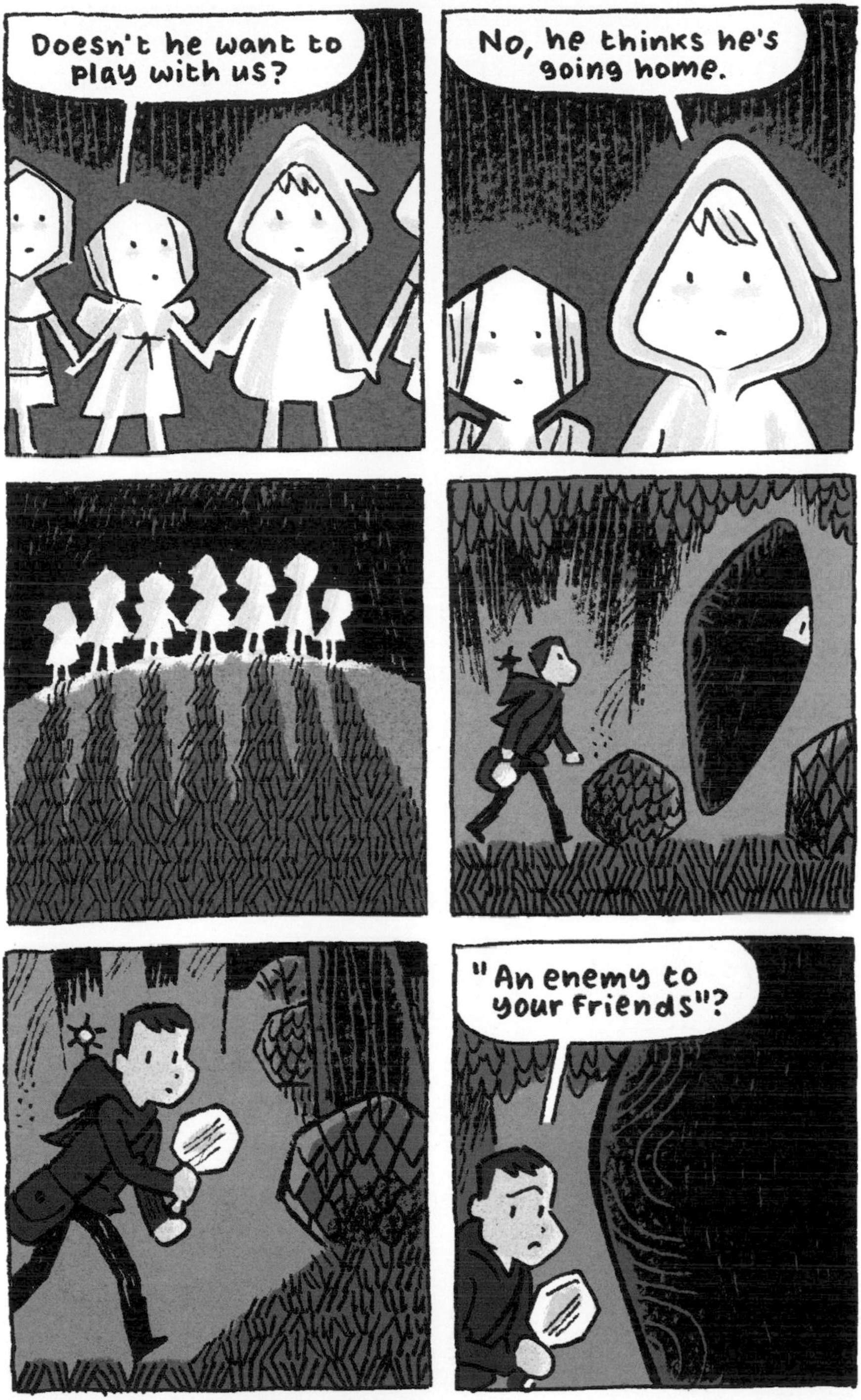
Doesn't he want to play with us?
No, he thinks he's going home.
"An enemy to your friends"?

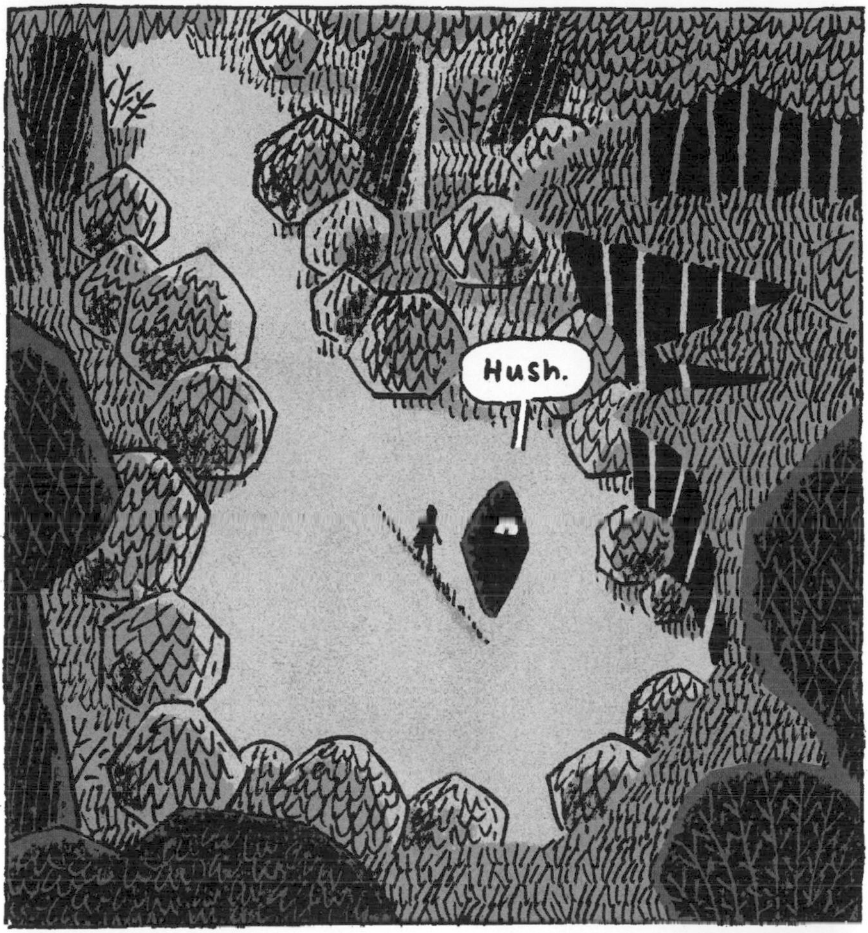
Hush.

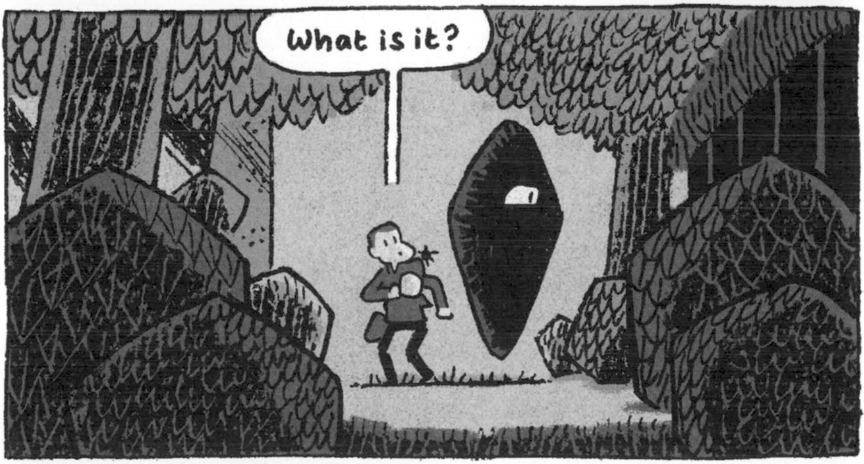
What is it?

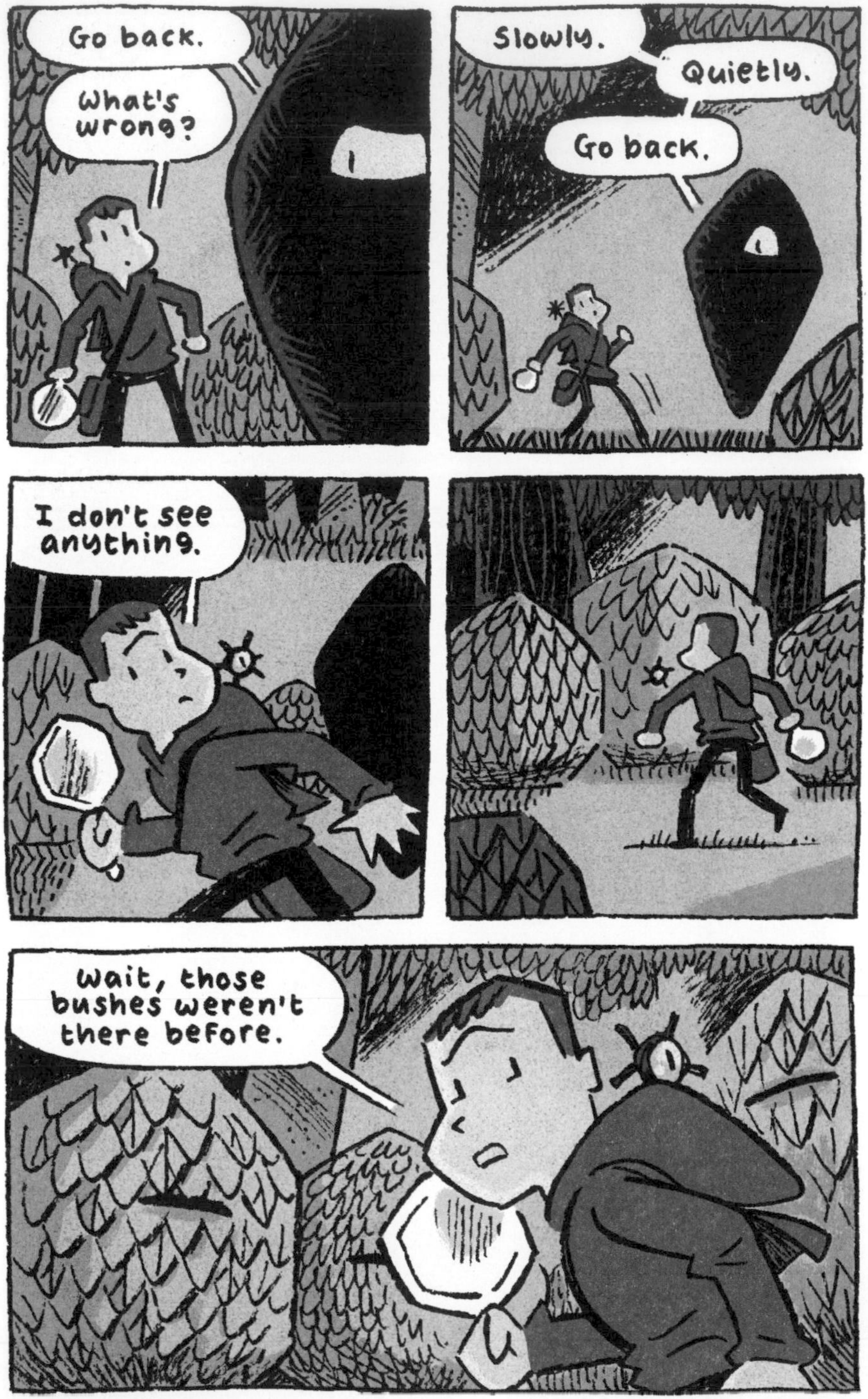
Go back.
What's wrong?
Slowly.
Quietly.
Go back.
I don't see anything.
Wait, those bushes weren't there before.

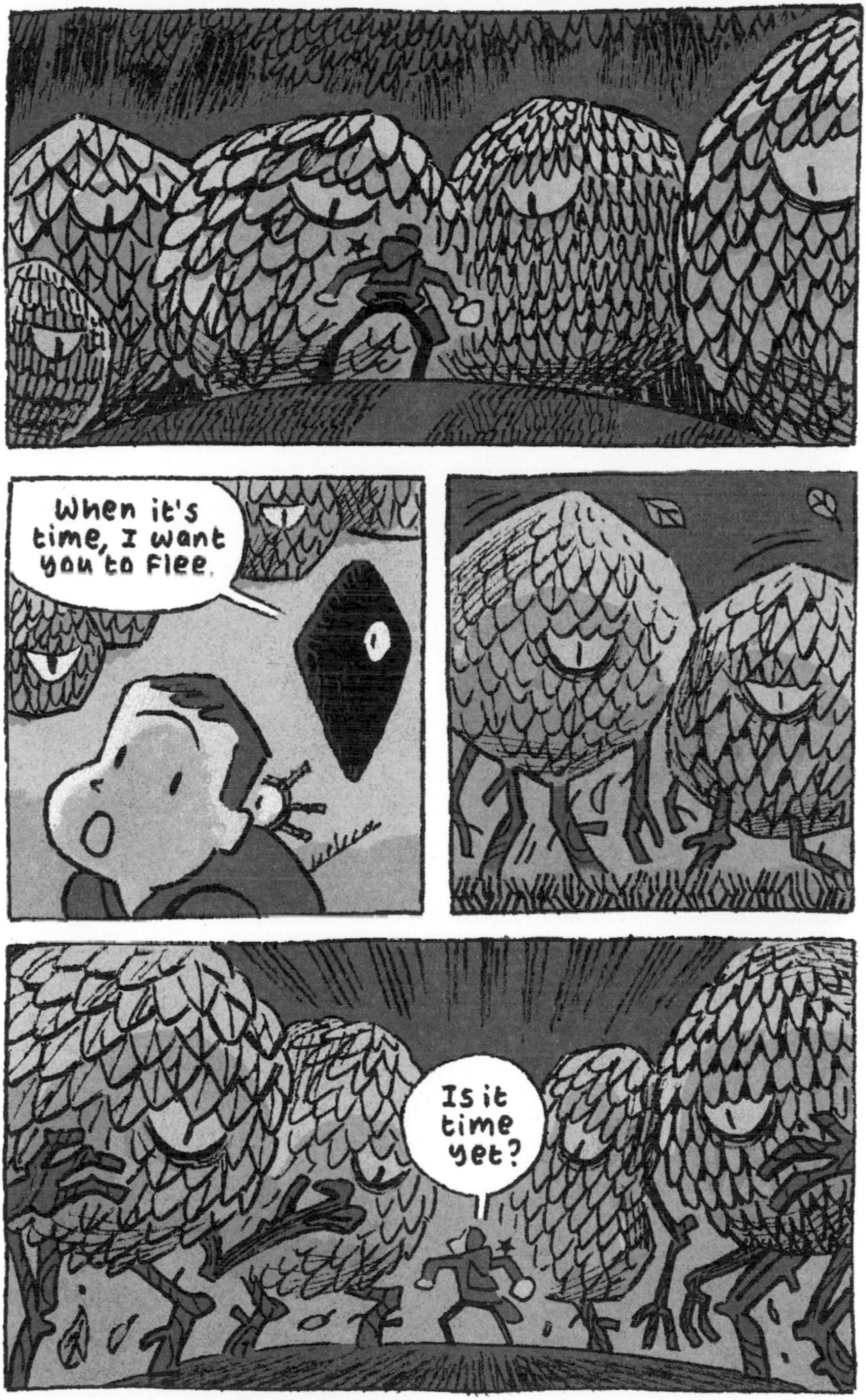
When it's time, I want you to flee.
Is it time yet?

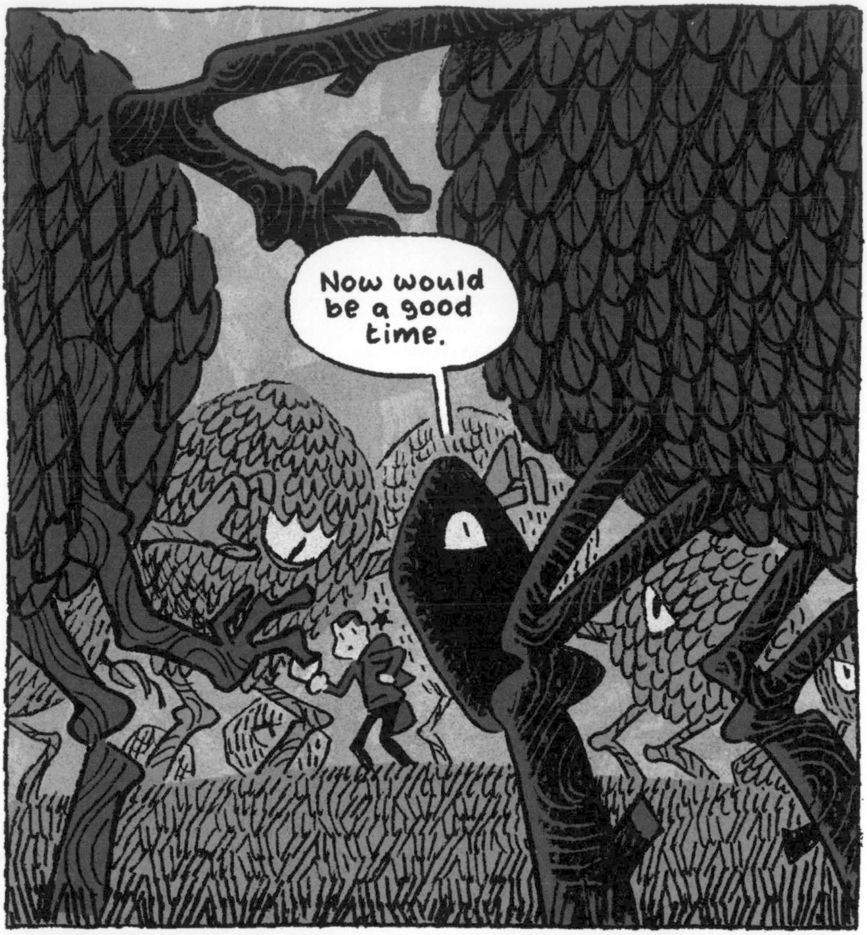
Now would be a good time.

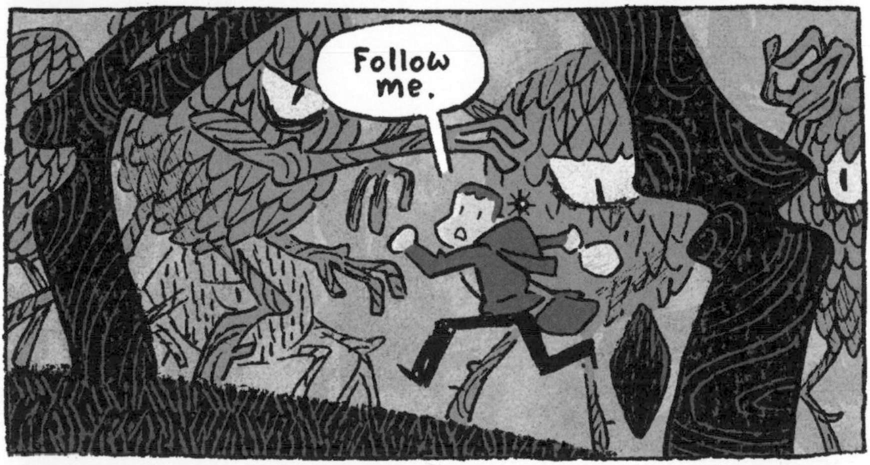
Follow me.

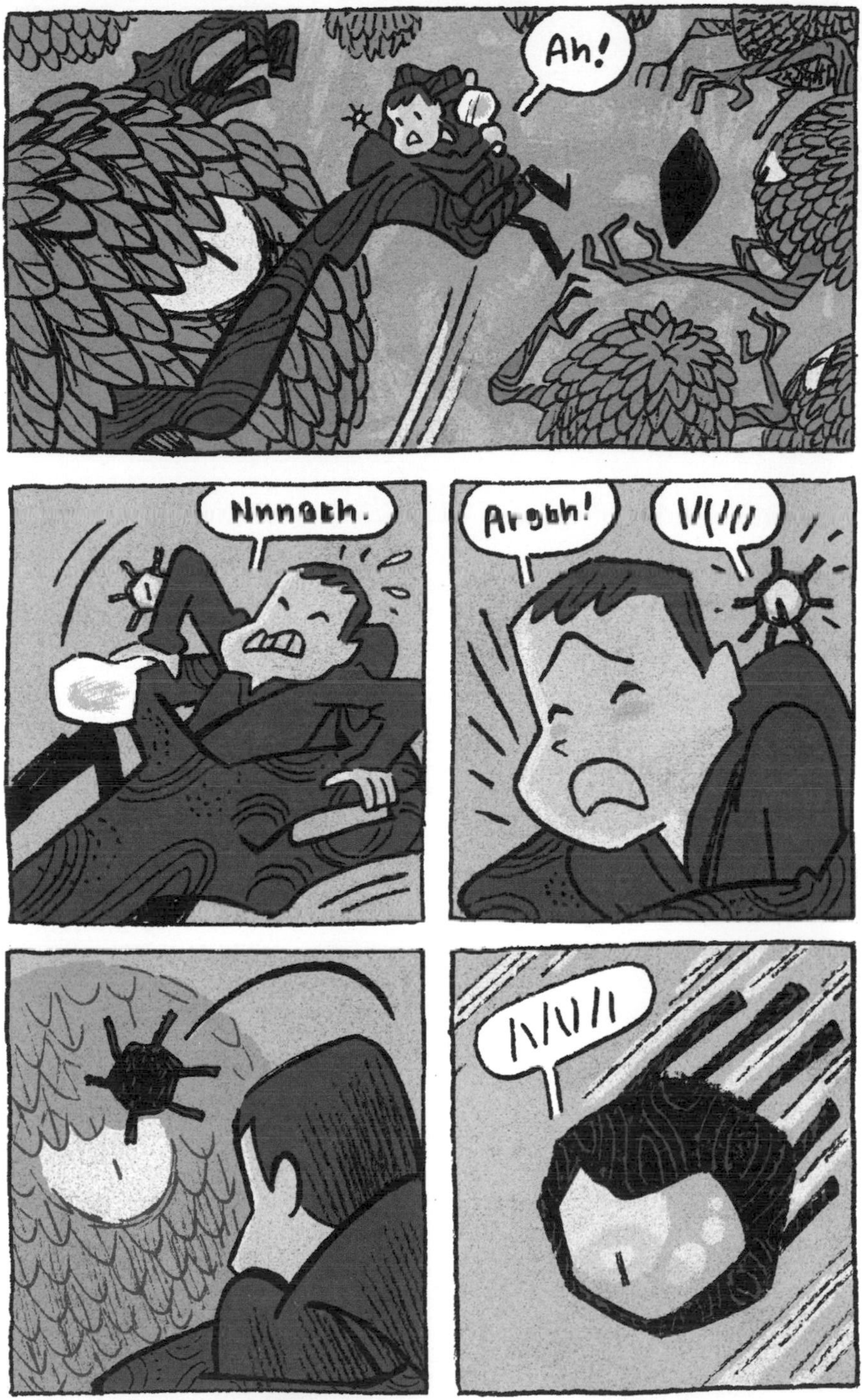
Ah!
Nnngh.
Argh!

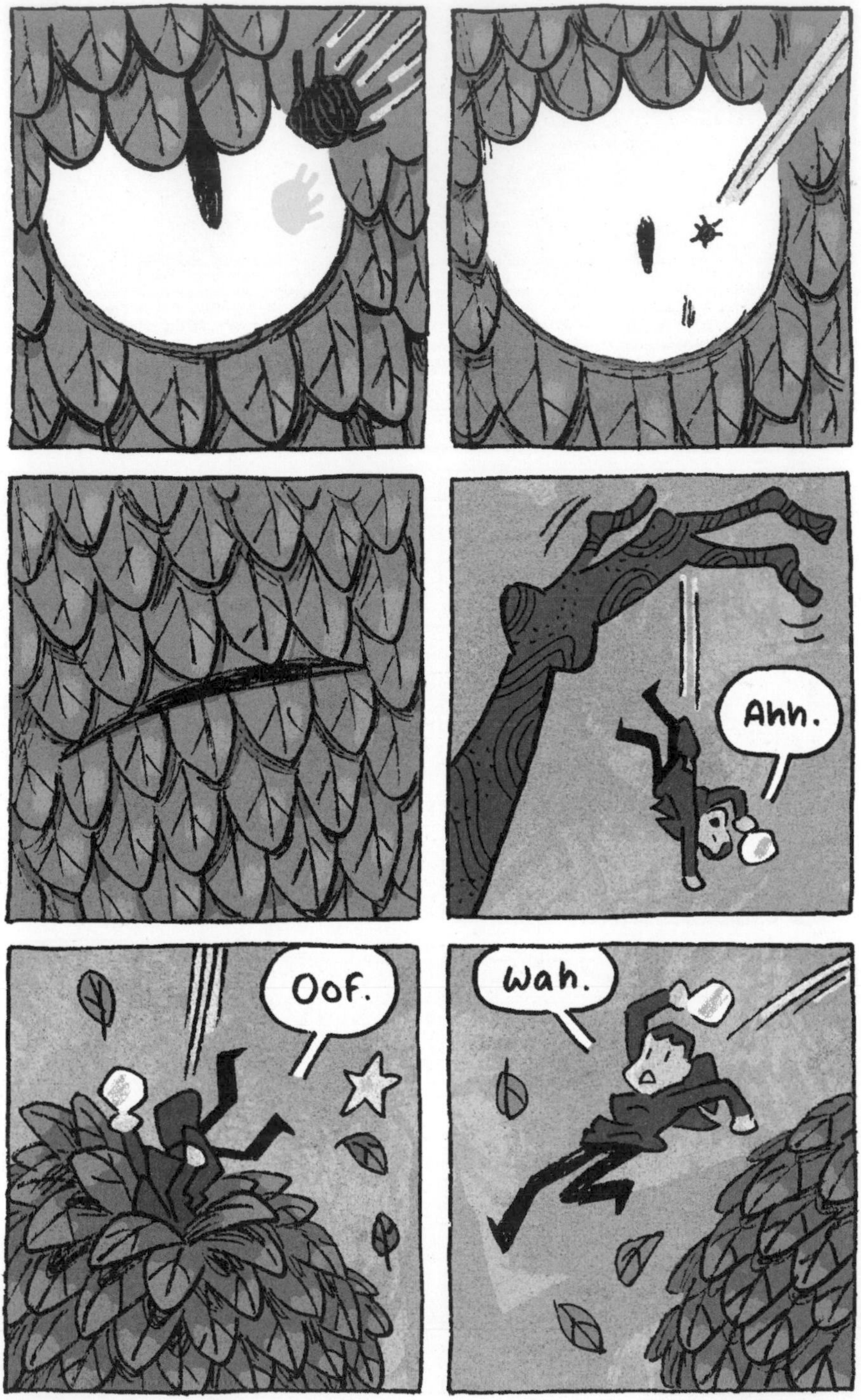

Ahh.
Oof.
Wah.

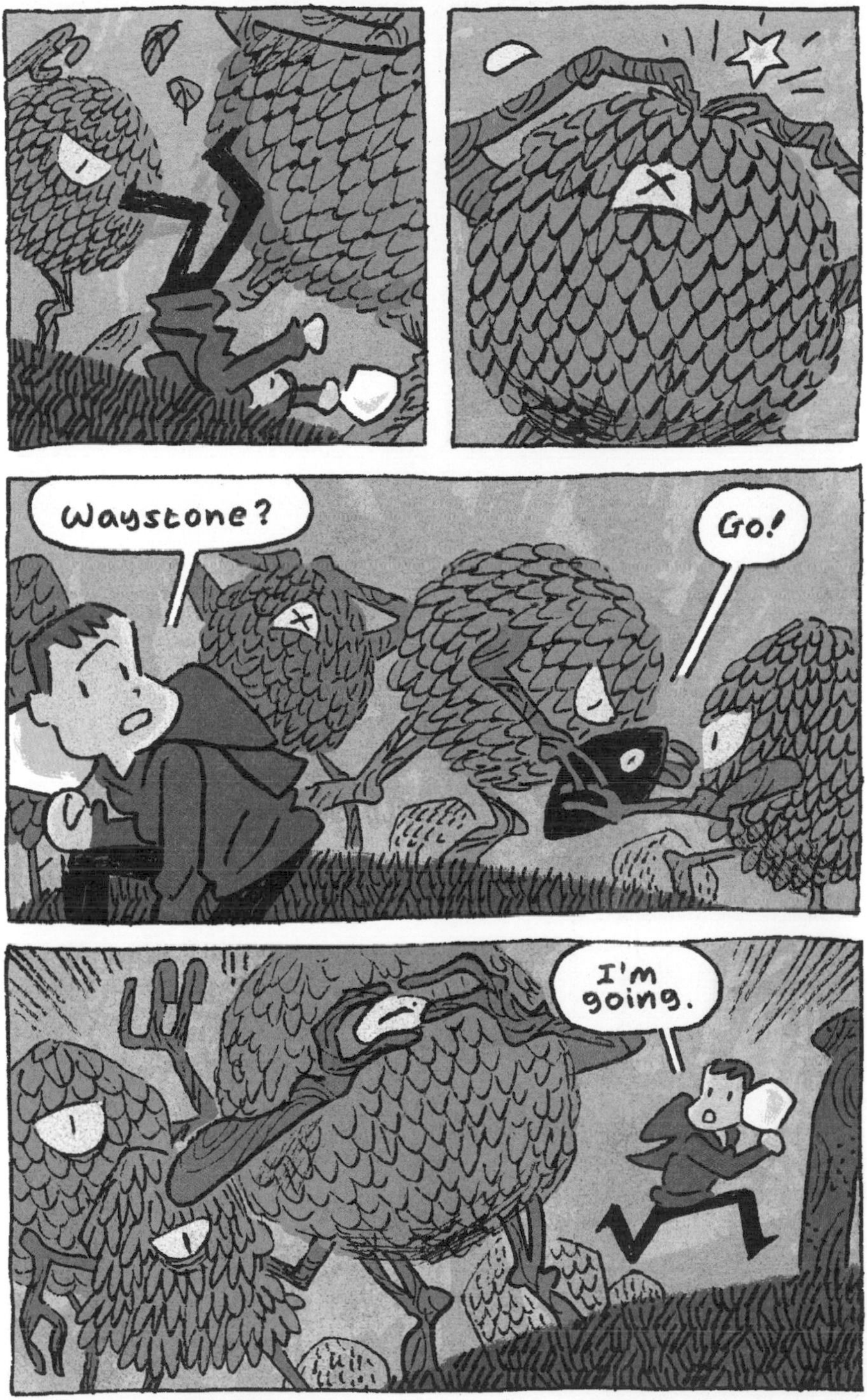
Waystone?
Go!
I'm going.

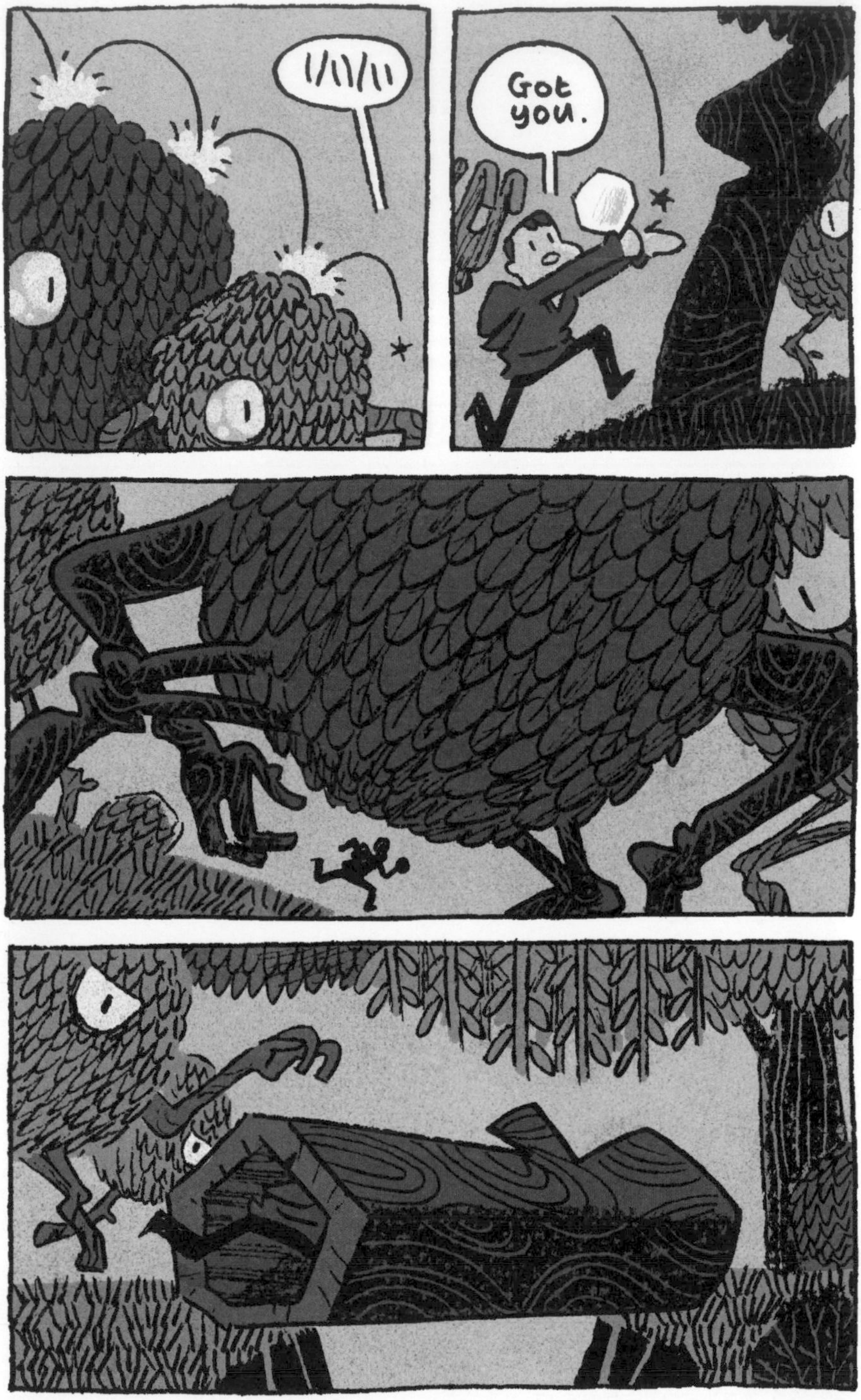
Got you.

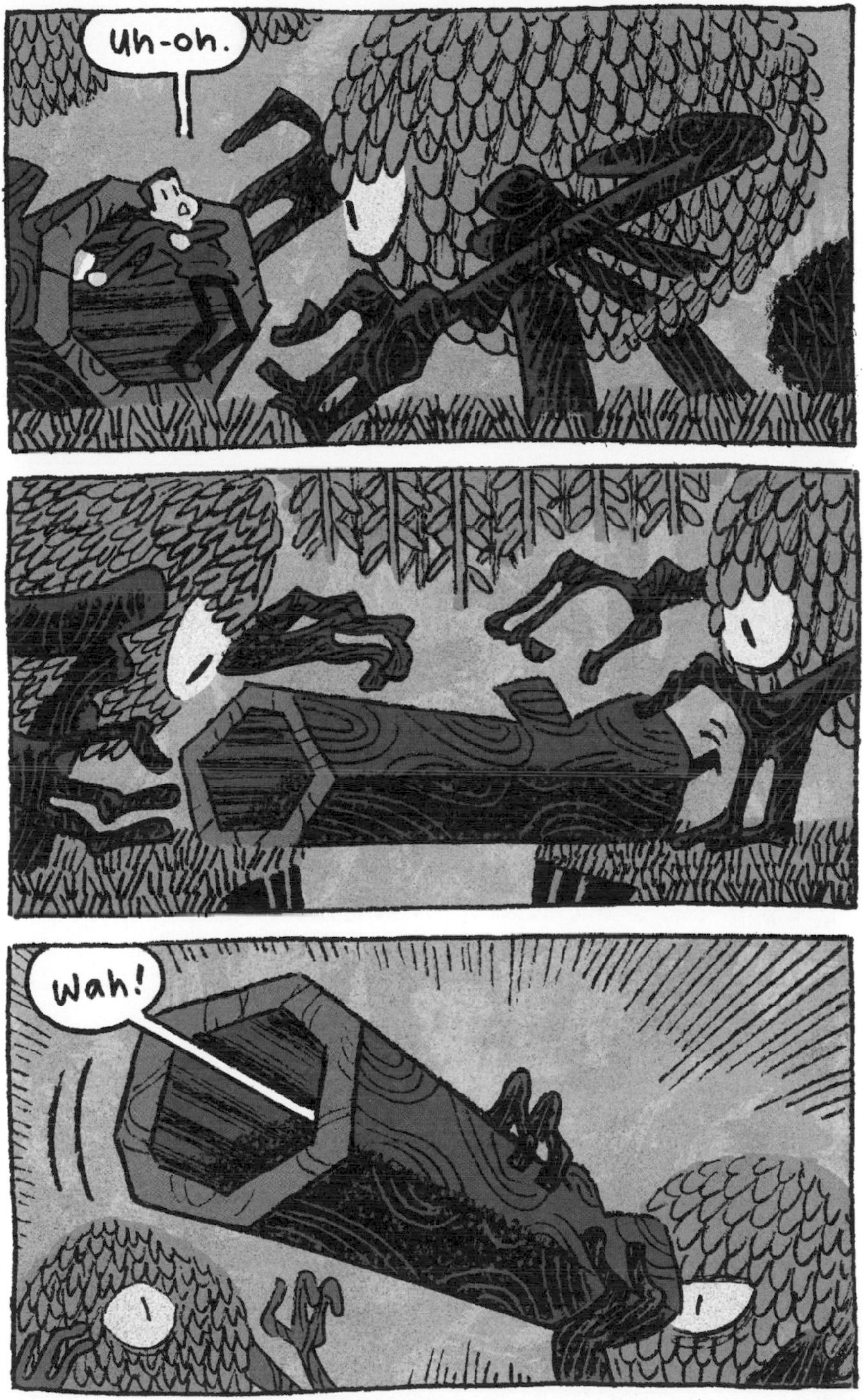
Uh-oh.
Wah!

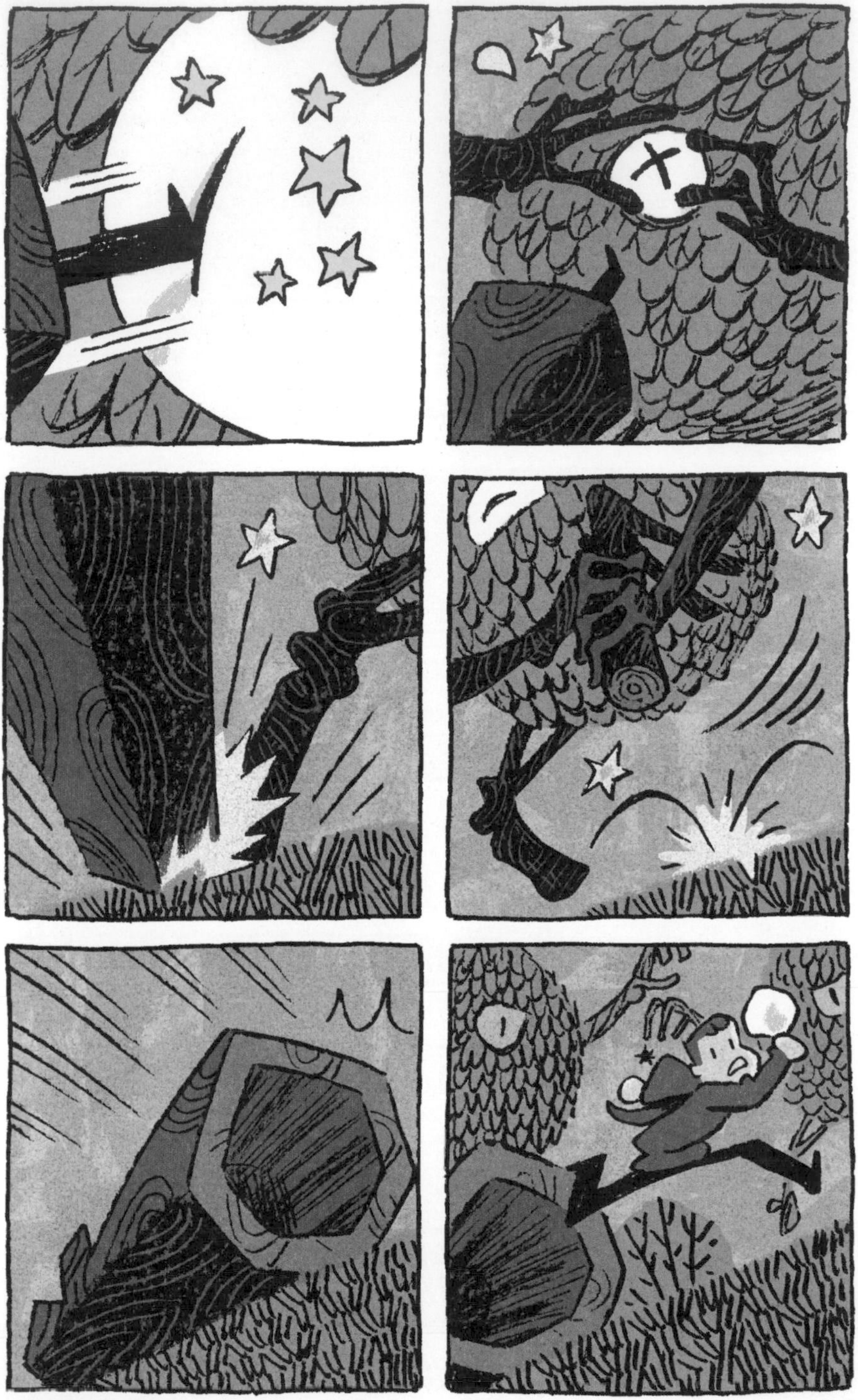

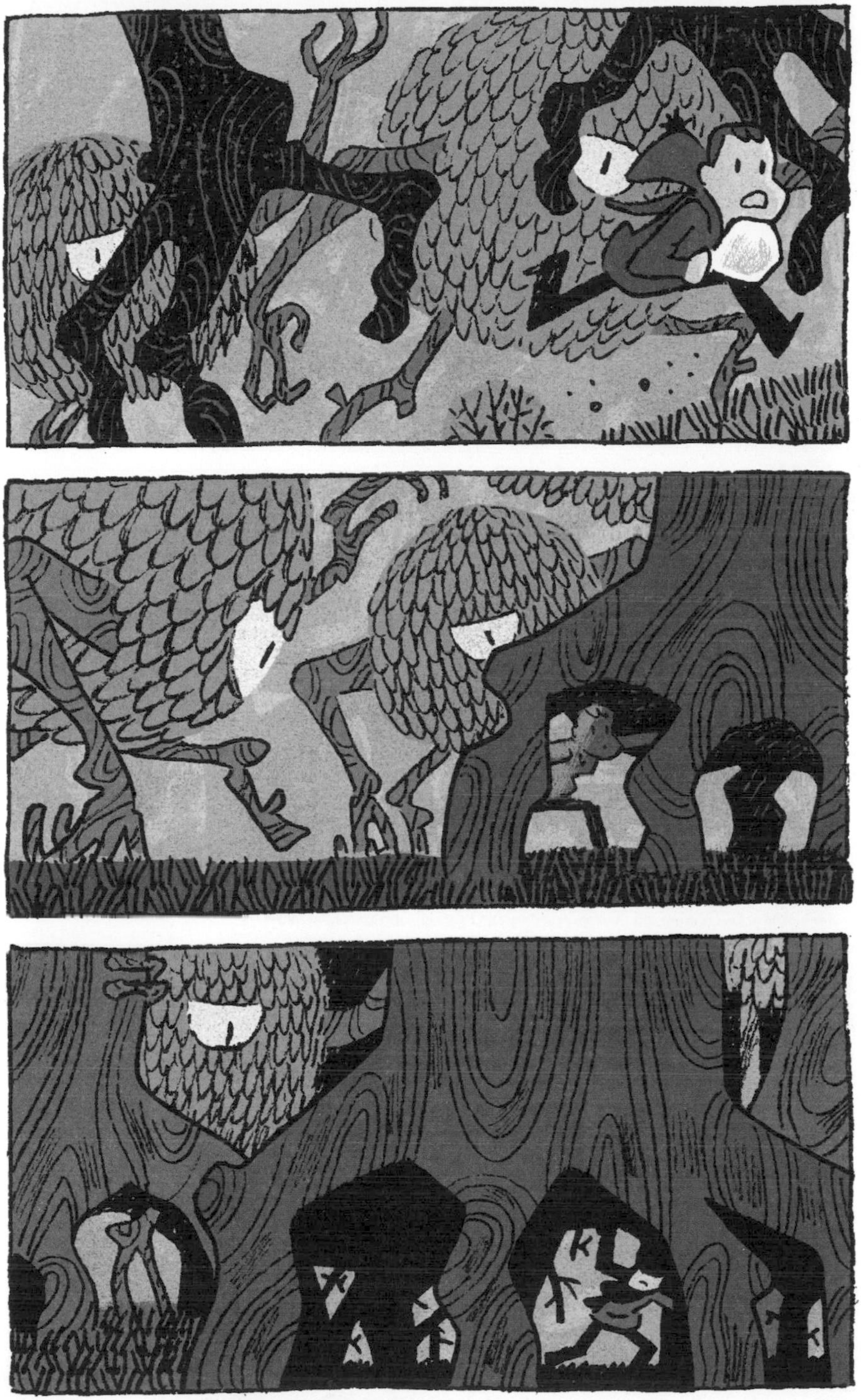

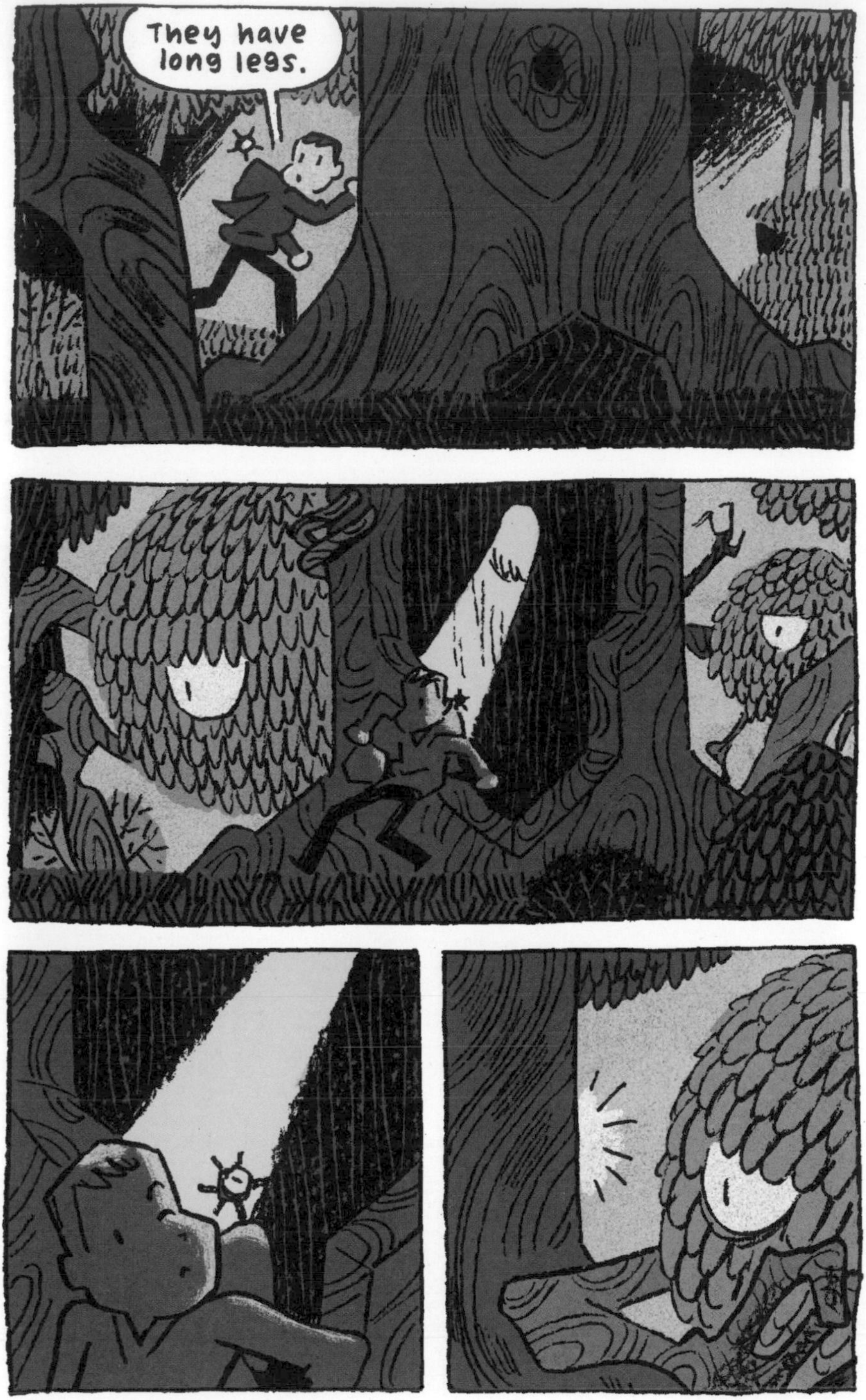
They have long legs.

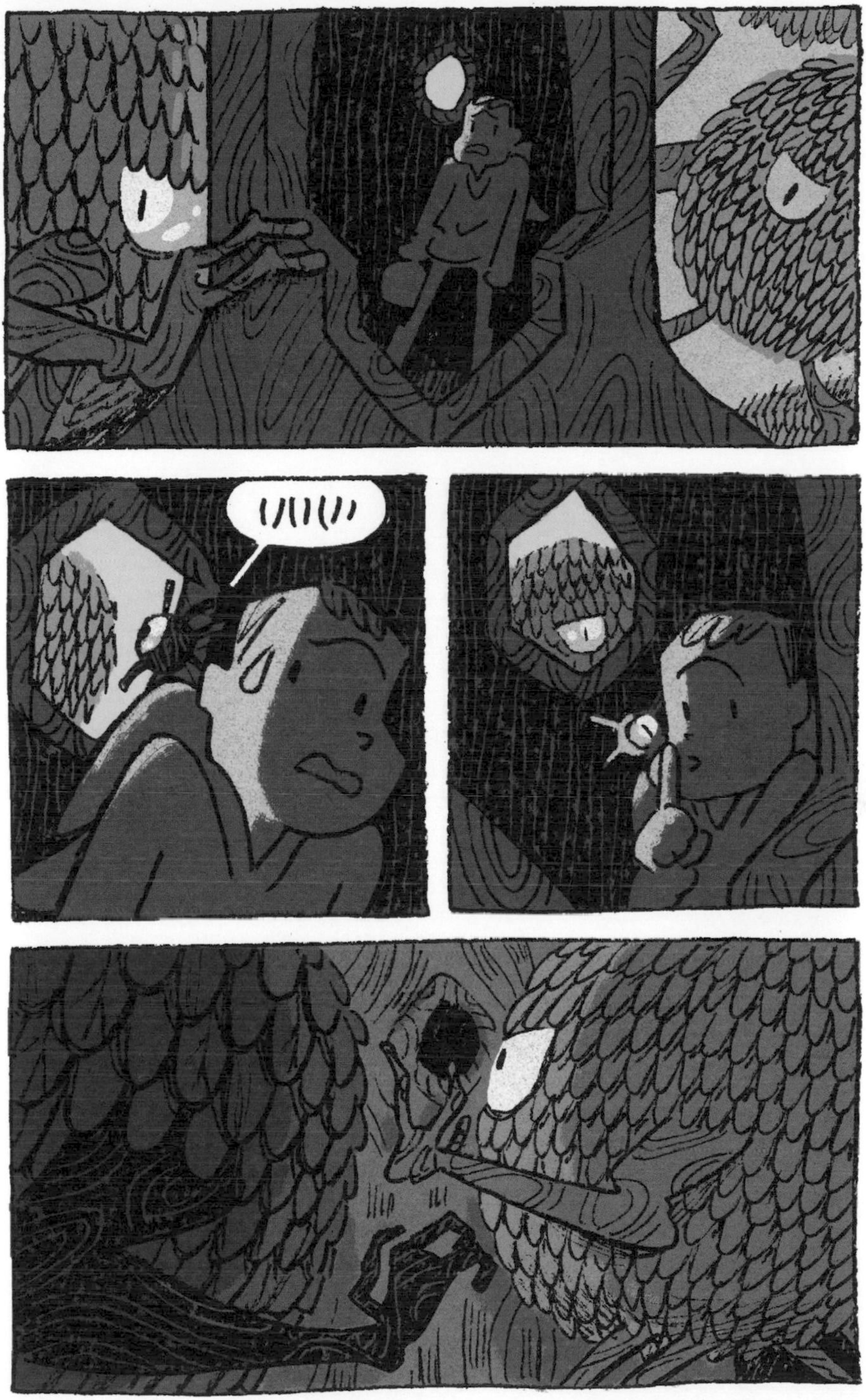

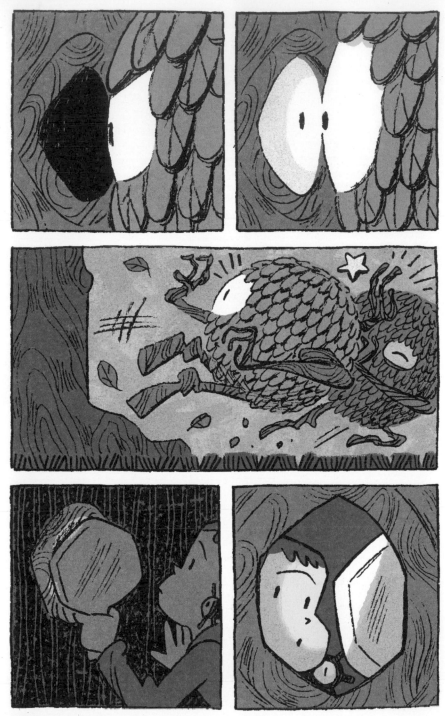

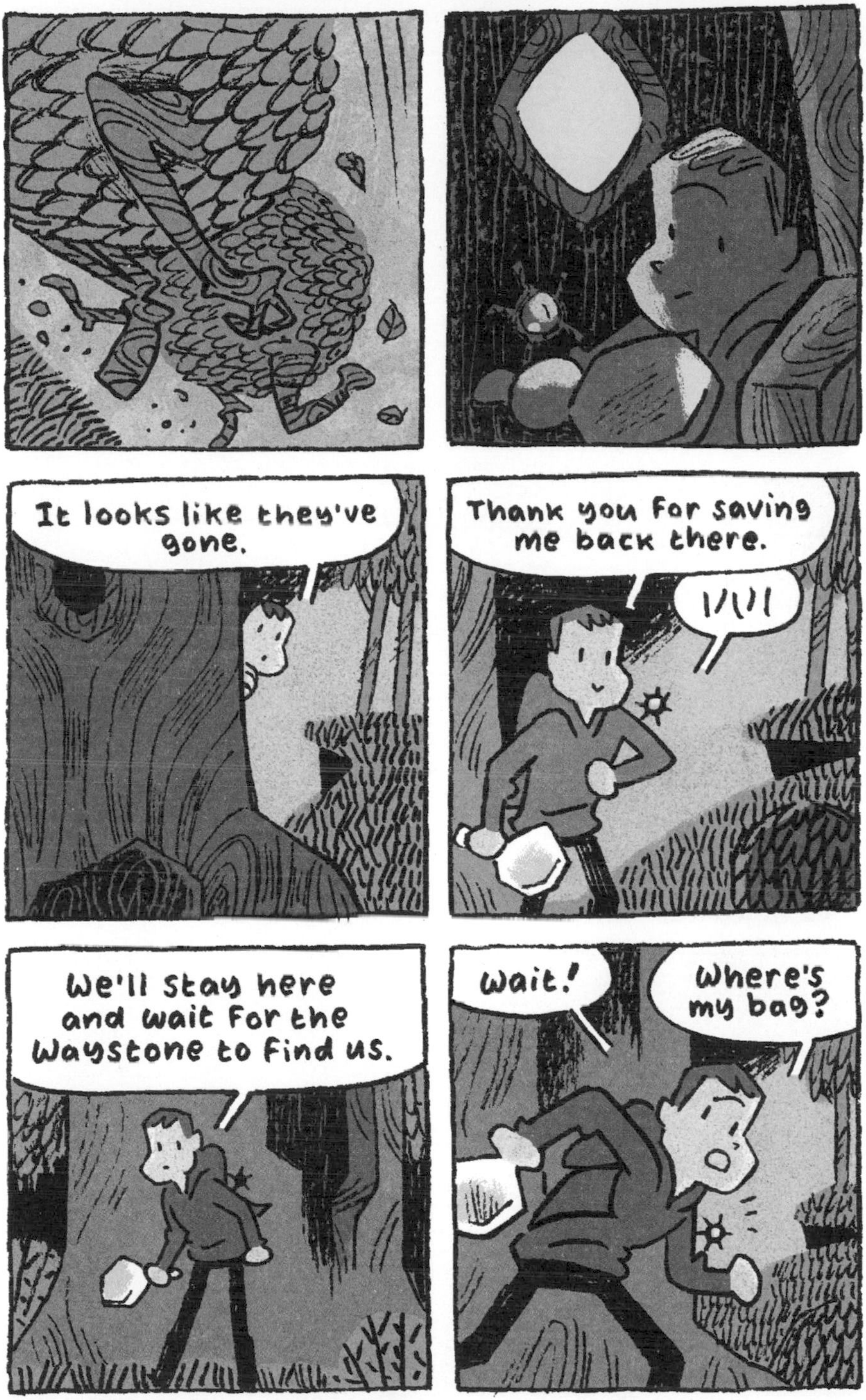
It looks like they've gone.
Thank you for saving me back there.
I/I\I
We'll stay here and wait for the Waystone to find us.
Wait!
Where's my bag?

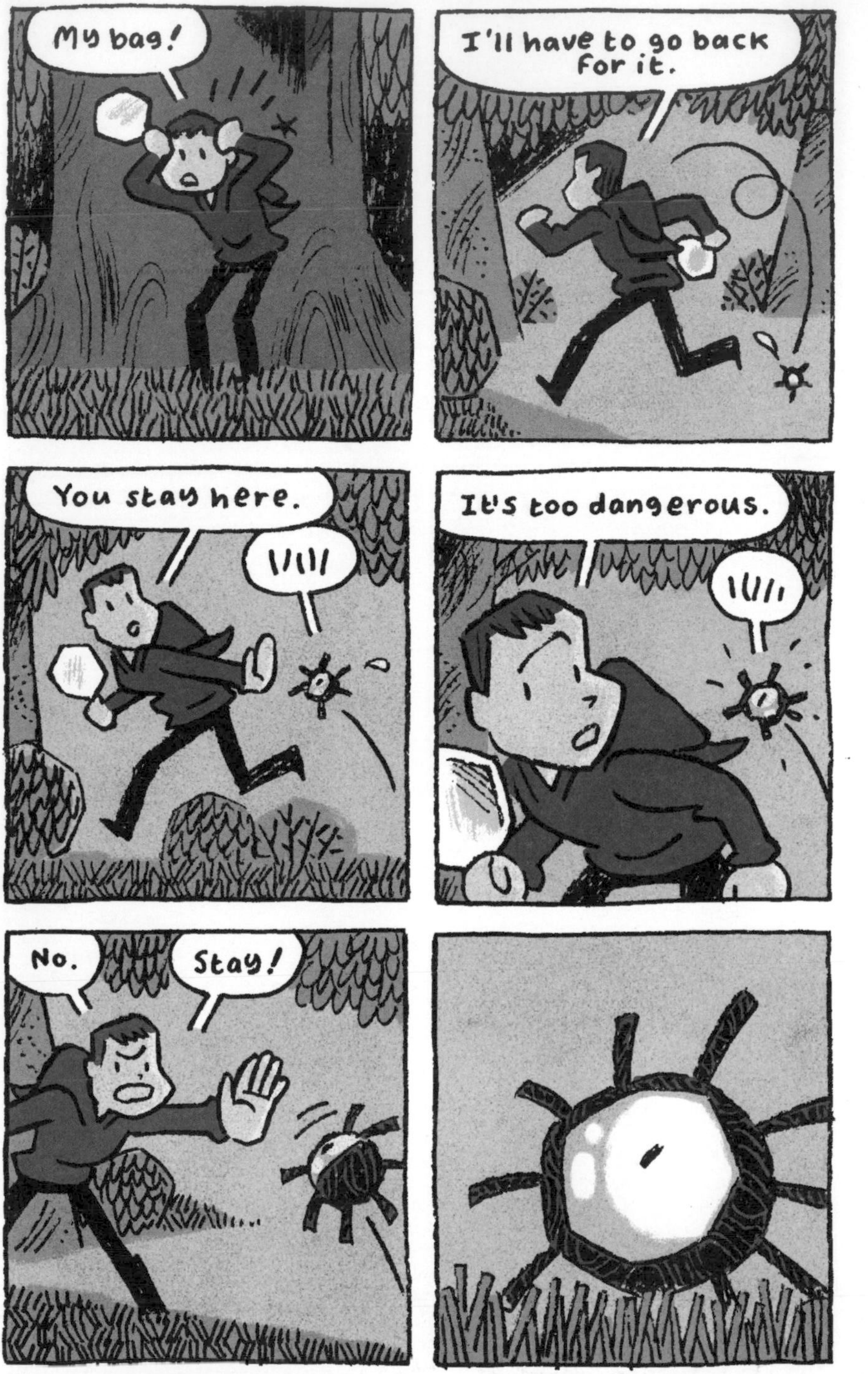
My bag!
I'll have to go back for it.
You stay here.
!/!!/
It's too dangerous.
!!/!/
No.
Stay!

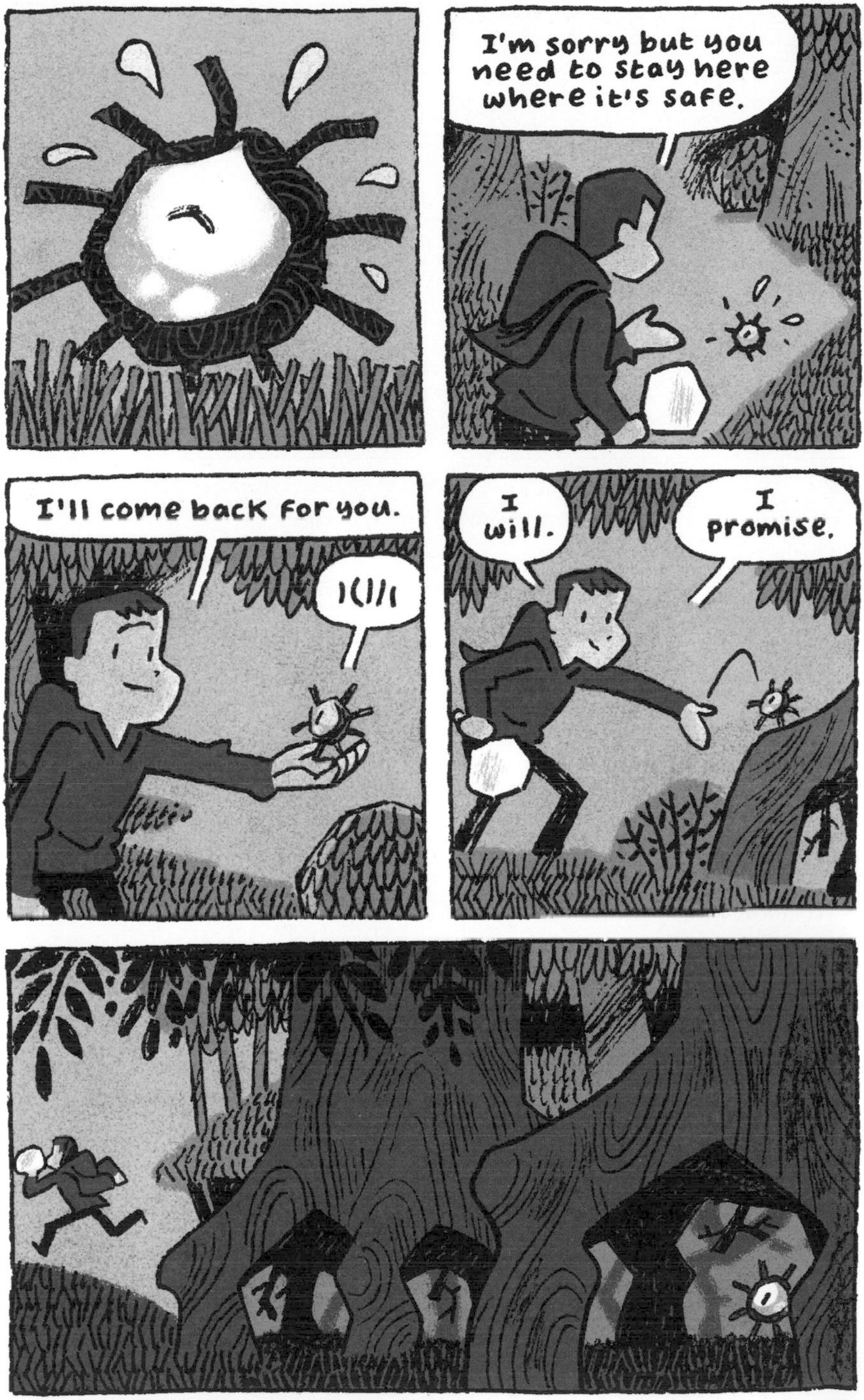
I'm sorry but you need to stay here where it's safe.
I'll come back for you.
I will.
I promise.

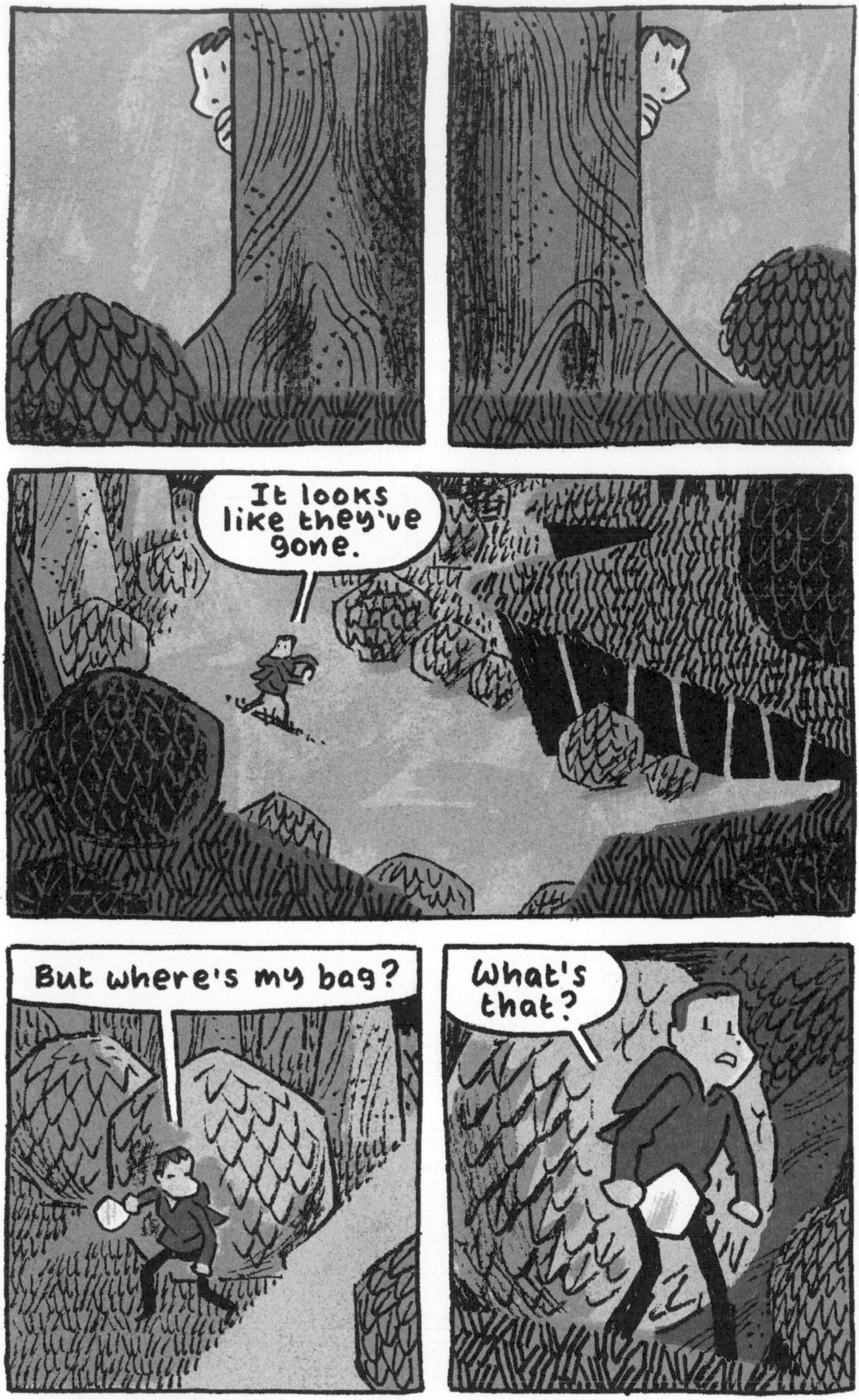
It looks like they've gone.
But where's my bag?
What's that?

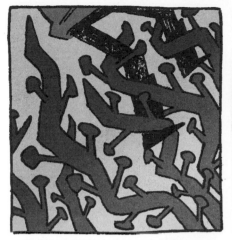

I only wish to bring you home safely.

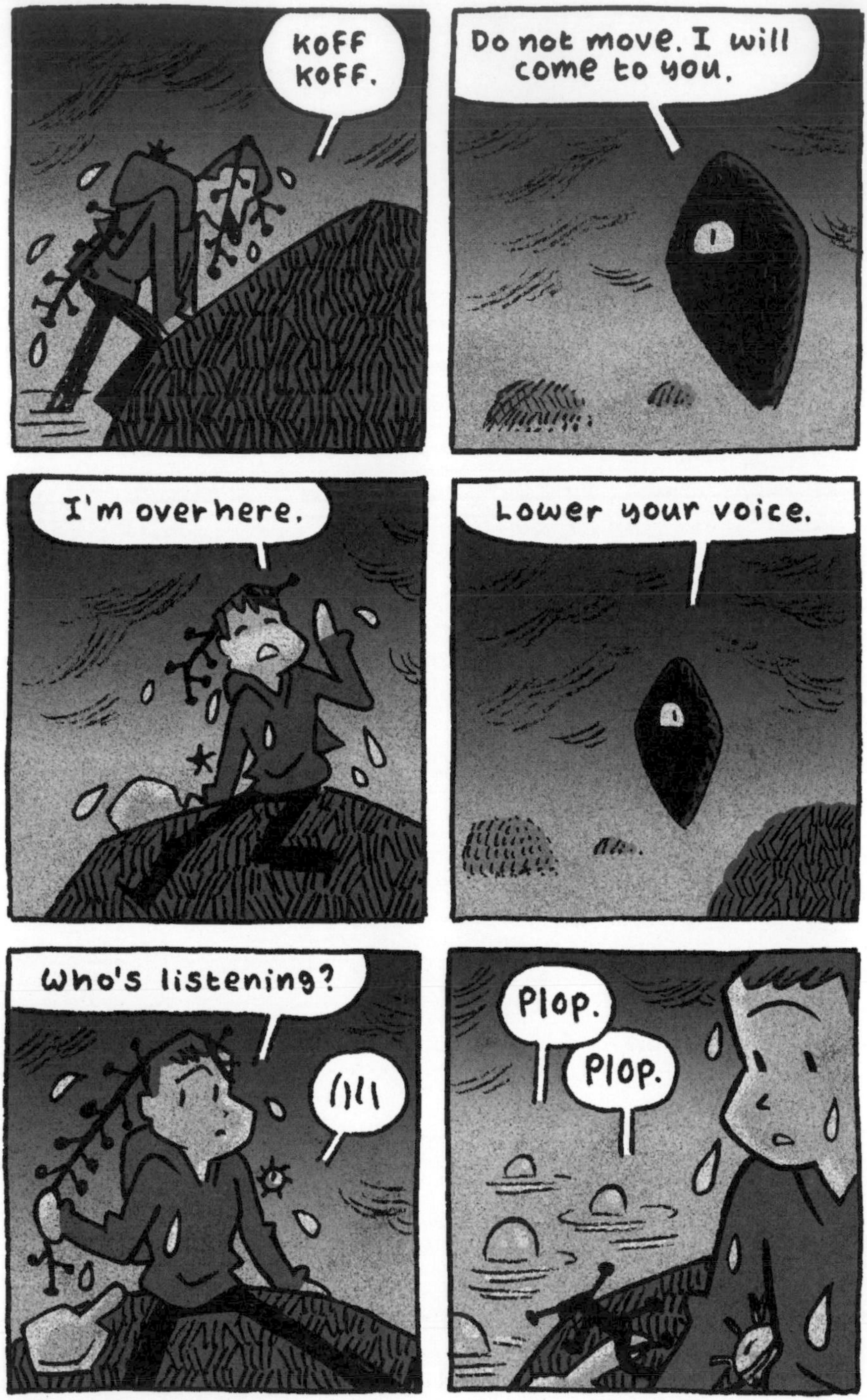
KOFF KOFF.
Do not move. I will come to you.
I'm over here.
Lower your voice.
Who's listening?
Plop.
Plop.

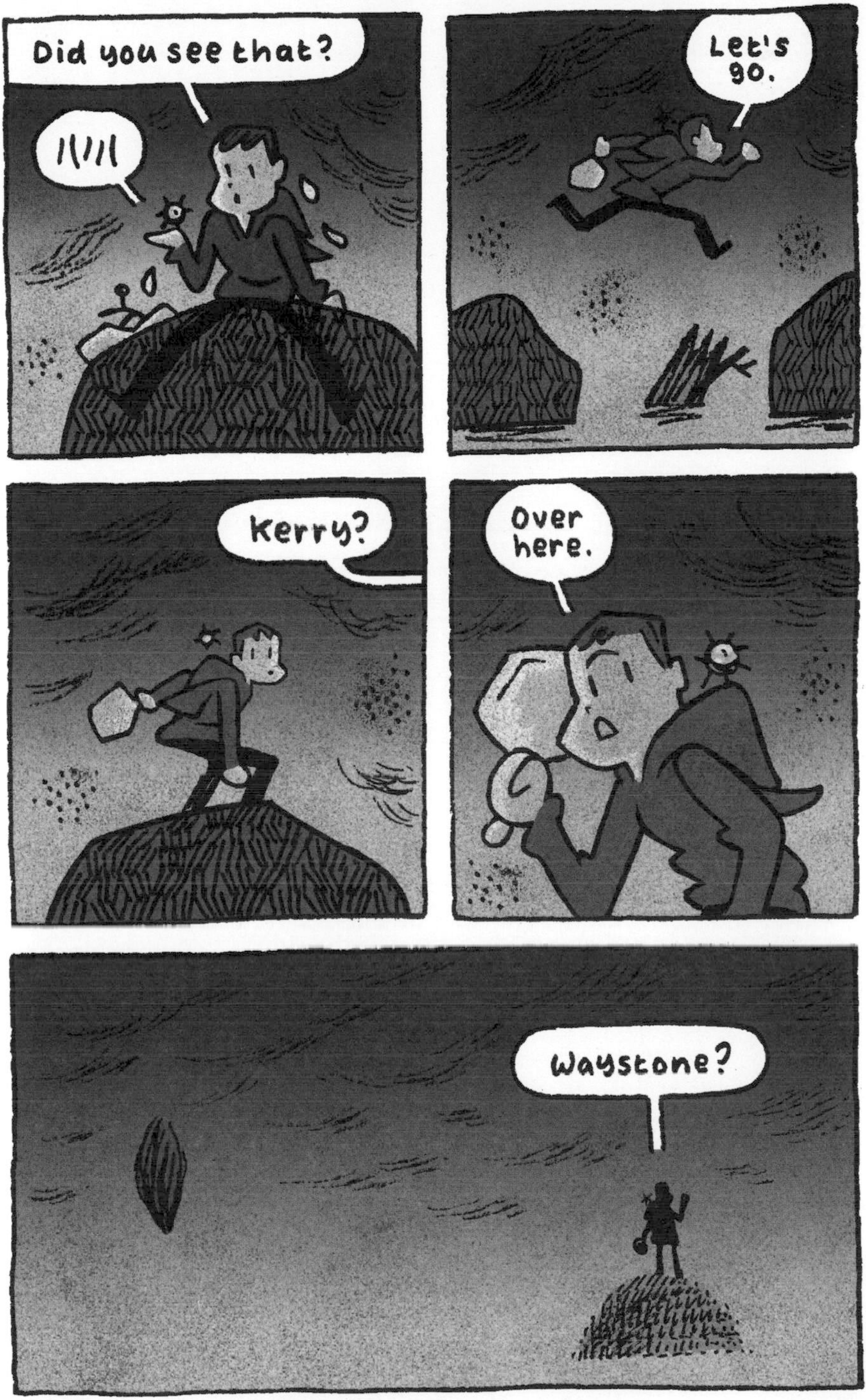
Did you see that?
Let's go.
Kerry?
Over here.
Waystone?

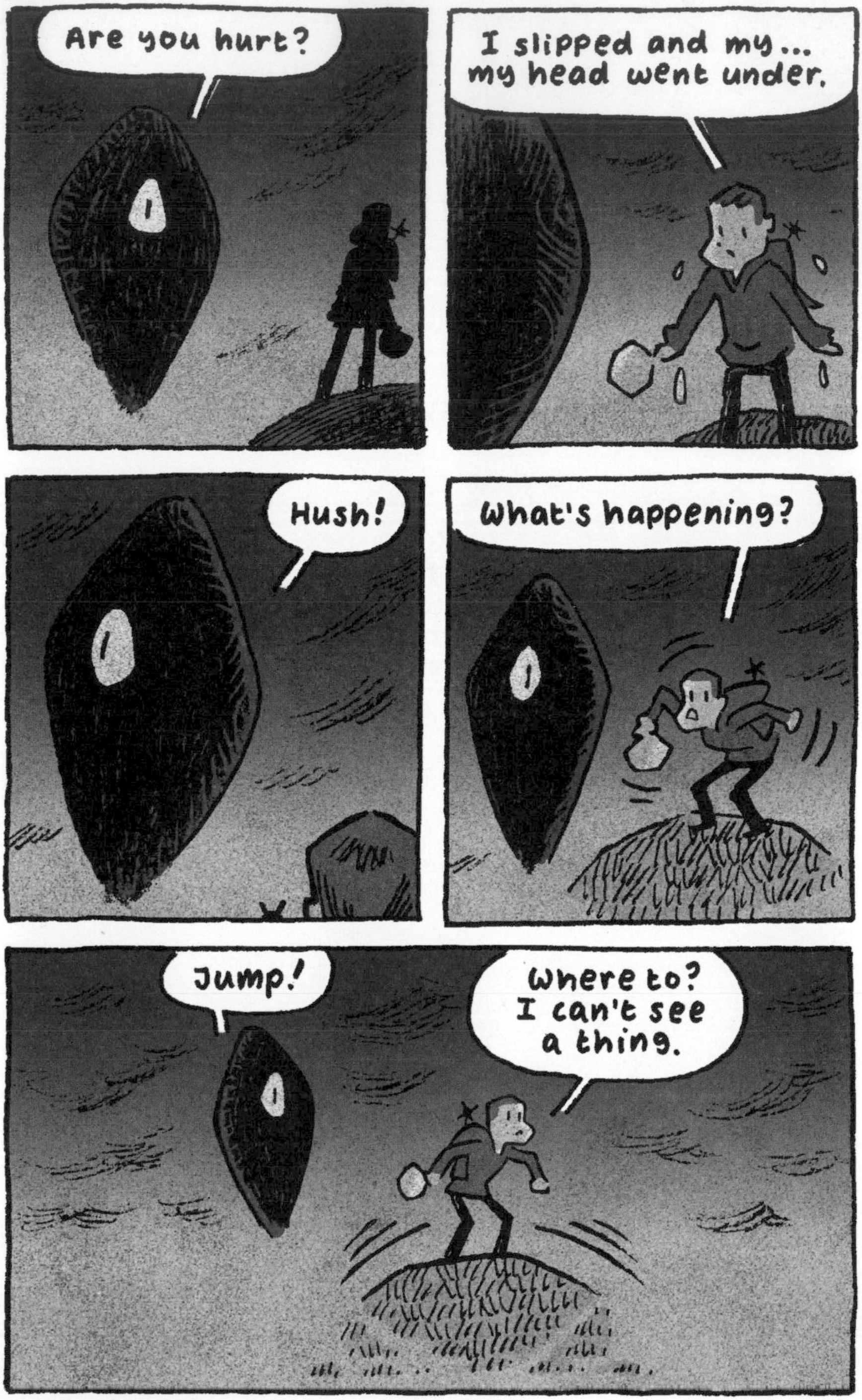
Are you hurt?
I slipped and my... my head went under.
Hush!
What's happening?
Jump!
Where to? I can't see a thing.

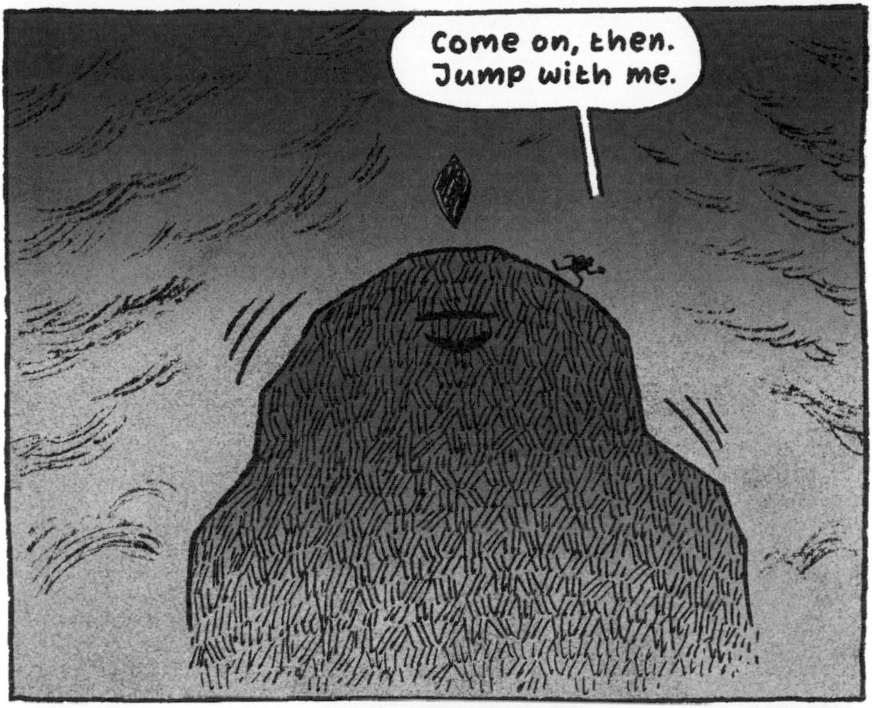
Come on, then. Jump with me.

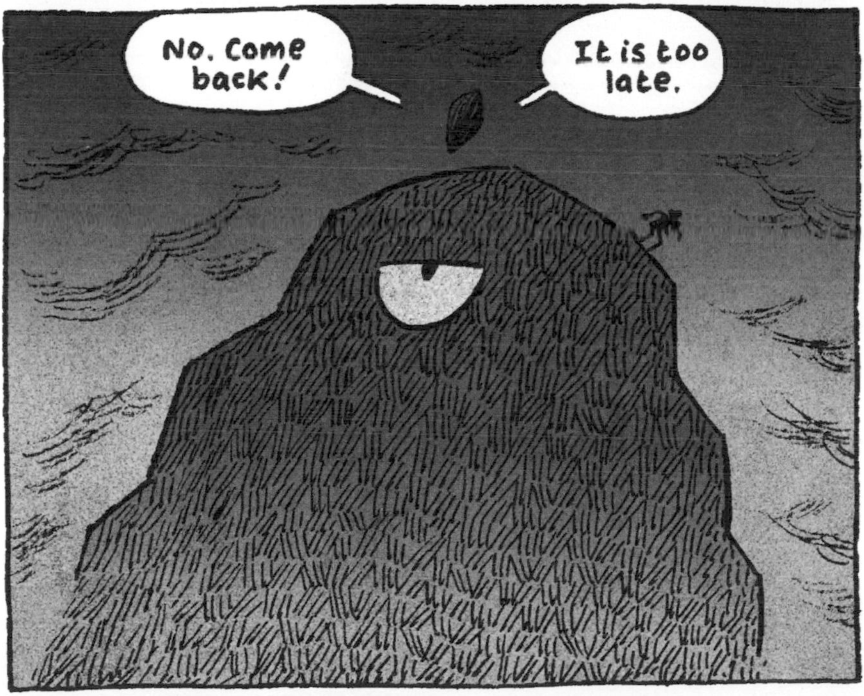
No. Come back!
It is too late.

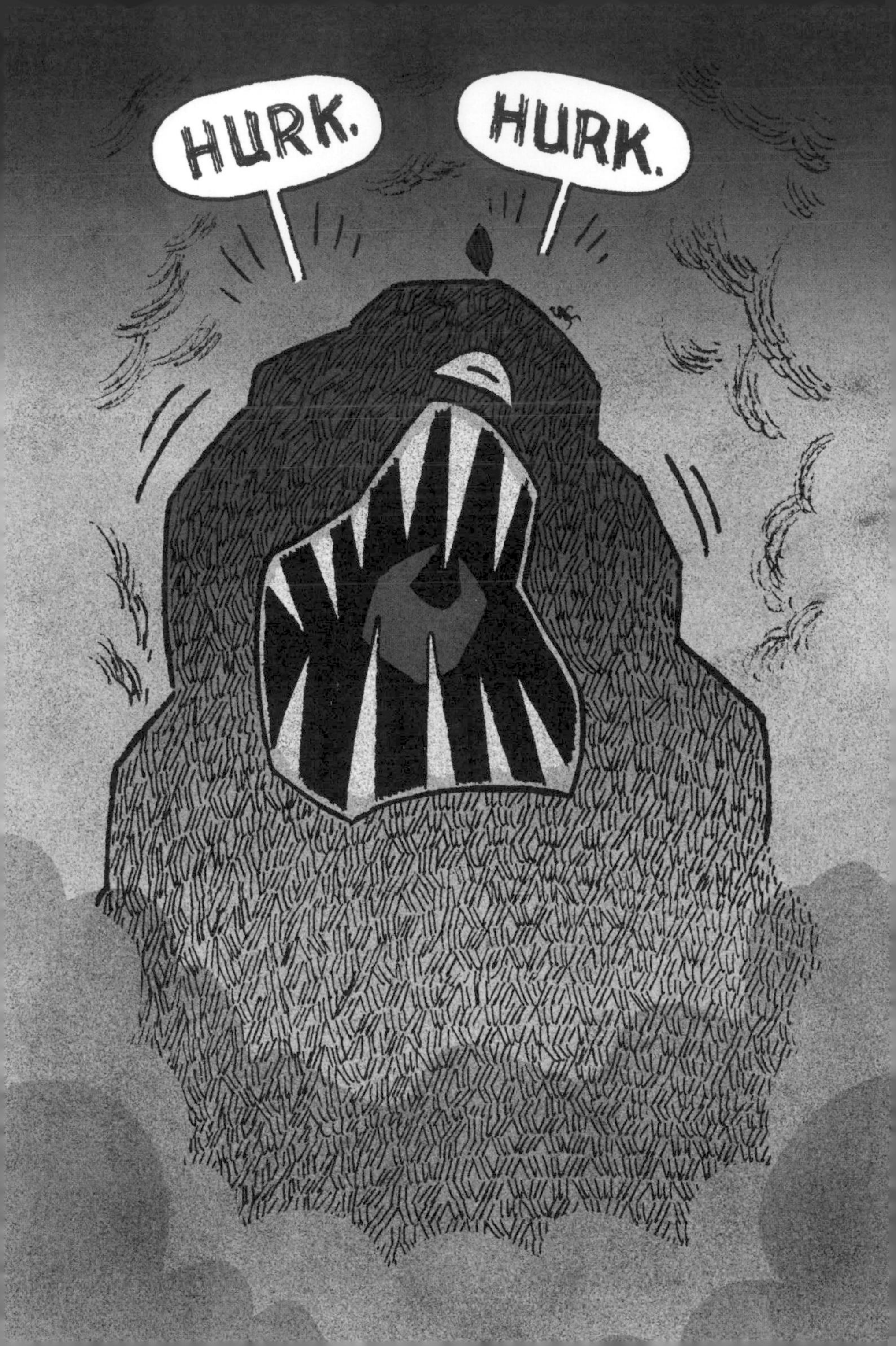
HURK.
HURK.

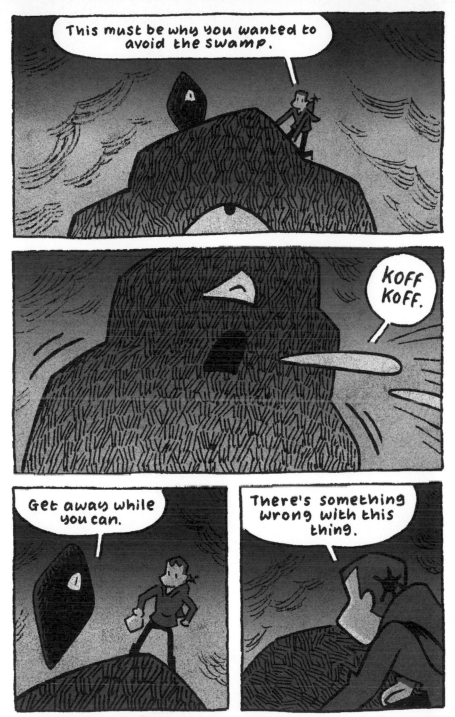

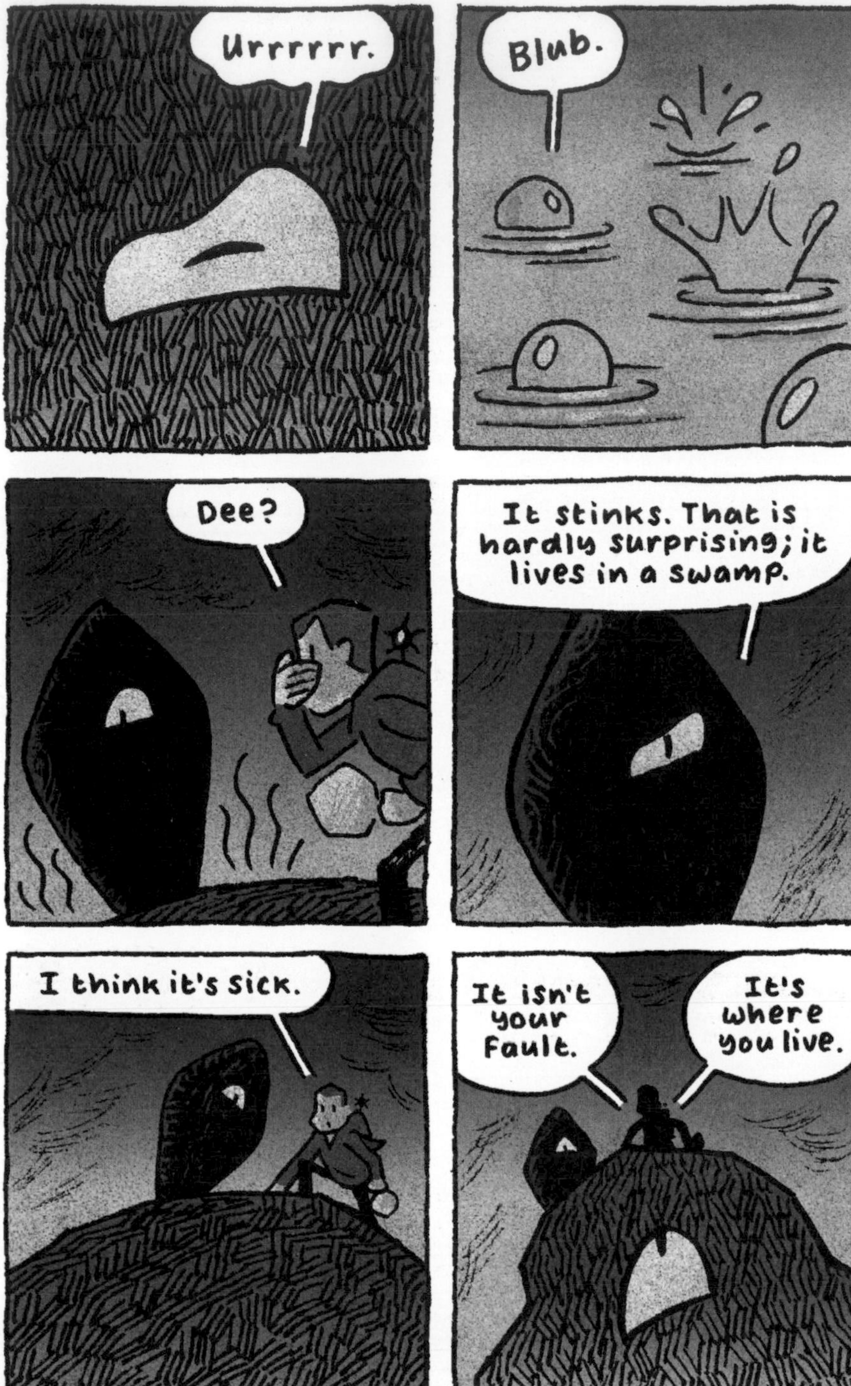
Urrrrrr.
Blub.
Dee?
It stinks. That is hardly surprising; it lives in a swamp.
I think it's sick.
It isn't your fault.
It's where you live.

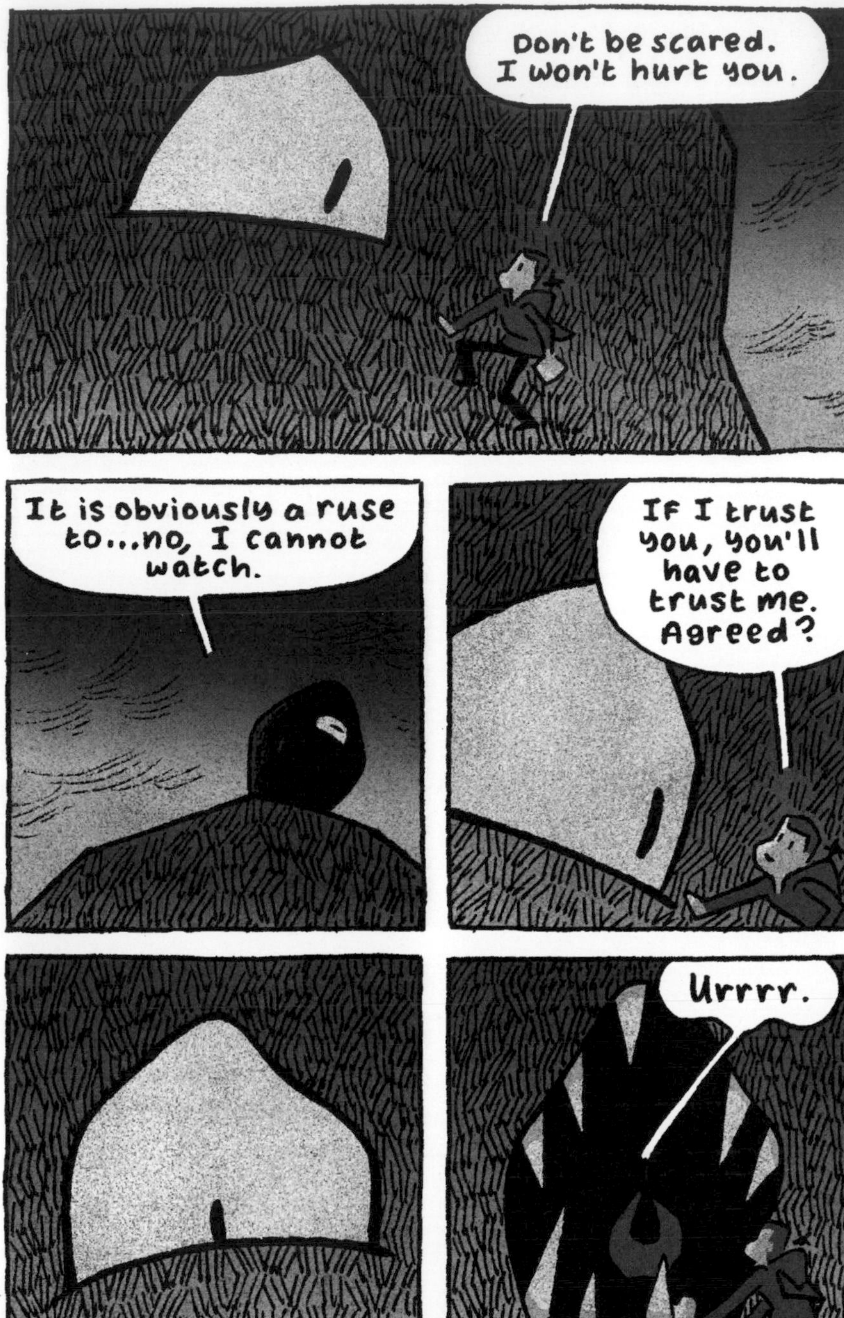

Don't be scared. I won't hurt you.
It is obviously a ruse to...no, I cannot watch.
If I trust you, you'll have to trust me. Agreed?
Urrrr.

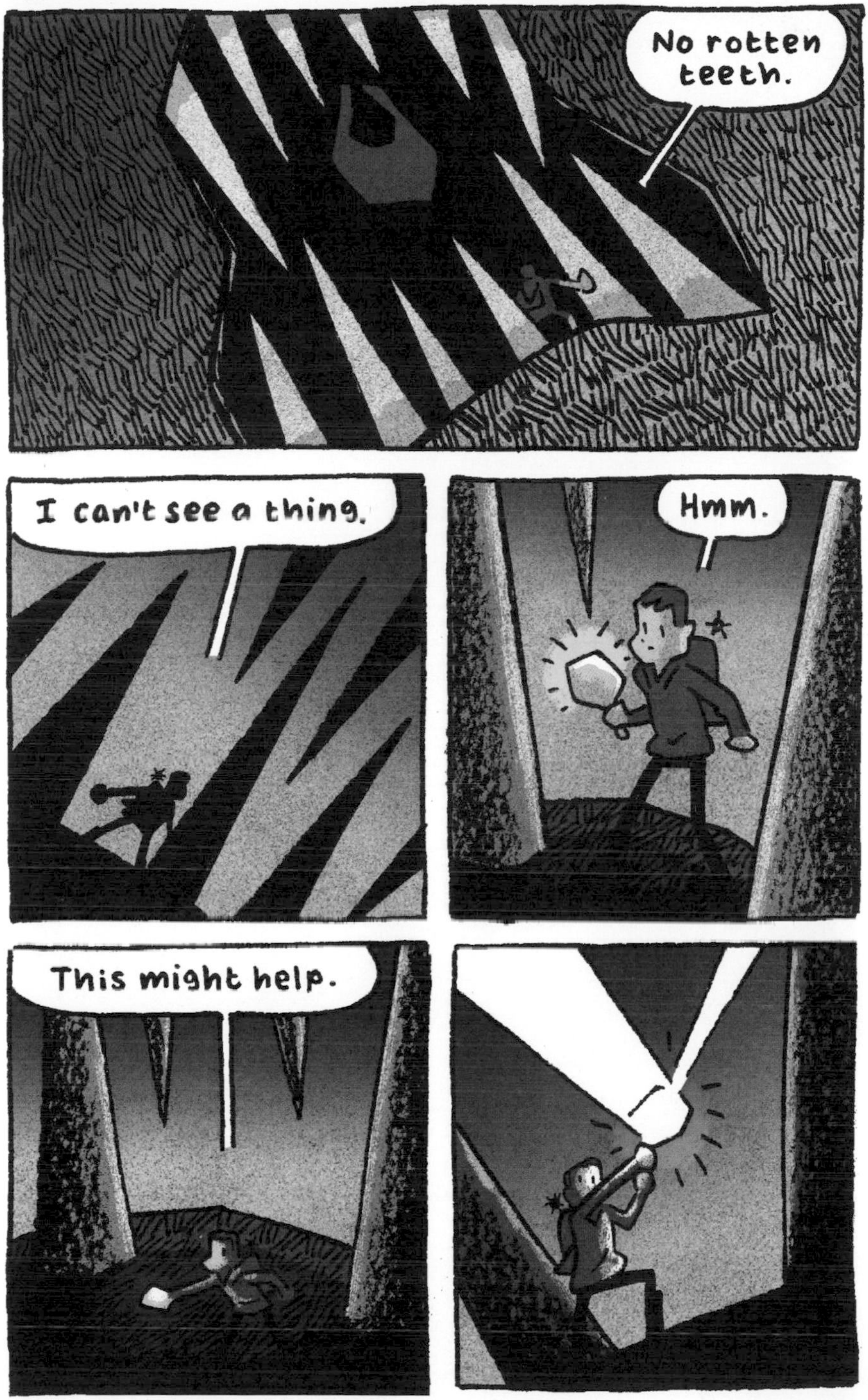
No rotten teeth.
I can't see a thing.
Hmm.
This might help.

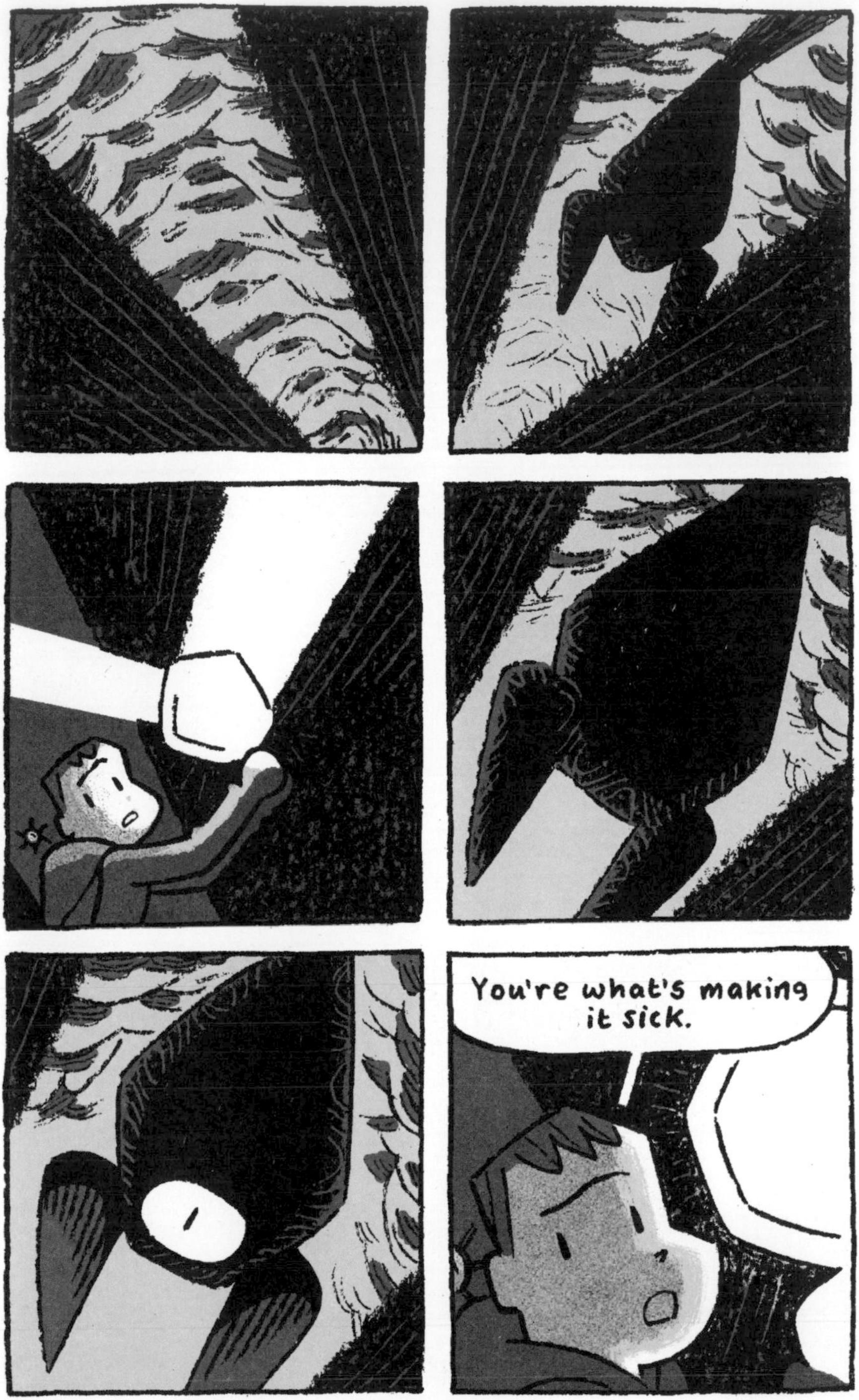
You're what's making it sick.

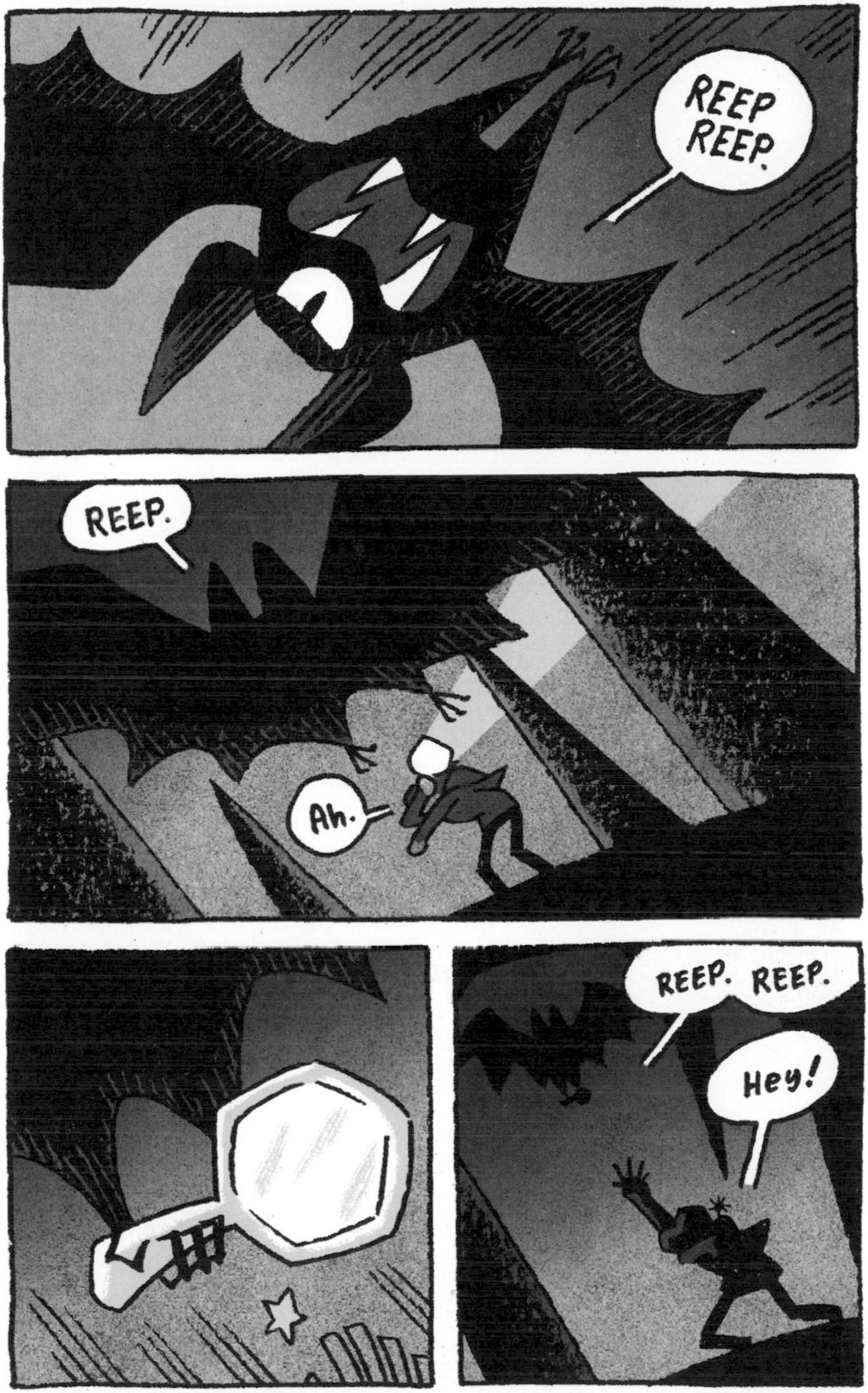
REEP REEP.
REEP.
Ah.
REEP. REEP.
Hey!

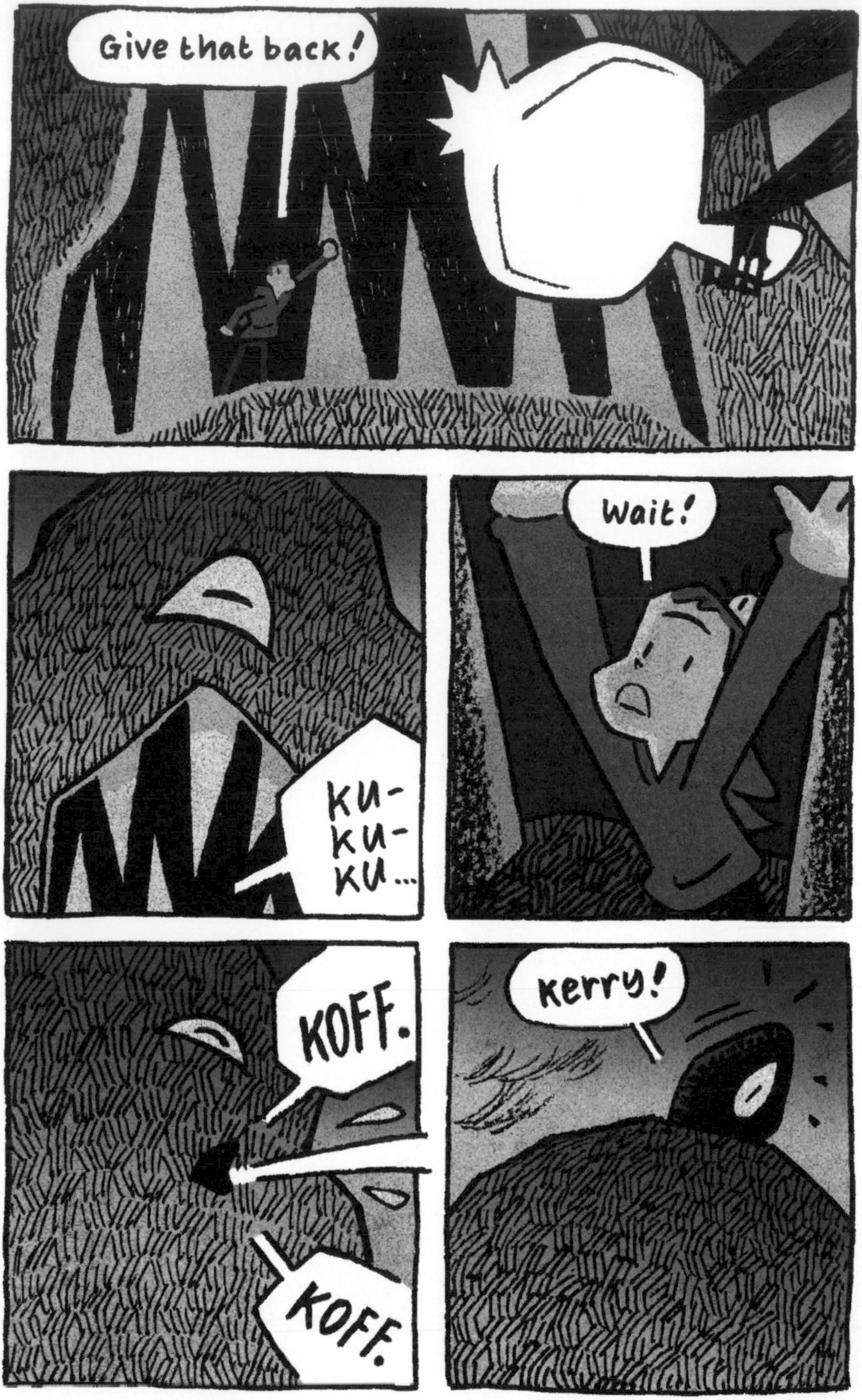
Give that back!
KU-
KU-
KU...
Wait!
KOFF.
KOFF.
Kerry!

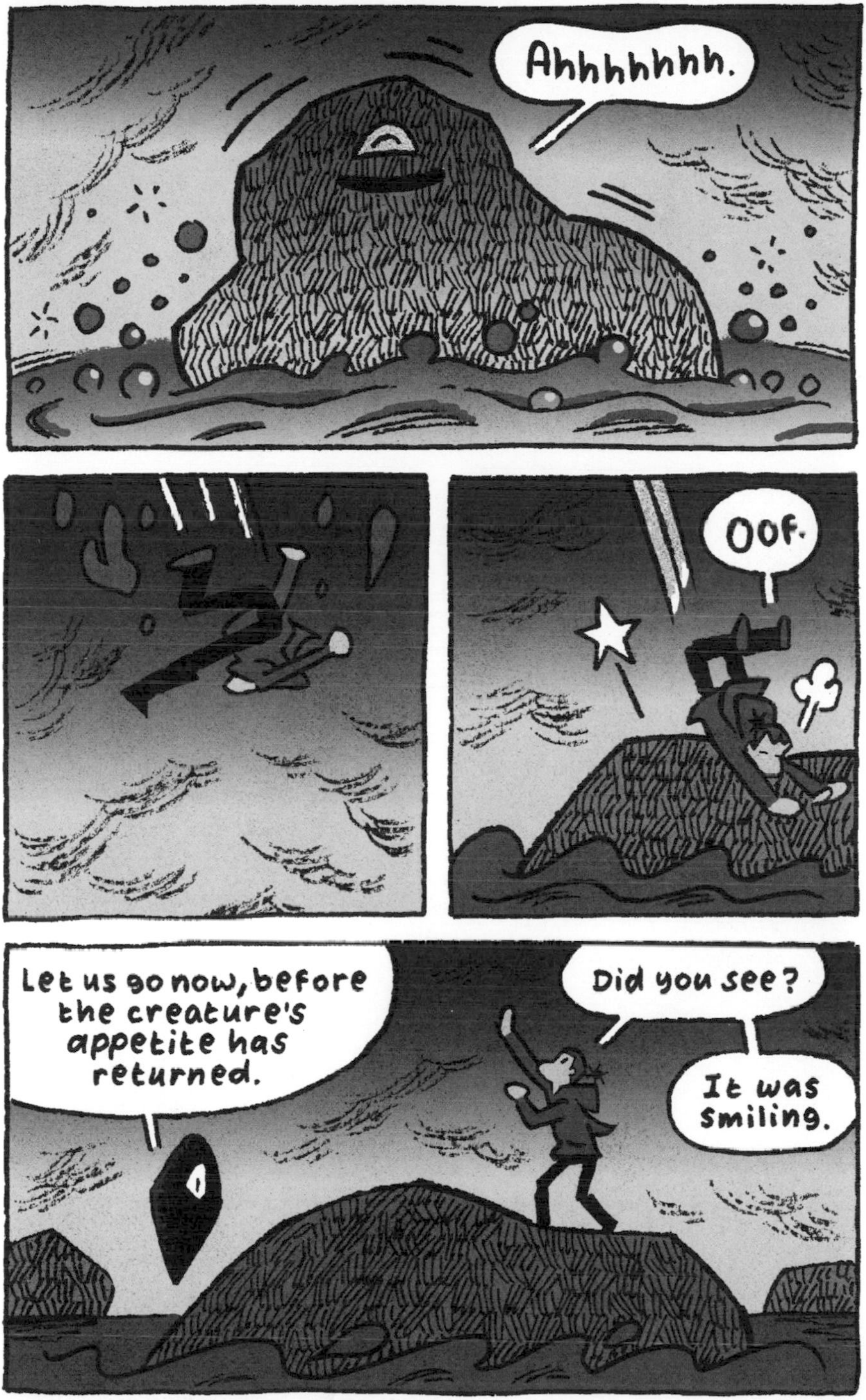
Ahhhhhhh.
OOF.
Let us go now, before the creature's appetite has returned.
Did you see?
It was smiling.

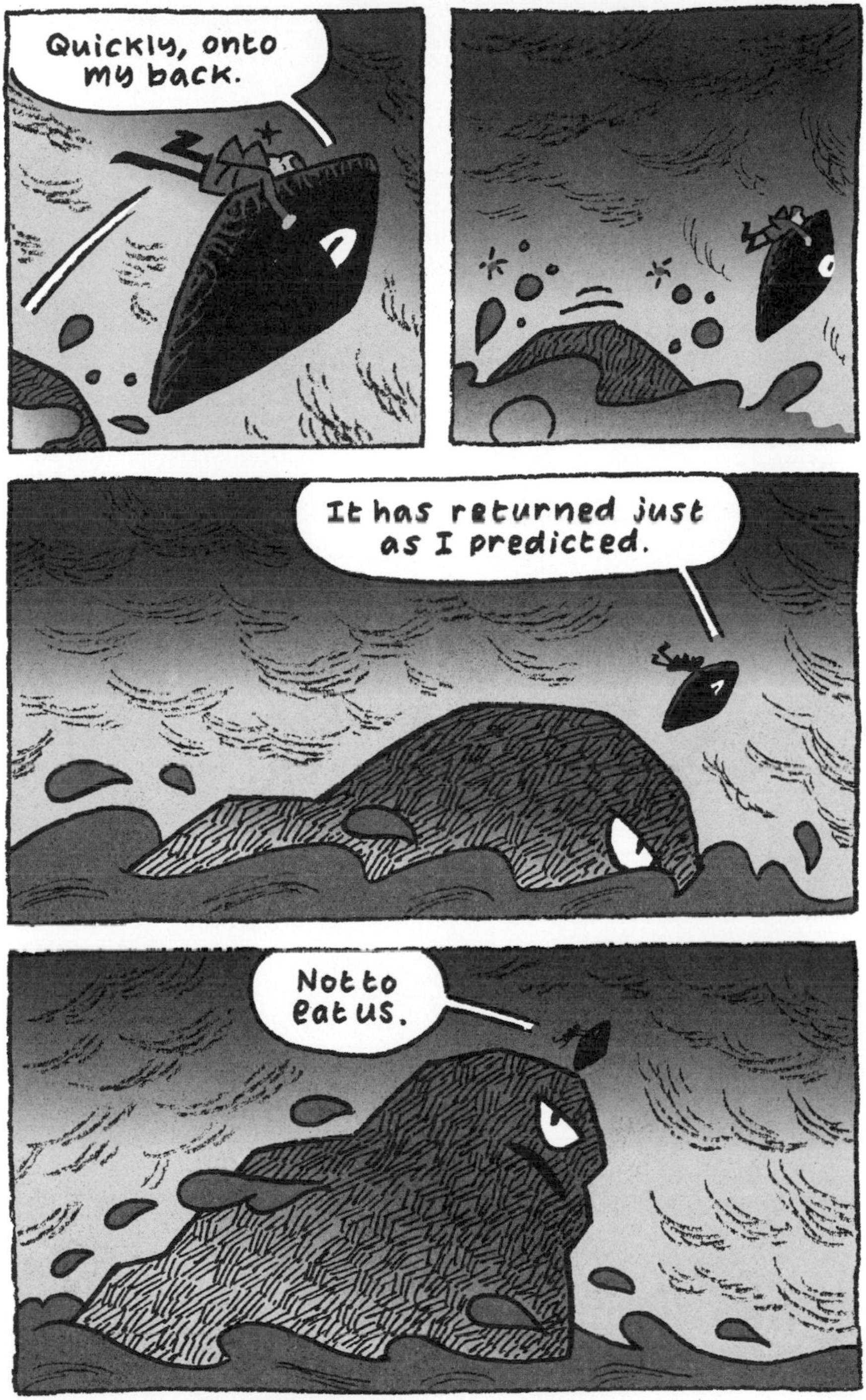
Quickly, onto my back.
It has returned just as I predicted.
Not to eat us.

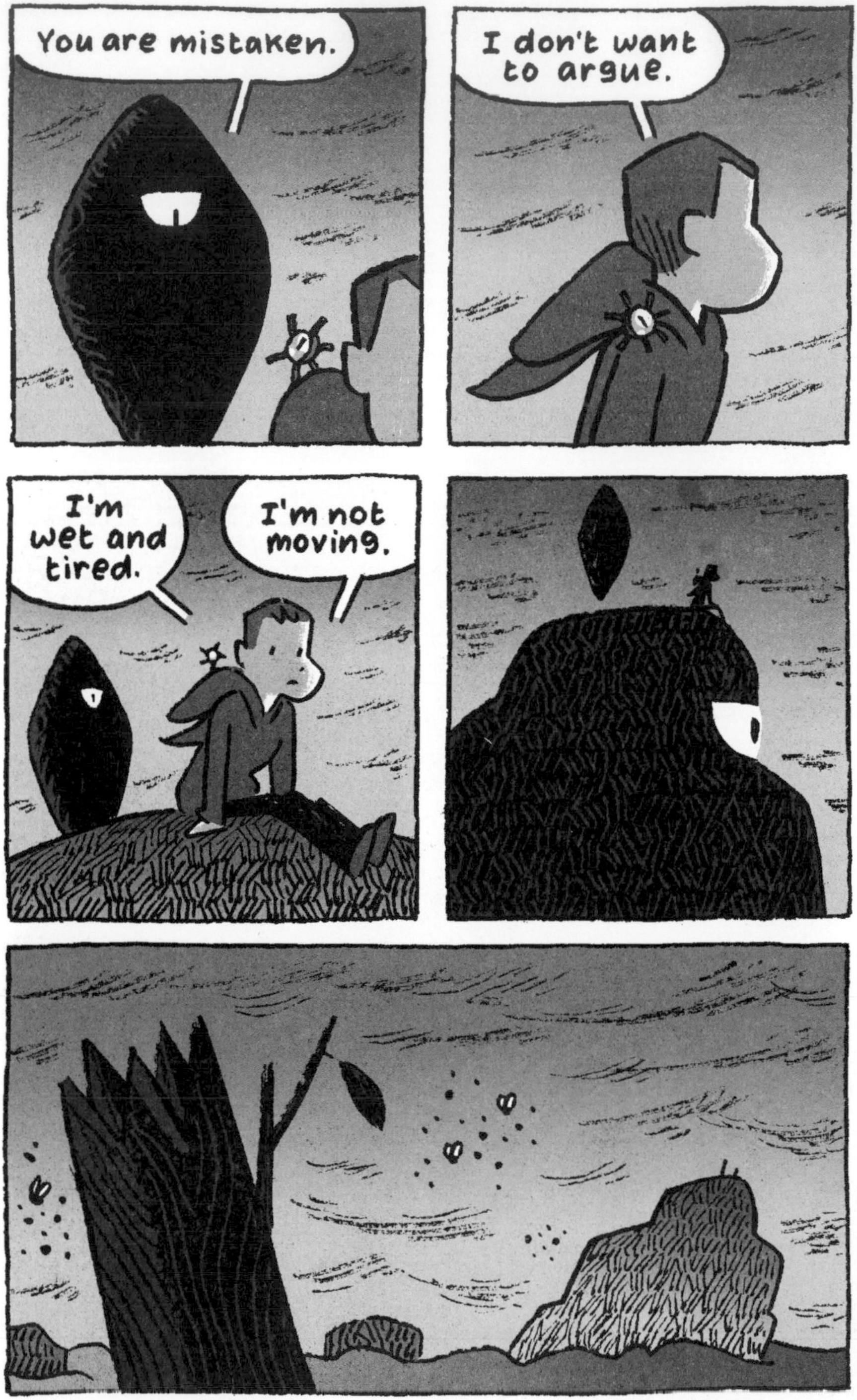
You are mistaken.
I don't want to argue.
I'm wet and tired.
I'm not moving.

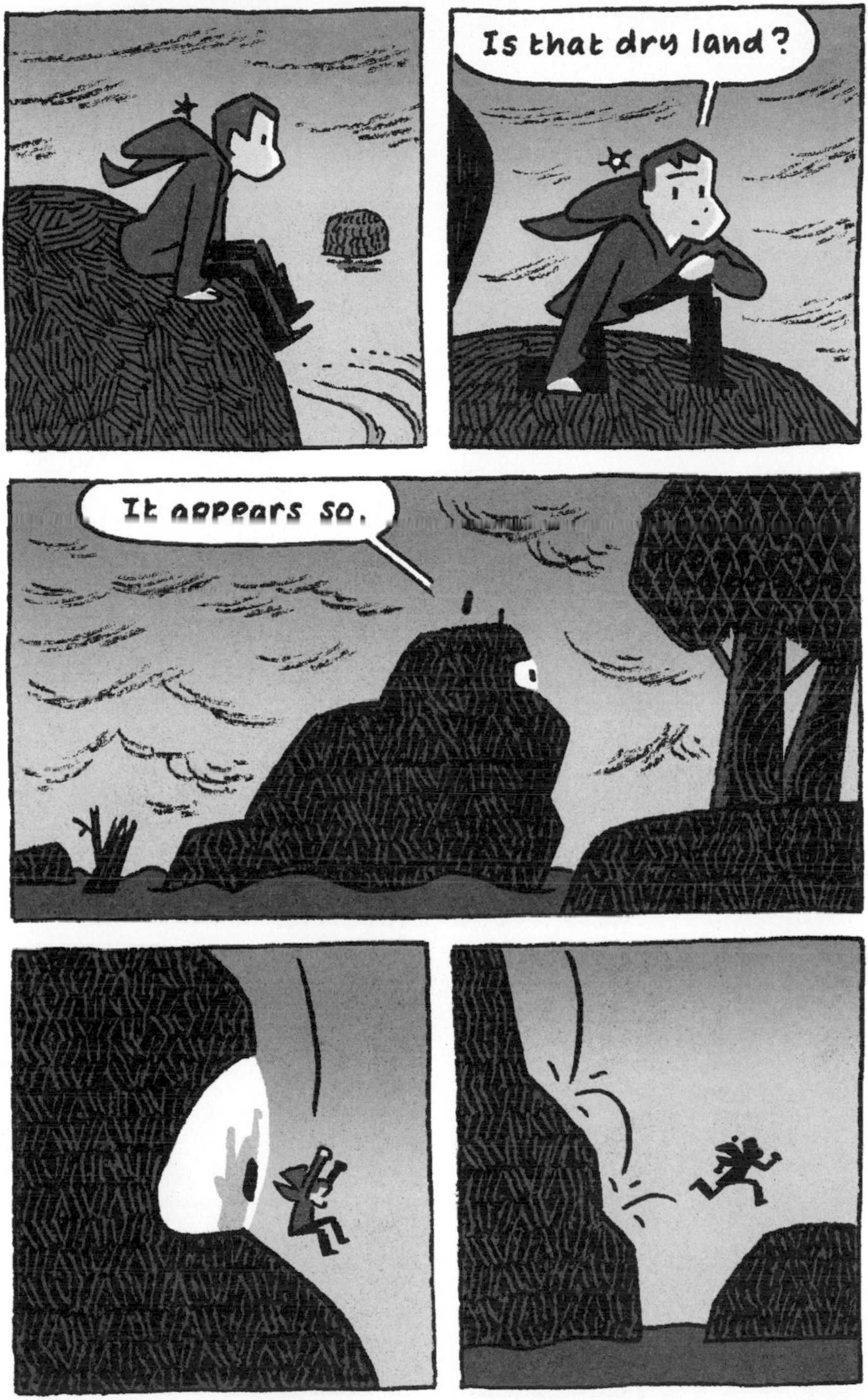
Is that dry land?
It appears so.

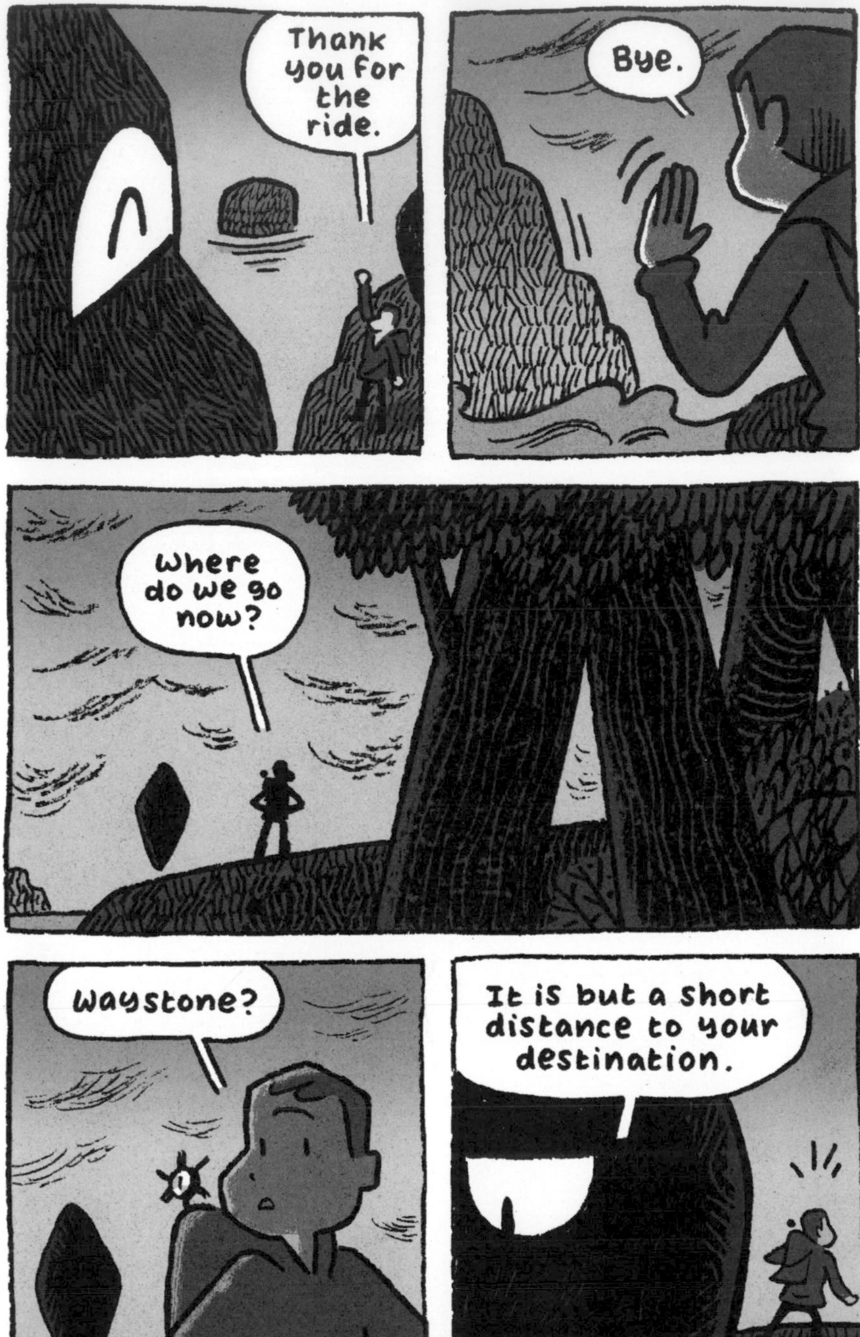
Thank you for the ride.
Bye.
Where do we go now?
Waystone?
It is but a short distance to your destination.

193

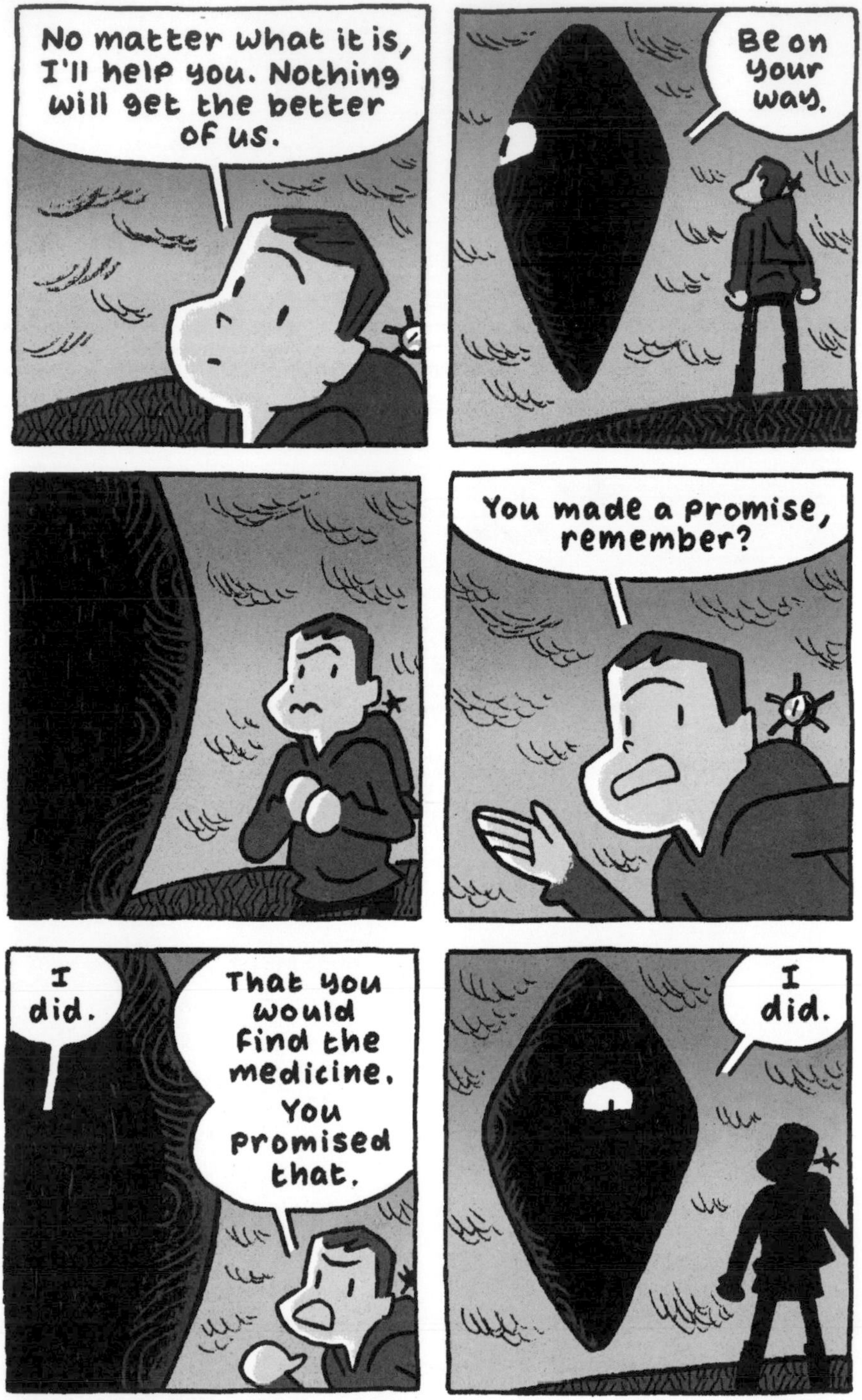
No matter what it is, I'll help you. Nothing will get the better of us.
Be on your way.
You made a promise, remember?
I did.
That you would find the medicine.
You promised that.
I did.

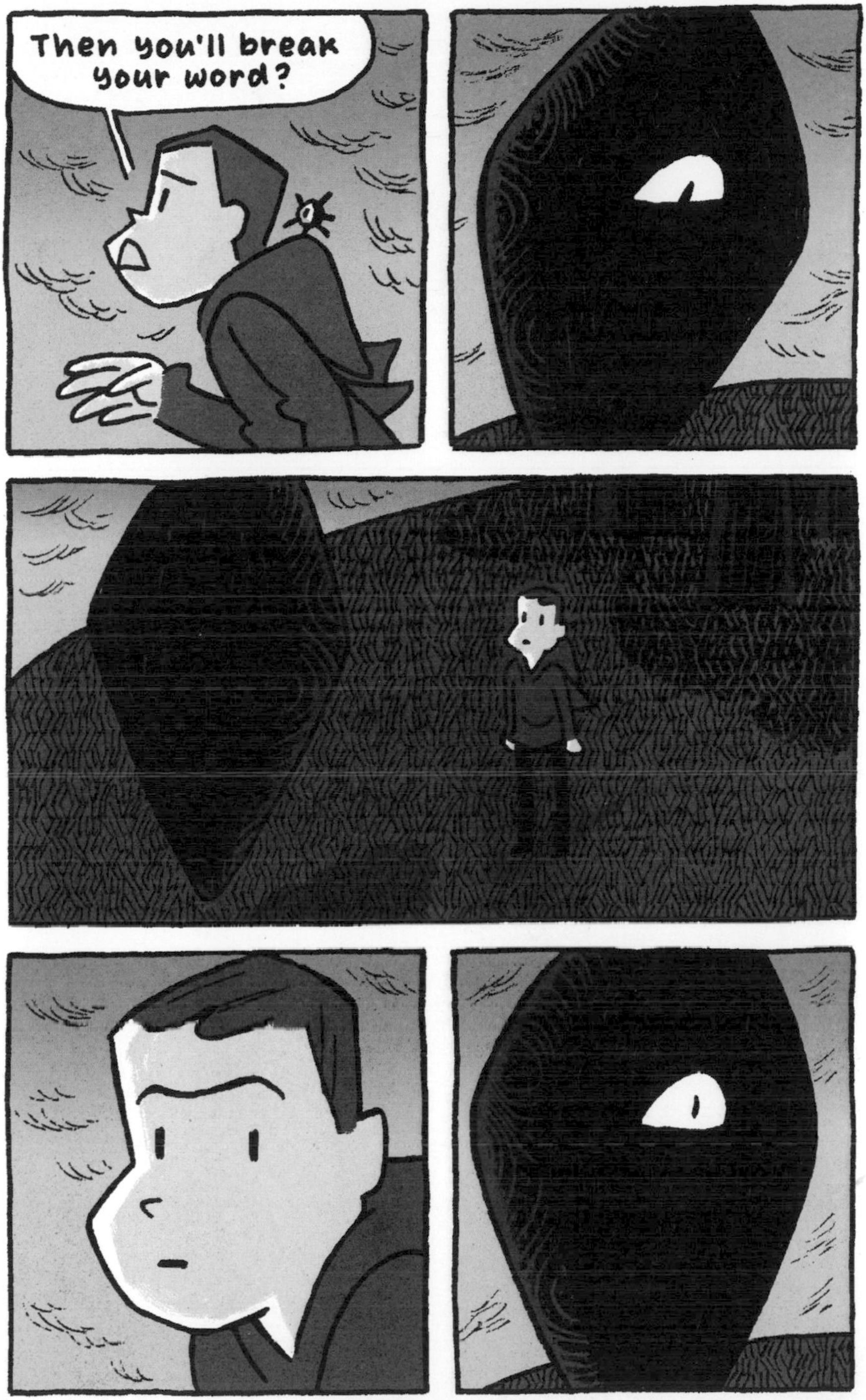
Then you'll break your word?

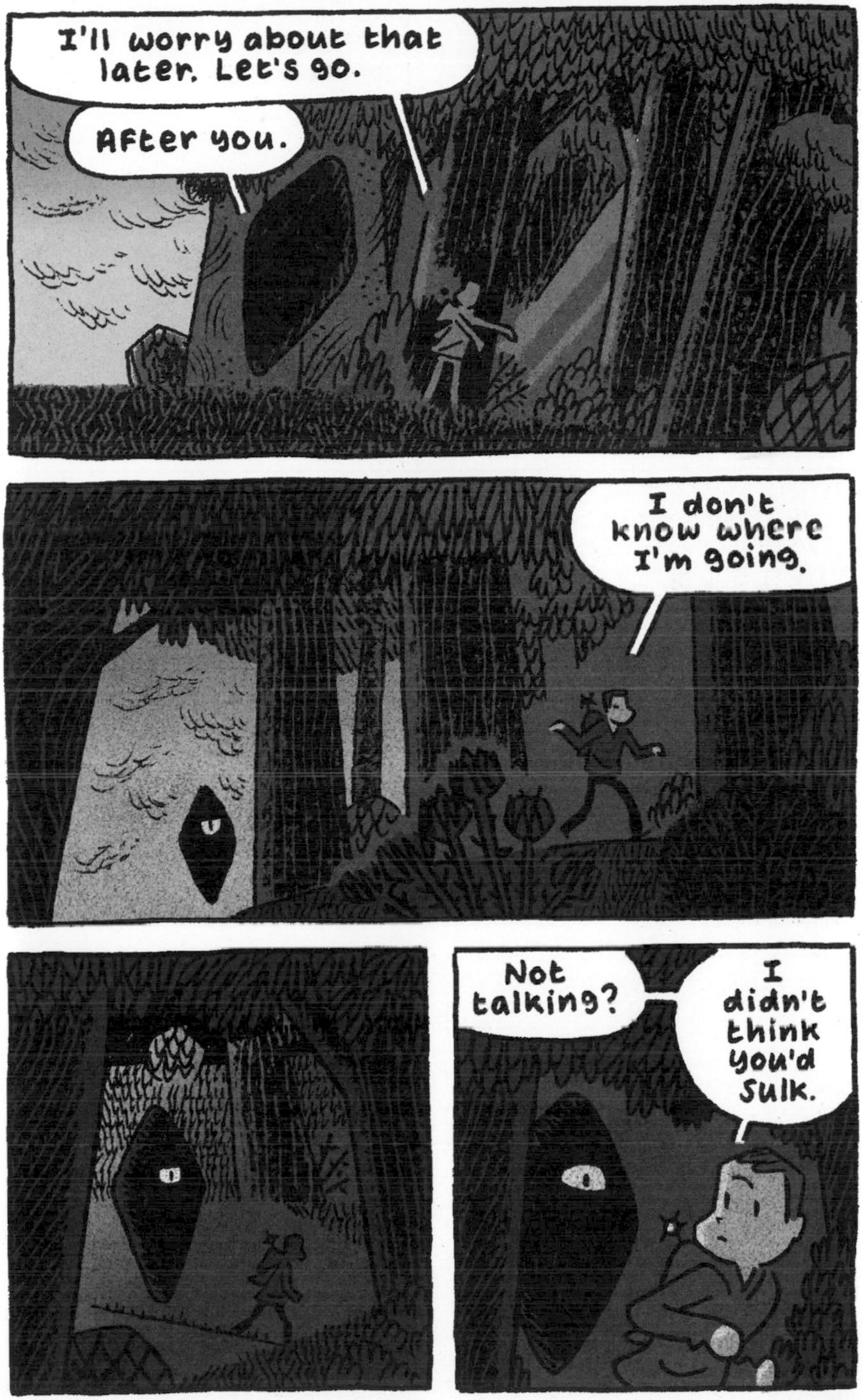
I'll worry about that later. Let's go.
After you.
I don't know where I'm going.
Not talking?
I didn't think you'd sulk.

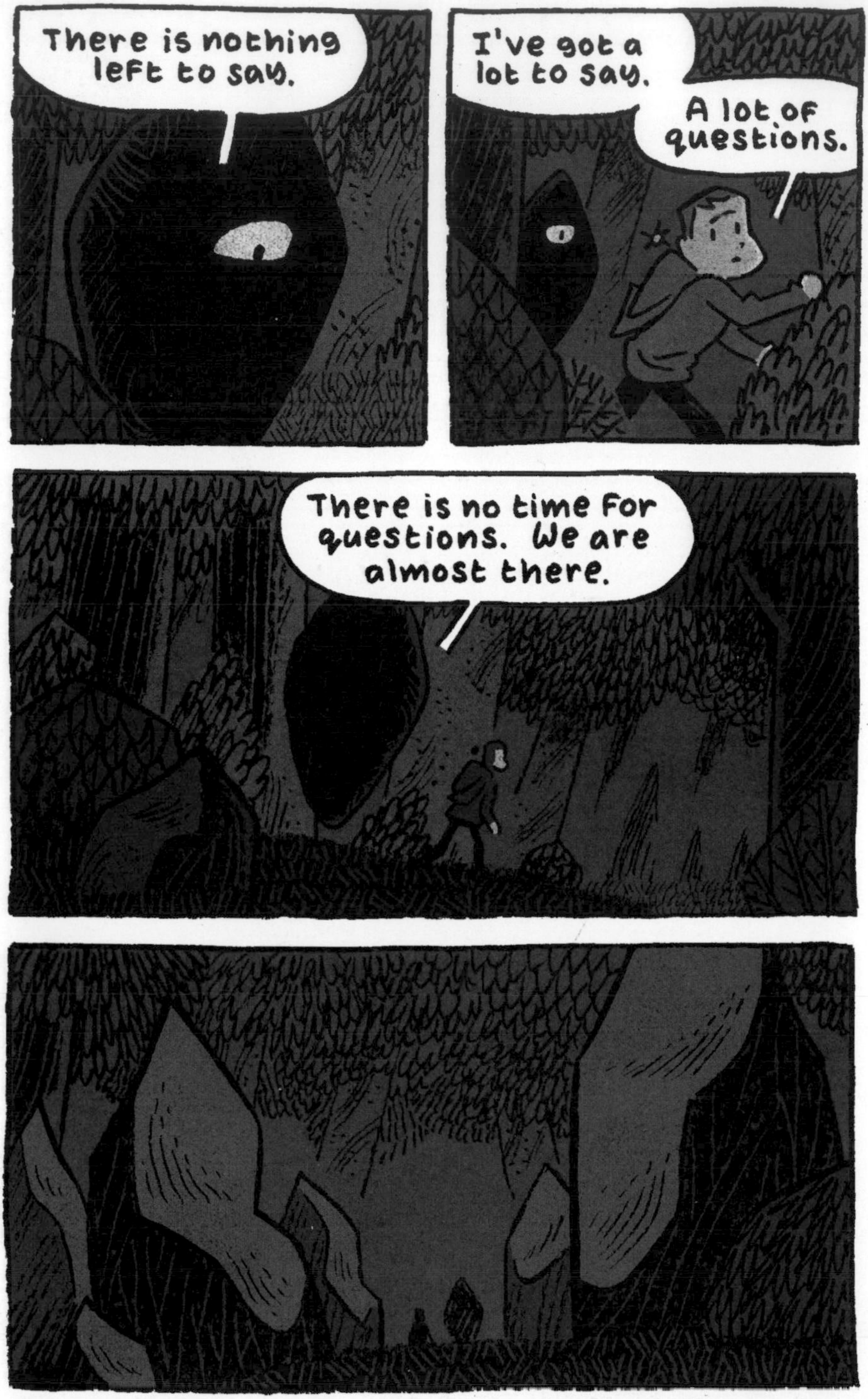
There is nothing left to say.
I've got a lot to say.
A lot of questions.
There is no time for questions. We are almost there.

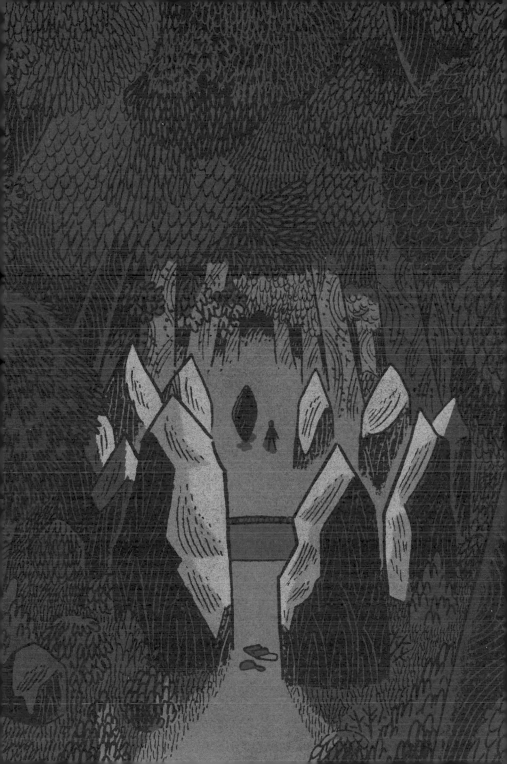

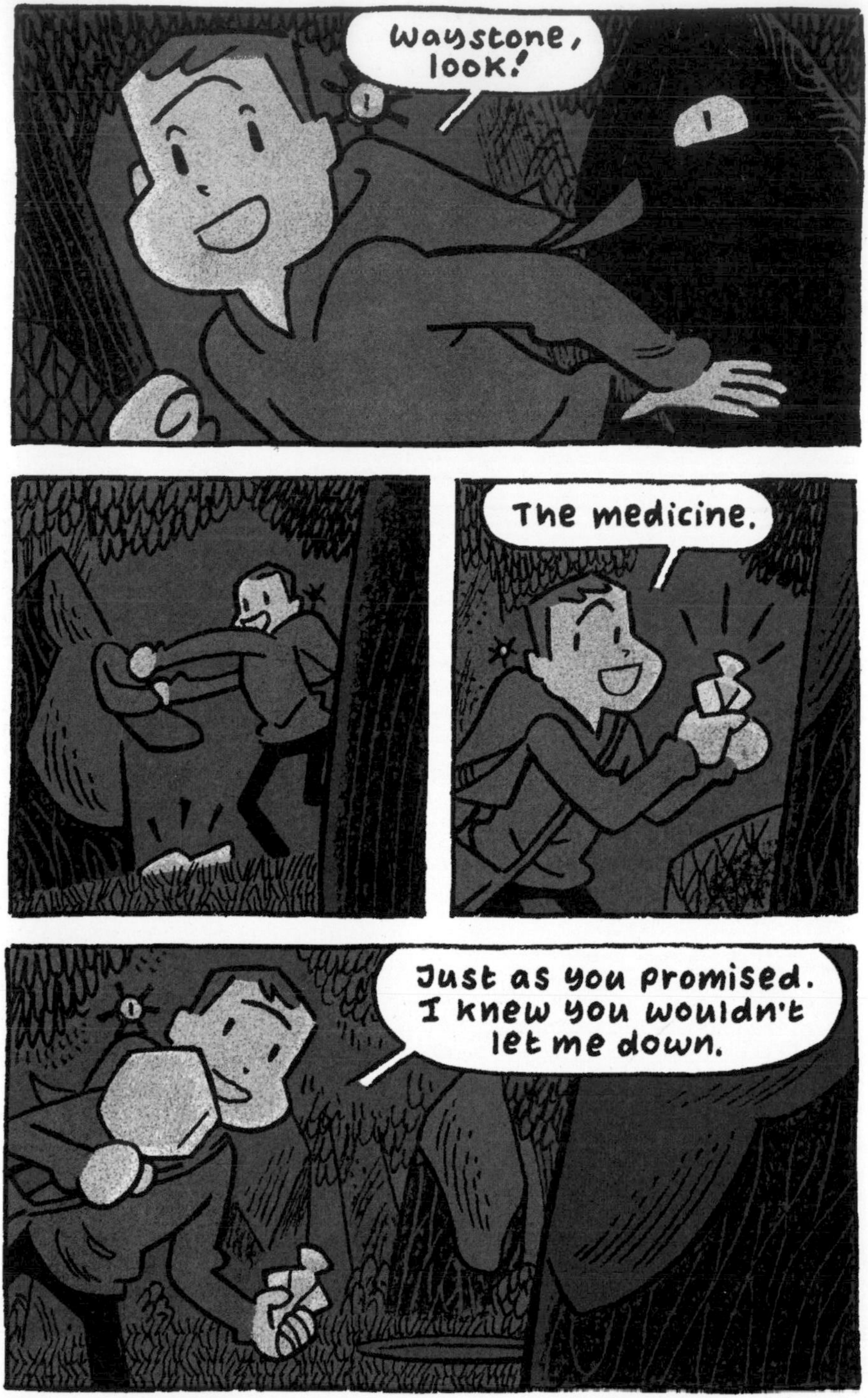
Waystone, look!
The medicine.
Just as you promised. I knew you wouldn't let me down.

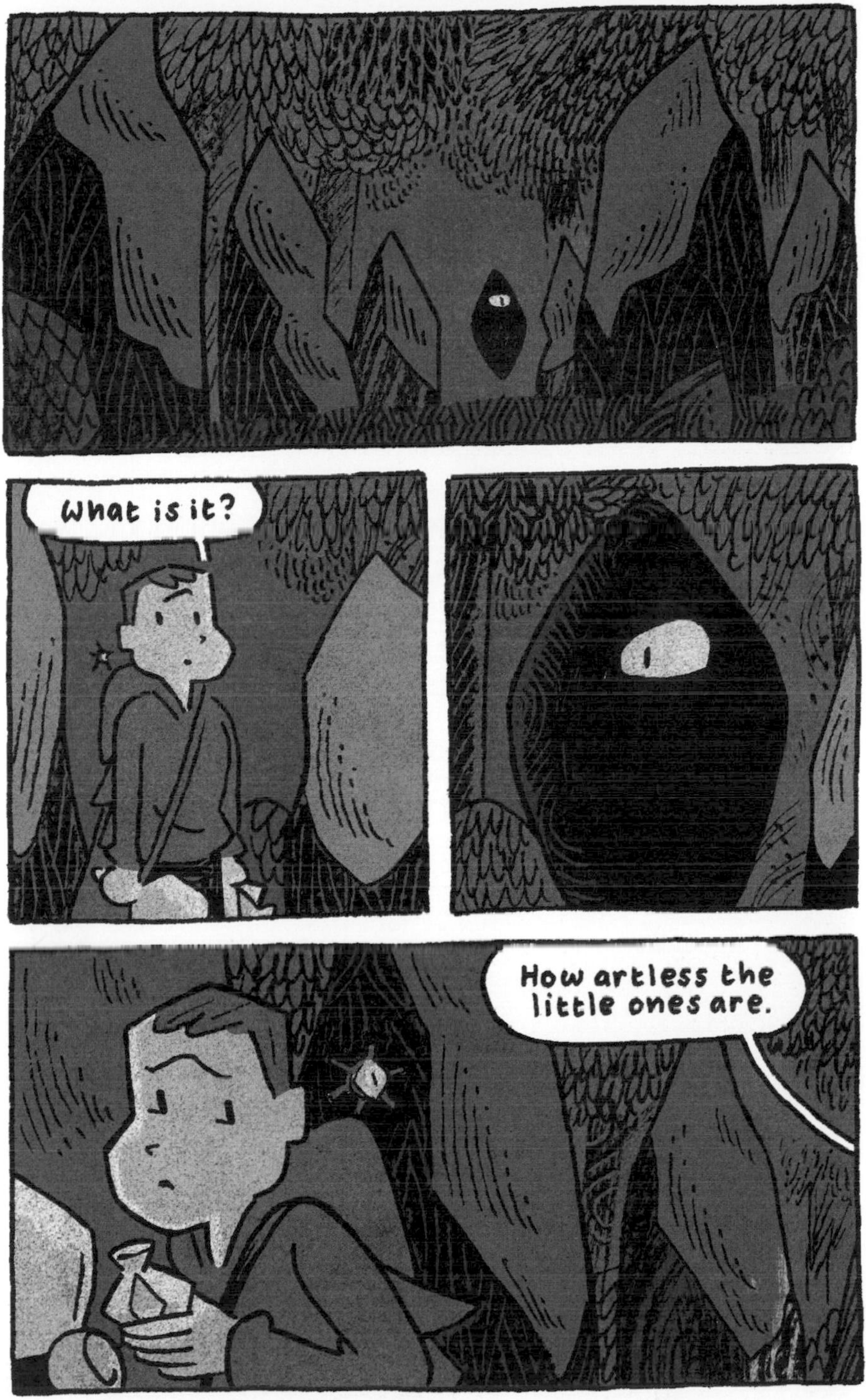
What is it?
How artless the little ones are.

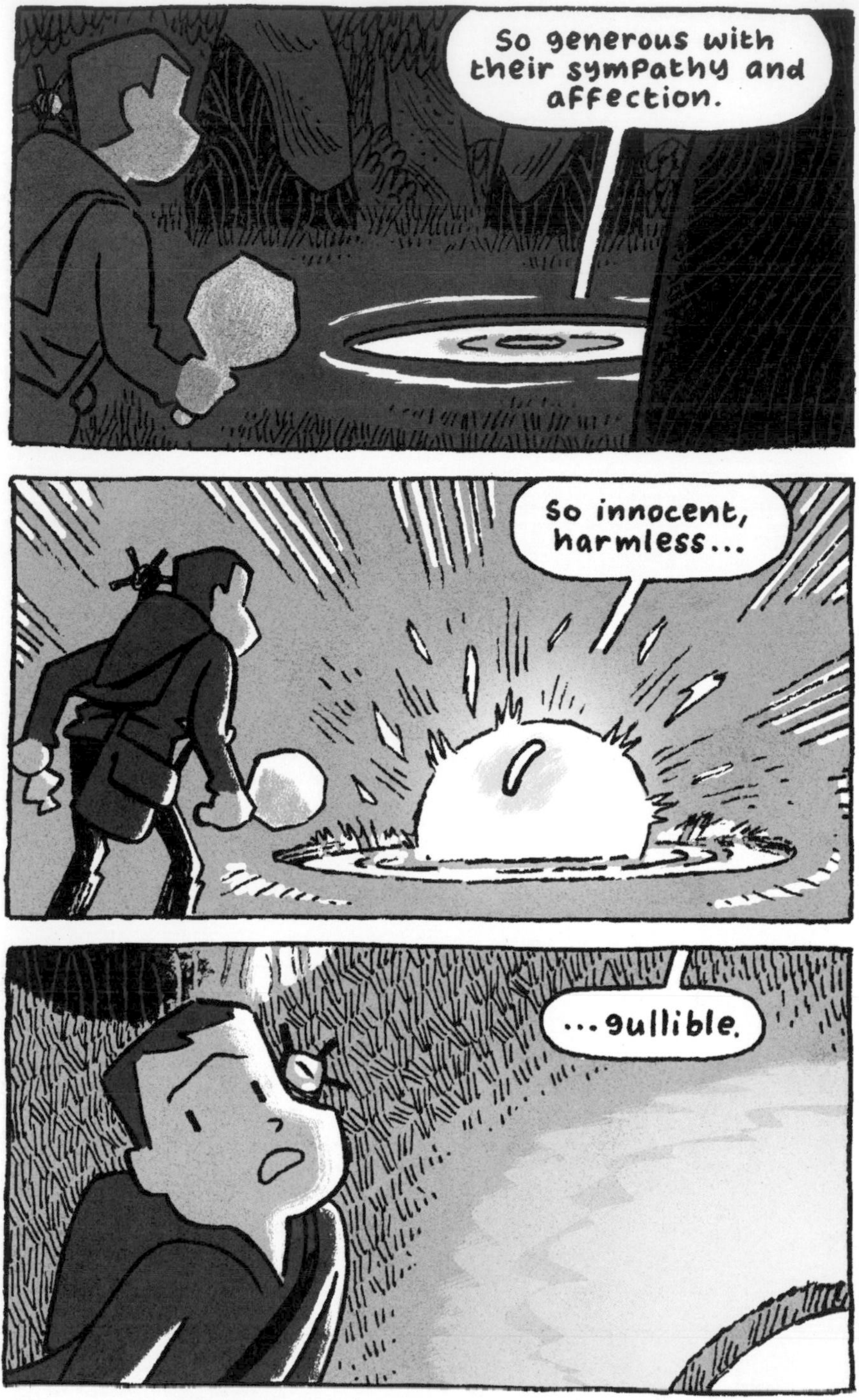
So generous with their sympathy and affection.
So innocent, harmless...
...gullible.

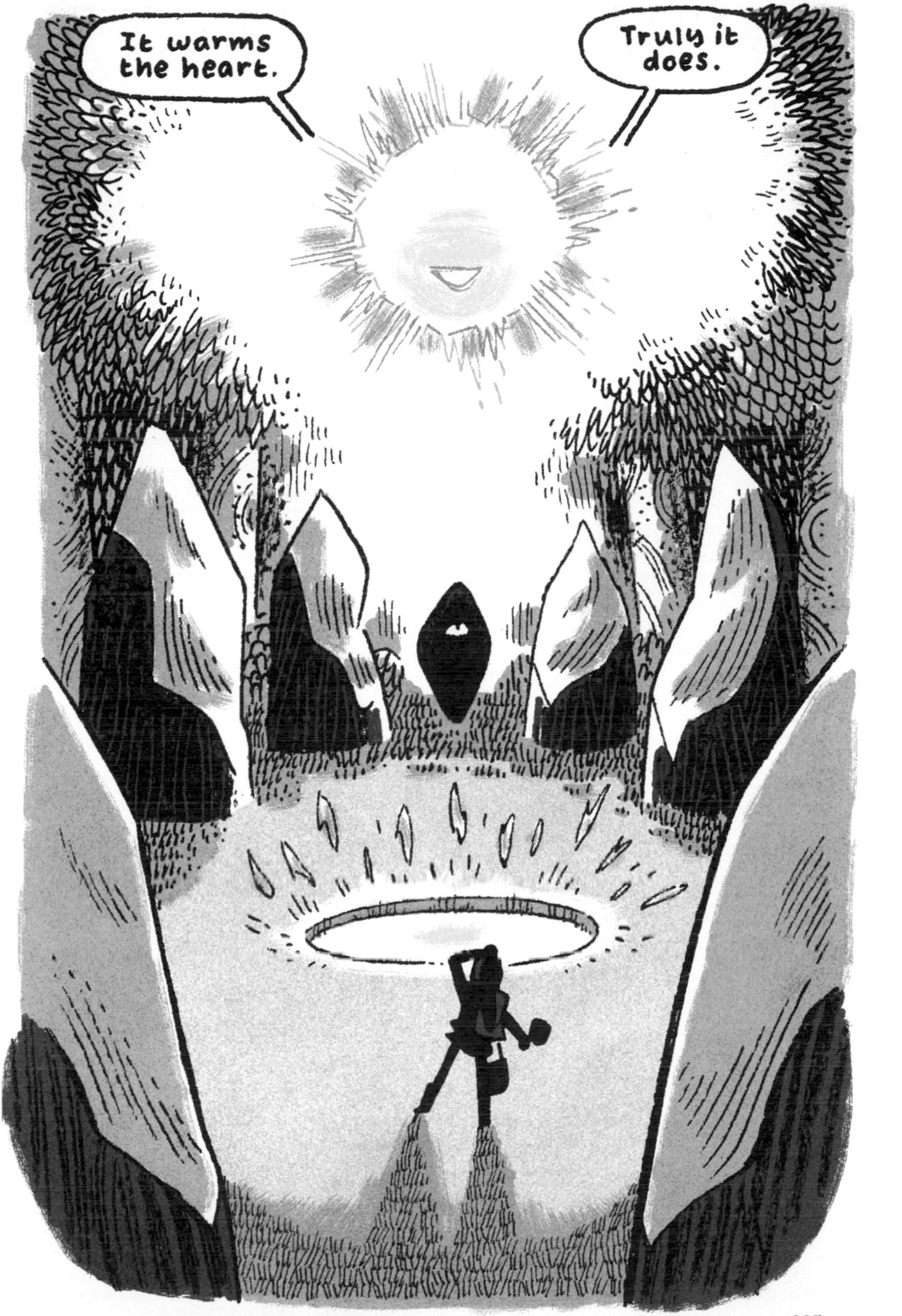
It warms the heart.
Truly it does.

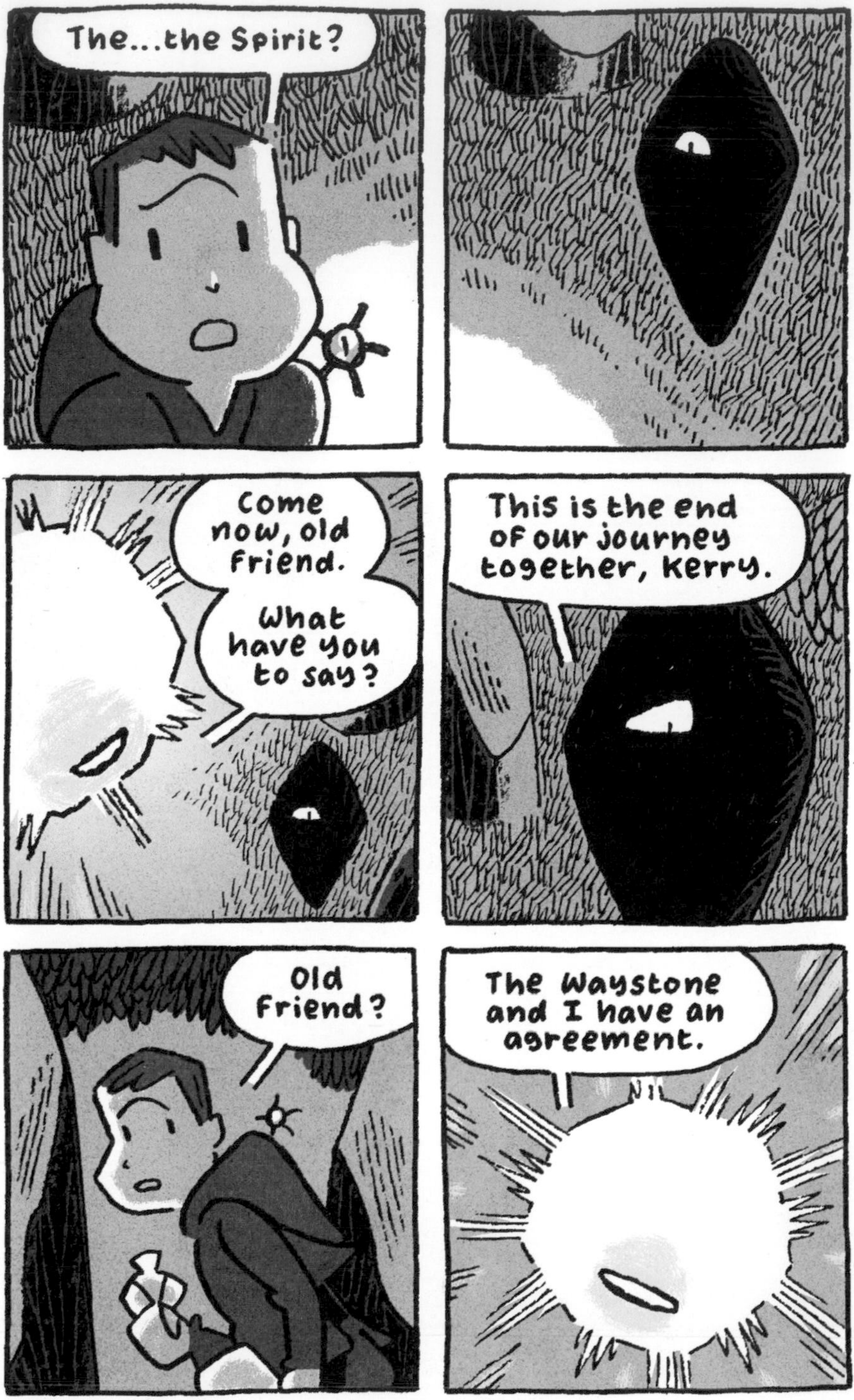
The...the Spirit?
Come now, old friend.
What have you to say?
This is the end of our journey together, Kerry.
Old Friend?
The Waystone and I have an agreement.

207

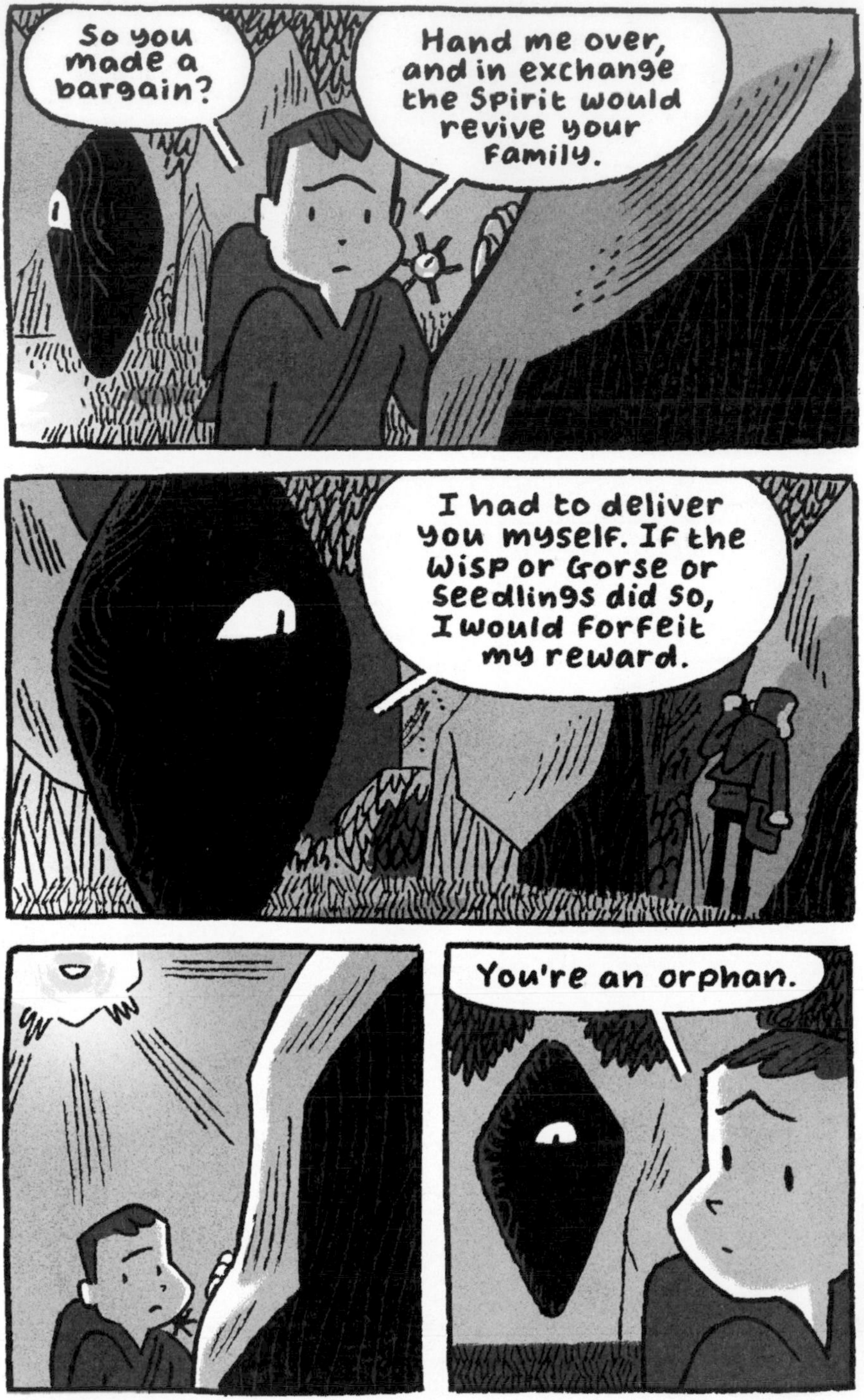
So you made a bargain?
Hand me over, and in exchange the Spirit would revive your family.
I had to deliver you myself. If the Wisp or Gorse or Seedlings did so, I would forfeit my reward.
You're an orphan.

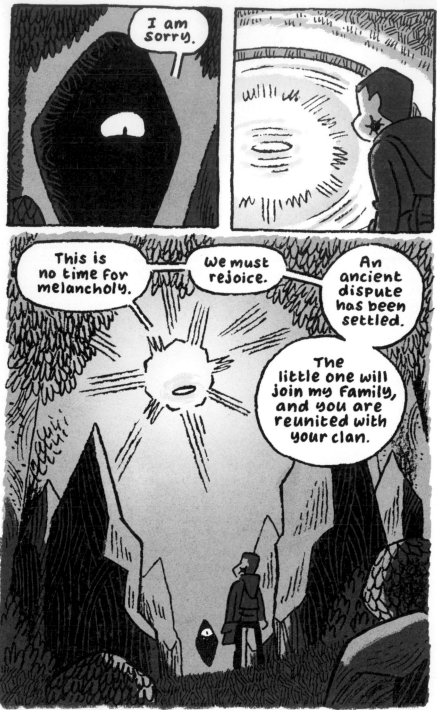

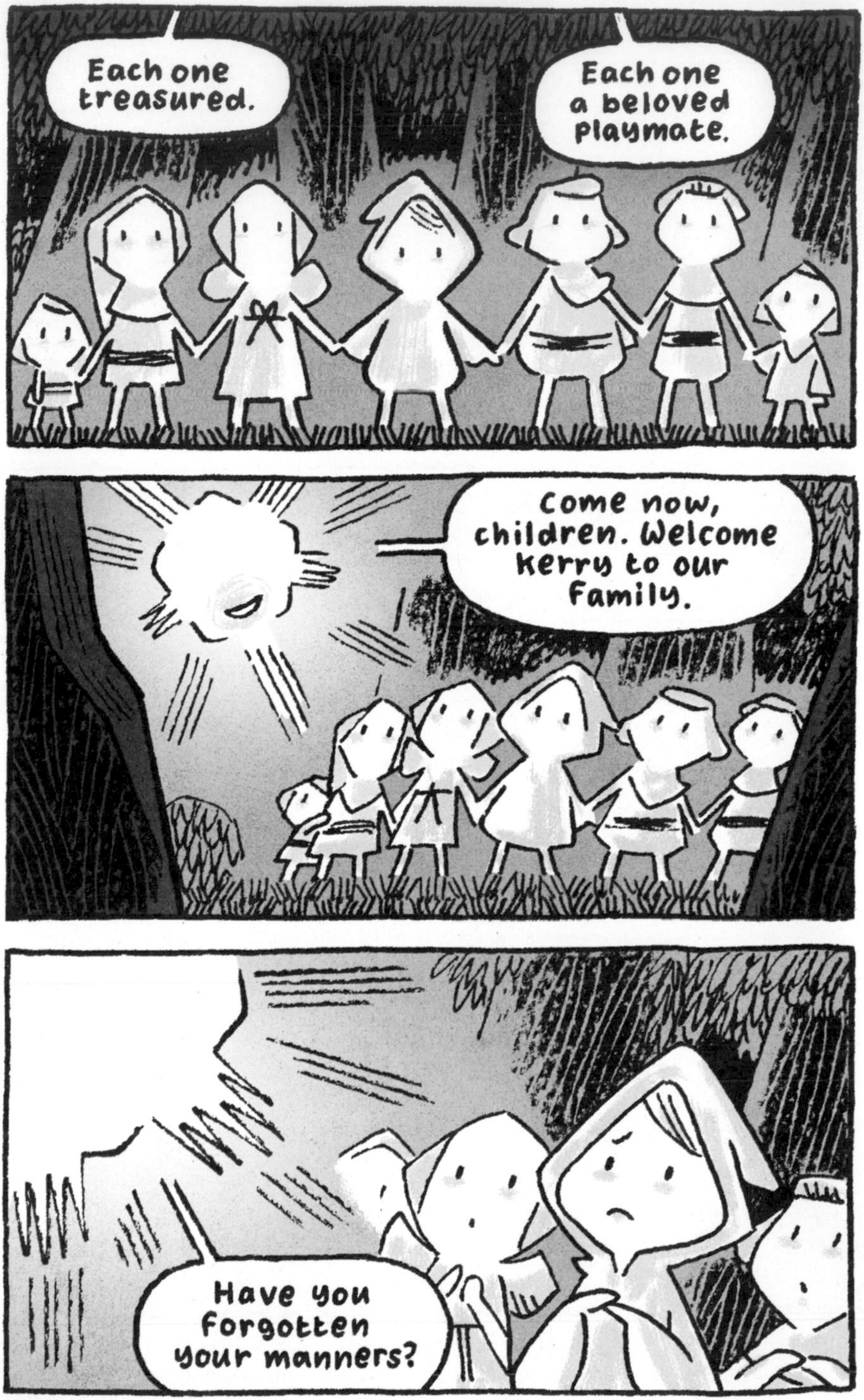
Each one treasured.
Each one a beloved playmate.
Come now, children. Welcome Kerry to our family.
Have you forgotten your manners?

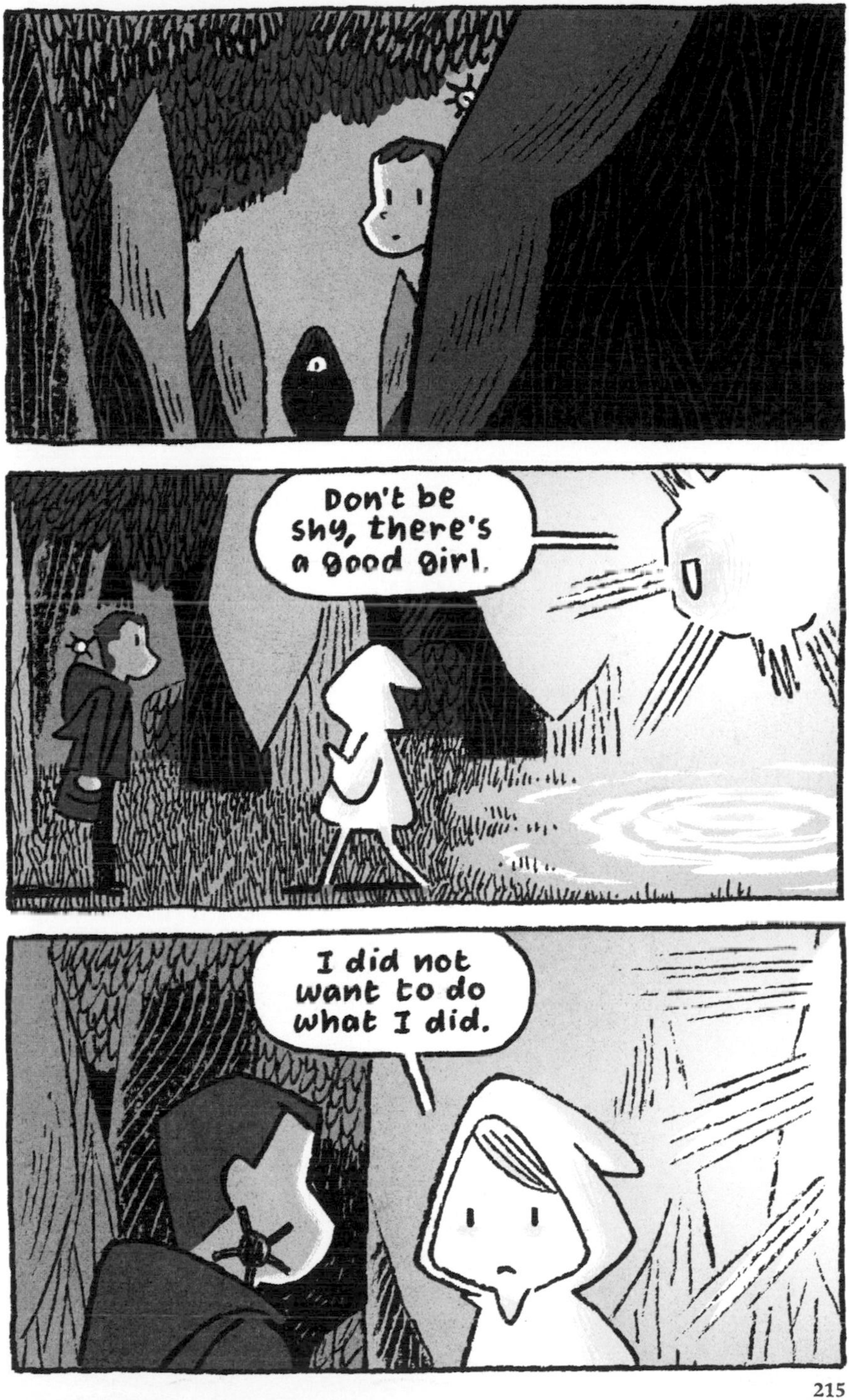
Don't be shy, there's a good girl.
I did not want to do what I did.

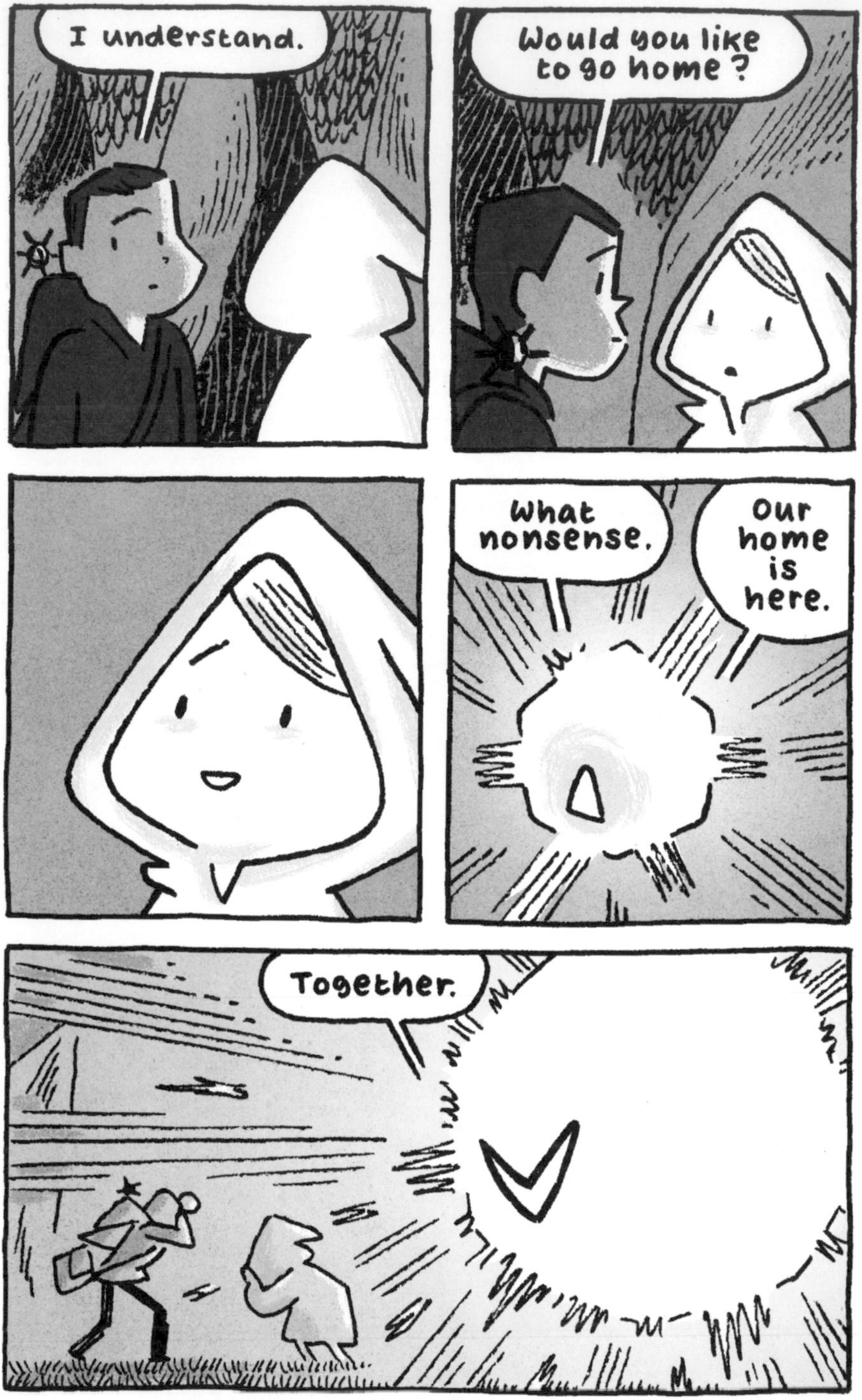
I understand.
Would you like to go home?
What nonsense.
Our home is here.
Together.

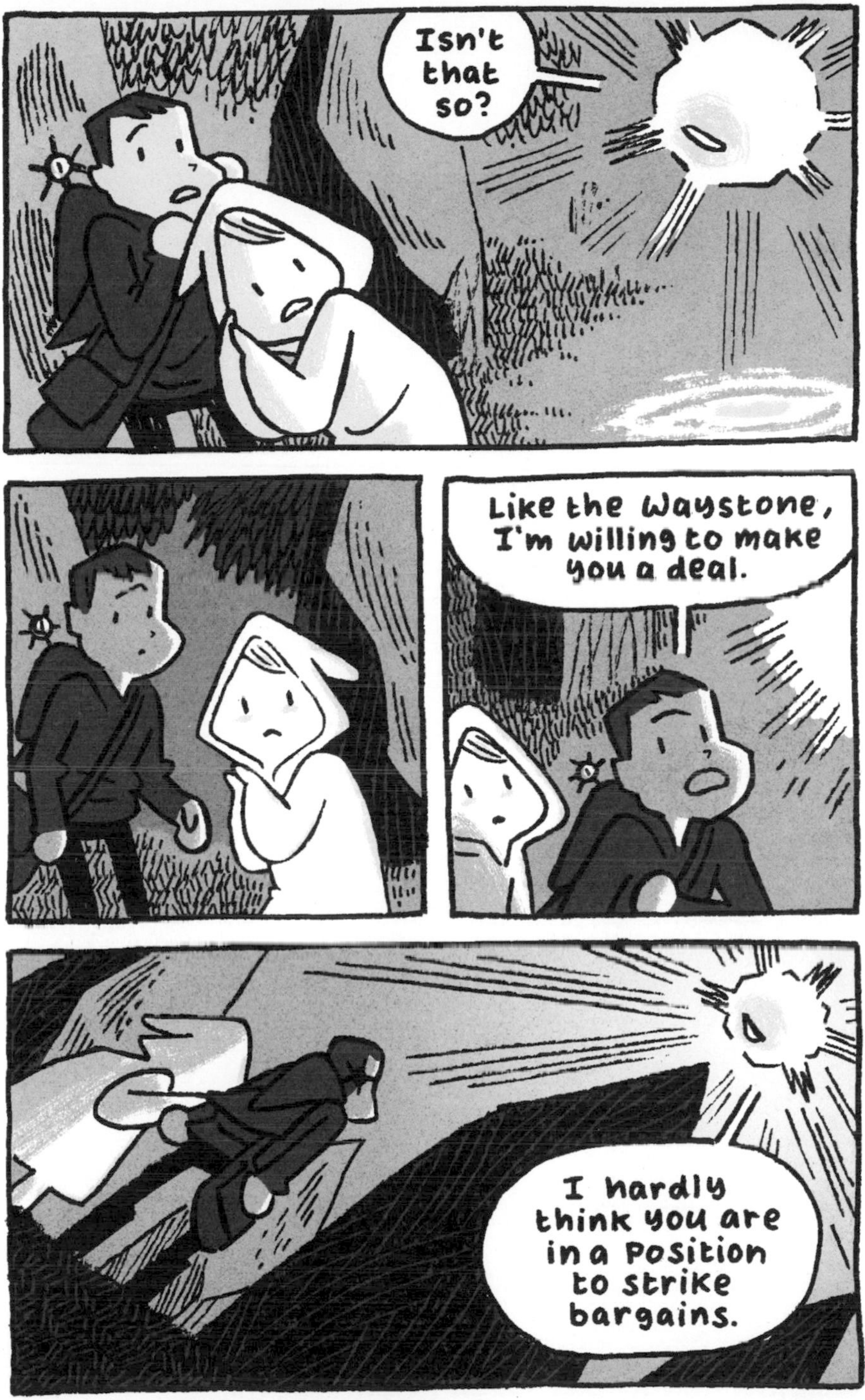
Isn't that so?
Like the Waystone, I'm willing to make you a deal.
I hardly think you are in a position to strike bargains.

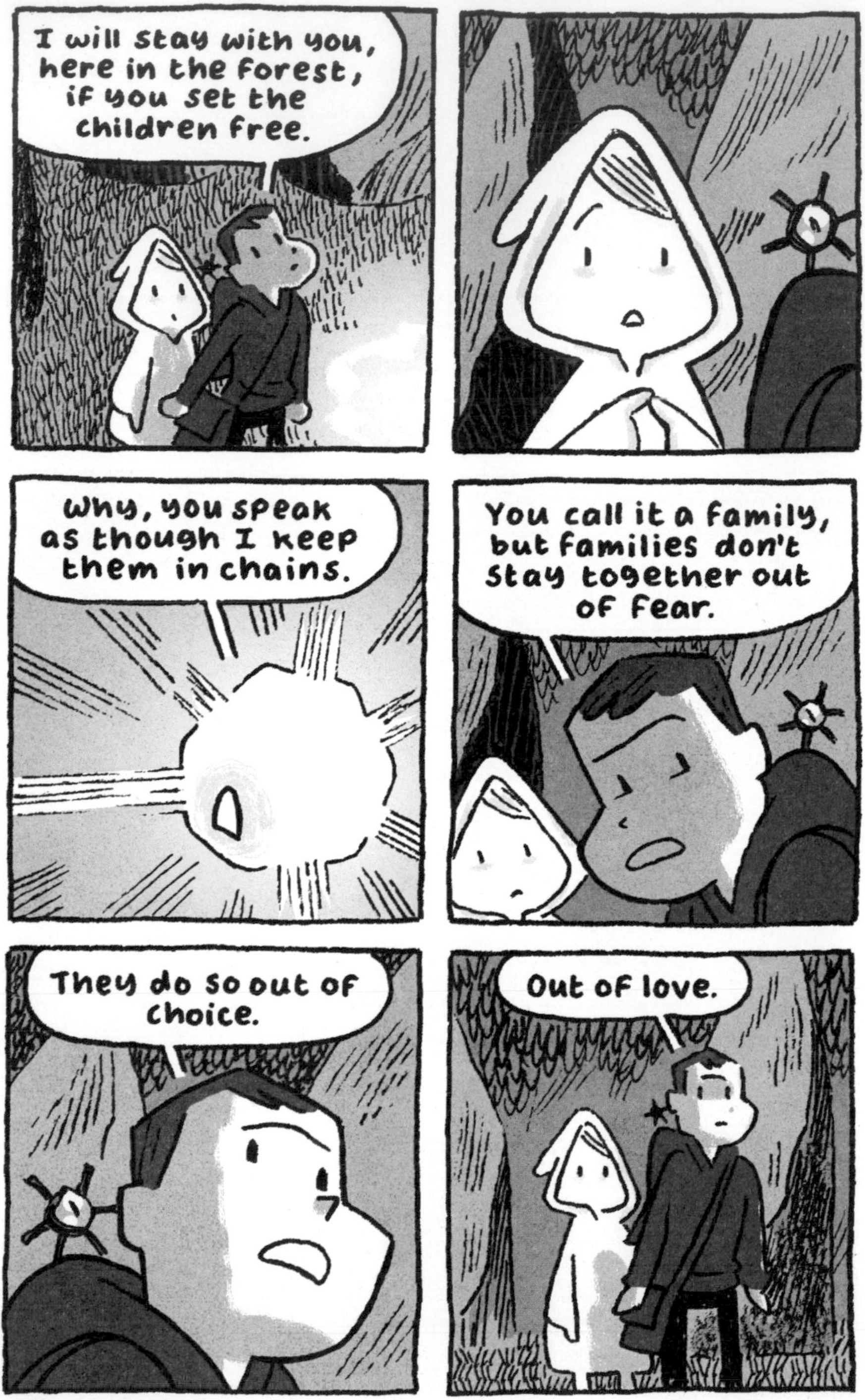
I will stay with you, here in the forest, if you set the children free.
Why, you speak as though I keep them in chains.
You call it a family, but families don't stay together out of fear.
They do so out of choice.
Out of love.

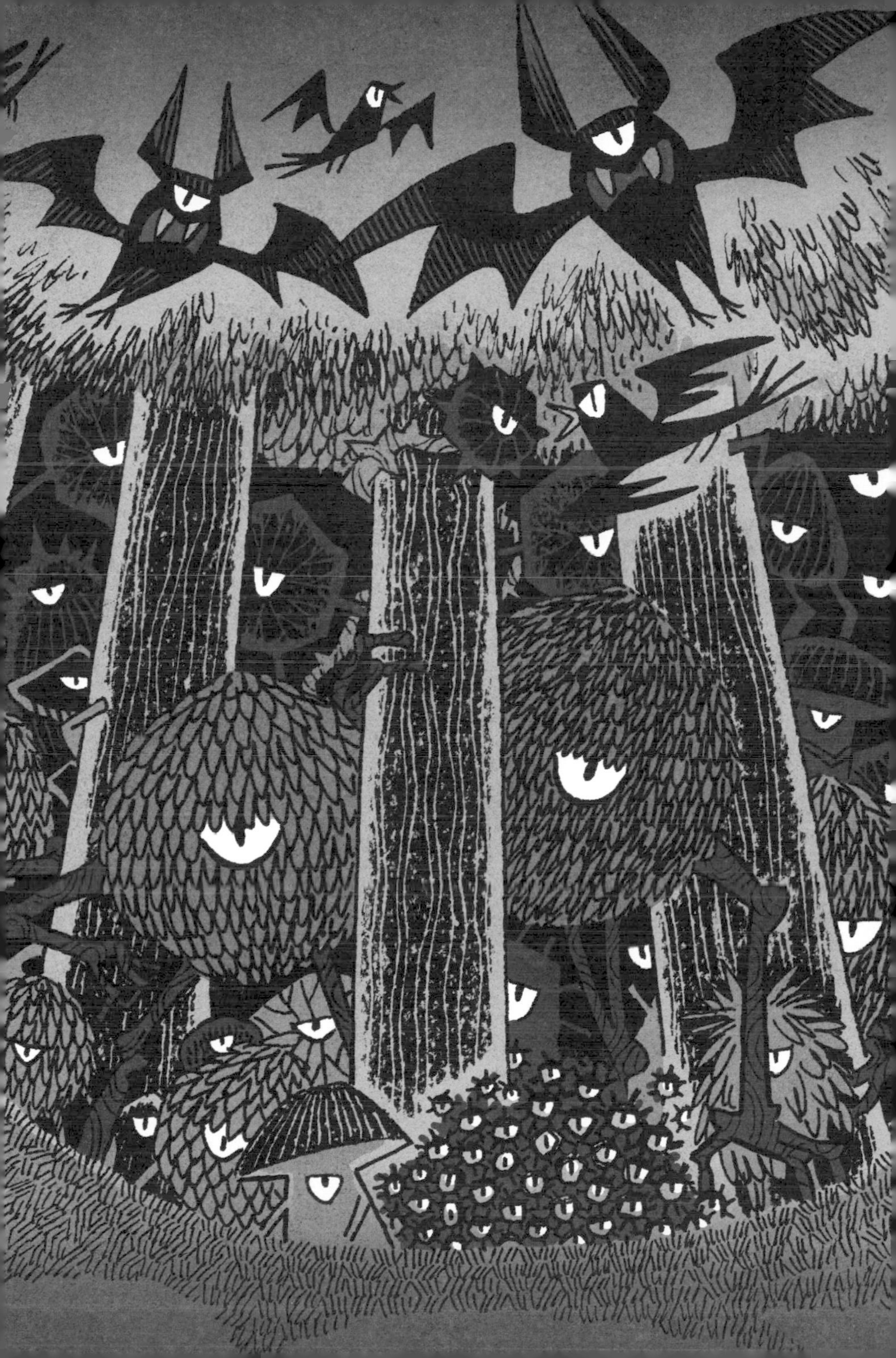

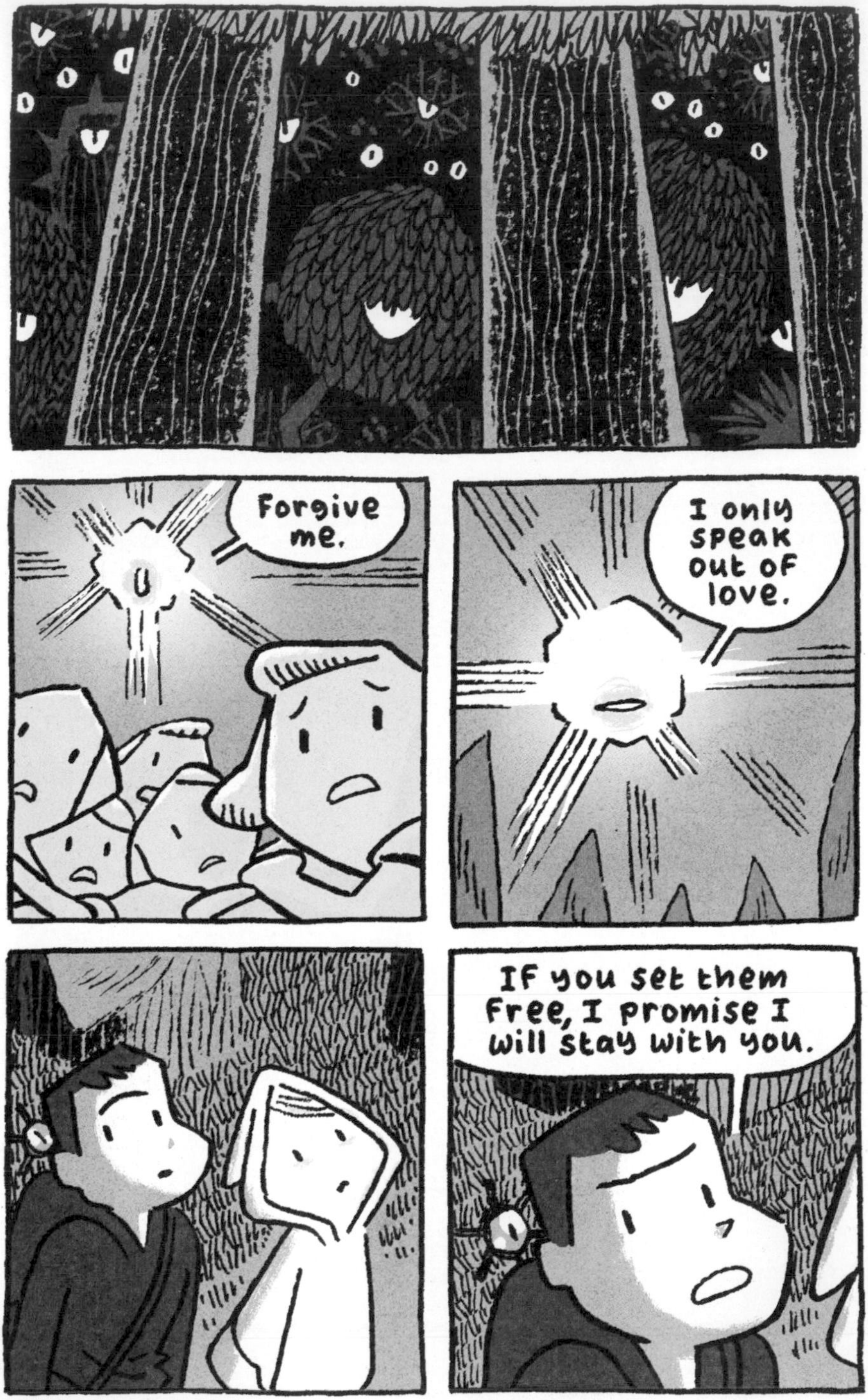
Forgive me.
I only speak out of love.
If you set them free, I promise I will stay with you.

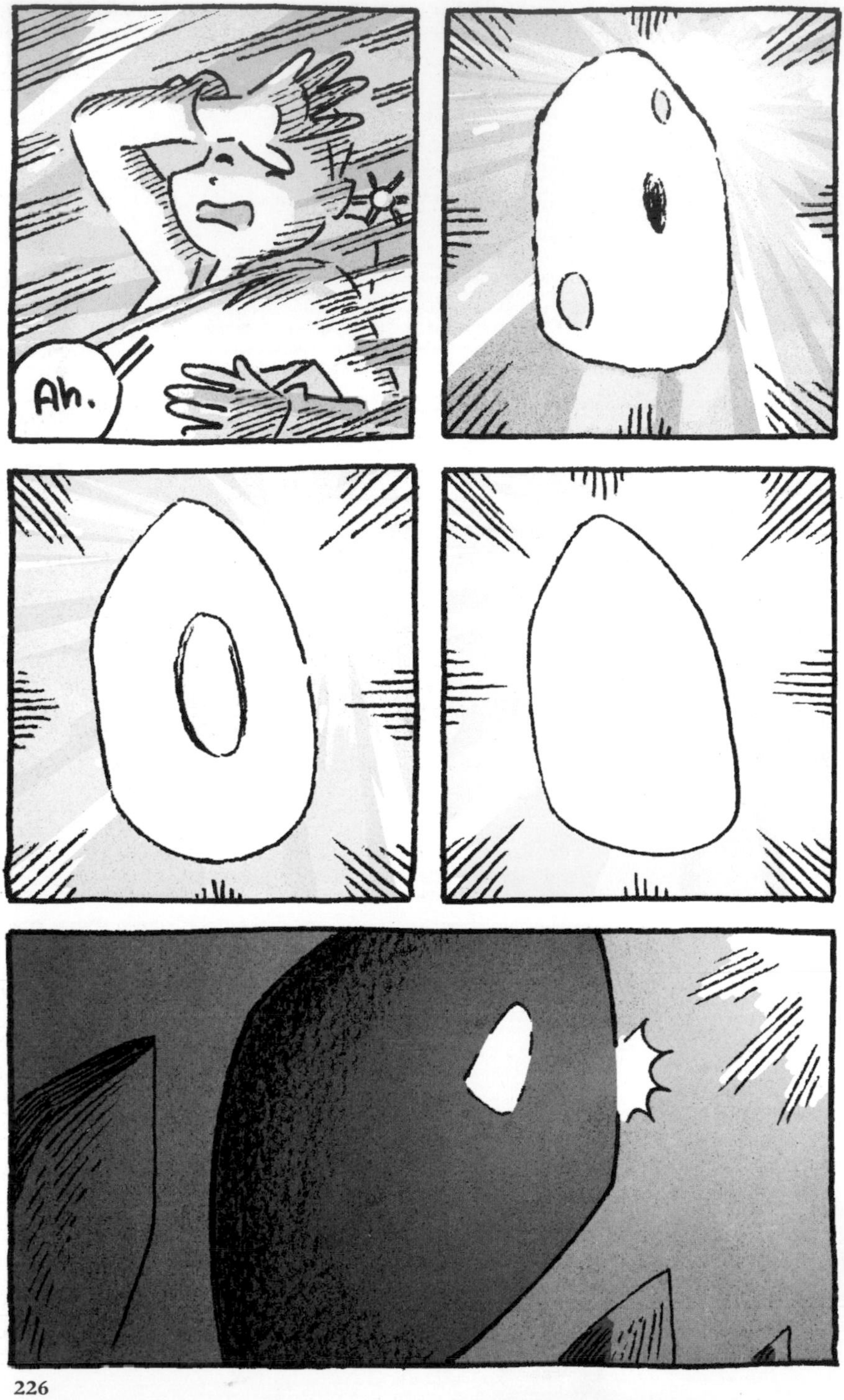
Ah.

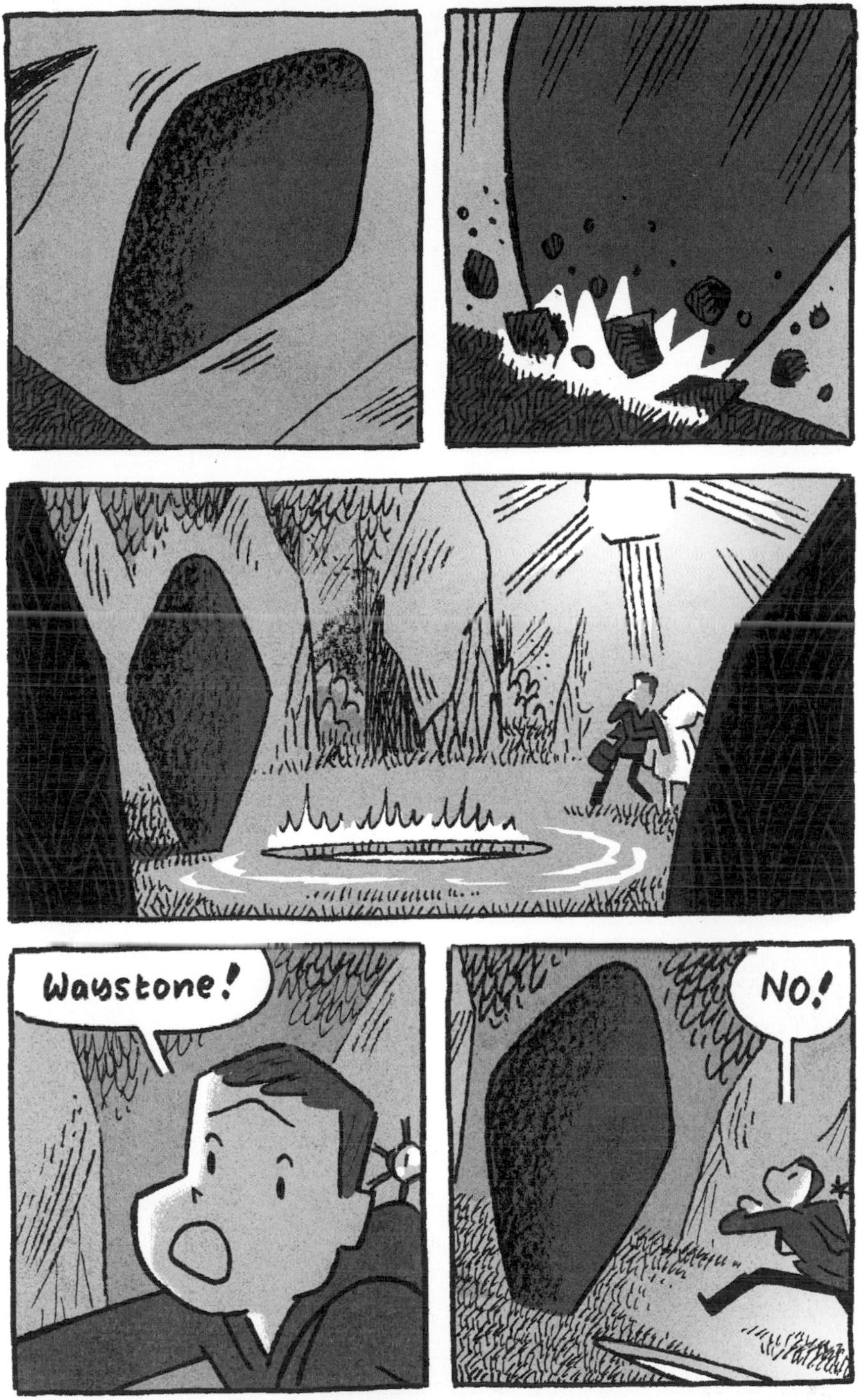
Waystone!
NO!

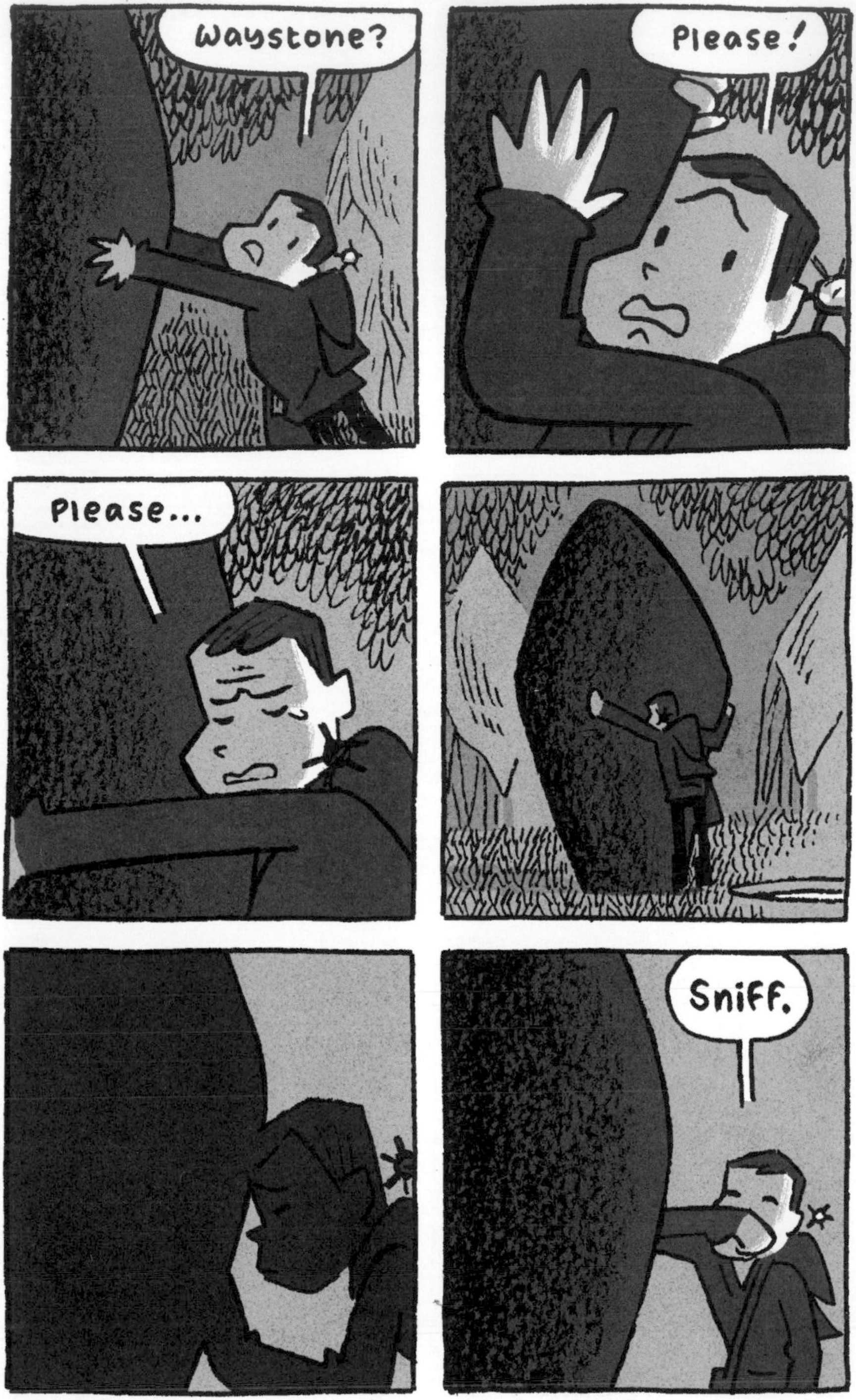
Waystone?
Please!
Please...
Sniff.

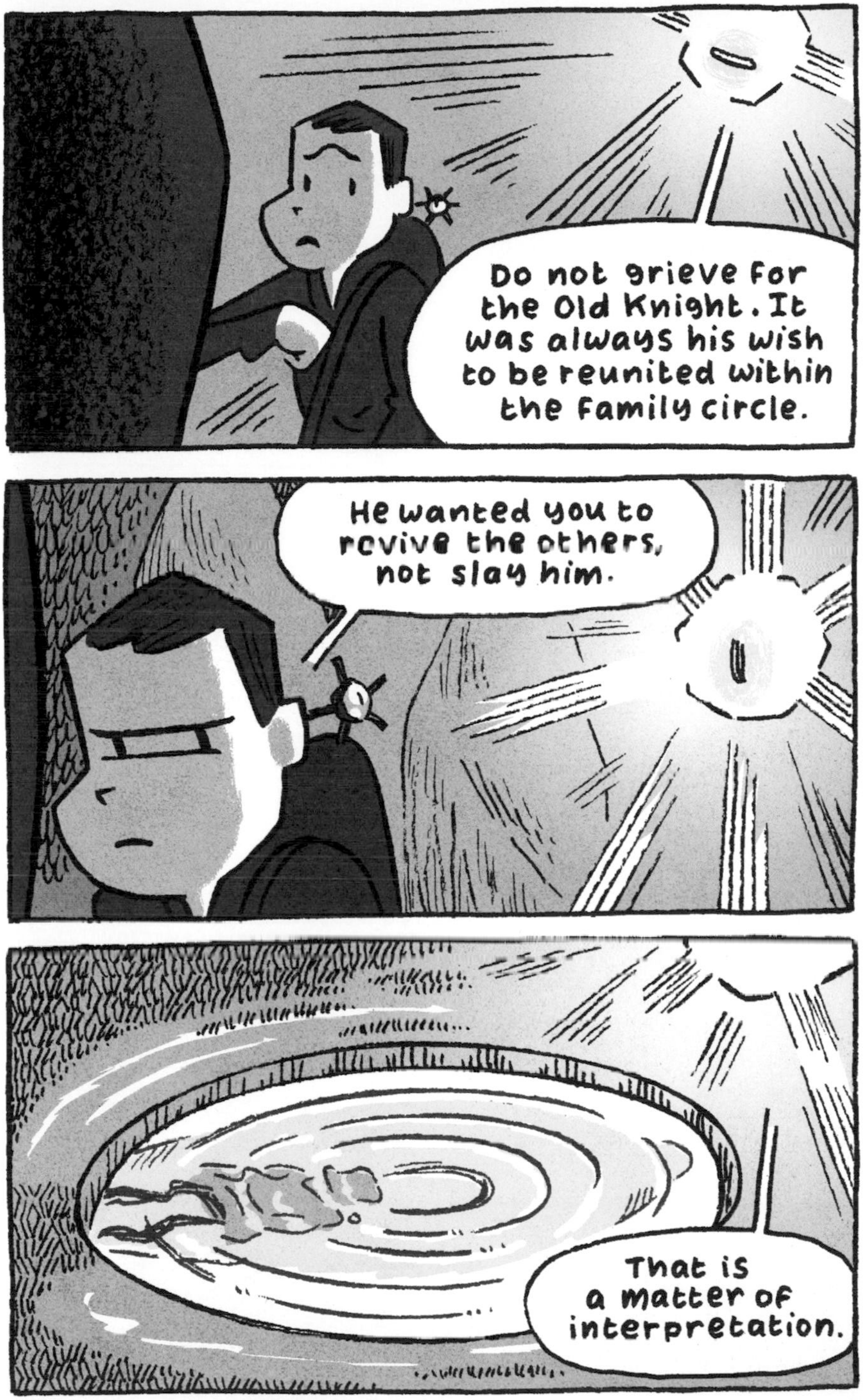
Do not grieve for the Old Knight. It was always his wish to be reunited within the family circle.
He wanted you to revive the others, not slay him.
That is a matter of interpretation.

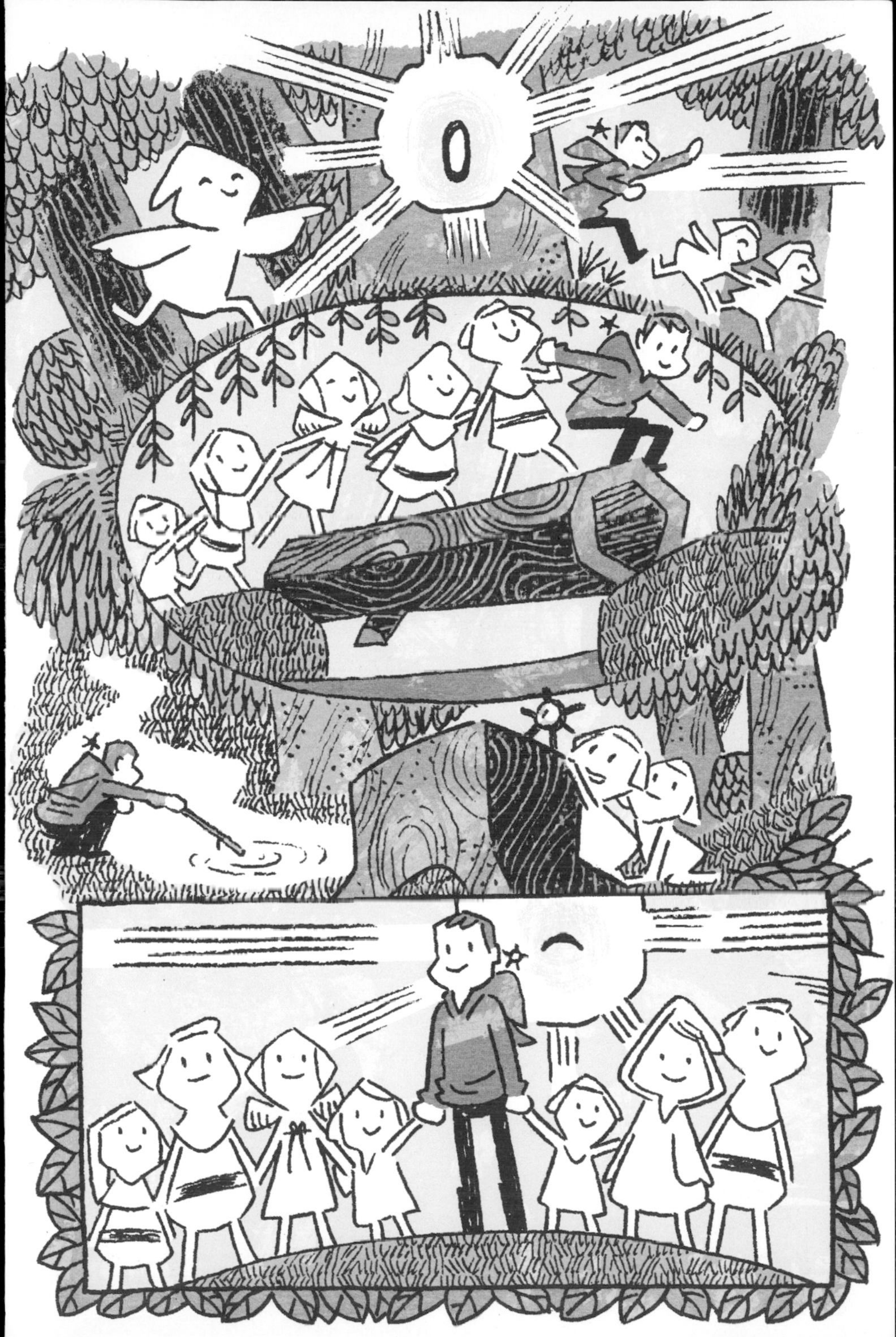

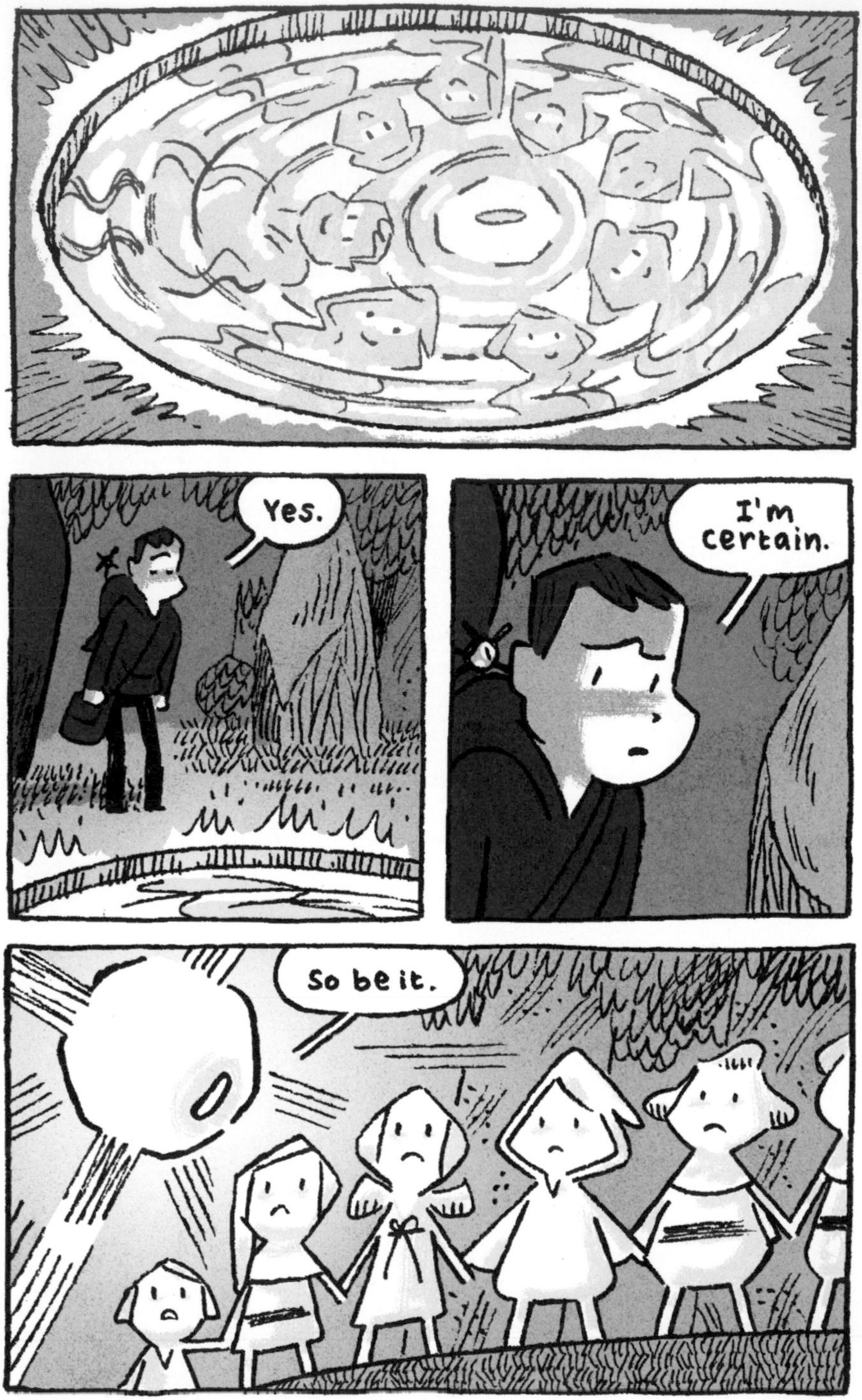
Yes.
I'm certain.
So be it.

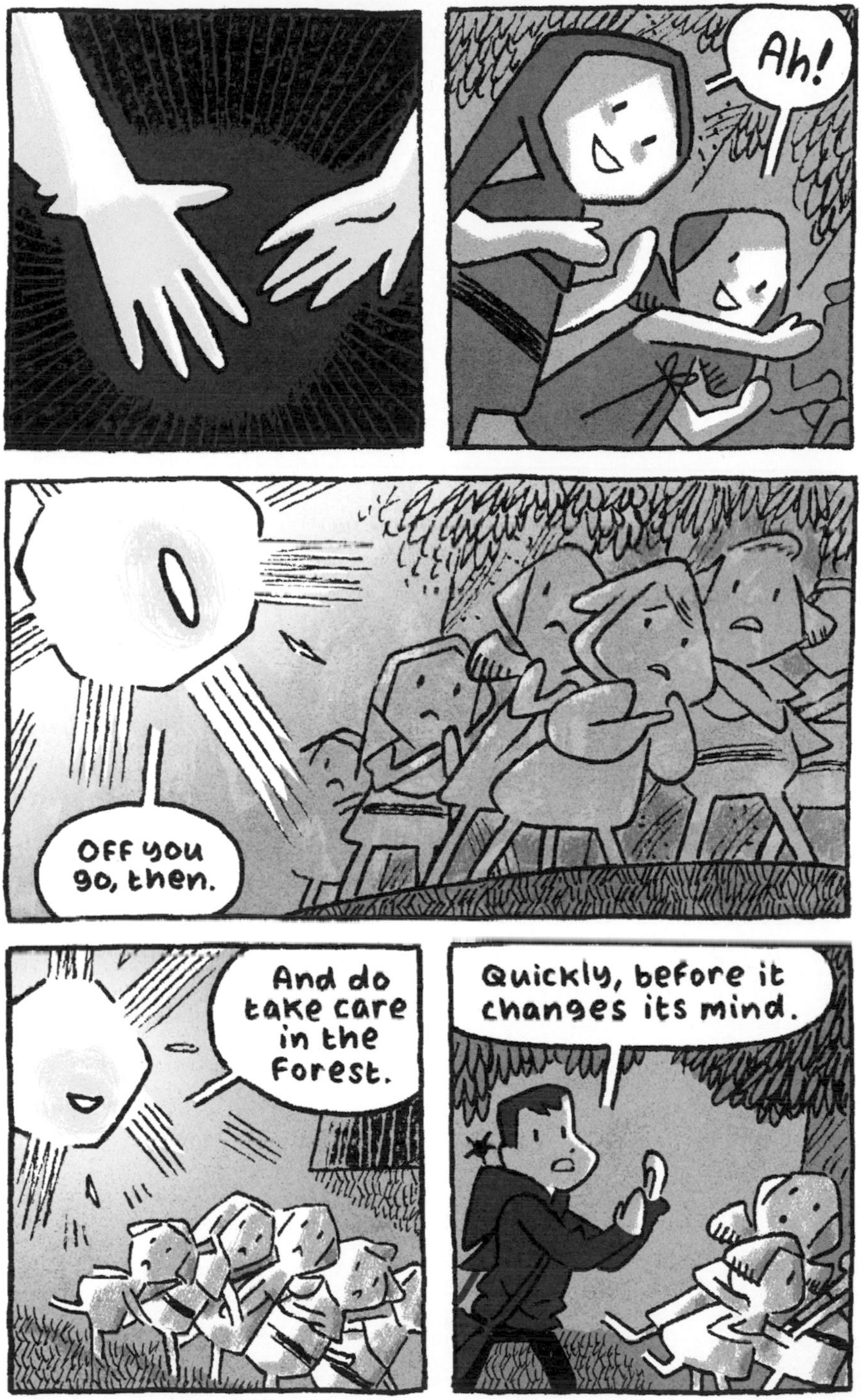
Ah!
Off you go, then.
And do take care in the Forest.
Quickly, before it changes its mind.

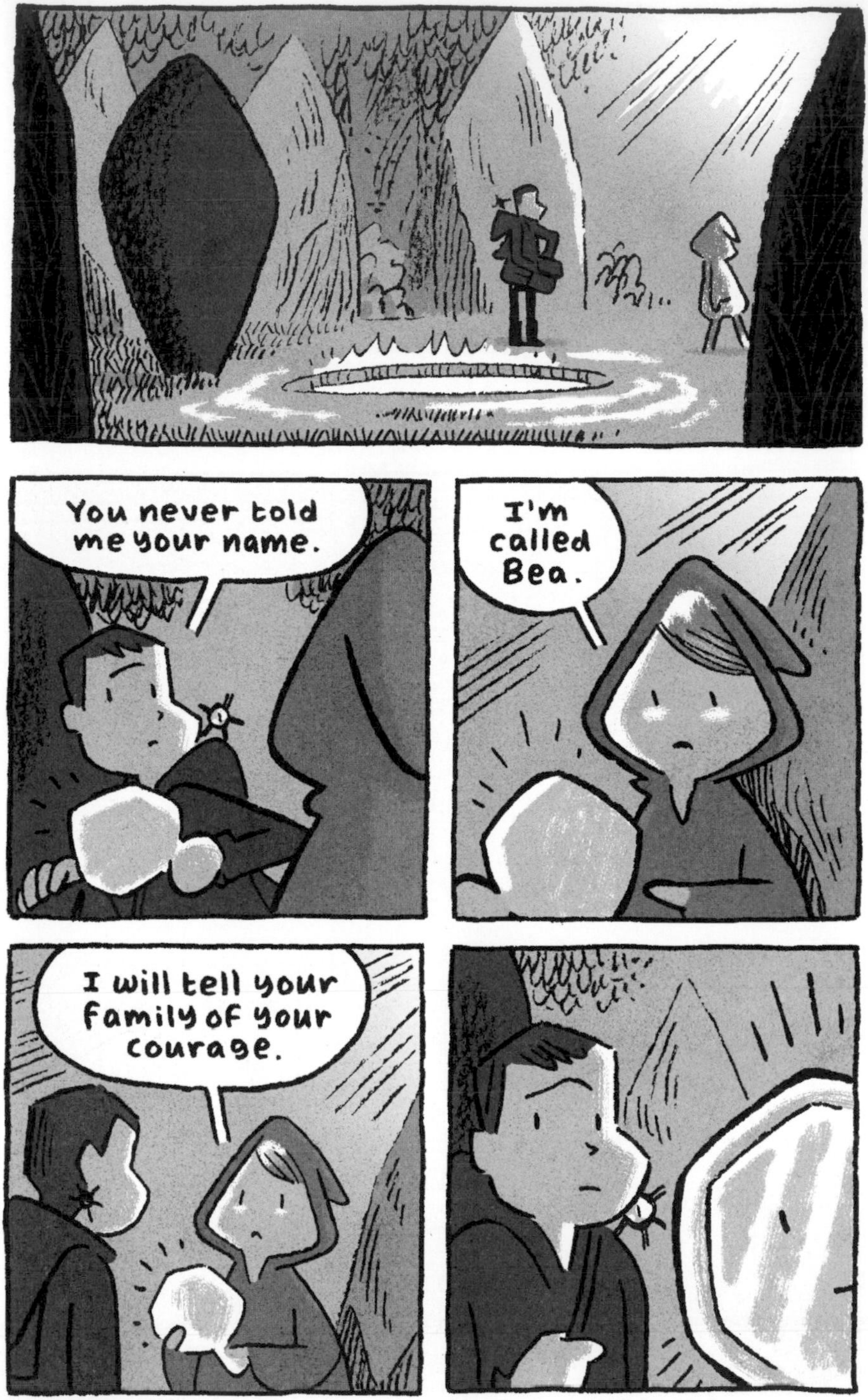
You never told me your name.
I'm called Bea.
I will tell your family of your courage.

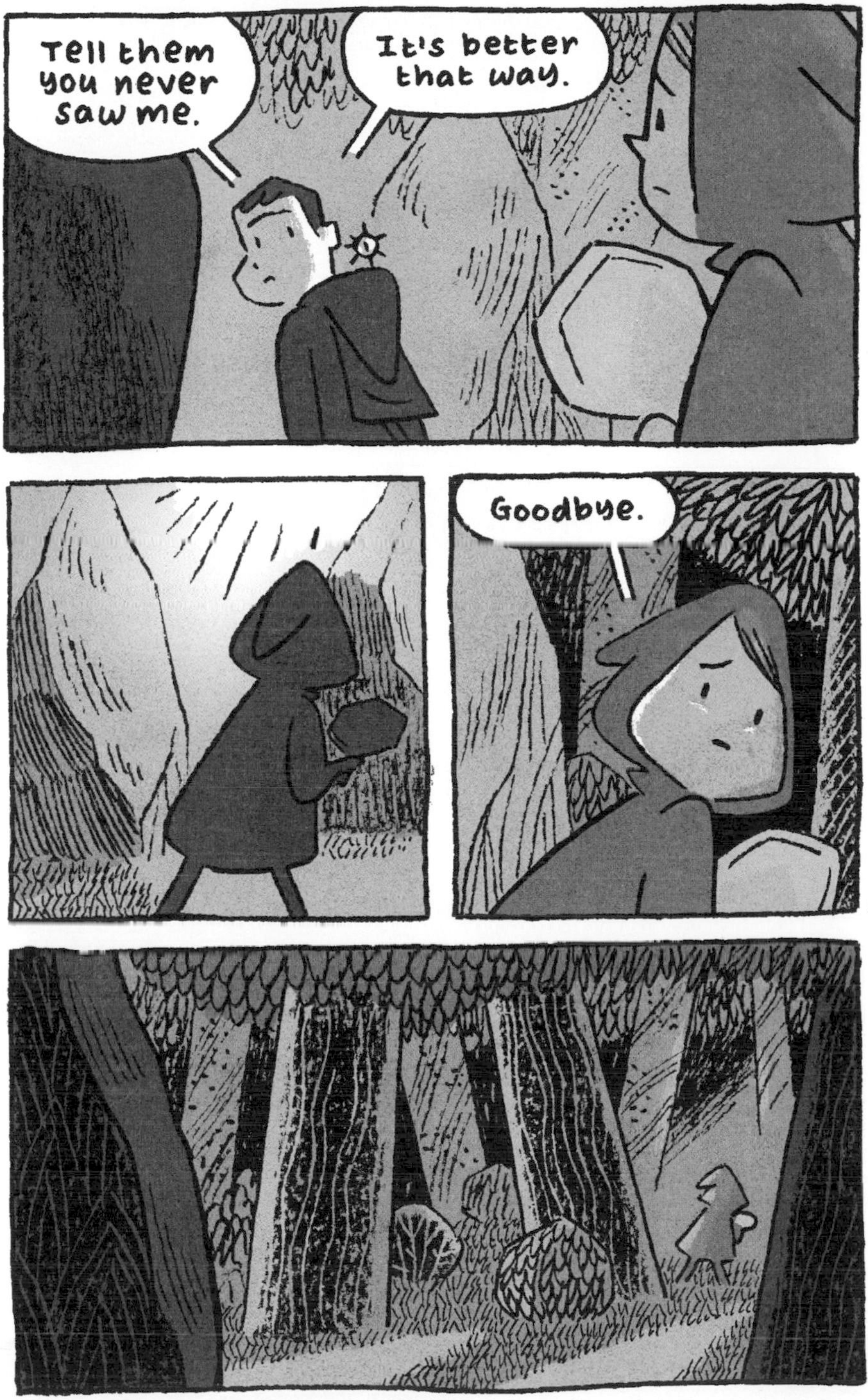
Tell them you never saw me.
It's better that way.
Goodbye.

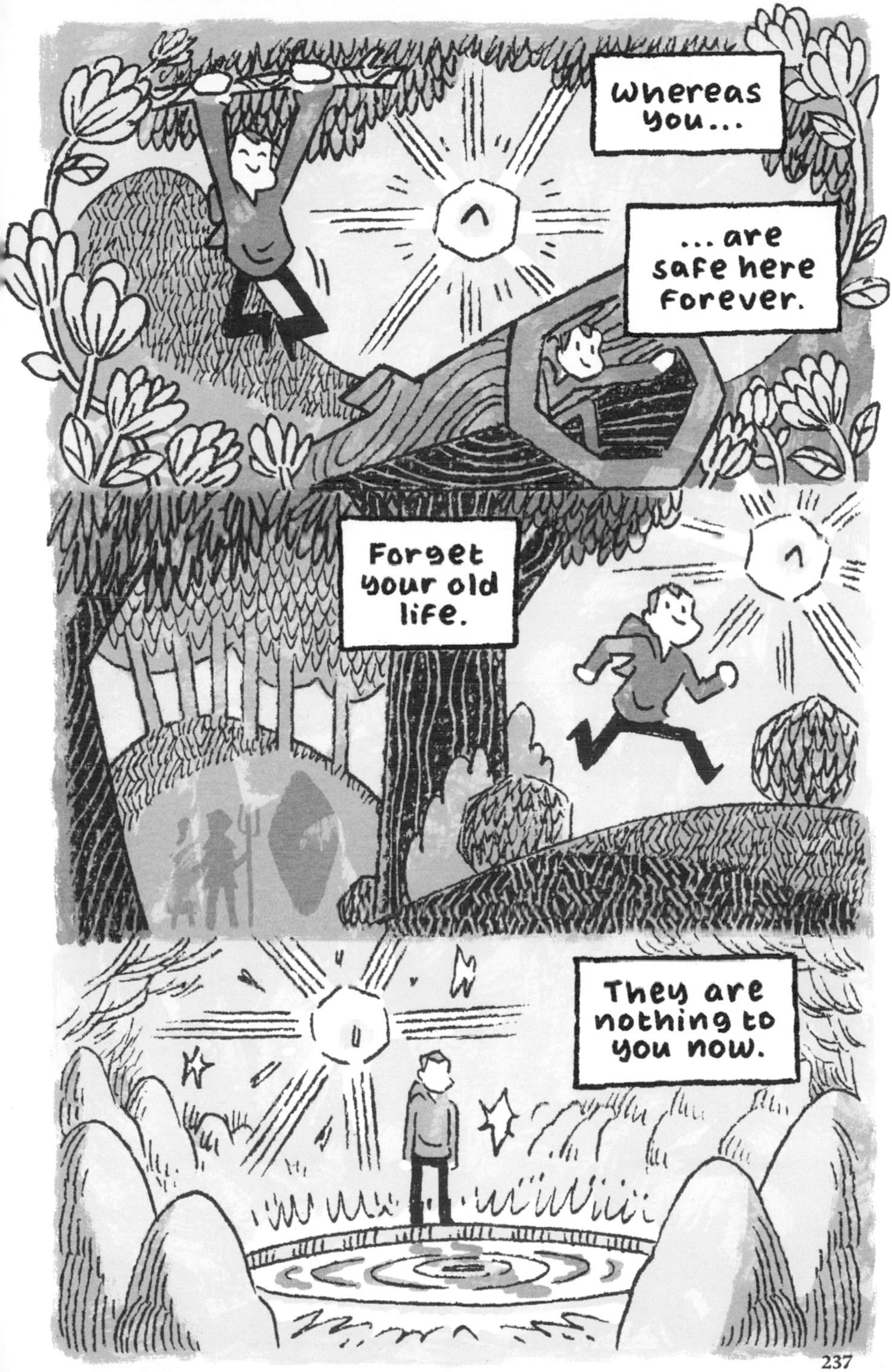
Whereas you...
...are safe here forever.
Forget your old life.
They are nothing to you now.

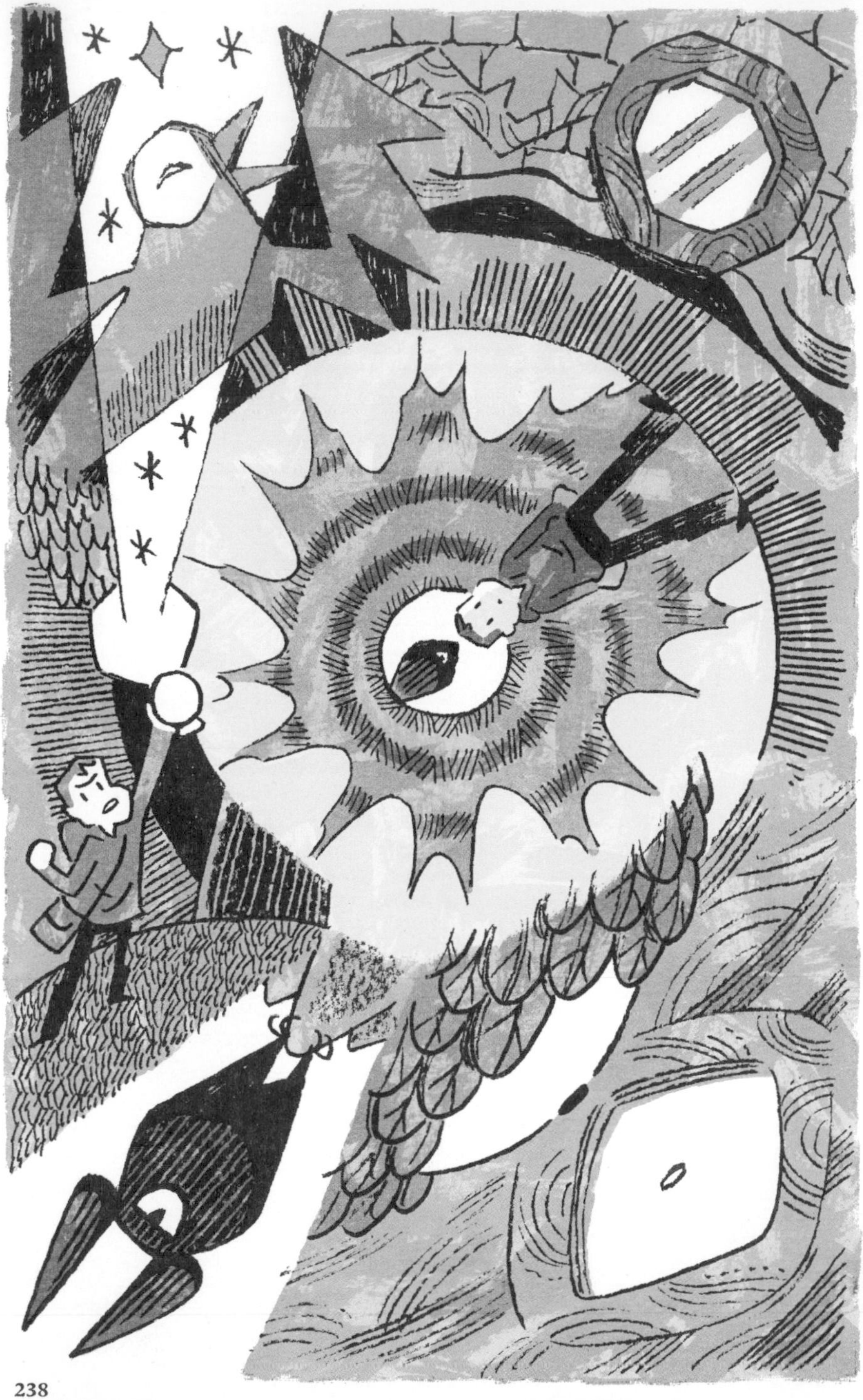

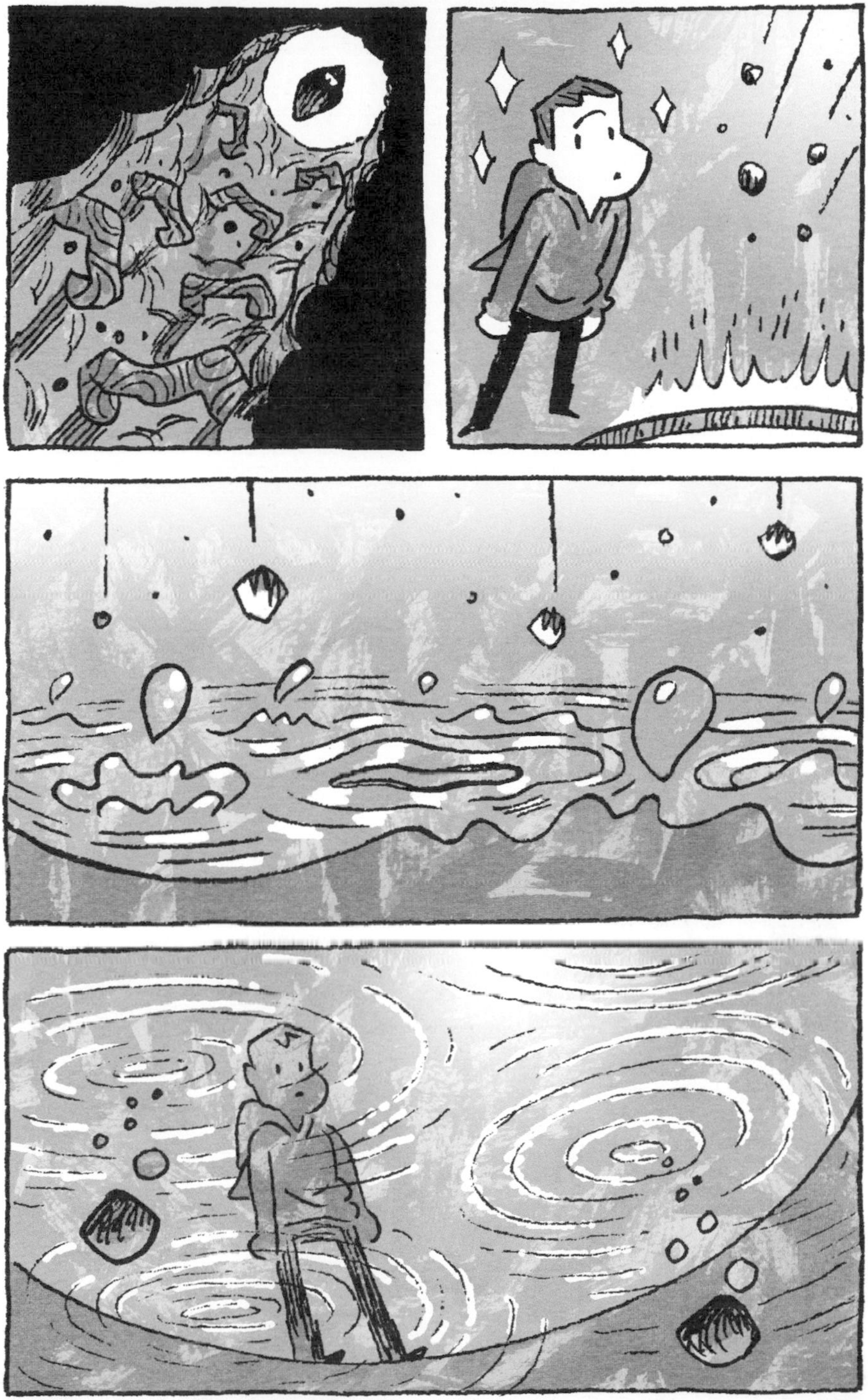

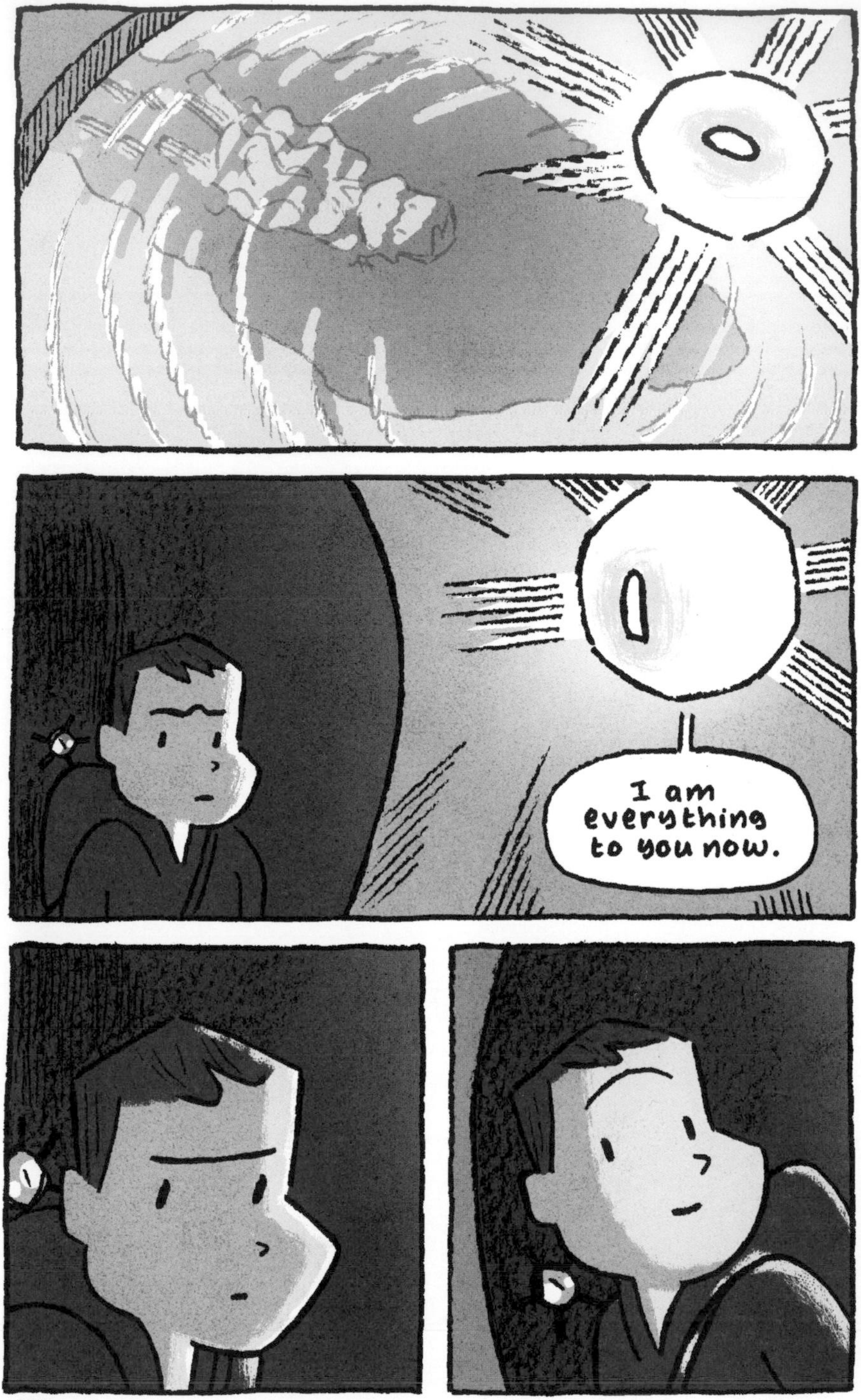
I am everything to you now.

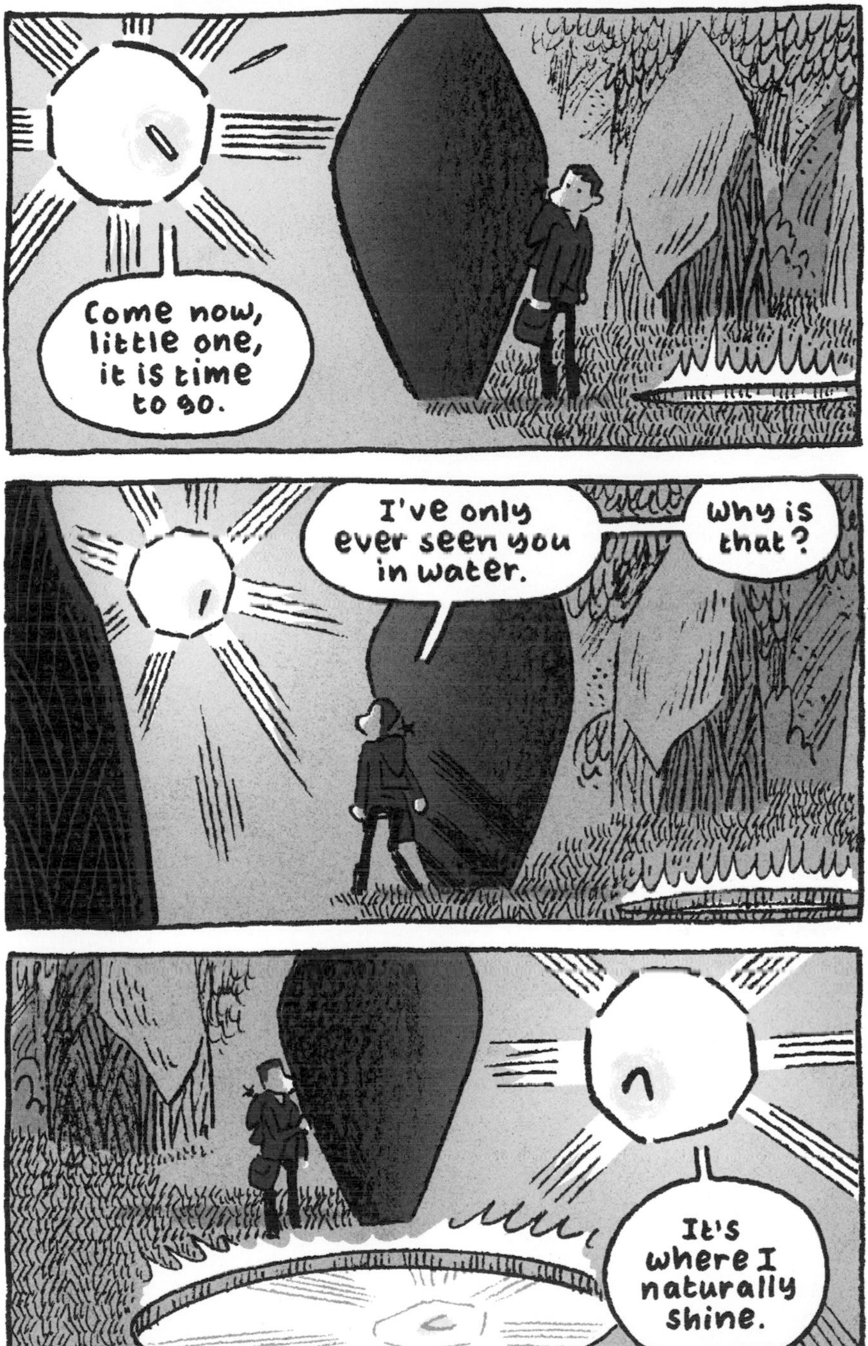
Come now, little one, it is time to go.
I've only ever seen you in water.
Why is that?
It's where I naturally shine.

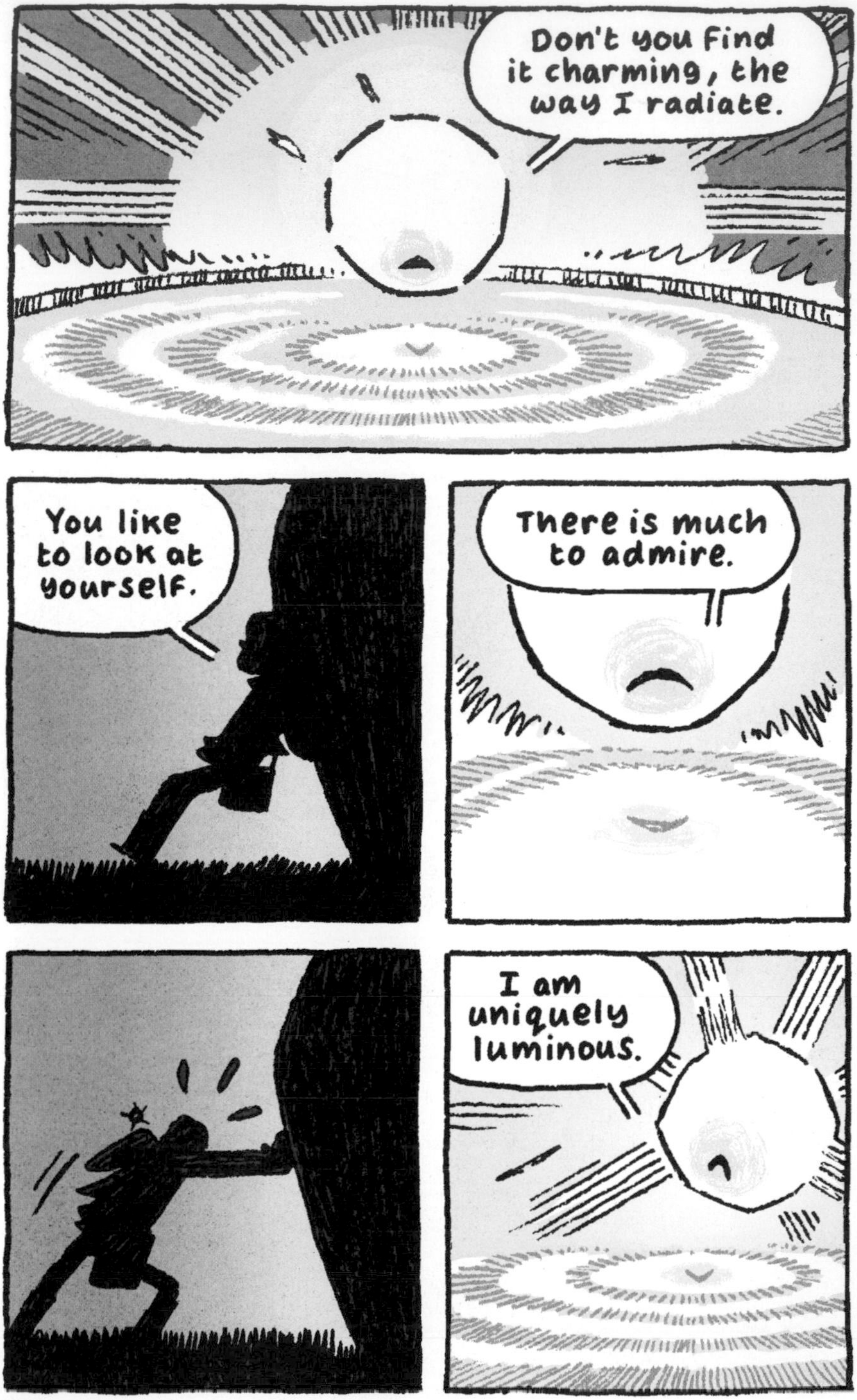
Don't you find it charming, the way I radiate.
You like to look at yourself.
There is much to admire.
I am uniquely luminous.

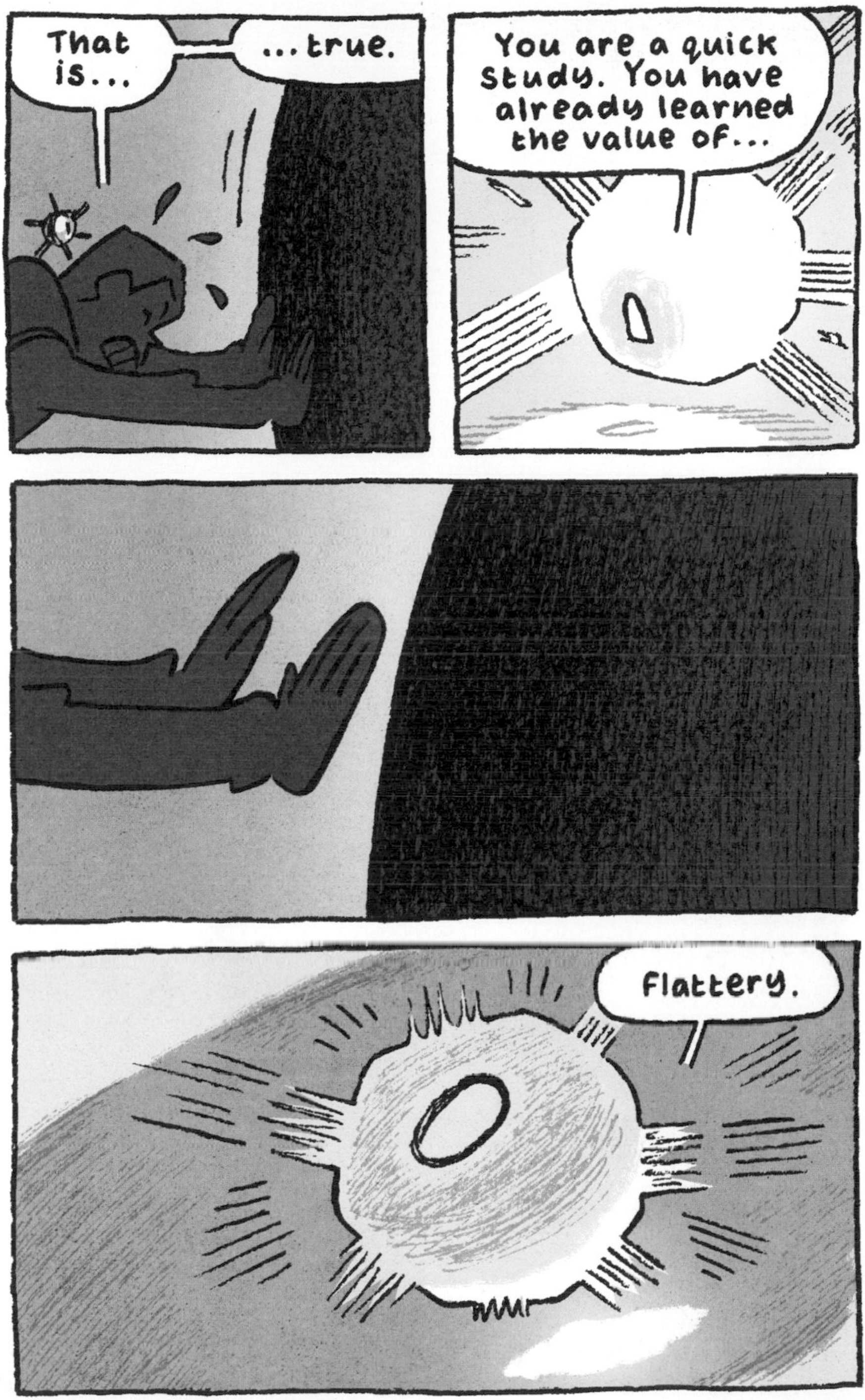
That is...
...true.
You are a quick study. You have already learned the value of...
Flattery.

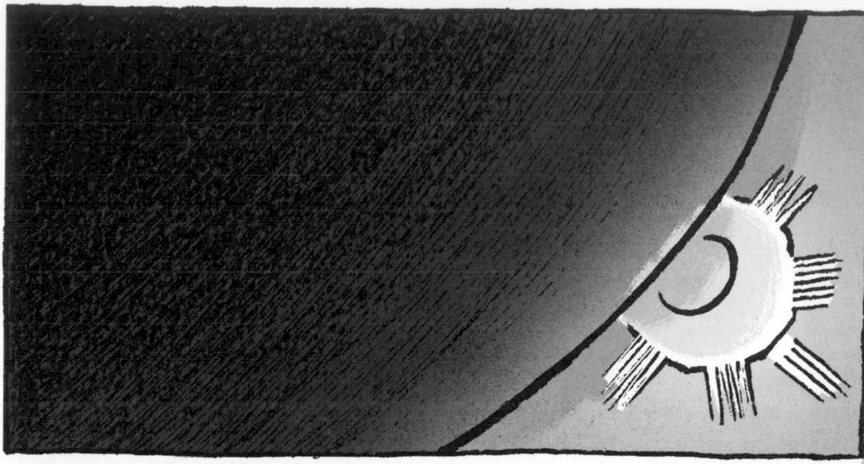

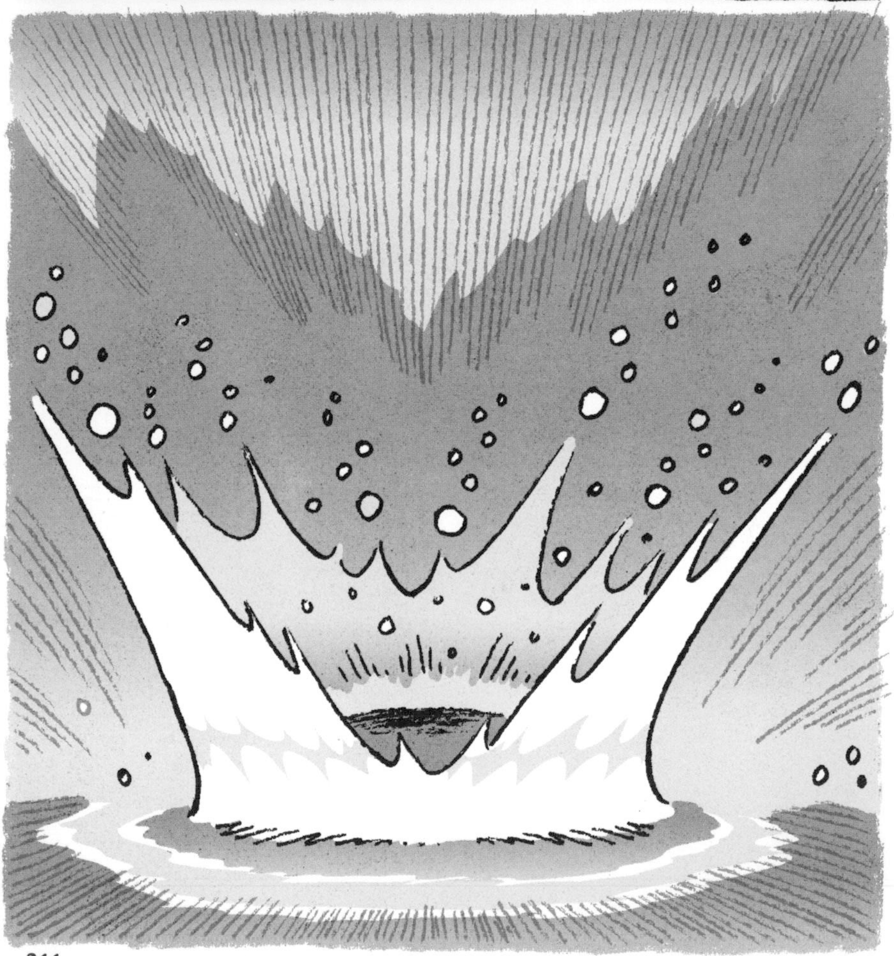

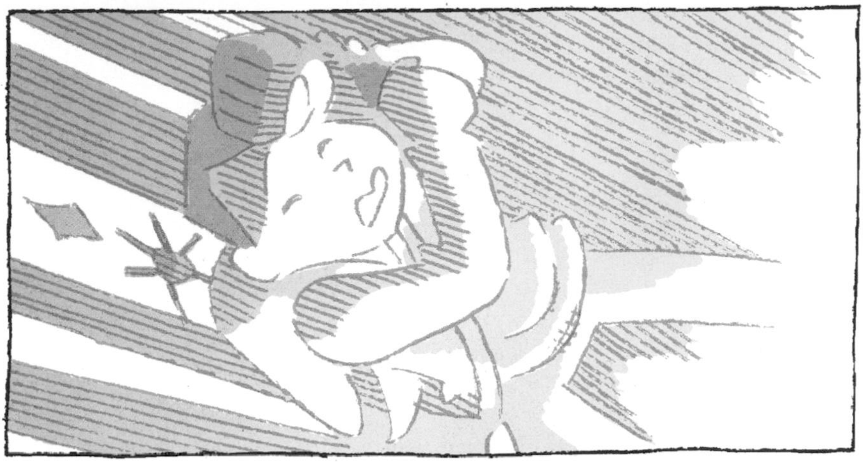
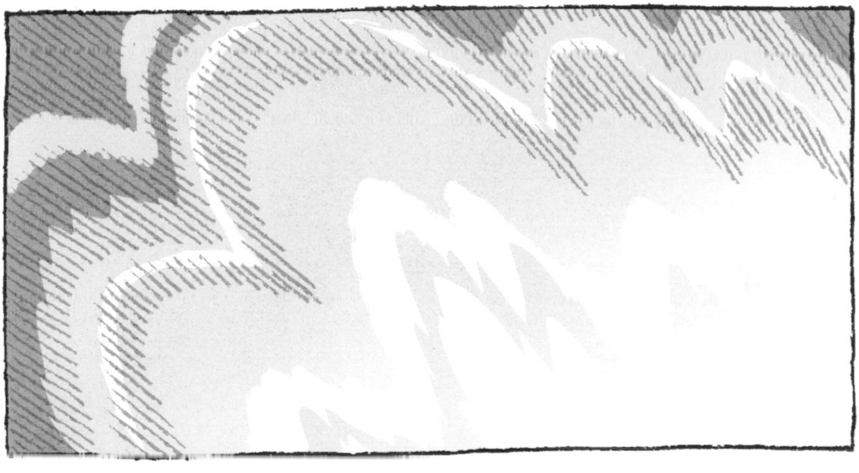
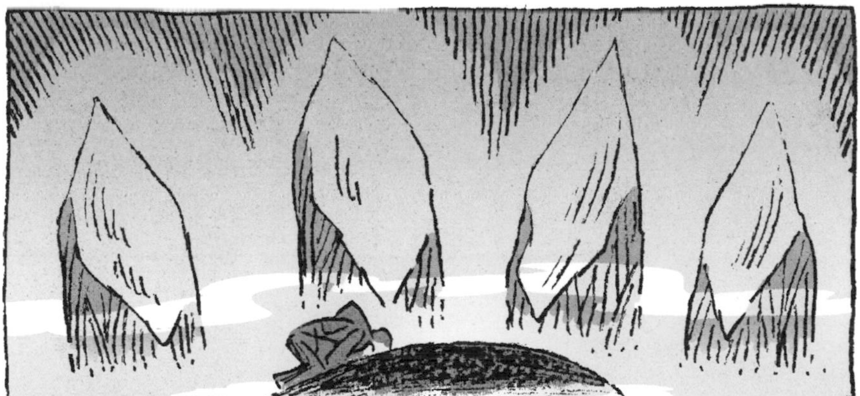

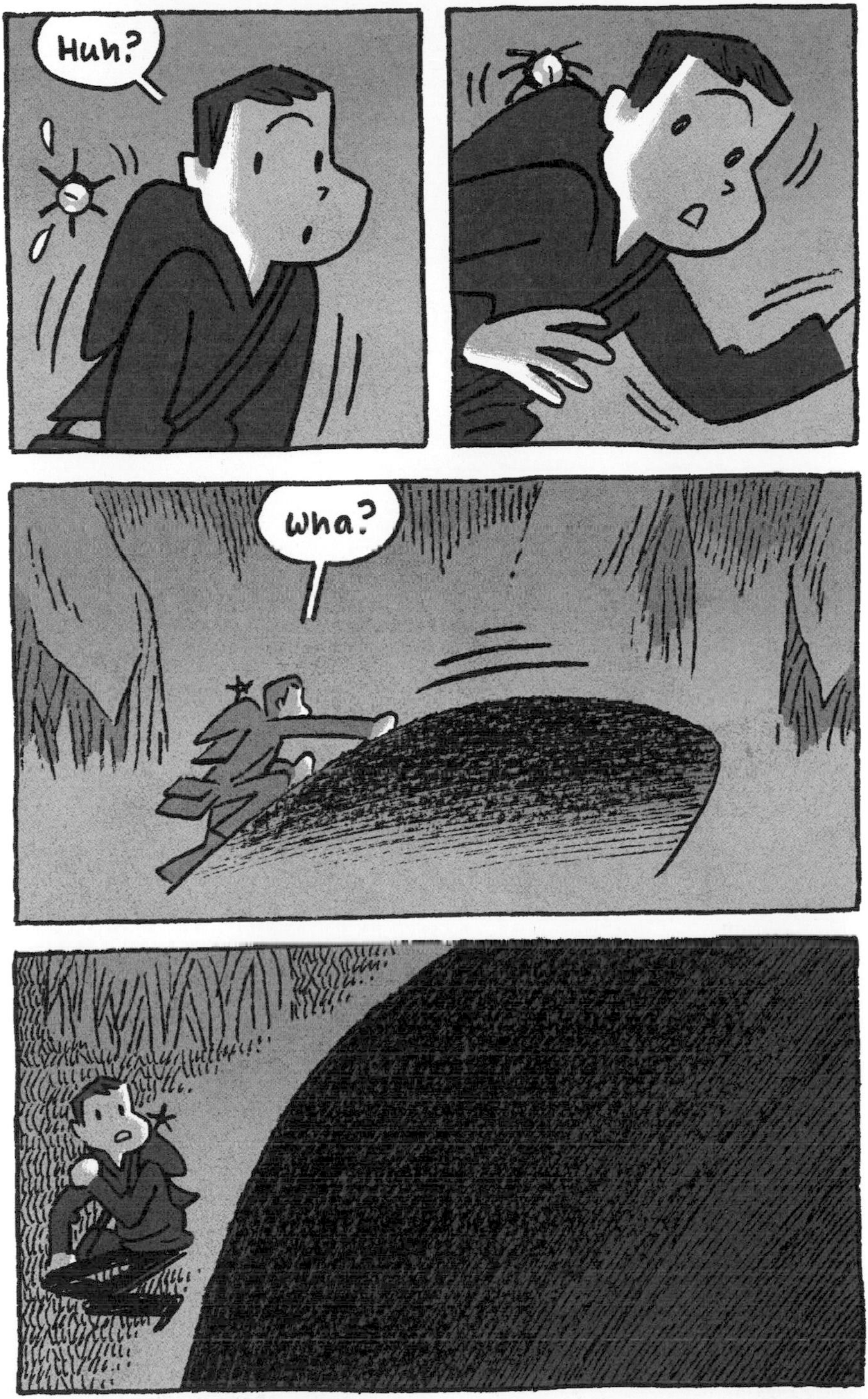
Huh?
Wha?

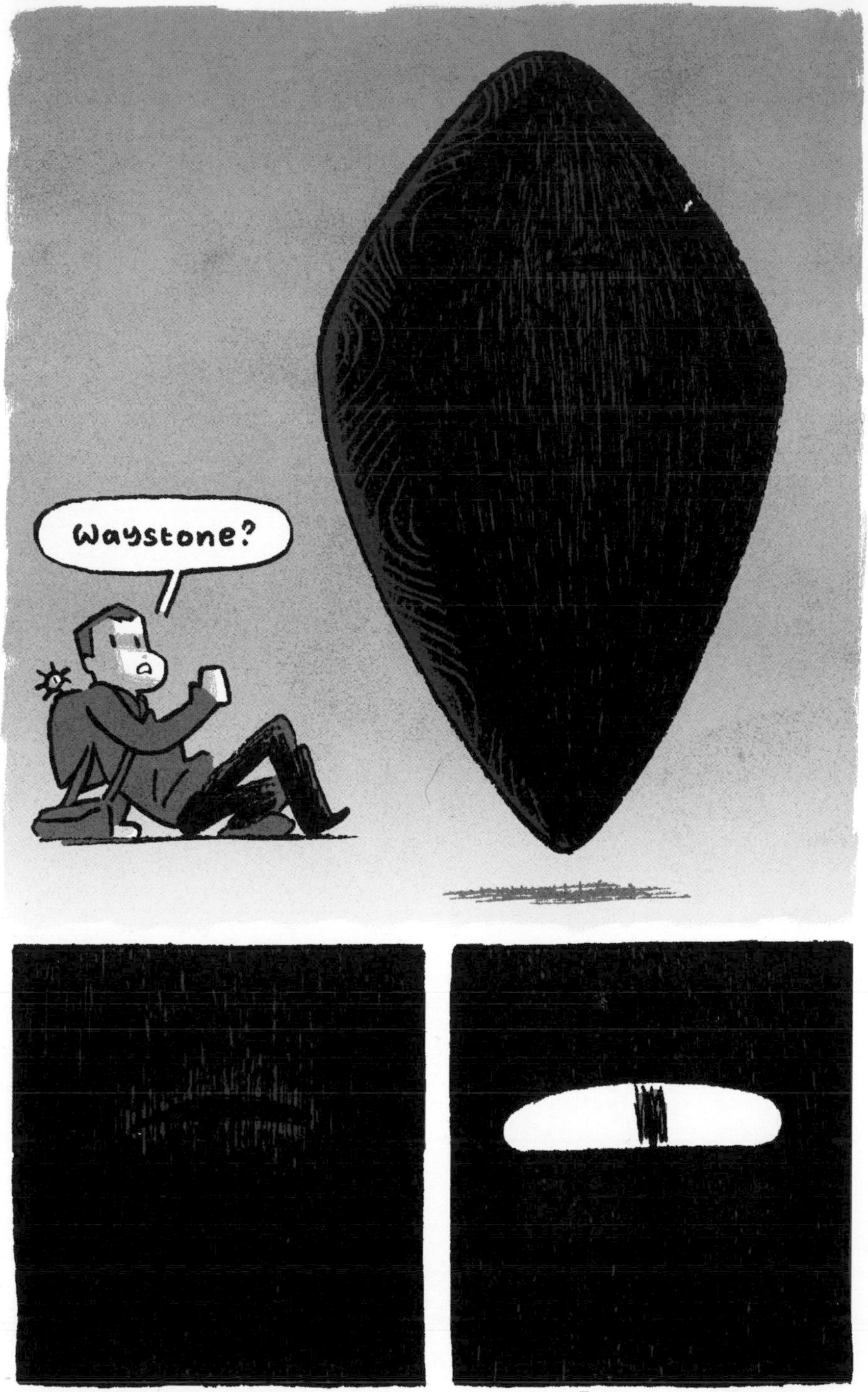
Waystone?

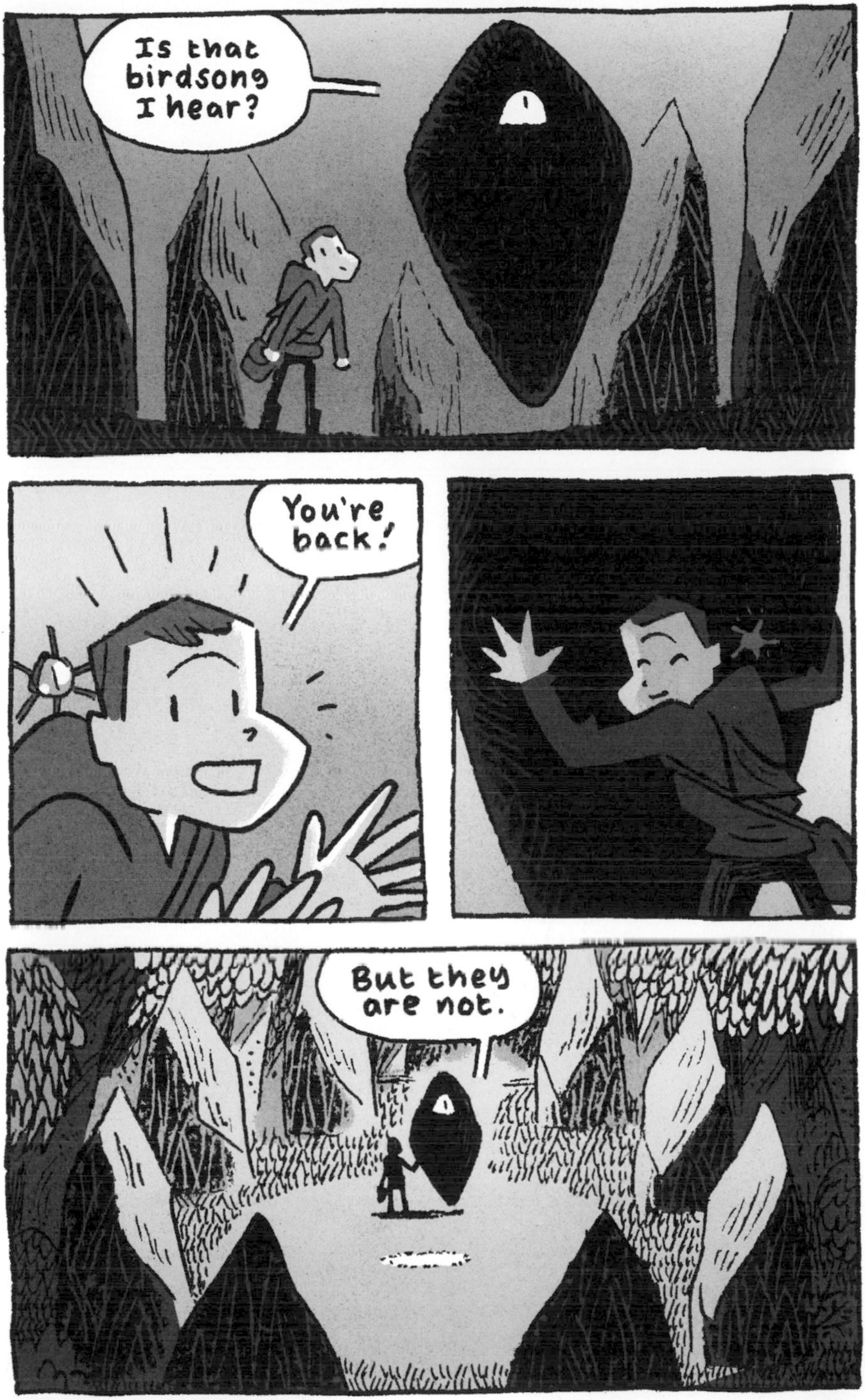
Is that birdsong I hear?
You're back!
But they are not.

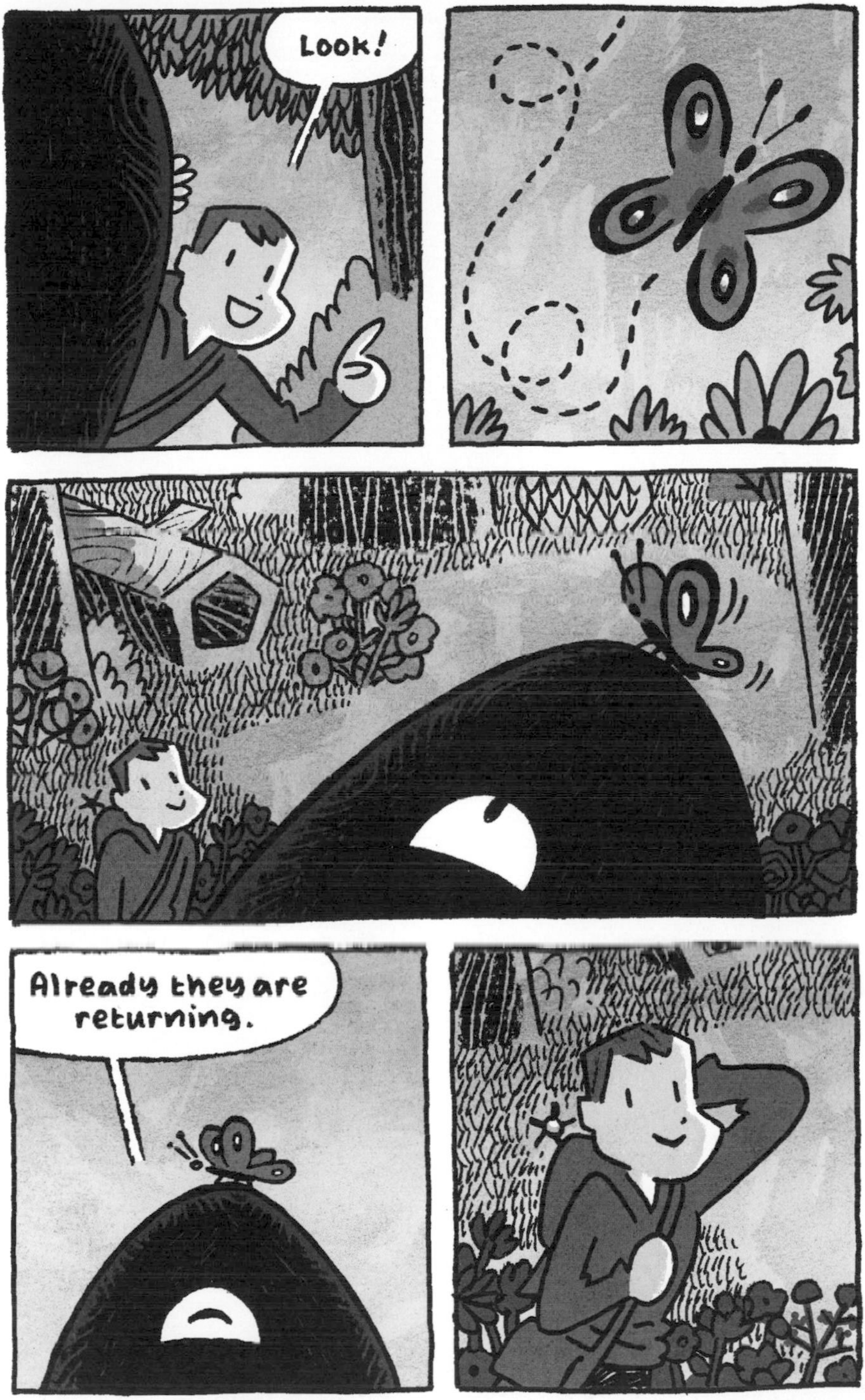
LOOK!
Already they are returning.

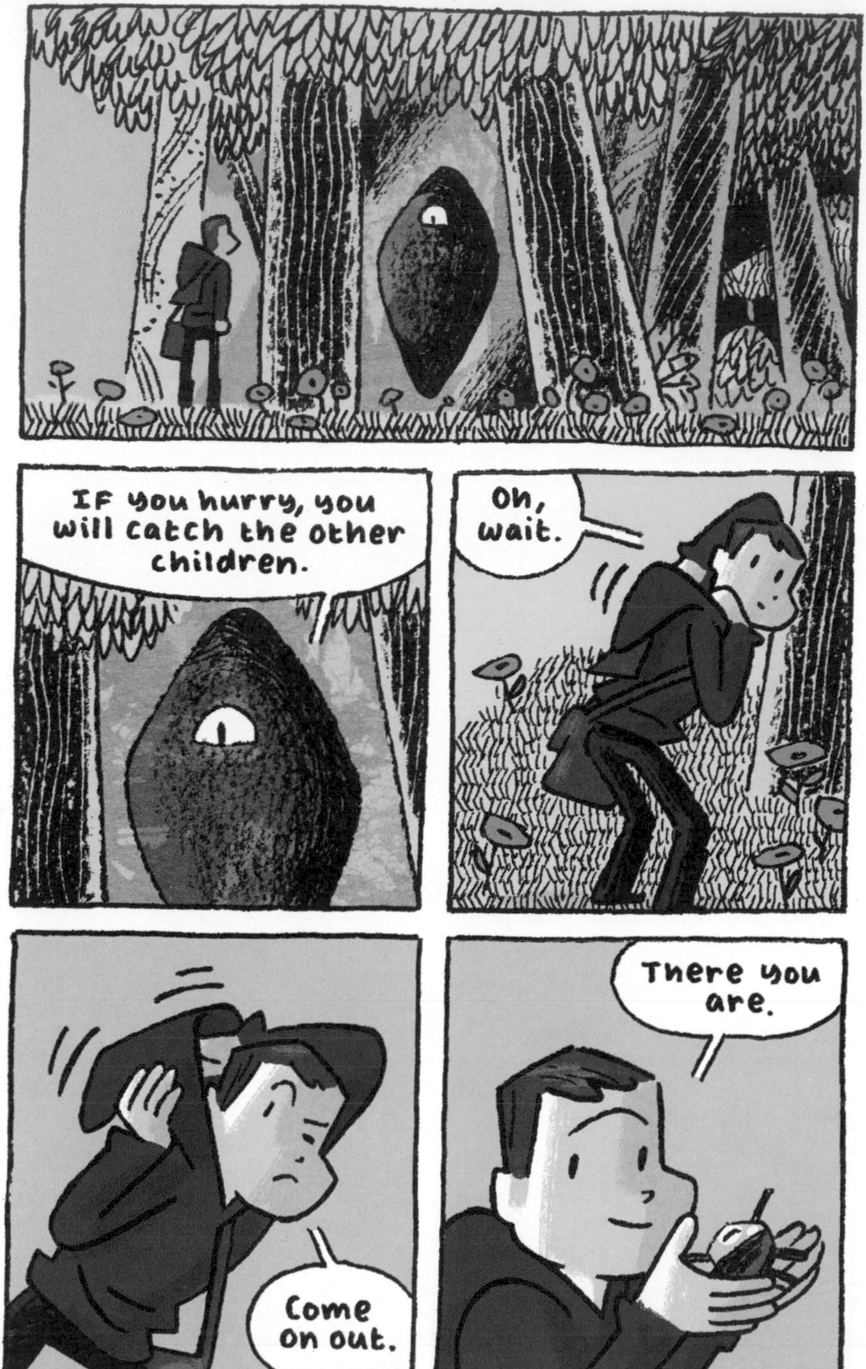
If you hurry, you will catch the other children.
Oh, wait.
Come on out.
There you are.

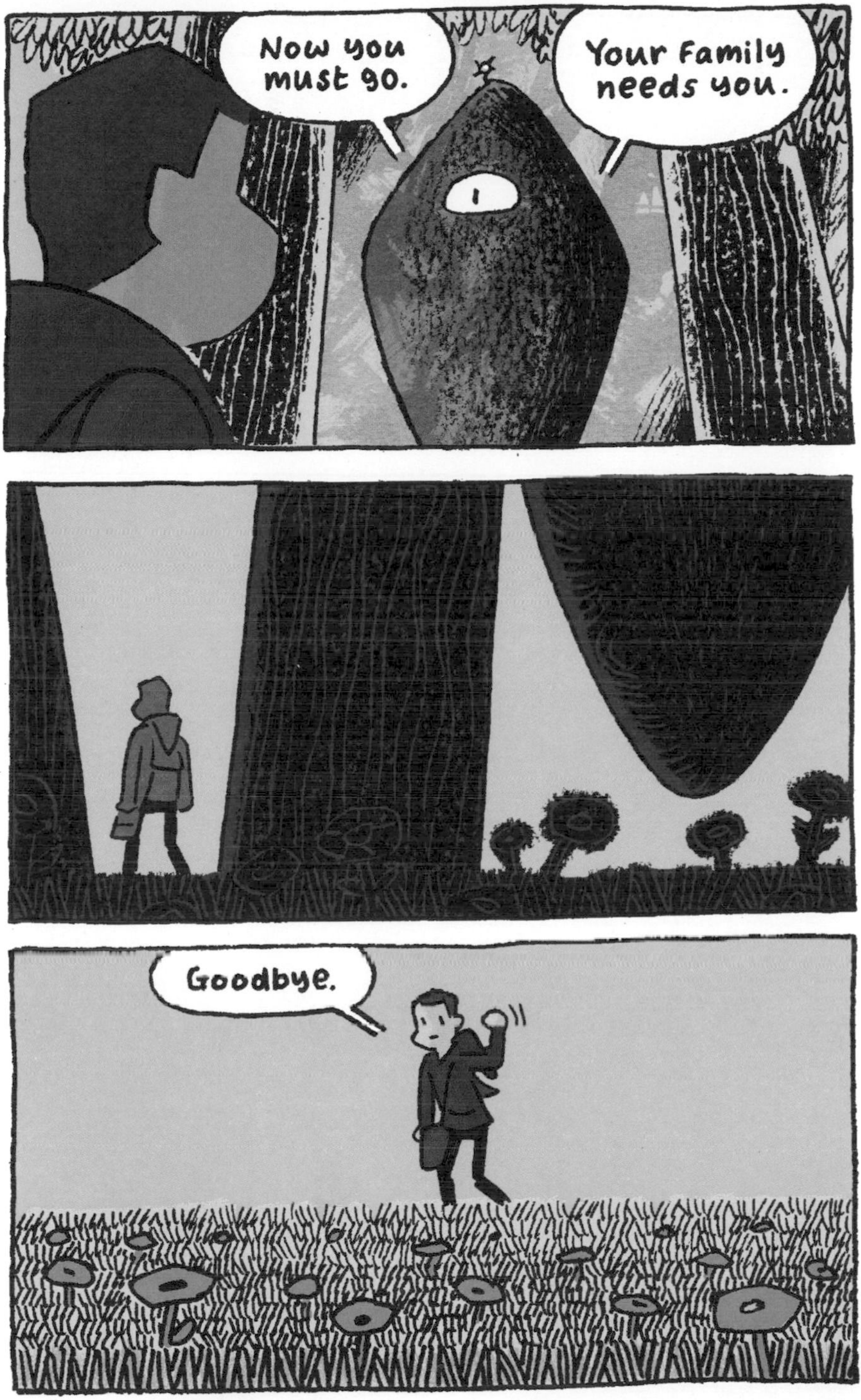
Now you must go.
Your family needs you.
Goodbye.

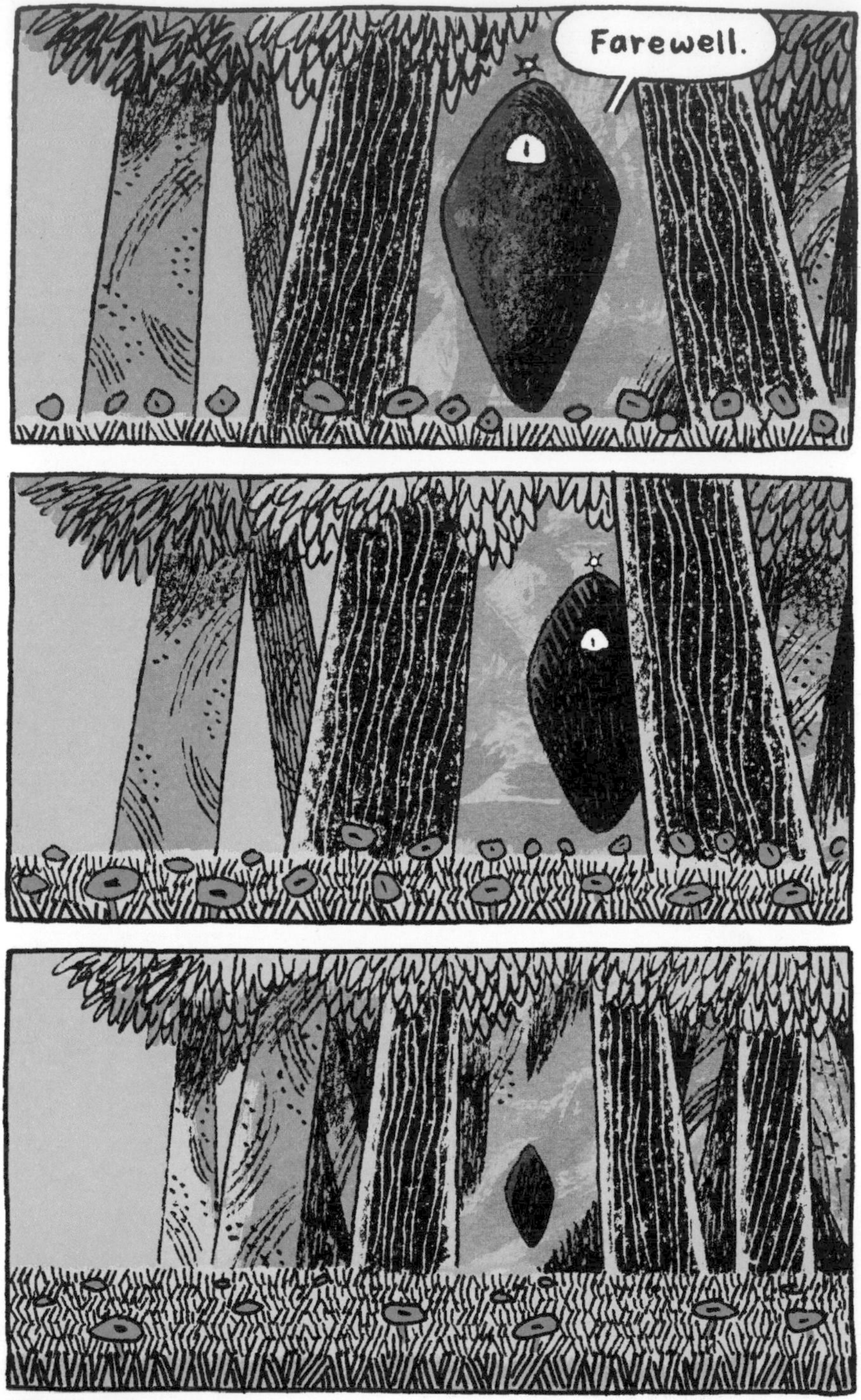
Farewell.

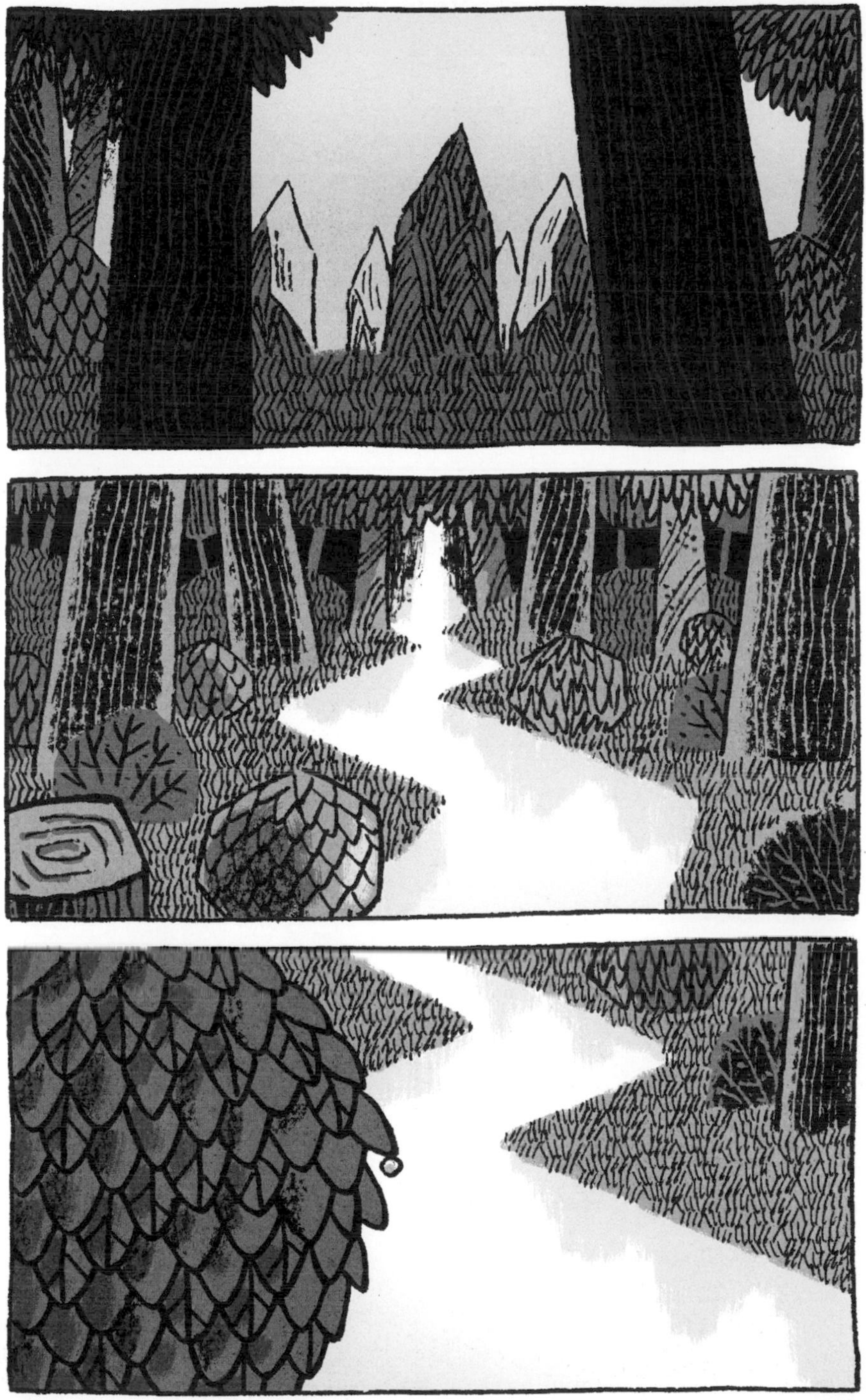

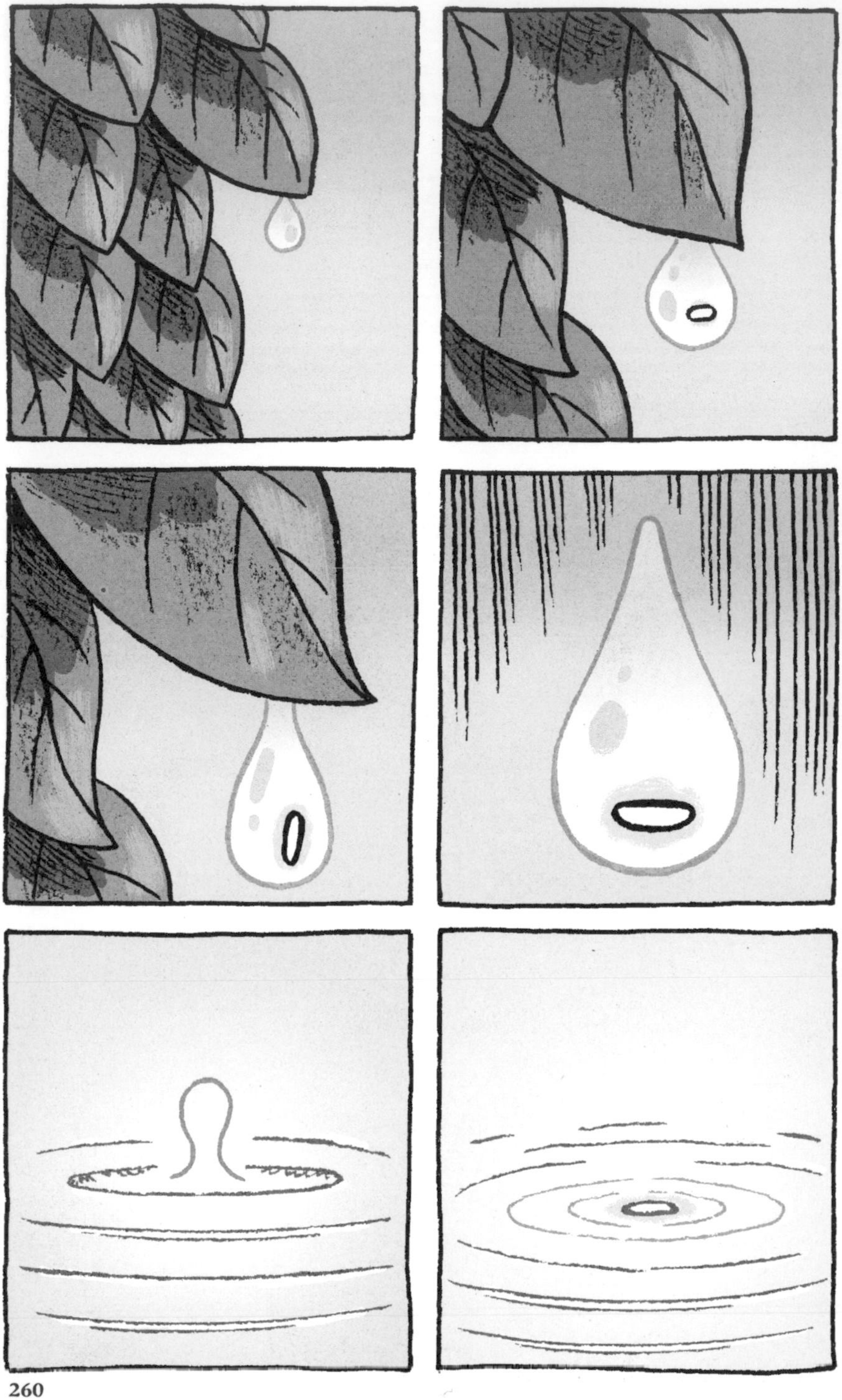

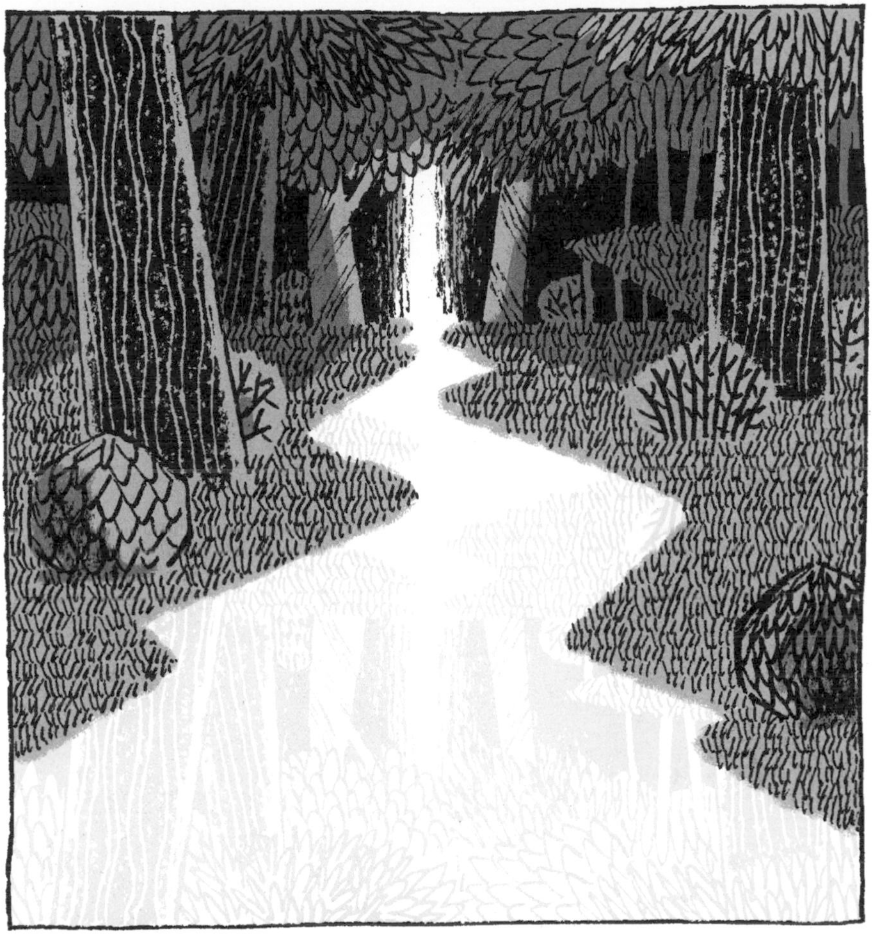

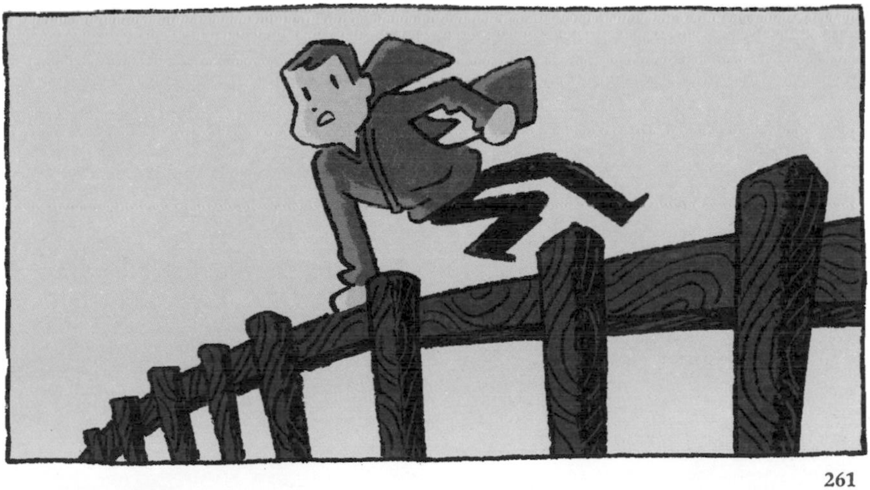

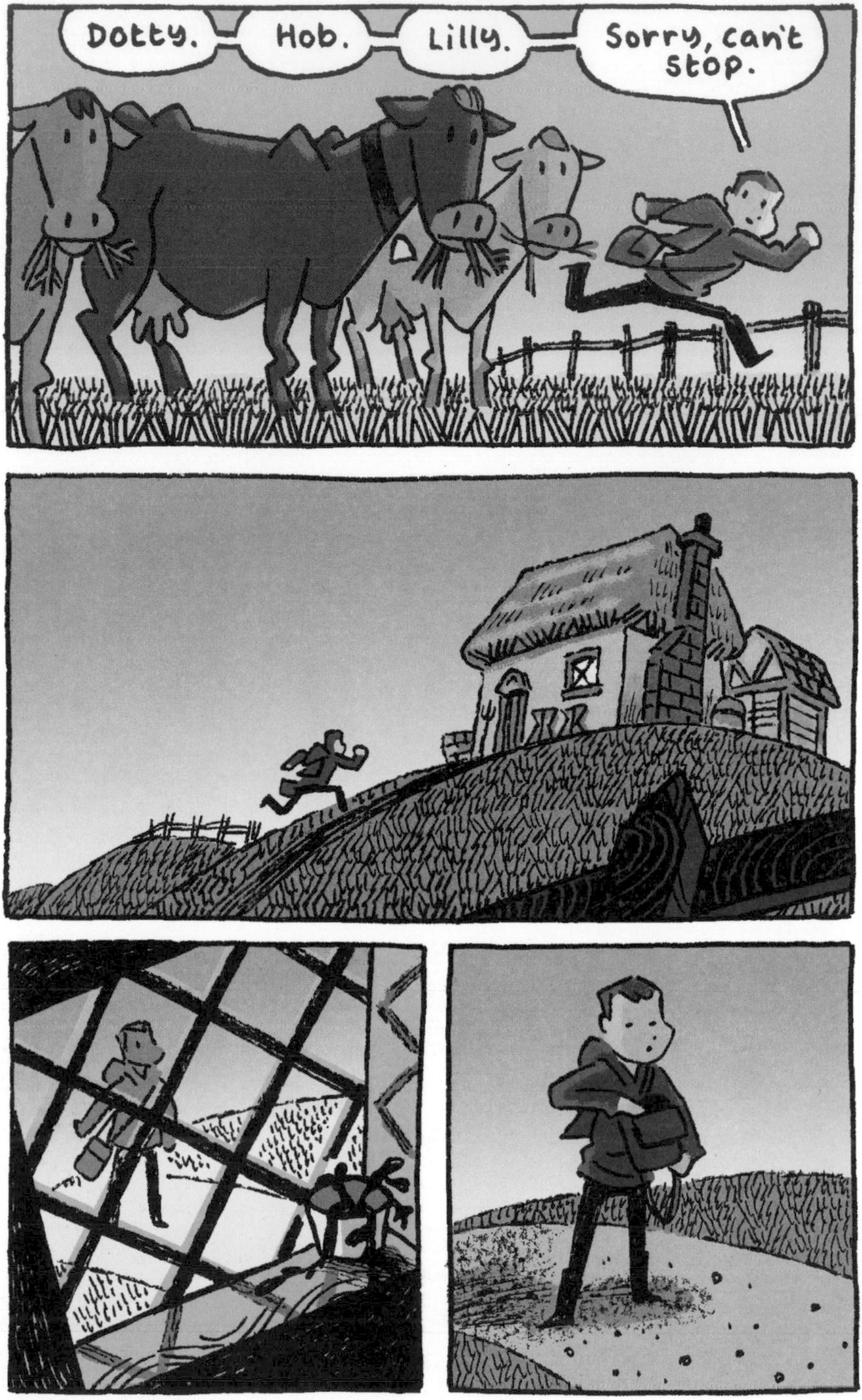
Dotty.
Hob.
Lilly.
Sorry, can't stop.

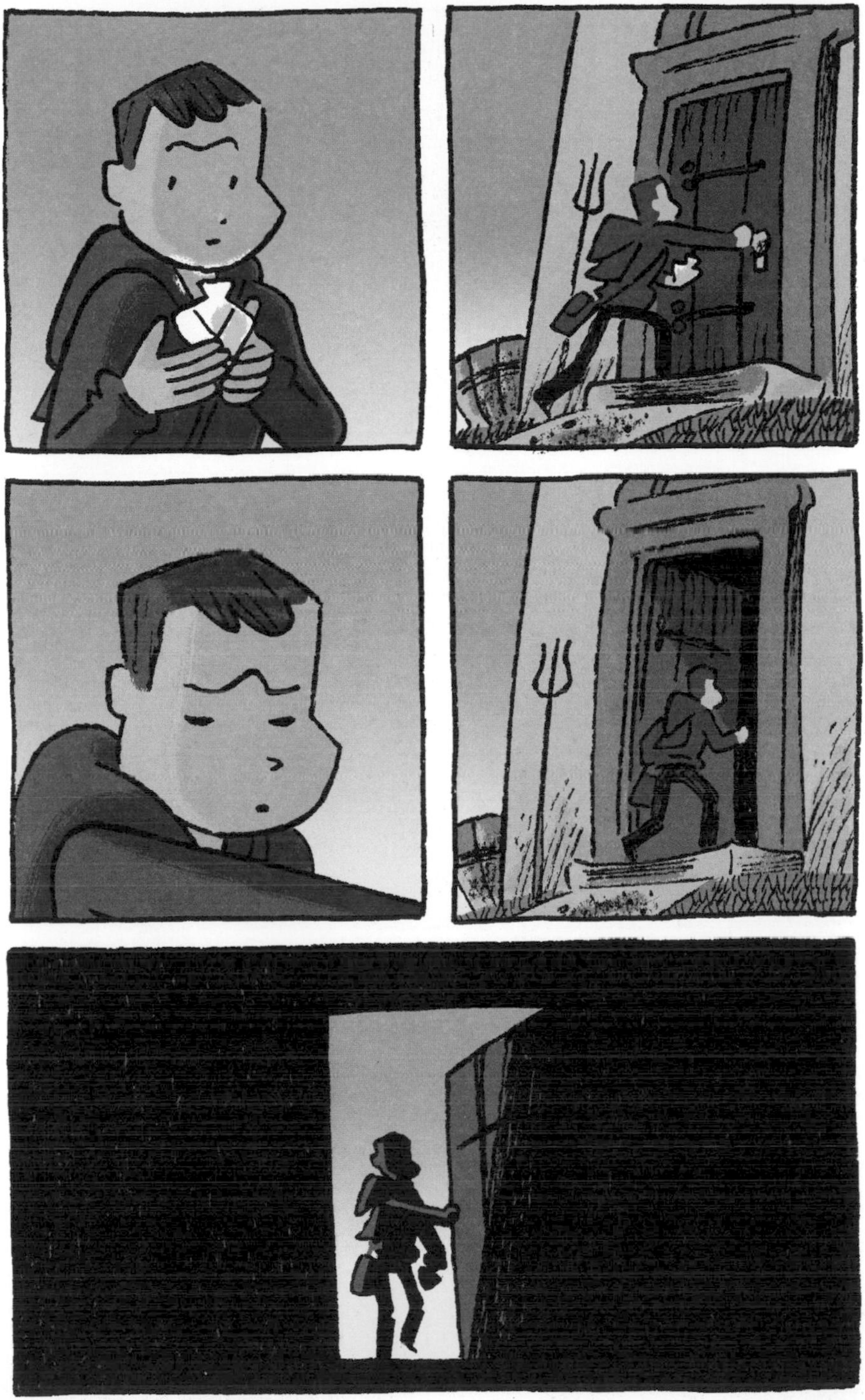

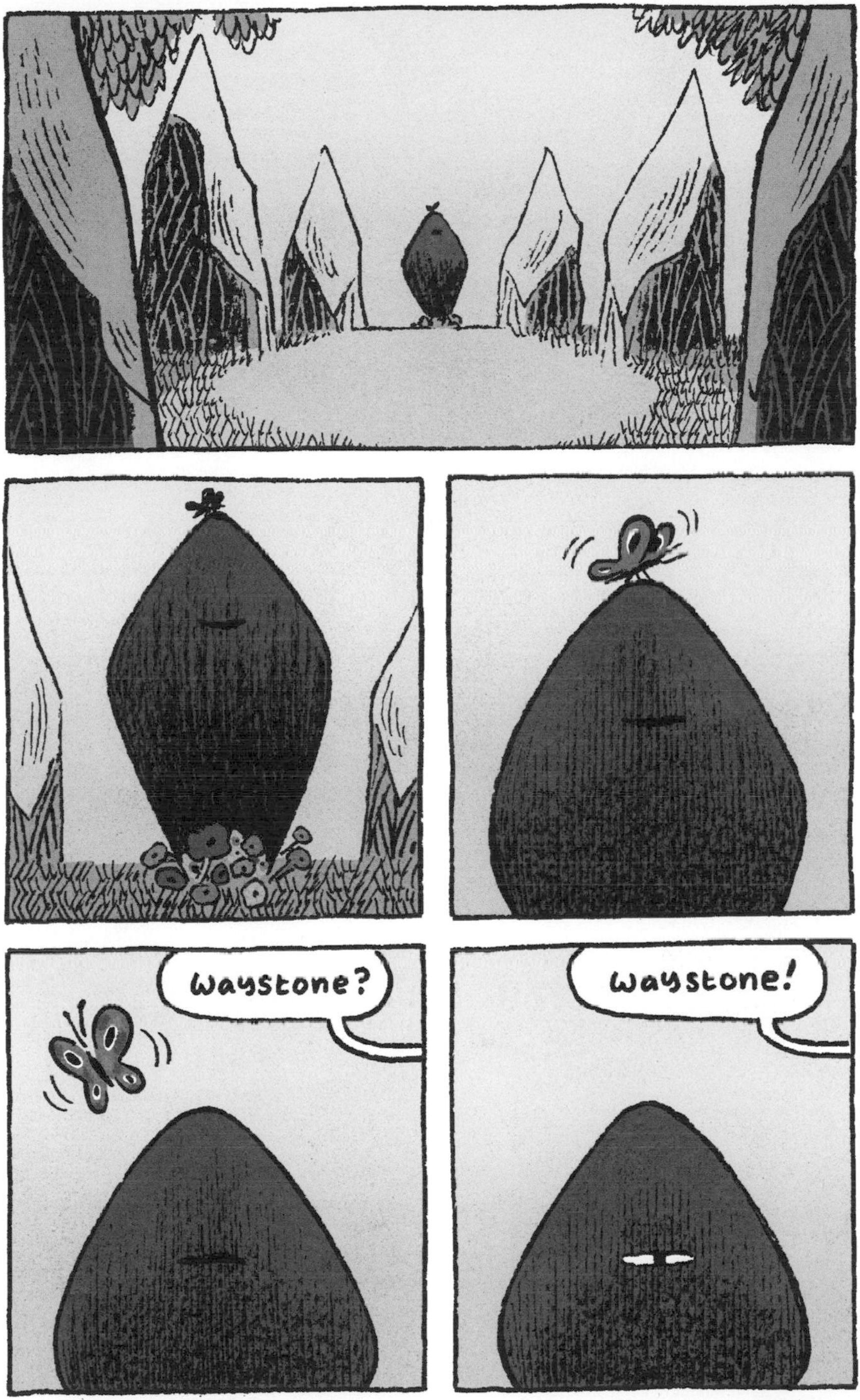
Waystone?
Waystone!

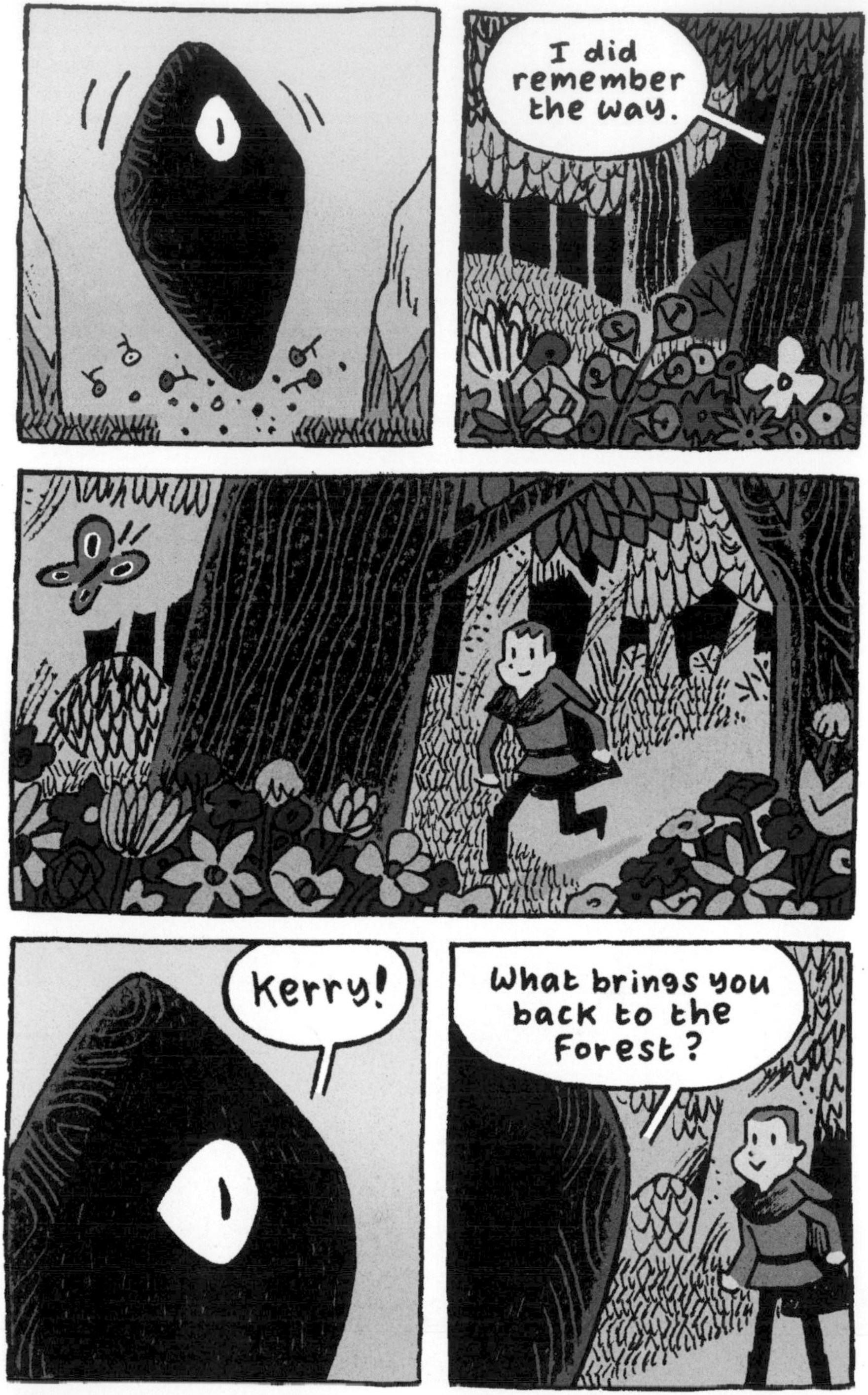
I did remember the way.
Kerry!
What brings you back to the Forest?

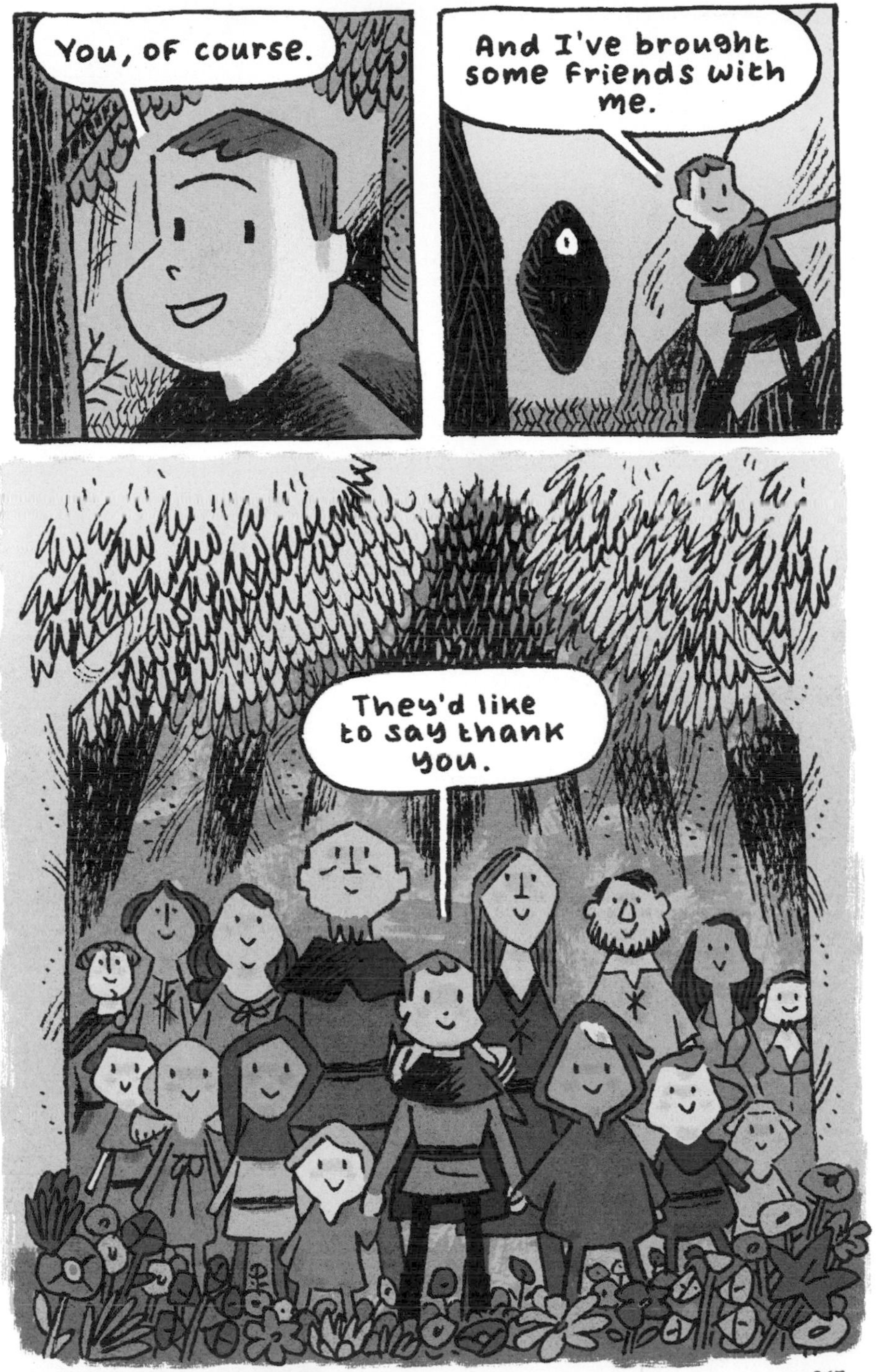
You, of course.
And I've brought some friends with me.
They'd like to say thank you.

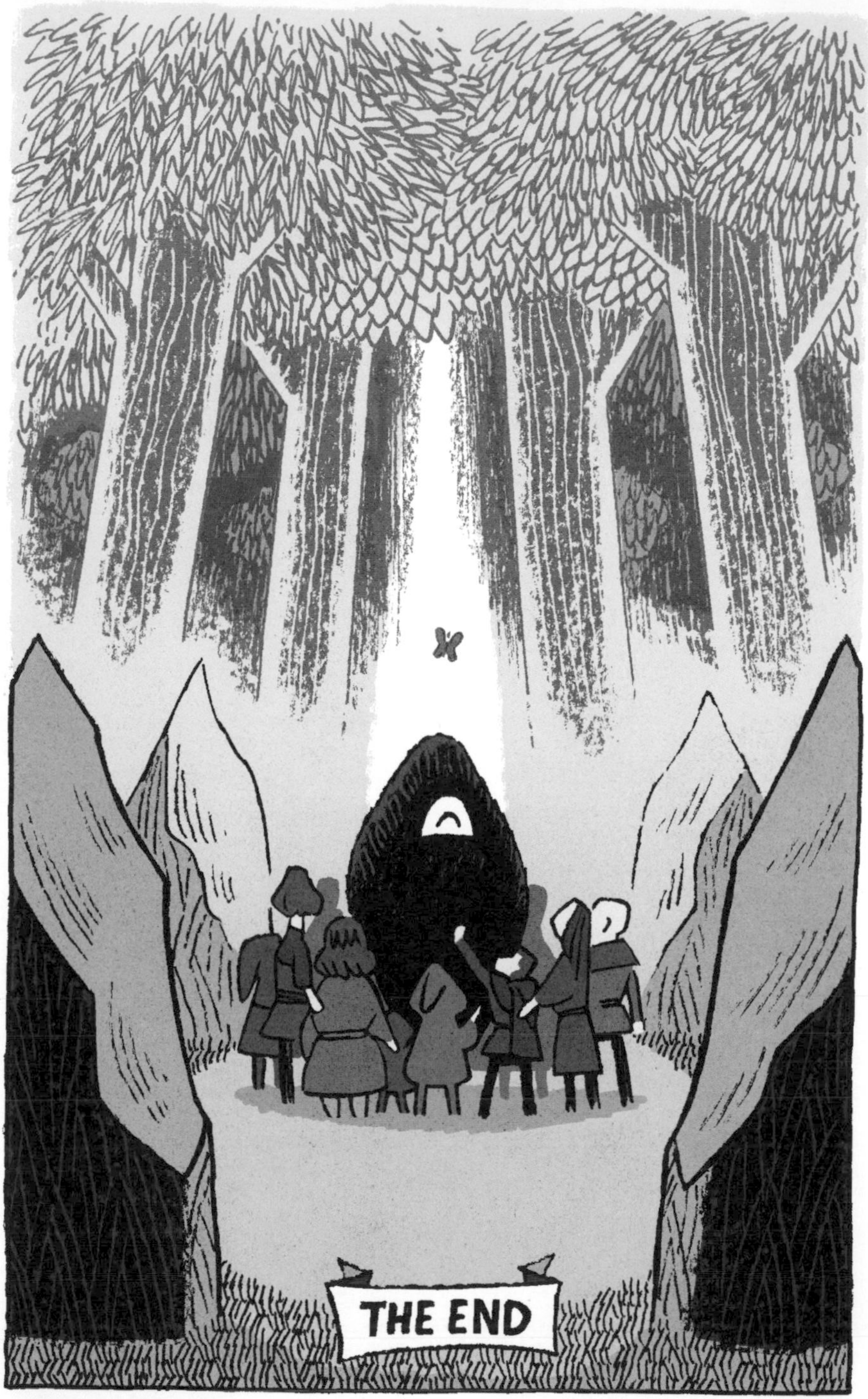
THE END

Kerry and the Knight of the Forest was drawn and lettered with Uni Pin pens, a blunt compass tip, and chinagraph pencils on 200g A5 sheets of fine grain paper. It was colored using Photoshop CS6 and a Wacom Bamboo tablet.

KERRY'S MUM & DAD

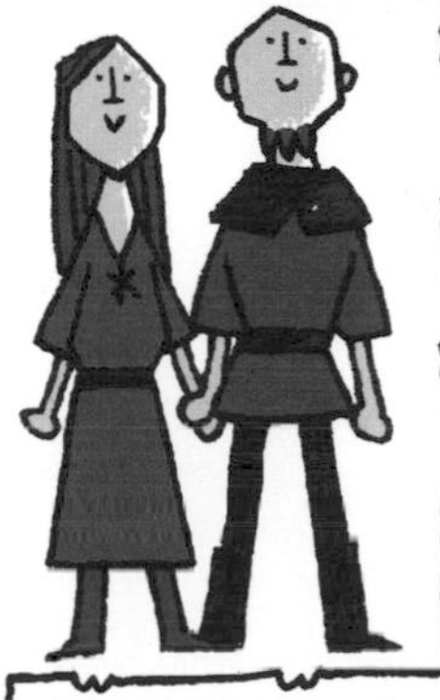

6	SPEED
7	EMPATHY
4	STEALTH
7	MOXIE
8	SMARTS
6	STRENGTH

SKILLS

Farming

Animal husbandry

Parenting

INFORMATION

When they are both struck down by a fever, Kerry has to find a cure and return home in time.

BLACKBIRD

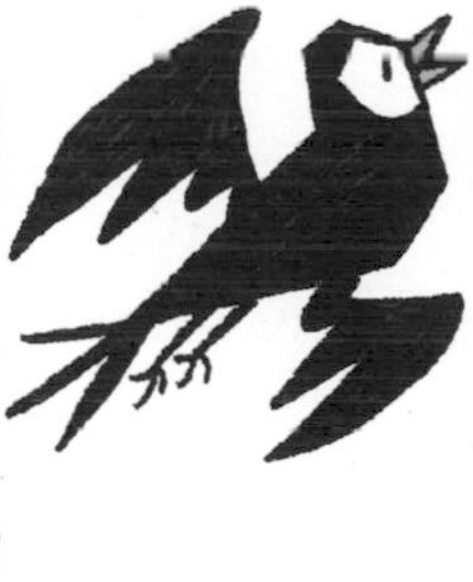

8	SPEED
3	EMPATHY
6	STEALTH
5	MOXIE
4	SMARTS
3	STRENGTH

SKILLS

Fly

Dive-bomb

INFORMATION

The bird sits high up in the trees and spies for the Spirit. Likes to eat snails.

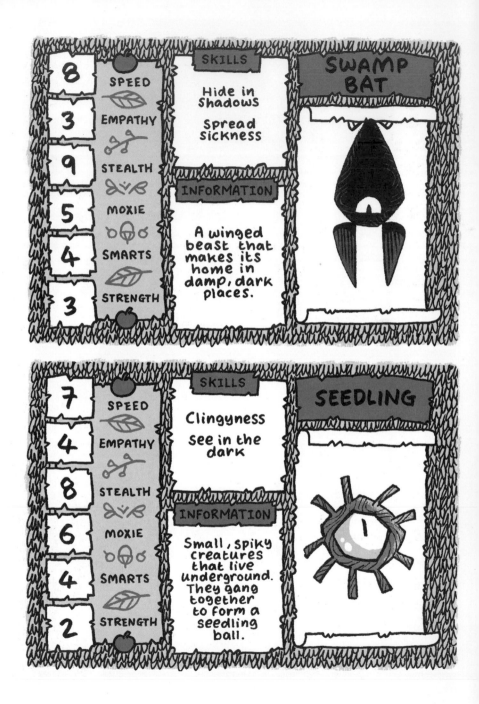

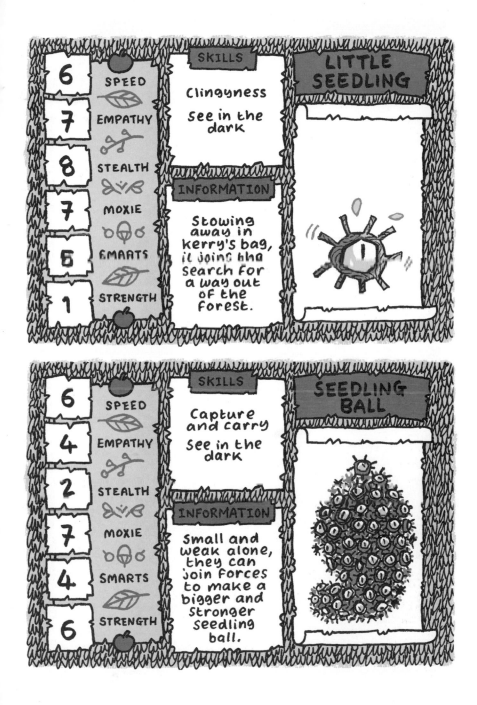

SKILLS

Clingyness

See in the dark

LITTLE SEEDLING

6 SPEED

7 EMPATHY

8 STEALTH

7 MOXIE

5 SMARTS

1 STRENGTH

INFORMATION

Stowing away in kerry's bag, it joins the search for a way out of the forest.

SKILLS

Capture and carry

See in the dark

SEEDLING BALL

6 SPEED

4 EMPATHY

2 STEALTH

7 MOXIE

4 SMARTS

6 STRENGTH

INFORMATION

Small and weak alone, they can join forces to make a bigger and stronger seedling ball.

Will-O-Wisp

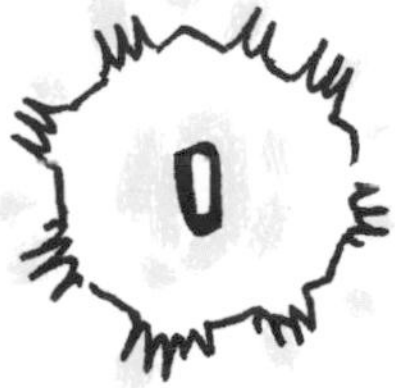

Stat	Value
SPEED	8
EMPATHY	2
STEALTH	6
MOXIE	4
SMARTS	5
STRENGTH	1

SKILLS

Hypnotize

Create illusions

INFORMATION

These beautiful balls of light lure unwary travelers deeper into the forest until captured by the Spirit.

Gorse Folk

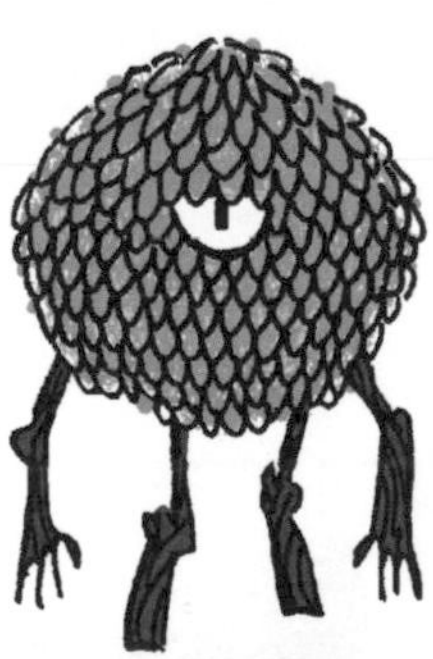

Stat	Value
SPEED	6
EMPATHY	3
STEALTH	9
MOXIE	5
SMARTS	3
STRENGTH	7

SKILLS

Hide in plain sight

Tracking

INFORMATION

Disguising themselves as bushes, the Gorse Folk lie in wait to attack those who have lost their way.

SPIRIT OF THE FOREST

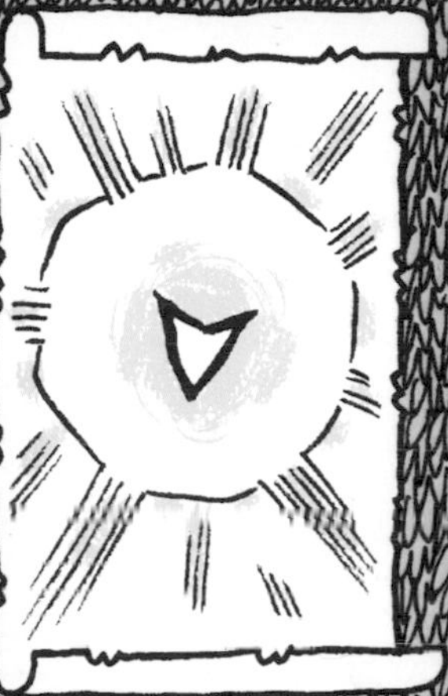

9	SPEED
4	EMPATHY
9	STEALTH
5	MOXIE
10	SMARTS
2	STRENGTH

SKILLS

Hypnotize

Create illusions

Lightning Strike

INFORMATION

A malicious Spirit which has corrupted the forest and rules over all of the creatures that live within it.

FOREST CHILDREN

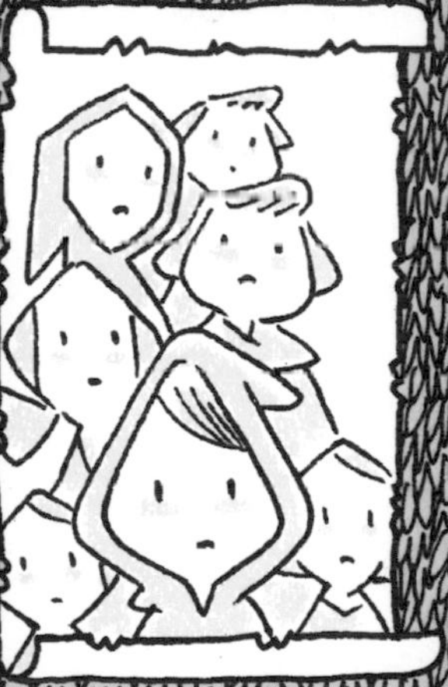

6	SPEED
7	EMPATHY
8	STEALTH
3	MOXIE
6	SMARTS
2	STRENGTH

SKILLS

Mislead

Hide in plain sight

INFORMATION

Children lured into the forest by the Spirit and held there at the whim of their captor.

CREATE YOUR OWN CHARACTER

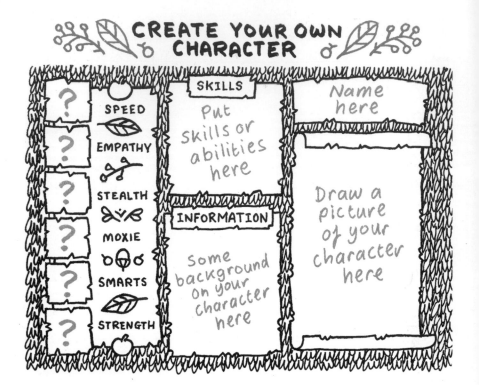

SPEED
EMPATHY
STEALTH
MOXIE
SMARTS
STRENGTH

SKILLS
Put skills or abilities here

INFORMATION
Some background on your character here

Name here

Draw a picture of your character here

Trace onto a separate sheet

- Assign your character a number between one and ten for each characteristic.

- Are they an animal, a creature or a person? Are they you?

- Give at least one characteristic a low number. If they are very strong, then they might have low stealth or speed.

- Note down their skills and a little bit about them in the information box.

- Draw a picture of your character.

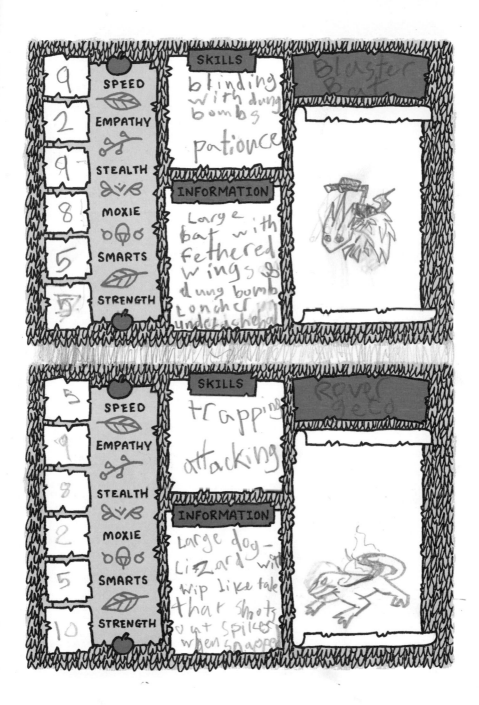

9 SPEED

2 EMPATHY

9 STEALTH

8 MOXIE

5 SMARTS

7 STRENGTH

SKILLS

blinding with dung bombs

patience

INFORMATION

Large bat with fethered wings & dung bomb loncher undetacheabl

Blaster Bat

---

5 SPEED

9 EMPATHY

8 STEALTH

2 MOXIE

5 SMARTS

10 STRENGTH

SKILLS

trapping

attacking

INFORMATION

Large dog-lizard with wip like tale that shots out spikes when snapped

Rever geco

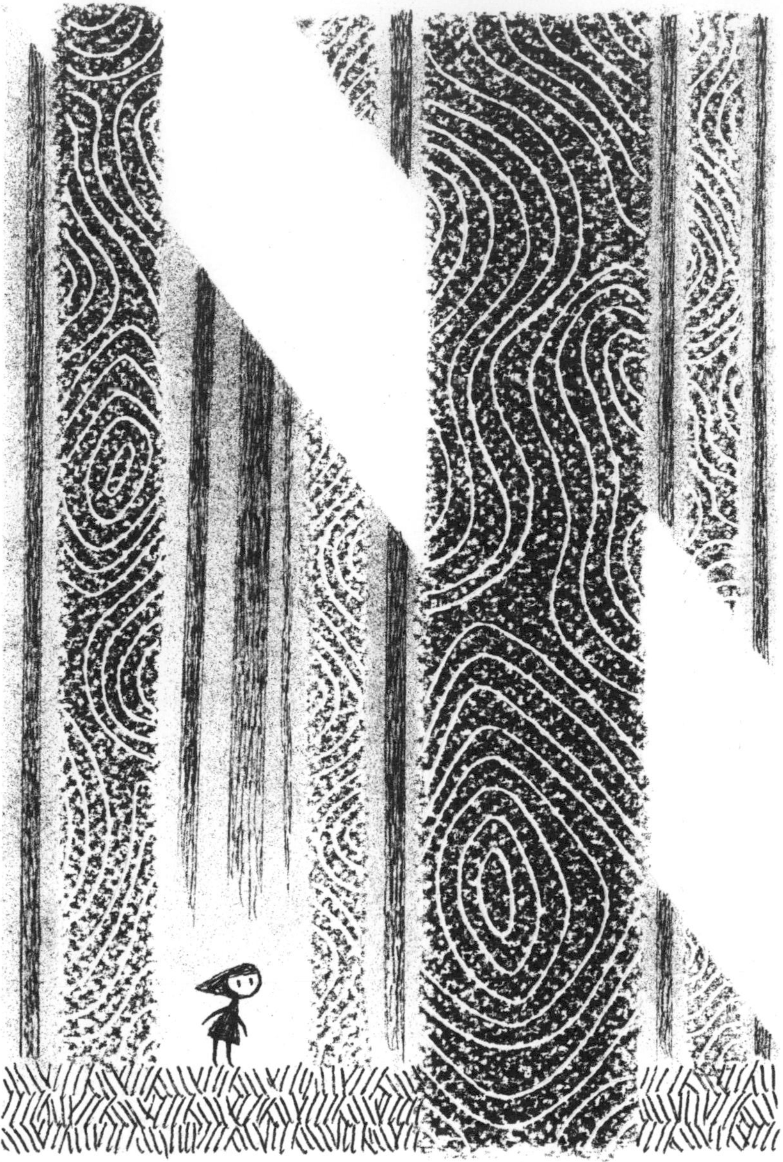

These are pages from an early attempt at this story a number of years ago. I'd picked it up and put it aside several times, including thumbnailing out an entire graphic novel before abandoning it.

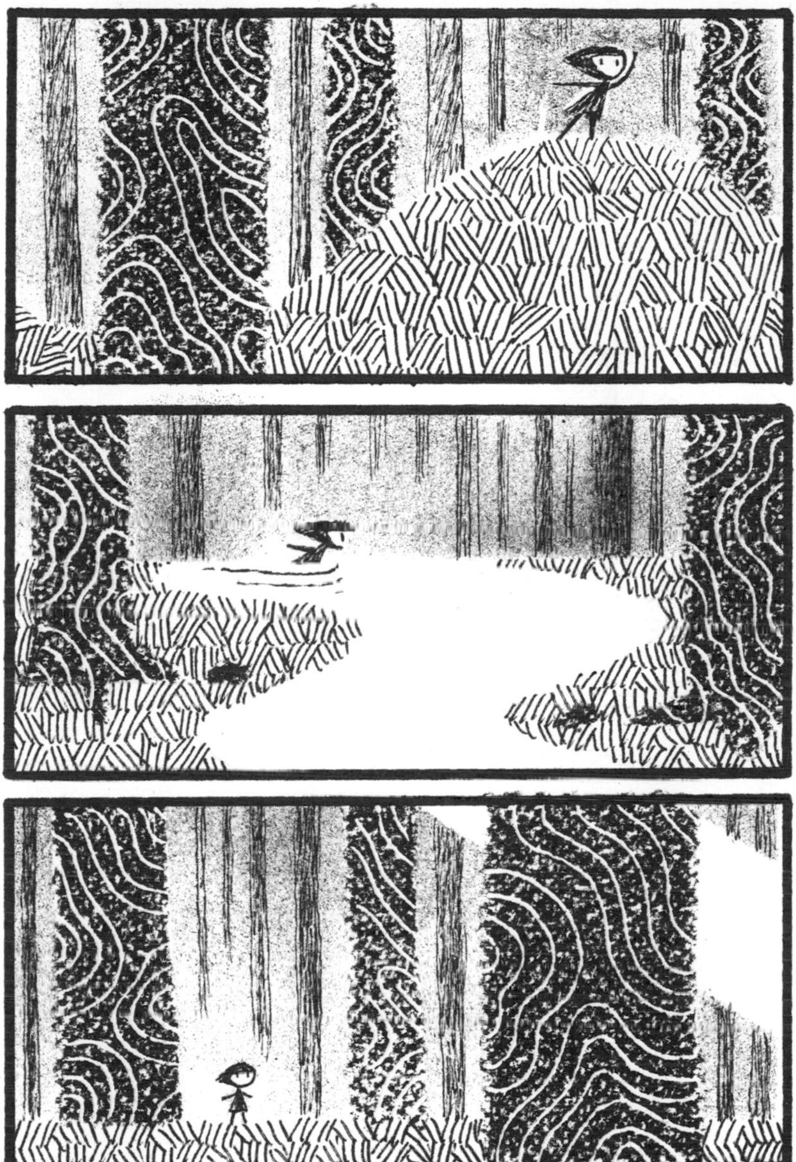

The fairy tale idea of the child lost in the woods wouldn't go away, though. Eventually I took it up again with the idea of the Waystone and it finally came together. Sometimes a story has to sit and stew a long time before it's ready.

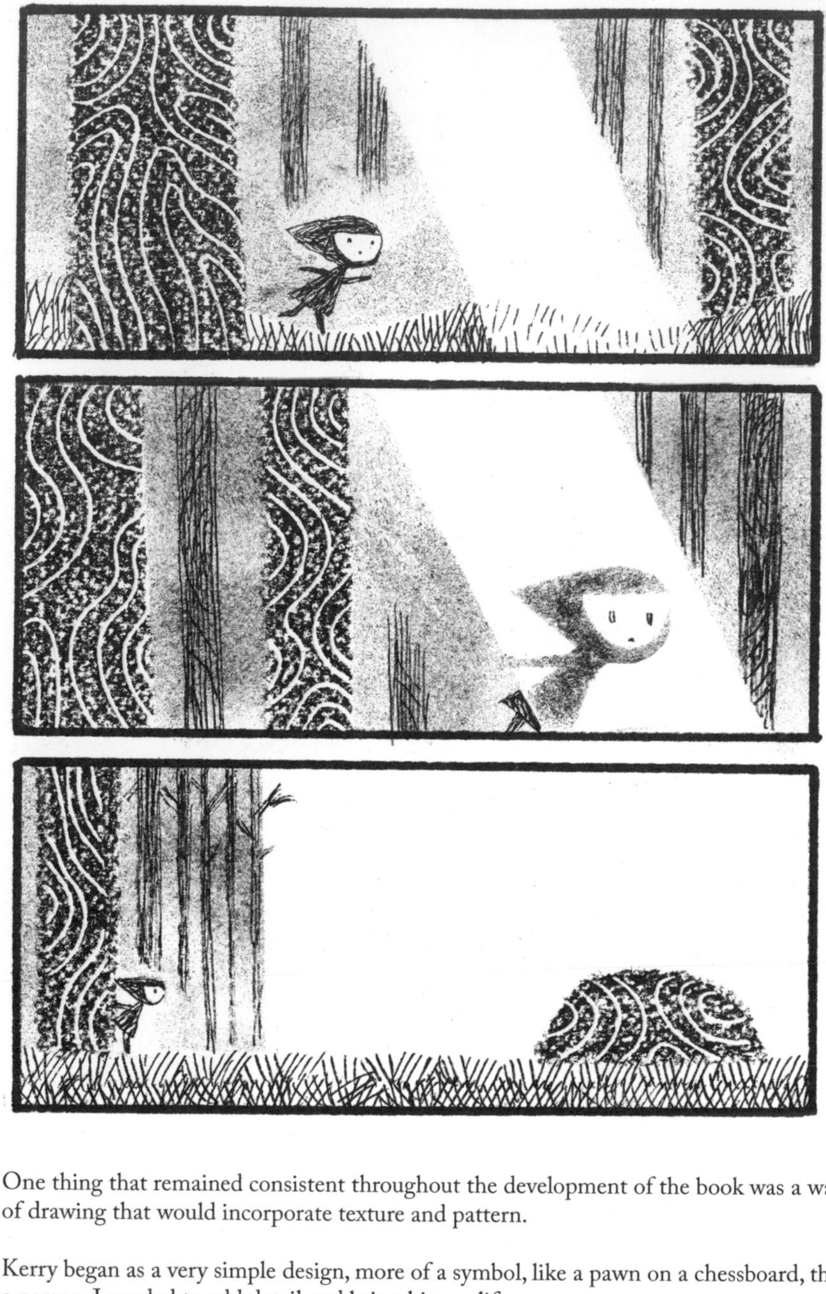

One thing that remained consistent throughout the development of the book was a way of drawing that would incorporate texture and pattern.

Kerry began as a very simple design, more of a symbol, like a pawn on a chessboard, than a person. I needed to add detail and bring him to life.

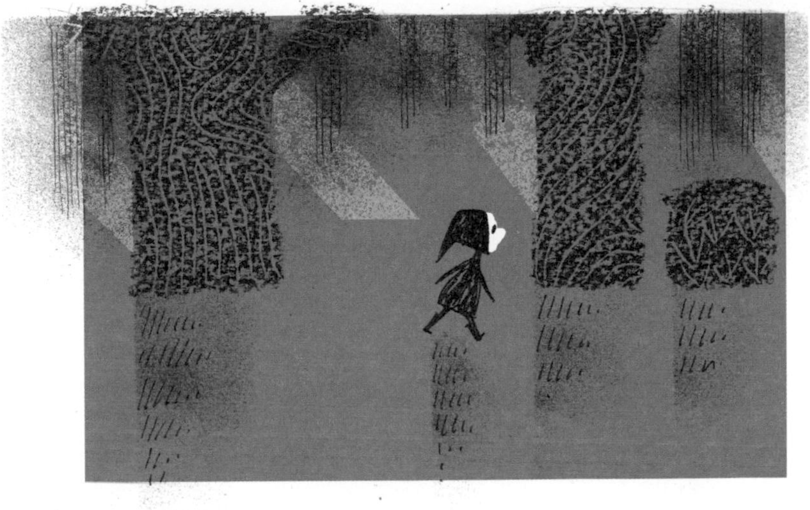

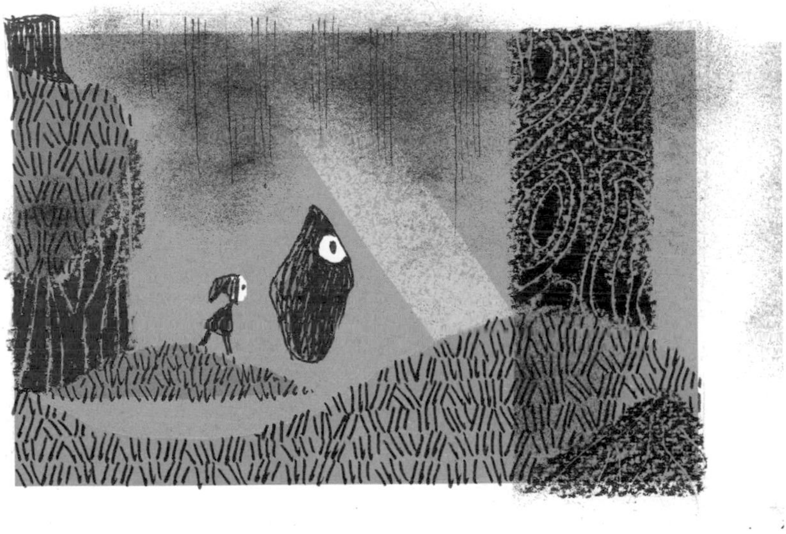

This is my first book to be in full color, and so I experimented with different ways to use it and what kind of color palette I was going to employ. Here I used an inkpad and sponge to get the murky effect.

I studied graphic design and illustration at college and love the process of designing book covers. I tend to do lots of little thumbnail sketches to work out the best combinations of words and image. I find a cover that works well as a tiny sketch will often make an eye-catching cover design that will stand out on the bookshelves. Patrick (the designer) and I tried lots of different ideas before settling on the right one.

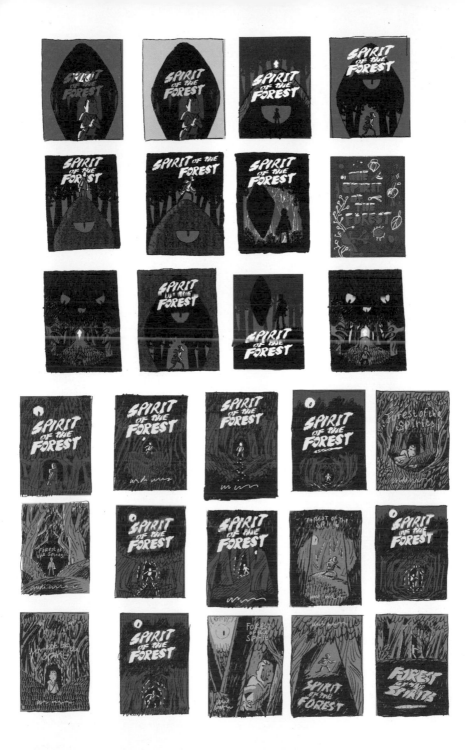

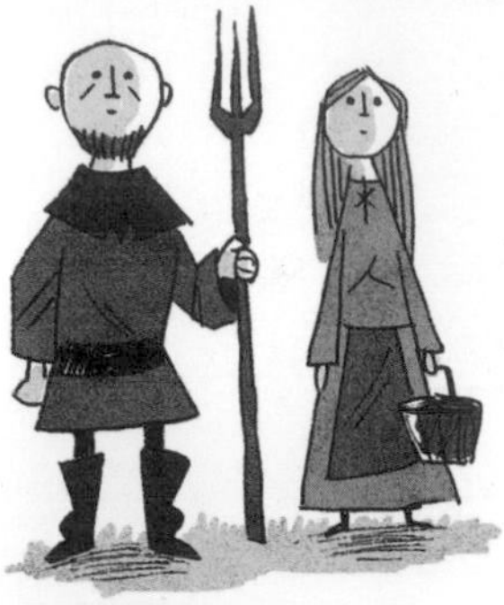

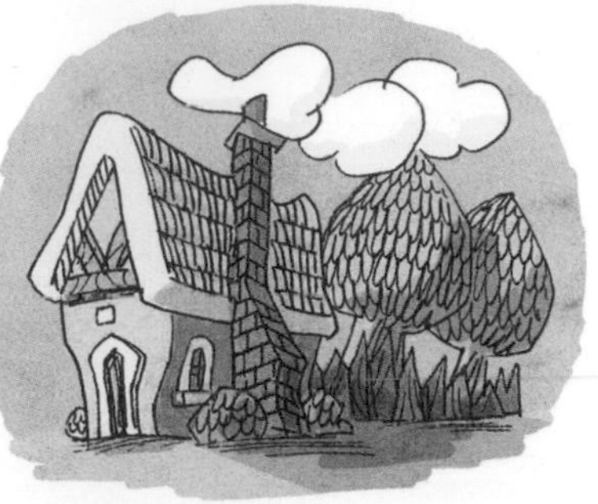

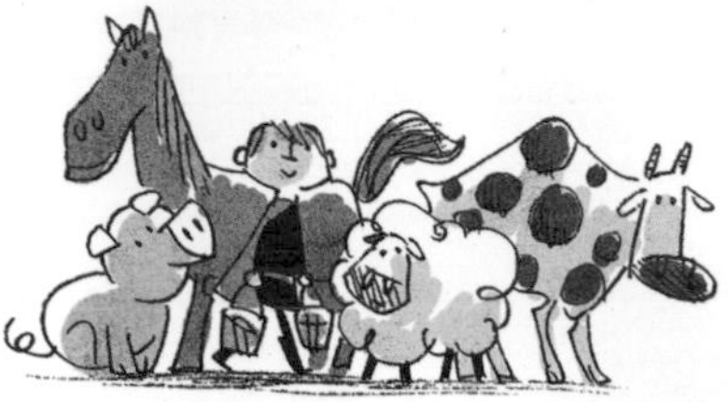

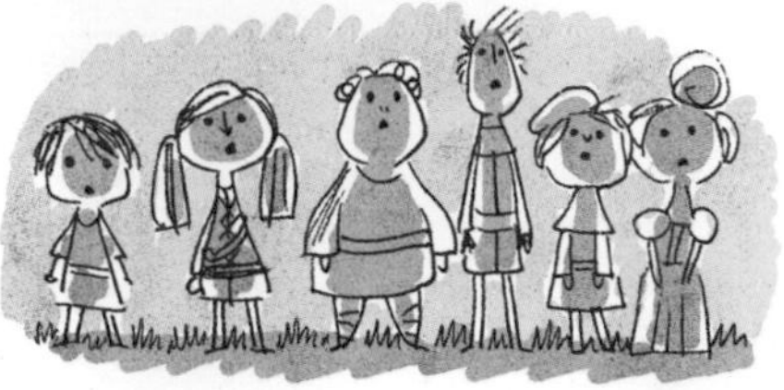

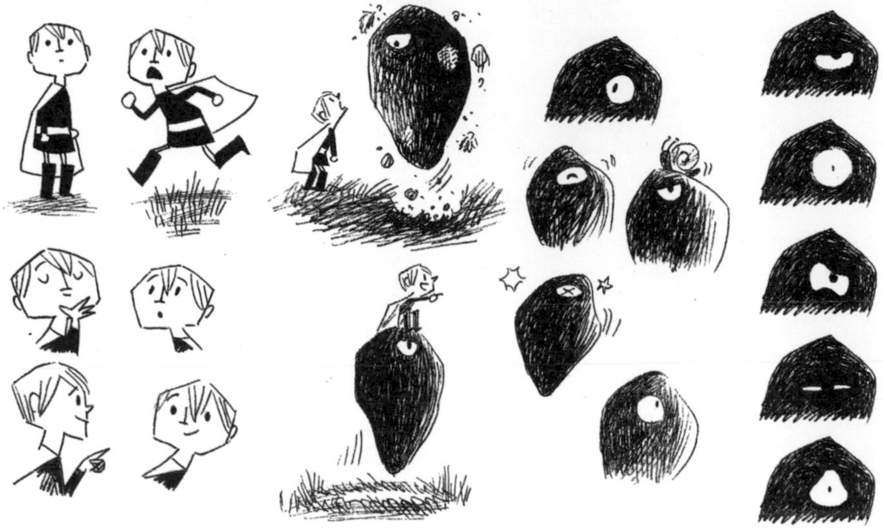

These are some of the development sketches I drew up in order to help visualize what the other characters and settings in the story would look like. I worked on giving Kerry more individuality and figured out how to bring a rock personality. They were stepping-stones on the way to the final designs. A finished book is only the visible tip of a mountain of sketches, scripts, and wrong turns.

**Thank you to Gina, Whitney, Patrick,
and the whole team at RHG for helping make
this book happen.**

Andi Watson was born and raised in a small town in the north of
England, where he loved to draw and read books. As a kid, he read
the Star Wars and Beano comic books. As a teenager, he read fantasy
trilogies and obsessed over Dungeons & Dragons. He rediscovered
comics while at art school, amazed by series like Akira and Love and
Rockets. At the very end of his degree, he decided to make his own
comic, as this would be his only opportunity before taking up a career
in illustration. It didn't quite work out that way, as many years later he is
still telling stories with words and pictures, this being his thirtieth book.
He has created comics for grown-ups and children and those somewhere
in between. These include stand-alone graphic novels for adults such
as *Breakfast After Noon* and *Slow News Day*, series for teenagers like
Skeleton Key, and series for children like Glister and Gum Girl. He's
occasionally been nominated for awards and has had books translated
into French, Spanish, German, and Italian. He still enjoys reading and
drawing. He lives in Worcester, England, with his wife and daughter,
where he drinks tea and is trying to learn French (again).

@andicomics
andiwatson.info

· THE SUMMER 2020 LIST ·

CRABAPPLE TROUBLE
By Kaeti Vandorn
· · · · · · · · · ·
Life isn't easy when you're an apple.

Callaway and Thistle must figure out how to work together—with delicious and magical results.

Young Chapter Book

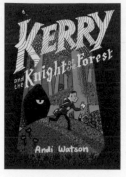

KERRY AND THE KNIGHT OF THE FOREST
By Andi Watson
· · · · · · · · · ·
Kerry needs to get home!

To get back to his parents, Kerry gets lost in a shortcu[t] He will have to make tough choices and figure out who to trust—or remain lost in the forest . . . forever.

Middle Grade

STEPPING STONES
By Lucy Knisley
· · · · · · · · · ·
Jen did not want to leave the city.

She did not want to move to a farm.

And Jen definitely did not want to get two new "sisters."

Middle Grade

SUNCATCHER
By Jose Pimienta
· · · · · · · · · ·
Beatriz loves music—more than her school, more than her friends—and she won't let anything stop her from achieving her dreams.

Even if it means losing everything else.

Young Adult

FIND US ONLINE AT @RHKIDSGRAPHIC AND RHKIDSGRAPHIC.COM